MW00425308

THE MONSTER BOOK OF
MONSTERS

THE MONSTER BOOK OF
MONSTERS

Edited and Introduced by

MICHAEL O'SHAUGHNESSY

BONANZA BOOKS
New York

This 1988 edition is published by Bonanza Books
distributed by Crown Publishers, Inc.,
225 Park Avenue South, New York, N.Y. 10003

Printed and Bound in Great Britain

Library of Congress Cataloging-in-Publication Data

The Monster book of monsters.
  1. Horror tales. 2. Monsters—Fiction.
I. O'Shaughnessy, Michael.
PN6120.95.H727M66 1988 808.83′872 88-2581
ISBN 0–517–66293–0
h g f e d c b a

INTRODUCTION
Here Be Monsters

When the men who made the ancient maps came to a region that was dangerous and little-known to explorers, they would write HERE BE MONSTERS. Think of this book as a dangerous corner of the library where fears take real shapes, for here are more monsters than you ever dreamed of, even in your worst nightmares.

Some of them are famous. King Kong, Dracula, the Abominable Snowman, Dr. Frankenstein's creation and The Beast from Twenty Thousand Fathoms are modern myths that haunt the twentieth-century imagination, but here they appear in new guises—modern variations on old themes that will intrigue as well as terrify. Then there are monsters that you may not have encountered before: Doctor Zombie's creatures, The Slime Beast, Mr. Waterman, the Purple-striped Grabber, and the extraordinary Aunt Nora. You'll like meeting *them*. And there are some human monsters too, a reminder that terror isn't just "out there" but right here inside ourselves.

Above all these are good *stories*, fifty in all. A dozen or so were nominated as the best stories of their particular years, and eight of the authors are consistently voted into the Top Twenty in polls by science fiction readers, with many Hugo and Nebula awards to their credit. And that's not to mention such world-class writers as Guy de Maupassant, Edgar Allan Poe, Victor Hugo, and Evelyn Waugh. Several of the tales have been made into movies, but there are rarities too, from magazines like the wonderful *Weird Tales*, and from little-known Victorian works. I think it makes a stimulating mix.

I have included as many different types of monsters as I could cram into these pages, all the way from Aliens to Zombies, and the only real problem was deciding what to leave out—the book could easily have been filled two or three times over. You'll notice, by the way, that under I for Insects there are some giant spiders; you may have heard that spiders, with eight legs, aren't actually insects, but in the story the Professor says they are so that's where they go. For this is nightmare-land, where the rules of zoology cease—alarmingly—to apply.

I hope you enjoy your visit.

—M.J.O'S

Monster Contents

The illustrations are by the following artists:
Ed Cartier (15, 147), Hannes Bok (72), artist unknown from *Famous Monsters of Filmland* (87), James Cawthorn (129, 241), nineteenth-century artist unknown (197), Gene Fawcette (208) Herman Vestal (249), artist unknown from *The Science Fiction Book* (261), John Giunta (317) and Kalvin Grey (347).

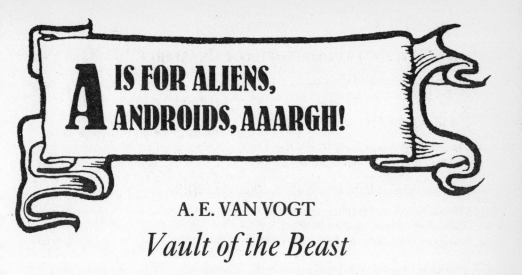

A IS FOR ALIENS, ANDROIDS, AAARGH!

A. E. VAN VOGT

Vault of the Beast

The creature crept. It whimpered from fear and pain. Shapeless, formless thing yet changing shape and form with each jerky movement, it crept along the corridor of the space freighter, fighting the terrible urge of its elements to take the shape of its surroundings. A gray blob of disintegrating stuff, it crept and cascaded, it rolled, flowed, and dissolved, every movement an agony of struggle against the abnormal need to become a stable shape. Any shape! The hard chilled-blue metal wall of the Earth-bound freighter, the thick, rubbery floor. The floor was easy to fight. It wasn't like the metal that pulled and pulled. It would be easy to become metal for all eternity.

But something prevented. An implanted purpose. A purpose that drummed from molecule to molecule, vibrated from cell to cell with an unvarying intensity that was like a special pain; Find the greatest mathematical mind in the solar system, and bring it to the vault of the Martian ultimate metal. The Great One must be freed. The prime number time lock must be opened!

That was the purpose that pressed on its elements. That was the thought that had been seared into its fundamental consciousness by the great and evil minds that had created it.

There was movement at the far end of the corridor. A door opened. Footsteps sounded. A man whistling to himself. With a metallic hiss, almost a sigh, the creature dissolved, looking momentarily like diluted mercury. Then it turned brown like the floor. It became the floor, a slightly thicker stretch of dark brown rubber spread out for yards.

It was ecstasy just to lie there and be flat and have shape, and to be so nearly dead that there was no pain. Death was sweet and desirable. And life such an unbearable torment. If only the life that was approaching would pass swiftly. If the life stopped, it would pull it into shape. Life could do that. Life was stronger than metal. The approaching life meant torture, struggle, pain.

The creature tensed its now flat, grotesque body—the body that could develop muscles of steel—and waited for the death struggle.

Spacecraftsman Parelli whistled happily as he strode along the gleaming corridor that led from the engine room. He had just received a wireless from the

9

hospital. His wife was doing well, and it was a boy. Eight pounds, the radiogram had said. He suppressed a desire to whoop and dance. A boy. Life sure was good.

Pain came to the thing on the floor. Primeval pain that sucked through its elements like burning acid. The brown floor shuddered in every molecule as Parelli strode over it. It had a tremendous urge to pull toward him, to take his shape. The thing fought its desire, fought with dread, and more consciously now that it could think with Parelli's brain. A ripple of floor rolled over the man.

Fighting didn't help. The ripple grew into a blob that momentarily seemed to become a human head. Gray nightmare of demoniac shape. The creature hissed metallically in terror, then collapsed palpitating with fear and pain and hate as Parelli strode on rapidly—too rapidly for its creeping pace. The thin sound died. The thing dissolved into brown floor, and lay quiescent yet quivering from its uncontrollable urge to live—live in spite of pain, in spite of terror. To live and fulfill the purpose of its creators.

Thirty feet up the corridor, Parelli stopped. He jerked his mind from its thoughts of child and wife. He spun on his heels, and stared uncertainly along the passageway from the engine room.

"Now what the devil was that?" he pondered aloud.

A queer, faint, yet unmistakably horrid sound was echoing through his consciousness. A shiver ran the length of his spine. That devilish sound.

He stood there, a tall, magnificently muscled man, stripped to the waist, sweating from the heat generated by the rockets that were decelerating the craft after its meteoric flight from Mars. Shuddering, he clenched his fists, and walked slowly back the way he had come.

The creature throbbed with the pull of him, a torment that pierced into every restless, agitated cell. Slowly it became aware of the inevitable, the irresistible need to take the shape of the life.

Parelli stopped uncertainly. The floor moved under him, a visible wave that reared brown and horrible before his incredulous eyes and grew into a bulbous, slobbering, hissing mass. A venomous demon head reared on twisted, half-human shoulders. Gnarled hands on apelike, malformed arms clawed at his face with insensate rage, and changed even as they tore at him.

"Good God!" Parelli bellowed.

The hands, the arms that clutched him grew more normal, more human, brown, muscular. The face assumed familiar lines, sprouted a nose, eyes, a red gash of mouth. The body was suddenly his own, trousers and all, sweat and all.

"—God!" his image echoed; and pawed at him with letching fingers and an impossible strength.

Gasping, Parelli fought free, then launched one crushing blow straight into the distorted face. A scream came from the thing. It turned and ran, dissolving as it ran, fighting dissolution, uttering half-human cries. Parelli chased it, his knees weak and trembling from funk and sheer disbelief. His arm reached out, and plucked at the disintegrating trousers. A piece came away in his hand, a cold, slimy, writhing lump like wet clay.

The feel of it was too much. His gorge rising in disgust, he faltered in his stride. He heard the pilot shouting from ahead: "What's the matter?"

Parelli saw the open door of the storeroom. With a gasp, he dived in, came out a moment later, an ato-gun in his fingers. He saw the pilot, standing with staring brown eyes, white face, and rigid body, facing one of the great windows.

"There it is!" the man cried.

A gray blob was dissolving into the edge of the glass, becoming glass. Parelli rushed forward, ato-gun poised. A ripple went through the glass, darkening it; and then, briefly, he caught a glimpse of a blob emerging on the other side of the glass into the cold of space. The officer came up beside him. The two of them watched the gray, shapeless mass creep out of sight along the side of the rushing freight liner.

Parelli sprang to life. "I got a piece of it!" he gasped. "Flung it down on the floor of the storeroom."

It was Lieutenant Morton who found it. A tiny section of floor reared up, and then grew amazingly large as it tried to expand into human shape. Parelli, with distorted, crazy eyes, scooped it up in a shovel. It hissed. It nearly became a part of the metal shovel, but couldn't because Parelli was so close. Parelli staggered with it behind his superior officer. He was laughing hysterically. "I touched it," he kept saying, "I touched it."

A large blister of metal on the outside of the space freighter stirred into sluggish life, as the ship tore into Earth's atmosphere. The metal walls of the freighter grew red, then whitehot, but the creature, unaffected, continued its slow transformation into gray mass. It realized vaguely that it was time to act.

Suddenly, it was floating free of the ship, falling slowly, heavily, as if somehow the gravitation of Earth had no serious effect upon it. A minute distortion inside its atoms started it falling faster, as in some alien way it suddenly became more subject to gravity. The earth was green below; and in the dim distance a city glittered in the sinking sun. The thing slowed and drifted like a falling leaf in a breeze toward the still-distant surface. It landed in an arroyo beside a bridge at the outskirts of the city.

A man walked over the bridge with quick, nervous steps. He would have been amazed, if he had looked back, to see a replica of himself climb from the ditch to the road, and start walking briskly after him.

Find the—greatest mathematician!

It was an hour later; and the pain of that thought was a continuous ache in the creature's brain, as it walked along the crowded street. There were other pains, too. The pain of fighting the pull of the pushing, hurrying mass of humanity that swarmed by with unseeing eyes. But it was easier to think, easier to hold form now that it had the brain and body of a man.

Find—mathematician!

"Why?" asked the man's brain of the thing. And the whole body shook with shock at such heretical questioning. The brown eyes darted in fright from side to side, as if expecting instant and terrible doom. The face dissolved a little in that brief moment of mental chaos, became successively the man with the hooked nose who swung by, and the tanned face of the tall woman who was looking into the shop window.

The process would have gone on, but the creature pulled its mind back from fear, and fought to readjust its face to that of the smooth-shaven young man who sauntered idly in from a side street. The young man glanced at him, looked away, then glanced back again startled. The creature echoed the thought in the man's brain: "Who the devil is that? Where have I seen that fellow before?"

Half a dozen women in a group approached. The creature shrank aside as they passed. Its brown suit turned the faintest shade of blue, the color of the nearest dress, as it momentarily lost control of its outer cells. Its mind hummed with the chatter of clothes and "My dear, didn't she look dreadful in that awful hat?"

There was a solid cluster of giant buildings ahead. The thing shook its human head consciously. So many buildings meant metal; and the forces that held metal together would pull and pull at its human shape. The creature comprehended the reason for this with the understanding of the slight man in a dark suit who wandered by dully. The slight man was a clerk; the thing caught his thought. He was thinking enviously of his boss who was Jim Brender, of the financial firm of J. P. Brender & Co.

The overtones of that thought made the creature turn abruptly and follow Lawrence Pearson, bookkeeper. If passersby had paid attention to him they would have been amazed after a moment to see two Lawrence Pearsons proceeding down the street, one some fifty feet behind the other. The second Lawrence Pearson had learned from the mind of the first that Jim Brender was a Harvard graduate in mathematics, finance, and political economy, the latest of a long line of financial geniuses, thirty years old, and head of the tremendously wealthy J. P. Brender & Co.

"Here I'm thirty, too," Pearson's thoughts echoed in the creature's mind, "and I've got nothing. Brender's got everything—everything while all I've got to look forward to is the same old boardinghouse till the end of time."

It was getting dark as the two crossed the river. The creature quickened its pace, striding forward aggressively. Some glimmering of its terrible purpose communicated itself in that last instant to the victim. The slight man turned, and let out a faint squawk as those steel-muscled fingers jerked at his throat, a single fearful snap. The creature's mind went black and dizzy as the brain of Lawrence Pearson died. Gasping, fighting dissolution, it finally gained control of itself. With one sweeping movement it caught the dead body and flung it over the concrete railing. There was a splash below, then a sound of gurgling water.

The thing that was now Lawrence Pearson walked on hurriedly, then more slowly till it came to a large, rambling brick house. It looked anxiously at the number, suddenly uncertain if it had remembered rightly. Hesitantly, it opened the door. A streamer of yellow light splashed out, and laughter vibrated in the thing's sensitive ears. There was the same hum of many thoughts and many brains, as there had been in the street. The creature fought against the inflow of thought that threatened to crowd out the mind of Lawrence Pearson. It found itself in a large, bright hall, which looked through a door into a room where a dozen people were sitting around a dining table.

"Oh, it's you, Mr. Pearson," said the landlady from the head of the table. She was a sharp-nosed, thin-mouthed woman at whom the creature stared with brief intentness. From her mind, a thought had come. She had a son who was a mathematics teacher in a high school. The creature shrugged. In one glance it penetrated the truth. This woman's son was as much of an intellectual lightweight as his mother. "You're just in time," she said incuriously. "Sarah, bring Mr.

Pearson's plate."

"Thank you, but I'm not feeling hungry," the creature replied; and its human brain vibrated to the first silent, ironic laughter that it had ever known. "I think I'll just lie down."

All night long it lay on the bed of Lawrence Pearson, bright-eyed, alert, becoming more and more aware of itself. It thought: "I'm a machine, without a brain of my own. I use the brains of other people. But somehow my creators made it possible for me to be more than just an echo. I use people's brains to carry out my purpose."

It pondered about these creators, and felt panic sweeping along its alien system, darkening its human mind. There was a vague physiological memory of pain and of tearing chemical action that was frightening.

The creature rose at dawn, and walked the streets till half-past nine. At that hour, it approached the imposing marble entrance of J. P. Brender & Co. Inside, it sank down in the comfortable chair initialed L. P., and began painstakingly to work at the books Lawrence Pearson had put away the night before. At ten o'clock, a tall young man in a dark suit entered the arched hallway and walked briskly through the row after row of offices. He smiled with easy confidence to every side. The thing did not need the chorus of "Good morning, Mr. Brender" to know that its prey had arrived. It rose with a lithe, graceful movement that would have been impossible to the real Lawrence Pearson, and walked briskly to the washroom. A moment later, the image of Jim Brender emerged from the door and walked with easy confidence to the door of the private office which Jim Brender had entered a few minutes before. The thing knocked, walked in—and simultaneously became aware of three things. First, it had found the mind after which it had been sent. Second, its image mind was incapable of imitating the finer subtleties of the razorsharp brain of the young man who was staring up with startled, dark-grey eyes. And third was the large metal bas-relief that hung on the wall.

With a shock that almost brought chaos, it felt the tug of that metal. And in one flash it knew that this was ultimate metal, product of the fine craft of the ancient Martians, whose metal cities, loaded with treasures of furniture, art and machinery, were slowly being dug up by enterprising human beings from the sands under which they had been buried for thirty or fifty million years. The ultimate metal! The metal that no heat would even warm, that no diamond or other cutting device could scratch, never duplicated by human beings, as mysterious as the ieis force which the Martians made from apparent nothingness.

All these thoughts crowded the creature's brain, as it explored the memory cells of Jim Brender. With an effort, the thing wrenched its mind from the metal, and fastened its gaze on Jim Brender. It caught full the flood of the wonder in his mind as he stood up.

"Good lord," said Jim Brender, "who are you?"

"My name's Jim Brender," said the thing, conscious of grim amusement, conscious, too, that it was progress for it to be able to feel such an emotion.

The real Jim Brender had recovered himself. "Sit down, sit down," he said heartily. "This is the most amazing coincidence I've ever seen."

He went over to the mirror that made one panel of the left wall. He stared, first at himself, then at the creature. "Amazing," he said. "Absolutely amazing."

"Mr. Brender," said the creature, "I saw your picture in the paper, and I thought our astounding resemblance would make you listen, where otherwise you might pay no attention. I have recently returned from Mars, and I am here to persuade you to come back to Mars with me."

"That," said Jim Brender, "is impossible."

"Wait," the creature said, "until I have told you why. Have you ever heard of the Tower of the Beast?"

"The Tower of the Beast!" Jim Brender repeated slowly. He went around his desk and pushed a button.

A voice from an ornamental box said, "Yes, Mr. Brender?"

"Dave, get me all the data on the Tower of the Beast and the legendary city of Li in which it is supposed to exist."

"Don't need to look it up," came the crisp reply. "Most Martian histories refer to it as the beast that fell from the sky when Mars was young—some terrible warning connected with it—the beast was unconscious when found—said to be the result of its falling out of sub-space. Martians read its mind, and were so horrified by its subconscious intentions they tried to kill it, but couldn't. So they built a huge vault, about fifteen hundred feet in diameter and a mile high—and the beast, apparently of these dimensions, was locked in. Several attempts have been made to find the city of Li, but without success. Generally believed to be a myth. That's all, Jim."

"Thank you!" Jim Brender clicked off the connection, and turned to his visitor. "Well?"

"It is not a myth. I know where the Tower of the Beast is; and I also know that the beast is still alive."

"Now, see here," said Brender good-humoredly, "I'm intrigued by your resemblance to me. But don't expect me to believe such a story. The beast, if there is such a thing, fell from the sky when Mars was young. There are some authorities who maintain that the Martian race died out a hundred million years ago, though twenty-five million is the conservative estimate. The only artifacts remaining of their civilization are their constructions of ultimate metal. Fortunately, toward the end they built almost everything from that indestructible metal."

"Let me tell you about the Tower of the Beast," said the thing quietly. "It is a tower of gigantic size, but only a hundred feet or so projected above the sand when I saw it. The whole top is a door, and that door is geared to a time lock, which in turn has been integrated along a line of ieis to the ultimate prime number."

Jim Brender stared; and the thing caught his startled thought, the first uncertainty, and the beginning of belief. "Ultimate," Brender said.

He snatched at a book from the little wall library beside his desk, and rippled through it. "The largest known prime is ah, here it is—is 230584300921393951. Some others, according to this authority, are 778443839397, 182521213001, and 78875943472201."

His frown deepened. "That makes the whole thing ridiculous. The ultimate prime would be an indefinite number." He smiled at the thing. "If there is a beast, and it is locked up in a vault of ultimate metal, the door of which is geared to a time lock, integrated along a line of ieis to the ultimate prime number—then the beast is caught. Nothing in the world can free it."

"To the contrary," said the creature. "I have been assured by the beast that it is within the scope of human mathematics to solve the problem, but that what is required is a born mathematical mind, equipped with all the mathematical training that Earth science can afford. You are that man."

"You expect me to release this evil creature—even if I could perform this miracle of mathematics?"

"Evil nothing!" snapped the thing. "That ridiculous fear of the unknown which made the Martians imprison it has resulted in a very grave wrong. The beast is a scientist from another space, accidentally caught in one of his experiments. I say 'his' when of course I do not know whether this race has a sexual differentiation."

"You actually talked with the beast?"

"It communicated with me by mental telepathy."

"It has been proven that thoughts cannot penetrate ultimate metal."

"What do humans know about telepathy? They cannot even communicate with each other except under special conditions." The creature spoke contemptuously.

"That's right. And if your story is true, then this is a matter for the Council."

"This is a matter for two men, you and me. Have you forgotten that the vault of the beast is the central tower to the great city of Li—billions of dollars' worth of treasure in furniture, art, and machinery? The beast demands release from its prison before it will permit anyone to mine that treasure. You can release it. We can share the treasure."

"Let me ask you a question," said Jim Brender. "What is your real name?"

"P-Pierce Lawrence!" the creature stammered. For the moment, it could think of no greater variation of the name of its first victim than reversing the two words, with a slight change on "Pearson." Its thoughts darkened with confusion as Brender went on.

"On what ship did you come from Mars?"

"O-on F4961," the thing stammered chaotically, fury adding to the confused state of its mind. It fought for control, felt itself slipping, suddenly felt the pull of the ultimate metal that made up the bas-relief on the wall, and knew by that tug that it was dangerously near dissolution.

"That would be a freighter," said Jim Brender. He pressed a button. "Carltons, find out if the F4961 had a passenger or person aboard named Pierce Lawrence. How long will it take?"

"A few minutes, sir."

Jim Brender leaned back. "This is mere formality. If you were on that ship, then I shall be compelled to give serious attention to your statements. You can understand, of course, that I could not possibly go into a thing like this blindly."

The buzzer rang. "Yes?" said Jim Brender.

"Only the crew of two was on the F4961 when it landed yesterday. No such person as Pierce Lawrence was aboard."

"Thank you." Jim Brender stood up. He said coldly, "Goodbye, Mr. Lawrence. I cannot imagine what you hoped to gain by this ridiculous story. However, it has been most intriguing, and the problem you presented was very ingenious indeed."

The buzzer was ringing. "What is it?"

"Mr. Gorson to see you, sir."

"Very well, send him right in."

The thing had greater control of its brain now, and it saw in Brender's mind that Gorson was a financial magnate, whose business ranked with the Brender firm. It saw other things, too; things that made it walk out of the private office, out of the building, and wait patiently until Mr. Gorson emerged from the imposing entrance. A few minutes later, there were two Mr. Gorsons walking down the street. Mr. Gorson was a vigorous man in his early fifties. He had lived a clean, active life; and the hard memories of many climates and several planets were stored away in his brain. The thing caught the alertness of this man on its sensitive elements, followed him warily, respectfully, not quite decided whether it would act. It thought: "I've improved a great deal from the primitive life that couldn't hold its shape. My creators, in designing me, gave to me powers of learning, developing. It is easier to fight dissolution, easier to be human. In handling this man, I must remember that my strength is invincible when properly used."

With minute care, it explored in the mind of its intended victim the exact route of his walk to his office. There was the entrance to a large building clearly etched on his mind. Then a long, marble corridor, into an automobile elevator up to the eighth floor, along a short corridor with two doors. One door led to the private entrance of the man's private office. The other to a storeroom used by the janitor. Gorson had looked into the place on various occasions; and there was in his mind, among other things, the memory of a large chest.

The thing waited in the storeroom till the unsuspecting Gorson was past the door. The door creaked. Gorson turned, his eyes widening. He didn't have a chance. A fist of solid steel smashed his face to a pulp, knocking the bones back into his brain. This time, the creature did not make the mistake of keeping its mind tuned to that of its victim. It caught him as he fell, forcing its steel fist back to a semblance of human flesh. With furious speed, it stuffed the bulky and athletic form into the large chest, and clamped the lid down tight. Alertly, it emerged from the storeroom, entered the private office of Mr. Gorson, and sat down before the gleaming desk of oak. The man who responded to the pressing of a button saw John Gorson sitting there, and heard John Gorson say:

"Crispins, I want you to start selling these stocks through the secret channels right away. Sell until I tell you to stop, even if you think it's crazy. I have information of something big on."

Crispins glanced down the row after row of stock names; and his eyes grew wider and wider. "Good lord, man!" he gasped finally, with that familiarity which is the right of a trusted adviser, "these are all gilt-edged stocks. Your whole fortune can't swing a deal like this."

"I told you I'm not in this alone."

"But it's against the law to break the market," the man protested.

"Crispins, you heard what I said. I'm leaving the office. Don't try to get in touch with me. I'll call you."

The thing that was John Gorson stood up, paying no attention to the bewildered thoughts that flowed from Crispins. It went out of the door by which it had entered. As it emerged from the building, it was thinking: "All I've got to do is kill half a dozen financial giants, start their stocks selling, and then—"

By one o'clock it was over. The exchange didn't close till three, but at one o'clock the news flashed on the New York tickers. In London, where it was getting dark, the papers brought out an extra. In Hankow and Shanghai, a dazzling new day was breaking as the newsboys ran along the streets in the shadows of skyscrapers, and shouted that J. P. Brender & Company had assigned; and that there was to be an investigation—

"We are facing," said the district court judge, in his opening address the following morning, "one of the most astounding coincidences in all history. An ancient and respected firm, with world-wide affiliations and branches, with investments in more than a thousand companies of every description, is struck bankrupt by an unexpected crash in every stock in which the firm was interested. It will require months to take evidence on the responsibility for the short-selling which brought about this disaster. In the meantime, I see no reason, regrettable as the action must be to all the old friends of the late J. P. Brender, and of his son, why the demands of the creditors should not be met, and the properties liquidated through auction sales and other such methods as I may deem proper and legal—"

Commander Hughes of Interplanetary Spaceways entered the office of his employer truculently. He was a small man, but extremely wiry; and the thing that was Louis Dyer gazed at him tensely, conscious of the force and power of this man.

Hughes began: "You have my report on this Brender case?"

The thing twirled the mustache of Louis Dyer nervously, then picked up a small folder, and read out loud:

"Dangerous for psychological reasons ... to employ Brender.... So many blows in succession. Loss of wealth and position ... No normal man could remain normal under ... circumstances. Take him into office ... befriend him ... give him a sinecure, or position where his undoubted great ability ... but not on a spaceship, where the utmost hardiness, both mental, moral, spiritual, and physical is required—"

Hughes interrupted: "Those are exactly the points which I am stressing. I knew you would see what I meant, Louis."

"Of course I see," said the creature, smiling in grim amusement, for it was feeling very superior these days. "Your thoughts, your ideas, your code, and your methods are stamped irrevocably on your brain and"—it added hastily—"you have never left me in doubt as to where you stand. However, in this case, I must insist. Jim Brender will not take an ordinary position offered by his friends. And it is ridiculous to ask him to subordinate himself to men to whom he is in every way superior. He has commanded his own space yacht; he knows more about the mathematical end of the work than our whole staff put together; and that is no reflection on our staff. He knows the hardships connected with space flying, and believes that it is exactly what he needs. I, therefore, command you, for the first time in our long association, Peter, to put him on space freighter F4961 in the place of Spacecraftsman Parelli who collapsed into a nervous breakdown after that curious affair with the creature from space, as Lieutenant Morton described it—By the way, did you find the ... er ... sample of that creature yet?"

"No, sir, it vanished the day you came in to look at it. We've searched the place high and low—queerest stuff you ever saw. Goes through glass as easy as light; you'd think it was some form of light stuff—scares me, too. A pure sympodial development—actually more adaptable of environment than anything hitherto discovered; and that's putting it mildly. I tell you, sir—But see here, you can't steer me off the Brender case like that."

"Peter, I don't understand your attitude. This is the first time I've interfered with your end of the work and—"

"I'll resign," groaned that sorely beset man.

The thing stifled a smile. "Peter, you've built up the staff of Spaceways. It's your child, your creation; you can't give it up, you know you can't—"

The words hissed softly into alarm; for into Hughes' brain had flashed the first real intention of resigning. Just hearing of his accomplishments and the story of his beloved job brought such a rush of memories, such a realization of how tremendous an outrage was this threatened interference. In one mental leap, the creature saw what this man's resignation would mean: The discontent of the men; the swift perception of the situation by Jim Brender; and his refusal to accept the job. There was only one way out—for Brender to get to the ship without finding out what had happened. Once on it, he must carry through with one trip to Mars, which was all that was needed.

The thing pondered the possibility of imitating Hughes' body. Then agonizingly realized that it was hopeless. Both Louis Dyer and Hughes must be around until the last minute.

"But, Peter, listen!" the creature began chaotically. Then it said, "Damn!" for it was very human in mentality. And the realization that Hughes took its words as a sign of weakness was maddening. Uncertainty descended like a black cloud over its brain.

"I'll tell Brender when he arrives in five minutes how I feel about all this!" Hughes snapped; and the creature knew that the worst had happened. "If you forbid me to tell him, then I resign. I—Good God, man, your face!"

Confusion and horror came to the creature simultaneously. It knew abruptly that its face had dissolved before the threatened ruin of its plans. It fought for control, leaped to its feet, seeing the incredible danger. The large office just beyond the frosted glass door—Hughes' first outcry would bring help. With a half sob, it sought to force its arm into an imitation of a metal fist, but there was no metal in the room to pull it into shape. There was only the solid maple desk. With a harsh cry, the creature leaped completely over the desk, and sought to bury a pointed shaft of stick into Hughes' throat.

Hughes cursed in amazement, and caught at the stick with furious strength. There was sudden commotion in the outer office, raised voices, running feet—

Brender parked his car near the ship. Then stood for a moment. It was not that he had any doubts. He was a desperate man, and therefore a long chance was in order. It wouldn't take very much time to find out if the Martian city of Li had been found. If it had been, then he would recover his fortune. He started to walk swiftly toward the ship.

As he paused beside the runway that led to the open door of F4961—a huge globe of shining metal, three hundred feet in diameter—he saw a man running toward him. He recognized Hughes.

The thing that was Hughes approached, fighting for calmness. The whole world was a flame of cross-pulling forces. It shrank from the thoughts of the people milling about in the office it had just left. Everything had gone wrong. It had never

intended to do what it now had to do. It had intended to spend most of the trip to
Mars as a blister of metal on the outer shield of the ship. With a tremendous effort,
it controlled itself. "We're leaving right away," it said.

Brender looked amazed. "But that means I'll have to figure out a new orbit
under the most difficult—"

"Exactly," the creature interrupted. "I've been hearing a lot about your
marvelous mathematical ability. It's time the words were proved by deeds."

Jim Brender shrugged. "I have no objection. But how is it that you're coming
along?"

"I always go with a new man."

It sounded reasonable. Brender climbed the runway, closely followed by
Hughes. The powerful pull of the metal was the first real pain the creature had
known for days. For a long month, it would now have to fight the metal, fight to
retain the shape of Hughes, and carry on a thousand duties at the same time. That
first pain tore along its elements, smashing the confidence that days of being
human had built up. And then, as it followed Brender through the door, it heard a
shout behind it. It looked back hastily. People were streaming out of several doors,
running toward the ship. Brender was several yards along the corridor. With a hiss
that was almost a sob, the creature leaped inside, and pulled the lever that clicked
the great door shut.

There was an emergency lever that controlled the antigravity plates. With one
jerk, the creature pulled the heavy lever hard over. Instantly, it experienced a
sensation of lightness and a sense of falling. Through the great plate window the
creature caught a flashing glimpse of the field below, swarming with people. White
faces turning upward, arms waving. Then the scene grew remote, as a thunder of
rockets vibrated through the ship.

"I hope," said Brender, as Hughes entered the control room, "you wanted me
to start the rockets."

"Yes," the thing replied thickly. "I'm leaving the mathematical end entirely in
your hands."

It didn't dare stay so near the heavy metal engines, even with Brender's body
there to help it keep its human shape. Hurriedly, it started up the corridor. The
best place would be the insulated bedroom.

Abruptly, it stopped in its headlong walk, teetering on tiptoes. From the control
room it had just left, a thought was trickling—a thought from Brender's brain. The
creature almost dissolved terror as it realized that Brender was sitting at the radio,
answering an insistent call from Earth.

It burst into the control room, and braked to a halt, its eyes widening with
humanlike dismay. Brender whirled from before the radio with a single twisting
step. In his fingers he held a revolver. In his mind, the creature read a dawning
comprehension of the whole truth. Brender cried: "You're the . . . thing that came
to my office, and talked about prime numbers and the vault of the beast."

He took a step to one side to cover an open doorway that led down another
corridor. The movement brought the telescreen into the vision of the creature. In
the screen was the image of the real Hughes. Simultaneously, Hughes saw the
thing.

"Brender," he bellowed, "it's the monster that Morton and Parelli saw on their trip from Mars. It doesn't react to heat or any chemicals, but we never tried bullets. Shoot, quick!" It was too much, metal, too much confusion. With a whimpering cry, the creature dissolved. The pull of the metal twisted it horribly into thick half metal. The struggle to be human left it a malignant structure of bulbous head, with one eye half gone and two snakelike arms attached to the half metal of the body. Instinctively, it fought closer to Brender, letting the pull of his body make it more human. The half metal became fleshlike stuff that sought to return to its human shape.

"Listen, Brender!" Hughes' voice was urgent. "The fuel vats in the engine room are made of ultimate metal. One of them is empty. We caught a part of this thing once before, and it couldn't get out of the small jar of ultimate metal. If you could drive it into the vat while it's lost control of itself, as it seems to do very easily—"

"I'll see what lead can do!" Brender rapped in a brittle voice.

Bang! The creature screamed from its half-formed slit of mouth, and retreated, its legs dissolving into gray dough.

"It hurts, doesn't it?" Brender ground out. "Get over into the engine room, you damned thing, into the vat!"

"Go on, go on!" Hughes was shouting from the telescreen.

Brender fired again. The creature made a slobbering sound, and retreated once more. But it was bigger again, more human. And in one caricature hand a caricature of Brender's revolver was growing.

It raised the unfinished, unformed gun. There was an explosion, and a shriek from the thing. The revolver fell, a shapeless, tattered blob, to the floor. The little gray mass of it scrambled frantically toward the parent body, and attached itself like some monstrous canker to the right foot.

And then, for the first time, the mighty and evil brains that had created the thing sought to dominate their robot. Furious, yet conscious that the game must be carefully played, the Controller forced the terrified and utterly beaten thing to its will. Scream after agonized scream rent the air, as the change was forced upon the unstable elements. In an instant, the thing stood in the shape of Brender, but instead of a revolver, there grew from one browned, powerful hand a pencil of shining metal. Mirror bright, it glittered in every facet like some incredible gem. The metal glowed ever so faintly, an unearthly radiance. And where the radio had been, and the screen with Hughes' face on it, there was a gaping hole. Desperately, Brender pumped bullets into the body before him, but though the shape trembled, it stared at him now, unaffected. The shining weapon swung toward him.

"When you are quite finished," it said, "perhaps we can talk."

It spoke so mildly that Brender, tensing to meet death, lowered his gun in amazement. The thing went on: "Do not be alarmed. This which you hear and see is an android, designed by us to cope with your space and number world. Several of us are working here under the most difficult conditions to maintain this connection, so I must be brief.

"We exist in a time world immeasurably more slow than your own. By a system of synchronization, we have geared a number of these spaces in such fashion that, though one of our days is millions of your years, we can communicate. Our purpose is to free Kalorn from the Martian vault. Kalorn was caught accidentally in a time warp of his own making and precipitated onto the planet you know as Mars. The Martians, needlessly fearing his great size, constructed a most diabolical prison, and we need your knowledge of the mathematics peculiar to your space and number world—and to it alone—in order to free him."

The calm voice continued, earnest but not offensively so, insistent but friendly. The speaker regretted that their android had killed human beings. In greater detail, he explained that every space was constructed on different numbers systems, some all negative, some all positive, some a mixture of the two, the whole an infinite variety, and every mathematics interwoven into the very fabric of the space it ruled.

Ieis force was not really mysterious. It was simply a flow from one space to another, the result of a difference in potential. This flow, however, was one of the universal forces, which only one other force could affect, the one he had used a few minutes before. Ultimate metal was *actually* ultimate. In their space they had a similar metal, built up from negative atoms. He could see from Brender's mind that the Martians had known nothing about minus numbers, so that they must have built it up from ordinary atoms. It could be done that way, too, though not so easily. He finished:

"The problem narrows down to this: Your mathematics must tell us how, with our universal force, we can short-circuit the ultimate prime number—that is, factor it—so that the door will open any time. You may ask how a prime can be factored when it is divisible only by itself and by one. That problem is, for your system, solvable only by your mathematics. Will you do it?"

Brender pocketed his revolver. His nerves were calm as he said, "Everything you have said sounds reasonable and honest. If you were desirous of making trouble, it would be the simplest thing in the world to send as many of your kind as you wished. Of course, the whole affair must be placed before the Council—"

"Then it is hopeless—the Council could not possibly accede—"

"And you expect me to do what you do not believe the highest governmental authority in the System would do?" Brender exclaimed.

"It is inherent in the nature of a democracy that it cannot gamble with the lives of its citizens. We have such a government here; and its members have already informed us that, in a similar condition, they would not consider releasing an unknown beast upon their people. Individuals, however, can gamble where governments must not. You have agreed that our argument is logical. What system do men follow if not that of logic?"

The Controller, through the creature, watched Brender's thoughts alertly. It saw doubt and uncertainty, opposed by a very human desire to help, based upon the logical conviction that it was safe. Probing his mind, it saw swiftly that it was unwise, in dealing with men, to trust too much to logic. It pressed on:

"To an individual we can offer—everything. In a minute, with your permission, we shall transfer this ship to Mars; not in thirty days, but in thirty seconds. The knowledge of how this is done will remain with you. Arrived at Mars you will find yourself the only living person who knows the whereabouts of the ancient city of Li, of which the vault of the beast is the central tower. In this city will be found literally billions of dollars' worth of treasure made of ultimate metal; and according to the laws of Earth, fifty percent will be yours. Your fortune re-established, you will be able to return to Earth this very day.

Brender was white. Malevolently, the thing watched the thoughts sweeping through his brain—the memory of the sudden disaster that had ruined his family. Brender looked up grimly.

"Yes," he said, "I'll do what I can."

A bleak range of mountains fell away into a valley of reddish gray sand. The thin winds of Mars blew a mist of sand against the building. *Such* a building! At a distance, it had looked merely big. A bare hundred feet projected above the desert, a hundred feet of height and *fifteen hundred feet of diameter*. Literally thousands of feet must extend beneath the restless ocean of sand to make the perfect balance of form, the graceful flow, the fairylike beauty which the long-dead Martians demanded of all their constructions, however massive. Brender felt suddenly small and insignificant as the rockets of his spacesuit pounded him along a few feet above the sand toward that incredible building.

At close range the ugliness of sheer size was miraculously lost in the wealth of the decorative. Columns and pilasters assembled in groups and clusters broke up the facades, gathered and dispersed again restlessly. The flat surface of wall and roof melted into a wealth of ornaments and imitation stucco work, vanished and broken into a play of light and shade.

The creature floated beside Brender. Its Controller said, "I see that you have been giving considerable thought to the problem, but this android seems incapable of following abstract thought, so I have no means of knowing the course of your speculations. I see, however, that you seem to be satisfied."

"I think I've got the answer," said Brender, "but first I wish to see the time lock. Let's climb."

They rose into the sky, dipping over the lip of the building. Brender saw a vast flat expanse; and in the center—He caught his breath!

The meager light from the distant sun of Mars shone down on a structure located at what seemed the exact center of the great door. The structure was about fifty feet high, and seemed nothing less than a series of quadrants coming together at the center, which was a metal arrow pointing straight up. The arrow head was not solid metal. Rather, it was as if the metal had divided in two parts, then curved together again. But not quite together. About a foot separated the two sections of metal. But that foot was bridged by a vague, thin, green flame of ieis force.

"The time lock!" Brender nodded. "I thought it would be something like that, though I expected it would be bigger, more substantial."

"Do not be deceived by its fragile appearance," answered the thing. "Theoretically, the strength of ultimate metal is infinite; and the ieis force can only be affected by the universal I have mentioned. Exactly what the effect will be, it is impossible to say as it involves the temporary derangement of the whole number system upon which that particular area of space is built. But now tell us what to do."

"Very well." Brender eased himself onto a bank of sand, and cut off his antigravity plates. He lay on his back, and stared thoughtfully into the blue-black sky. For the time being all doubts, worries and fears were gone from him. He relaxed, and read, "The Martian mathematic, like that of Euclid and Pythagoras, was based on endless magnitude. Minus numbers were beyond their philosophy.

On Earth however, beginning with Descartes, an analytical mathematic was evolved. Magnitude and perceivable dimensions were replaced by that of variable-values between positions in space.

"For the Martians, there was only one number between 1 and 3. Actually, the totality of such numbers is an infinite aggregate. And with the introduction of the idea of the square root of minus one—or i—and the complex numbers, mathematics definitely ceased to be a simple thing of magnitude, perceivable in picture. Only the intellectual step from the infinitely small quantity to the lower limit of every possible finite magnitude brought out the conception of a variable number which oscillated beneath any assignable number that was not zero.

"The prime number, being a conception of pure magnitude, had no reality in *real* mathematics, but in this case was rigidly bound up with the reality of the ieis force. The Martians knew ieis as a pale-green flow about a foot in length and developing say a thousand horsepower. (It was actually 12.171 inches and 1021.23 horsepower, but that was unimportant.) The power produced never varied, the length never varied, from year end to year end, for tens of thousands of years. The Martians took the length as their basis of power and called it one 'rb.' And because of the absolute invariability of the flow they decided it was eternal.

"They decided furthermore that nothing could be eternal without becoming prime. Their whole mathematic was based on numbers which could be factored, that is, disintegrated, destroyed, rendered less than they had been; and numbers which could not be factored, disintegrated, or divided into smaller groups.

"Any number which could be factored was incapable of being infinite. Contrariwise, the infinite number must be prime.

"Therefore, they built a lock and integrated it along a line of ieis, to operate when the ieis ceased to flow—which would be at the end of Time, provided it was not interfered with. To prevent interference, they buried the motivating mechanism of the flow in ultimate metal, which could not be destroyed or corroded in any way. According to their mathematic, that settled it."

"But you have the answer," said the voice of the thing eagerly.

"Simply this: The Martians set a value on the flow of one 'rb.' If you interfere with that flow to no matter what small degree, you no longer have an 'rb.' You have something less. The flow, which is a universal, becomes automatically less than a universal, less than infinite. The prime number ceases to be prime. Let us suppose that you interfere with it to the extent of ultimate prime *minus one*. You will then have a number divisible by two. As a matter of fact, the number, like most large numbers, will immediately break into thousands of pieces, i.e., it will be divisible by tens of thousands of smaller numbers. If the present time falls anywhere near one of those breaks, the door would open immediately if you can so interfere with the flow that one of the factors occurs in immediate time."

"That is very clear," said the Controller with satisfaction, and the image of Brender was smiling triumphantly. "We shall now use this android to manufacture a universal; and Kalorn shall be free very shortly." He laughed aloud. "The poor android is protesting violently at the thought of being destroyed, but after all it is only a machine, and not a very good one at that. Besides, it is interfering with my proper reception of your thoughts. Listen to it scream, as I twist it into shape."

The cold-blooded words chilled Brender, pulled him from the heights of his abstract thought. Because of the prolonged intensity of his thinking, he saw with sharp clarity something that had escaped him before.

"Just a minute," he said. "How is it that the robot, introduced from your world, is living at the same time rate as I am, whereas Kalorn continues to live at your time rate?"

"A very good question." The face of the creature was twisted into a triumphant sneer, as the Controller continued. "Because, my dear Brender, you have been duped. It is true that Kalorn is living in our time rate, but that was due to a short-coming in our machine. The machine which Kalorn built, while large enough to transport him, was not large enough in its adaptive mechanism to adapt him to each new space as he entered it. With the result that he was transported but not adapted. It was possible, of course, for us, his helpers, to transport such a small thing as the android, though we have no more idea of the machine's construction than you have.

"In short, we can use what there is of the machine, but the secret of its construction is locked in the insides of our own particular ultimate metal, and in the brain of Kalorn. Its invention by Kalorn was one of those accidents which, by the law of averages, will not be repeated in millions of our years. Now that you have provided us with the method of bringing Kalorn back, we shall be able to build innumerable interspace machines. Our purpose is to control all spaces, all worlds—particularly those which are inhabited. We intend to be absolute rulers of the entire Universe."

The ironic voice ended, and Brender lay in his prone position the prey of horror. The horror was twofold, partly due to the Controller's monstrous plan, and partly to the thought that was pulsing in his brain. He groaned, as he realized that his warning thought must be ticking away on the automatic receiving brain of the robot. "Wait," his thought was saying, "that adds a new factor. Time—"

There was a scream from the creature as it was forcibly dissolved. The scream choked to a sob, then silence. An intricate machine of shining metal lay there on that great gray-brown expanse of sand and ultimate metal.

The metal glowed; and then the machine was floating in the air. It rose to the top of the arrow, and settled over the green flame of ieis.

Brender jerked on his antigravity screen, and leaped to his feet. The violent action carried him some hundred feet into the air. His rockets sputtered into staccato fire, and he clamped his teeth against the pain of acceleration. Below him, the great door began to turn, to unscrew, faster and faster, till it was like a flywheel. Sand flew in all directions in a miniature storm.

At top acceleration, Brender darted to one side. Just in time. First, the robot machine was flung off that tremendous wheel by sheer centrifugal power. Then the door came off, and, spinning now at an incredible rate, hurtled straight into the air and vanished into space.

A puff of black dust came floating out of the blackness of the vault. Suppressing his horror, yet perspiring from awful relief, he rocketed to where the robot had fallen into the sand. Instead of glistening metal, a time-dulled piece of junk lay there. The dull metal flowed sluggishly and assumed a quasi-human shape. The flesh remained gray and in little rolls as if it were ready to fall apart from old age.

The thing tried to stand up on wrinkled legs, but finally lay still. Its lips moved, mumbled:

"I caught your warning thought, but I didn't let them know. Now, Kalorn is dead. They realized the truth as it was happening. End of Time came—"

It faltered into silence; and Brender went on, "Yes, end of time came when the flow became momentarily less than eternal—came at the factor point which occurred a few minutes ago."

"I was ... only partly ... within its ... influence, Kalorn all the way ... Even if they're lucky ... 'twill be years before ... they invent another machine ... and one of their years is billions ... of yours ... I didn't tell them ... I caught your thought ... and kept it ... from them—"

"But why did you do it—Why?"

"Because they were hurting me. They were going to destroy me. Because ... I liked ... being human. I was ... somebody!"

The flesh dissolved. It flowed slowly into a pool of lava-like gray. The lava crinkled, split into dry, brittle pieces. Brender touched one of the pieces. It crumbled into a fine powder of dust. He gazed out across that grim, deserted valley of sand, and said aloud, pityingly, "Poor Frankenstein."

He turned and flew toward the distant spaceship.

FREDERIK POHL
We Never Mention Aunt Nora

Mary Lynne Edkin brought the man home to meet her brother.

It was uncomfortable for everyone. Mary Lynne's brother Alden looked up from his chair. He snapped his fingers and the sound on the trivision obediently diminished to a merely obtrusive level.

He held out his hand. "Pleased to meet you," he said, but it was obviously a lie.

Mary Lynne got that expression on her face.

"Al," she said dangerously.

Her brother shrugged and snapped his fingers twice more. The set shut itself off.

Mary Lynne's expression cleared. She was not a pretty girl, but she was a pleasant-looking one. The no-midriff fashion was kind to her; she still had a nice figure.

"Al," she said, but smiling now, "Al, guess what! Jimmy and I want to get married!"

"Oh-ho," said her brother, and he stood up in order to take a better look.

Even standing, he had to look up at this man James Croy. Croy was *big*. Six feet ten or eleven at the least, and his hair was snow white. Still, thought Alden Edkin, the man's face didn't look old. Maybe he was platinum blond. Al snorted, for he didn't hold with men dyeing their hair, common though the practice was.

He asked accusingly, "How come I never met him before?"

"Now, Al—"

"How come?"

Mary Lynne blushed. "Well, Al, there hasn't been much chance for you to meet."

"Oh-ho," said her brother again. "You just met him yourself."

"But I love him, Al!" cried Mary Lynne, clutching at the tall man's arm. "He's—he—oh, I can't explain it. But I love him!"

"Sure you do," said her brother. "You love him. But what do you know about him?"

"I know enough!"

Alden said sternly, "Family, Mary Lynne! Marriage isn't just between two people. We come of good stock and we can't marry just anybody. Think of the children you may have! Our family—"

"Our family!" echoed his sister. "What's so special about our family? How many times have you said that Aunt Nora—"

"Mary Lynne!" Alden warned. She paused. He said, "No offense, Mr. Croy. But what do we know? You may be after her money, for all we can tell."

The large man cleared his throat and straightened the crease in his Bermudas. He said modestly, "I assure you, Mr. Edkin, I am not interested in money."

"But you'd say that anyhow. Wouldn't you? Not that there's much *cash*. But there's this big house—Mary Lynne's and mine. And, Mary, you have to think of what Mother and Dad would want. They didn't leave you this big house—it will be yours when I'm gone—so that some adventurer could come along and—"

"Alden!" Mary Lynne was furious. She turned to the man she loved apologetically, but he was merely looking politely concerned. She whirled on her brother. "Apologize to Jimmy!"

There was a marked silence.

"Well," said her brother at last, talking to the wall, "there's one good thing. Being that she's under age, she can't—"

He stopped and waited.

They all waited. The big house that Mother and Dad had left them happened to be on the lip of the takeoff pits for the Moon rocket. The screeching howl of the night rocket's takeoff rattled the windows and made the trivision set moan shrilly in resonance.

But it only lasted for a few seconds.

"—can't get married without my consent," Alden Edkin finished.

"Alden!" cried his sister again, but it was more a sob than a protest.

Alden Edkin merely looked obstinate. He was good at it.

James Croy cleared his throat. "Sir," he said, "I know that what you say is true. We cannot marry without your consent. I hope that you'll give it."

"Don't hold your breath." Edkin sat down and glanced longingly at the trivision set. "As I say, we don't know anything about you."

"That's easily taken care of, Mr. Edkin," said Croy, smiling. "I'm an orphan. No ties, no family. Until recently, I was a draftsman for Amalgamated Luna, in the rocket engine department."

"Until recently? You don't even have a job?"

"Not exactly, sir. But I was fortunate enough to design a rather good firing chamber. They've adopted it for the Mars rocket."

Edkin nodded thoughtfully. "You sold them the design?"

Croy shook his head. "Not outright. But the royalties are—well, ample. I assure you that I can support Mary Lynne in adequate style. And I should mention that the royalty contract runs for thirty years, with cost-of-living increases."

"Um." Alden Edkin found that he was beginning to relax slightly. This Croy was, in his way, not without a certain charm.

Edkin said in a warmer tone, "Well, money isn't the only consideration. Still . . . Say, what about making some coffee, Mary Lynne? I'm sure our guest would enjoy it."

She looked at him in some surprise, shrugged, patted her proposed fiancé's arm and left the room.

Edkin said, "I hope you won't pay any attention to what Mary Lynne said about Aunt Nora."

"Of course not," said Croy and smiled. He had a very nice smile. His eyes were deep-set, somber and serious, and the smile beneath them was like sunlight bursting out from under a cloud.

Edkin was momentarily dazzled. He shook his head to clear it; for a second, he had almost thought he could see *through* the man. But that was nonsense.

Croy was saying, "I don't drink coffee, Mr. Edkin, but I'm glad Mary Lynne's out of the room. I hope we can get better acquainted."

"Sure," said Edkin testily. "Well, sit down and tell me something about yourself. Where was your family when you had one?"

"We're originally from Portland, Mr. Edkin."

"Portland, Maine? Say, I was stationed near Presq'Isle when I was in the Army."

"No," said Croy regretfully, "Portland, Oregon. After my parents passed away, I attended several schools, graduating from the University of California."

"Oh, we know lots of people there!" exclaimed Edkin. "Our cousins on my mother's side have some friends who teach at Berkeley. Perhaps you know them—Harold Sizeland and—"

"Sorry," Croy apologized. "I was at the Los Angeles campus. But let's not talk about *me*, Mr. Edkin. Mary Lynne tells me you're in credit maintenance."

"That's right." Actually he was a loan collector; it was close enough.

Croy leaned confidentially closer. "You can help me, Mr. Edkin. I'm planning a sort of surprise for Mary Lynne."

"Surprise?"

"Here," said Croy, reaching into his pocket. He pulled out several sheets of legal cap, stapled into a blue folder. "Since you're in the financial line," he said, "you'll know if this is all right. What it is, it's a kind of trust agreement for Mary Lynne."

Edkin scowled. "You're taking a lot for granted, Croy. I haven't agreed to anything."

"Of course not. But won't you look this over for me? You see, it puts all the royalties from my firing chamber in her name. Irrevocably. So that if anything happened to me, or there was, well, anything serious—" he didn't say the word "divorce," but he shrugged it—"she'll be well provided for. I'd appreciate your opinion of the contract."

Edkin glanced at the papers suspiciously.

He was ready to stand up and order from the house this brash young giant who interrupted his trivision programs and proposed to carry off his sister. But something hit him in the eye. And what that something happened to be was a neatly typed line specifying Mary Lynne's guaranteed minimum annual income from the trust agreement.

Thirty-five thousand dollars a year.

Edkin swallowed.

Attached to the certificate of agreement was a notarized copy of the Amalgamated Luna royalty contract. Unless it was a fake, the thirty-five-thousand-dollar figure was exactly right.

Mary Lynne came back into the room, and nearly dropped the coffee tray.

"Hi there, Mary Lynne!" greeted her brother, looking up from where he was patting Croy on the shoulder. "Coffee, eh? Good!"

She stared at him unbelievingly. He bobbed his head, winked conspiratorially at Croy, jammed the papers in his pocket and stood up.

"Coffee, eh?" he repeated, carrying chairs toward the table. "Your young man won't drink it, Mary Lynne. But surely he'll have some cake, eh? Or a drink? Some tea? Perhaps a glass of chocolate milk—Mary Lynne will be glad to warm it. No?"

He shrugged and sat down, smiling. "No matter," he observed. "Now tell me. When would you two lovebirds like the happy event to take place?"

Three days later, the marriage was performed. It was the minimum legal waiting period.

Alden Edkin, as it happened, was a bachelor who believed that every man who glanced at his sister was a prospective rapist—and that those who proposed marriage were after her money besides. Still, he was not an idiot.

He had taken certain precautions.

First, he took a copy of the trust agreement to Mr. Senutovitch in his company's legal department. Mr. Senutovitch read the papers over with real enjoyment.

"Ah, bully stuff, Edkin," he said sentimentally. He leaned back and gazed at the ceiling while the arms of his reclining chair sighed faintly and adjusted to his position. "It's a pleasure to read the work of a master."

"You think it's all legal. Mr. Senutovitch?"

"Legal?" Mr. Senutovitch coughed gently. "Did you notice the classic language of the operative clause? That's Paragraph Three: 'Does hereby devise, grant, give, bestow and convey, without let or distraint, absolutely.' Oh, it's a grand piece of work."

"And irrevocable?"

Mr. Senutovitch smiled. "Quite irrevocable."

"You're sure, Mr. Senutovitch?"

The lawyer said mildly, "Edkin, I wrote this company's Chattel Lien Form. I'm sure."

The other precaution Edkin took was to drop into his company's Credit Reference Library and put through the name of Croy, James T., for a report.

It would take a few days for the credit report to come through, and meanwhile the ceremony would be performed and the couple off on their honeymoon. But at least, Edkin consoled himself, when it did come through, it would be a comprehensive document. The company took an expansive view of what a credit report should cover.

The company, moreover, was not to be deceived by any such paltry devices as a change of name—or, for that matter, of fingerprints, retinal patterns or blood type. If a man could change his basic genetic construction, he might fool the company, but not with anything less; the Credit Reference Library was hooked in by direct wire with the F.B.I. office in Washington—for the convenience of the F.B.I., not of the company. There would be no secrets left to Mr. Croy. And therefore no secret worries for Alden Edkin.

And then Edkin stood by, fighting a manly urge to weep, as his sweet young sister gave herself in wedlock to this white-haired giant with the deep, penetrating eyes. The ceremony was performed before Father Hanover at Trinity Episcopal Church. There were few witnesses, though Mr. Senutovitch showed up, wrung the bridegroom's hand warmly and left without a word.

In the empty house, Alden Edkin took a deep breath, let it out, and put through a phone call to their only surviving relative. It was the least he could do.

A plump face over the fur collar of a lounging robe peered out of the phone's screen at him.

"Aunt Nora?" said Edkin tentatively. "My, you're looking well."

"You lie," she said shrilly. "I look *old*. What do you want? If it's money, I won't give you a—"

"No, nothing like that, Aunt Nora."

"Then what? You sorry you threw me out of the house twenty years ago? Is that what you called up to say?"

"Aunt Nora," said Edkin boldly, "I say let bygones be bygones. I called you up to tell you the news about Mary Lynne—my sister—your niece."

"Well? Well? What about her?"

"She just got married, Aunt Nora," said Edkin, beaming.

"What about it? People do, you know. There's nothing strange."

Edkin was shocked. Such a lack of family feeling! And from *her*, who should feel herself lucky beyond imagining that anyone in the family called her up at all. He was angry enough to say what he had vowed he would never refer to.

"At least," he said icily, "she got *married*."

Pause.

Thinly: "What do you mean by that?"

"You know perfectly well, Aunt Nora."

In the tiny screen, her face was a doll's face, an angry doll; it flushed red. She must have been shaking the phone, Edkin thought distractedly; rings of color haloed the edge of the screen.

She cried, "You're a sanctimonious jerk, Alden Edkin! You forbade me to associate with your sister—my own niece!—so I wouldn't corrupt her . . . when she was three months old and the good Lord Himself couldn't corrupt her, because she didn't so much as know which end was up! And now, just because she's getting married, you call me up. Hoping, no doubt, that because I'm getting old and absent-minded, I'll send along a little check for ten thousand dollars or so as a wedding present. Well, you're wrong! If Mary Lynne wants to call me up, I'll talk to her—but not to you! Understand?"

And the little screen flashed red and orange as she hung up.

Edkin pushed down the off button and shrugged. Aunt Nora! Who could account for her moods? A product of her sordid past, of course, but— It had been a mistake to call her up. Definitely.

Virtuously, Alden Edkin went to bed.

The following morning, he got the report from the Credit Reference Library. It had received special priority. The paper it was typed on flamed with warning red.

Alden Edkin was waiting at the airfield when the honeymooners returned from their Grand Tour.

He had been champing at the bit for six weeks—six long weeks and not a word from them, six weeks when they were out of touch with the world. Because they *wanted* it that way!

It was Alden Edkin's conviction that he knew *why* James Croy wanted it that way. He stood there by the customs gate, grinding his teeth, a plump angry man with a face that was rapidly turning purple.

He saw them coming down the wheeled steps from the plane and he bawled, "Mary Lynne! Mary Lynne, come down here this minute! Get away from that monster Croy!"

Mary Lynne, her arm adoringly on the arm of her husband, shuddered. "Oh-oh," she muttered. "Storm clouds rising. Batten down all hatches."

Croy tsked solicitously. "Poor man, he's upset, isn't he? But you mustn't worry."

"I'm not worried, darling."

"Of course not, of course not. Trust me." Croy nodded approvingly. "I've got to stop off for a second. A little errand— But I'll be right back and then I'm sure we can straighten out whatever's troubling your brother." Gently he kissed her ear. "My darling," he whispered, soft as a moth's wing.

And then that perfect gentleman, James Croy, bowed to the brother-in-law who was raging impotently across the customs gate, turned on his heel and disappeared into the men's room.

The men's room had a North Entrance, a South Entrance, a Mezzanine Entrance and a Service Entrance to the floor below. It is not a matter of record which door Croy used to come out, but it was not the one by which he had gone in.

The policemen finally went away. "Sorry," said the sergeant, curt and somewhat bored—he had been with Missing Persons for a good long time. "Probably he'll turn up."

But it wasn't true, and both he and Alden Edkin knew it. And when he had left, Edkin told his sister what the red-bordered credit report had shown.

Across the top was printed in bold letters *Zero Credit Rating Zero.*

"You can't fool Consolidated Credit," snapped Edkin. "They know. And this man Croy—why, he's a monster. Mary Lynne! He preys on women."

"Oh, no," wept his sister. But she was already in her heart convinced.

"Oh, yes! He is! Listen to this! Four years ago, in Miami, he married a girl named Doris L. Cockingham. There's no record of a divorce! He just married her—set up a trust for her with the royalties from an electric underwater lung, left her pregnant and disappeared. Eh?"

"I don't believe you," sobbed his sister.

"Then listen to this! Eleven months later, in Troy, New York, he married Marsha Gutknecht. Revolting! Can you *understand* a man like that? Loose morals, bigamy—why, he'd *never* get credit with a record like that."

"There must be some perfectly simple explanation," whimpered Mary Lynne. "When Jim comes back—"

"He won't be back!" said her brother brutally. "Get used to that idea, Mary Lynne! The Gutknecht woman never saw him again, and she was pregnant, too. He *meant* to run away! He used false names. Told different stories to each of them. But he couldn't fool Consolidated Credit. He put four hundred thousand dollars in trust for this woman and took off and never gave her another thought. How do you like that, Mary Lynne?"

"Jim wouldn't—"

"Jim did! And again the following year. Whitefish Bay, Wisconsin—a girl named Deloris Bennyhoff. Then in Jim Thorpe, Pennsylvania—" He crumpled the paper in rage. "Ah, what's the use? Five women! He married them, runs off, leaves them pregnant. And what do you have to say to that, Mary Lynne?"

Mary Lynne looked at her brother through blurred eyes.

In a faint, faint voice, she said, "Well, at least he runs true to form, Alden."

Oh, they looked for him. But they couldn't find him. The police couldn't find him, private detectives couldn't find him, even Consolidated Credit couldn't find him. Jim Croy was gone—probably forever, at least under that name. And while they were looking, events took their natural course, and Mary Lynne made reservations at the hospital and began to pack a little bag.

And Aunt Nora phoned.

Her plump face peered somberly out of the phone screen. "I'm coming east," she announced.

"You're not!" croaked Alden, wincing already. "I mean—"

"Thursday," she said. "On the six o'clock plane."

"But, Aunt Nora—" It was the last thing he wanted! So many years of cutting her out of the family circle because of the indiscretion of her youth, and now—

"Meet me," she said, and hung up.

There was nothing to be done about it. Aunt Nora showed up at the house her sister had left the children just as Mary Lynne gasped, checked her wristwatch, gasped again and reached for her ready-packed bag.

"Hello, Aunt Nora," said Alden distractedly. "Mary Lynne, aren't you ready yet? Good-by, Aunt Nora. Make yourself at home."

"Wait!" cried Aunt Nora, but she was talking to a closed door.

She sighed, shook her head irritably and took off her coat. Men were so foolish about babies! There would be plenty of time; she would unpack her bag, get settled in, and then, with full leisure, proceed to the hospital. And she was willing to bet that she would be there well before the baby arrived.

She was right—though what she found in the upper bureau drawer of her room made her hurry to the hospital sooner than she'd planned.

"Alden!" she gasped. "The picture! I saw the picture—"

"Hello, Aunt Nora," said Edkin gloomily. "Lord, but this takes a long time!"

"It just seems long," snapped Nora and waved a picture under his nose. It was inscribed in white ink: *For Mary Lynne, from Jimmy, with love.* "Who's this?"

Edkin said guiltily, "Mary's—ah—husband. He's away just now."

"I bet he is! That's not any Jimmy! That's Sam!"

"Sam?"

"*My* Sam. The one who left me in a delicate condition years ago! And the only difference is, now he marries them!"

Alden, hardly listening, said soothingly, "That was a long time ago, Aunt Nora. We don't worry about it now. Besides, you gave the baby up for adoption, didn't you? I never even saw him—or her? What was it, a boy?"

She said shortly, "No."

"A girl, then."

"Guess again," said Aunt Nora in a more peculiar tone. "And it wasn't exactly adoption."

Her tone was peculiar enough to attract his full attention. He looked at her queerly, but she didn't seem to be joking. Funny. He didn't have the faintest idea of what she meant—

Until an endless twenty minutes later.

Until the white-faced nurse came out of the delivery room wheeling a bassinet; until, without a word, the nurse pointed a shaking finger, and Edkin saw what it was that his sister had—with the help of what called itself James Croy—brought into an unsuspecting world.

CHARLES BEAUMONT
Last Rites

Somewhere in the church a baby was shrieking. Father Courtney listened to it, and sighed, and made the Sign of the Cross. Another battle, he thought, dismally. Another grand tug of war. And who won this time, Lord? Me? Or that squalling infant, bless its innocence?

"In the Name of the Father, and of the Son, and of the Holy Ghost. Amen."

He turned and made his way down the pulpit steps, and told himself, Well, you ought to be used to it by now, Heaven knows. After all, you're a priest, not a monologist. What do you care about "audience reaction"? And besides, who ever listens to these sermons of yours, anyway—even under the best of conditions? A few of the ladies in the parish (though you're sure they never hear or understand a word), and, of course, Donovan. But who else?

Screech away, little pink child! Screech until you—no.

No, no. Ahh!

He walked through the sacristy, trying not to think of Donovan, or the big city churches with their fine nurseries and sound-proof walls and amplifiers that amplified . . .

One had what one had: It was God's will.

And were things really so bad? Here there was the smell of forests, wasn't there? And in what city parish could you see wild flowers growing on the hills like bright lava? Or feel the earth breathing?

He opened the door and stepped outside.

The fields were dark-silver and silent. Far above the fields, up near the clouds, a rocket launch moved swiftly, dragging its slow thunder behind it.

Father Courtney blinked.

Of course things were not so bad. Things would be just fine, he thought, and I would not be nervous and annoyed at little children, if only—

Abruptly he put *his* hands together. "Father," he whispered, "let him be well. Let that be Your will!"

Then, deciding not to wait to greet the people, he wiped his palms with a handkerchief and started for the rectory.

The morning was very cold. A thin film of dew coated each pebble along the path, and made them all glisten like drops of mercury. Father Courtney looked at the pebbles and thought of other walks down this path, which led through a wood to Hidden River, and of himself laughing; of excellent wine and soft cushions and himself arguing, arguing; of a thousand sweet hours in the past.

He walked and thought these things and did not hear the telephone until he had reached the rectory stairs.

A chill passed over him, unaccountably.

He went inside and pressed a yellow switch. The screen blurred, came into focus. The face of an old man appeared, filling the screen.

"Hello, Father."

"George!" The priest smiled and waved his fist, menacingly. "George, why haven't you contacted me?" He sputtered. "Aren't you out of that bed yet?"

"Not yet, Father."

"Well, I expected it, I knew it. *Now* will you let me call a doctor?"

"No—" The old man in the screen shook his head. He was thin and pale. His hair was profuse, but very white, and there was something in his eyes. "I think I'd like you to come over, if you could."

"I shouldn't," the priest said, "after the way you've been treating all of us. But, if there's still some of that Chianti left . . ."

George Donovan nodded. "Could you come right away?"

"Father Yoshida won't be happy about it."

"Please. Right away."

Father Courtney felt his fingers draw into fists. "Why?" he asked, holding onto the conversational tone. "Is anything the matter?"

"Not really," Donovan said. His smile was brief. "It's just that I'm dying."

"And I'm going to call Doctor Ferguson. Don't give me any argument, either. This nonsense has gone far—"

The old man's face knotted. "No," he said, loudly. "I forbid you to do that."

"But you're ill, man. For all we know, you're *seriously* ill. And if you think I'm going to stand around and watch you work yourself into the hospital just because you happen to dislike doctors, you're crazy."

"Father, listen—*please.* I have my reasons. You don't understand them, and I don't blame you. But you've got to trust me. I'll explain everything, if you'll promise me you won't call *anyone.*"

Father Courtney breathed unsteadily; he studied his friend's face. Then he said, "I'll promise you this much. I won't contact a doctor until I've seen you."

"Good." The old man seemed to relax.

"I'll be there in fifteen minutes."

"With your Little Black Bag?"

"Certainly not. You're going to be all right."

"Bring it, Father. Please. Just in case."

The screen blurred and danced and went white.

Father Courtney hesitated at the blank telephone.

Then he walked to a table and raised his fists and brought them down hard, once.

You're going to get well, he thought. It isn't going to be too late.

Because if you are dying, if you really are, and I could have prevented it . . .

He went to the closet and drew on his overcoat.

It was thick and heavy, but it did not warm him. As he returned to the sacristy he shivered and thought that he had never been so cold before in all his life.

The helicar whirred and dropped quickly to the ground. Father Courtney removed the ignition key, pocketed it, and thrust his bulk out the narrow door, wheezing.

A dull rumbling sifted down from the sky. The wake of fleets a mile away, ten miles, a hundred.

It's raining whales in our backyard, the priest thought, remembering how Donovan had described the sound once to a little girl.

A freshet of autumn leaves burst against his leg, softly, and for a while he stood listening to the rockets' dying rumble, watching the shapes of gold and red that scattered in the wind, like fire.

Then he whispered, "Let it be Your will," and pushed the picket gate.

The front door of the house was open.

He walked in, through the livingroom, to the study.

"George."

"In here," a voice answered.

He moved to the bedroom, and twisted the knob.

George Donovan lay propped on a cloudbank of pillows, his thin face white as the linen. He was smiling.

"I'm glad to see you, Father," he said, quietly.

The priest's heart expanded and shrank and began to thump in his chest.

"The Chianti's down here in the night-table," Donovan gestured. "Pour some: morning's a good enough time for a dinner wine."

"Not now, George."

"Please. It will help."

Father Courtney pulled out the drawer and removed the half-empty bottle. He got a glass from the bookshelf, filled it. Dutifully, according to ritual, he asked. "For you?"

"No," Donovan said. "Thank you all the same." He turned his head. "Sit over there, Father, where I can see you."

The priest frowned. He noticed that Donovan's arms were perfectly flat against the blanket, that his body was rigid, outlined beneath the covering. No part of the old man moved except the head, and that slowly, unnaturally.

"That's better. But take off your coat—it's terribly hot in here. You'll catch pneumonia."

The room was full of cold winds from the open shutters.

Father Courtney removed his coat.

"You've been worried, haven't you?" Donovan asked.

The priest nodded. He tried to sense what was wrong, to smell the disease, if there was a disease, if there was anything.

"I'm sorry about that." The old man seemed to sigh. His eyes were misted, webbed with distance, lightly. "But I wanted to be alone. Sometimes you have to be alone, to think, to get things straight. Isn't that true?"

"Sometimes, I suppose, but—"

"No. I know what you're going to say, the questions you want to ask. But there's not enough time . . ."

Father Courtney arose from the chair, and walked quickly to the telephone extension. He jabbed a button. "I'm sorry, George," he said, "but you're going to have a doctor."

The screen did not flicker.

He pressed the button again, firmly.

"Sit down," the tired voice whispered. "It doesn't work. I pulled the wires ten minutes ago."

"Then I'll fly over to Milburn—"

"If you do, I'll be dead when you get back. Believe that: I know what I'm talking about."

The priest clenched and unclenched his stubby fingers, and sat down in the chair again.

Donovan chuckled. "Drink up," he said. "We can't have good wine going to waste, can we?"

The priest put the glass to his lips. He tried to think clearly. If he rushed out to Milburn and got Doctor Ferguson, perhaps there'd be a chance. Or— He took a deep swallow.

No. That wouldn't do. It might take hours.

Donovan was talking now; the words lost—a hum of locusts in the room, a far-off murmuring; then, like a radio turned up: "Father, how long have we been friends, you and I?"

"Why . . . twenty years," the priest answered. "Or more."

"Would you say you know me very well by now?"

"I believe so."

"Then tell me first, right now, would you say that I've been a good man?"

Father Courtney smiled. "There've been worse," he said, and thought of what this man had accomplished in Mount Vernon, quietly, in his own solid way, over the years. The building of a decent school for the children—Donovan had shamed the people into it. The new hospital—Donovan's doing, his patient campaigning. Entertainment halls for the young; a city fund for the poor; better teachers, better doctors—all, all because of the old man with the soft voice, George Donovan.

"Do you mean it?"

"Don't be foolish. And don't be treacly, either. Of course I mean it."

In the room, now, a strange odor fumed up, suddenly.

The old man said, "I'm glad." Still he did not move. "But, I'm sorry I asked. It was unfair."

"I don't have the slightest idea what you're talking about."

"Neither do I, Father, completely. I thought I did, once, but I was wrong."

The priest slapped his knees, angrily. "Why won't you let me get a doctor? We'll have plenty of time to talk afterwards."

Donovan's eyes narrowed, and curved into what resembled a smile. "You're my doctor," he said. "The only one who can help me now."

"In what way?"

"By making a decision." The voice was reedy: it seemed to waver and change pitch.

"What sort of a decision?"

Donovan's head jerked up. He closed his eyes and remained this way for a full minute, while the acrid smell bellied and grew stronger and whorled about the room in invisible currents.

"'. . . the gentleman lay graveward with his furies . . .' Do you remember that, Father?"

"Yes," the priest said. "Thomas, isn't it?"

"Thomas. He's been here with me, you know, really; and I've been asking him things. On the theory that poets aren't entirely human. But he just grins. 'You're dying of strangers,' he says; and grins. Bless him." The old man lowered his head. "He disappointed me."

Father Courtney reached for a cigarette, crumpled the empty pack, laced and unlaced his fingers. He waited, remembering the times he had come to this house, all the fine evenings. Ending now?

Yes. Whatever else he would learn, he knew that, suddenly: they were ending.

"What sort of a decision, George?"

"A theological sort."

Father Courtney snorted and walked to a window. Outside, the sun was hidden behind a curtain of gray. Birds sat black and still on the telephone lines, like notes of music; and there was rain.

"Is there something you think you haven't told me?" he asked.

"Yes."

"About yourself?"

"Yes."

"I don't think so, George." Father Courtney turned. "I've known about it for a long time."

The old man tried to speak.

"I've known very well. And now I think I understand why you've refused to see anyone."

"No," Donovan said. "You don't. Father, listen to me: it isn't what you think."

"Nonsense." The priest reverted to his usual gruffness. "We've been friends for too many years for this kind of thing. It's *exactly* what I think. You're an intelligent, well-read, mule-stubborn old man who's worried he won't get to Heaven because sometimes he has doubts."

"That isn't—"

"Well, rubbish! Do you think I don't ask questions, myself, once in a while? Just because I'm a priest, do you think I go blindly on, never wondering, not even for a minute?"

The old man's eyes moved swiftly, up and down.

"Every intelligent person doubts, George, once in a while. And we all feel terrible about it, and we're terribly sorry. But I assure you, if this were enough to damn us, Heaven would be a wilderness." Father Courtney reached again for a cigarette. "So you've shut yourself up like a hermit and worried and stewed and endangered your life, and all for nothing." He coughed. "Well, that's it, isn't it?"

"I wish it were," Donovan said, sadly. His eyes kept dancing. There was a long pause; then he said, "Let me pose you a theoretical problem, Father. Something I've been thinking about lately."

Father Courtney recalled the sentence, and how many times it had begun the evenings of talk—wonderful talk! These evenings, he realized, were part of his life now. An important part. For there was no one else, no one of Donovan's intelligence, with whom you could argue any subject under the sun—from Frescobaldi to baseball, from Colonization on Mars to the early French symbolists, to agrarian reforms, to wines, to theology . . .

The old man shifted in the bed. As he did, the acrid odor diminished and swelled and pulsed. "You once told me," he said, "that you read imaginative fiction, didn't you?"

"I suppose so."

"And that there were certain concepts you could swallow—such as parallel worlds, mutated humans, and the like—but that other concepts you couldn't swallow at all. Artificial life, I believe you mentioned, and time travel, and a few others."

The priest nodded.

"Well, let's take one of these themes for our problem. Will you do that? Let's take the first idea."

"All right. Then the doctor."

"We have this man, Father," Donovan said, gazing at the ceiling. "He looks perfectly ordinary, you see, and it would occur to no one to doubt this; but he is not ordinary. Strictly speaking, he isn't even a man. For, though he lives, he isn't alive. You follow? He is a thing of wires and coils and magic, a creation of other men. He is a machine . . ."

"George!" The priest shook his head. "We've gone through this before: it's foolish to waste time. I came here to help you, not to engage in a foolish discussion."

"But that's how you *can* help me," Donovan said.

"Very well," the priest sighed. "But you know my views on this. Even if there were a logical purpose to which such a creature might be put—and I can't think of any—I still say they will never create a machine that is capable of abstract thought. Human intelligence is a spiritual thing—and spiritual things can't be duplicated by men."

"You really believe that?"

"Of course I do. Extrapolation of known scientific advances is perfectly all right; but this is something else entirely."

"Is it?" the old man said. "What about Pasteur's discovery? Or the X-Ray? Did Roentgen correlate a lot of embryonic data, Father, or did he come upon something brand new? What do you think even the scientists themselves would have said to the idea of a machine that would see through human tissue? They would have said, It's fantastic. And it was, too, and is. Nevertheless, it exists."

"It's not the same thing."

"No . . . I suppose that's true. However, I'm not trying to convince you of my thesis. I ask merely that you accept it for the sake of the problem. Will you?"

"Go ahead, George."

"We have this man, then. He's artificial, but he's perfect: great pains have been taken to see to this. Perfect, no detail spared, however small. He looks human, and he acts human, and for all the world knows, he *is* human. In fact, sometimes even he, our man, gets confused. When he feels a pain in his heart, for instance, it's difficult for him to remember that he has no heart. When he sleeps and awakes refreshed, he must remind himself that this is all controlled by an automatic switch somewhere inside his brain, and that he doesn't *actually* feel refreshed. He must think, I'm not real, I'm not real, I'm not real!

"But this becomes impossible, after a while. Because he doesn't believe it. He begins to ask, Why? *Why* am I not real? Where is the difference, when you come right down to it? Humans eat and sleep—as I do. They talk—as I do. They move and work and laugh—as I do. What they think, I think, and what they feel, I feel. Don't I?

"He wonders, this mechanical man does, Father, what would happen if all the people on earth were suddenly to discover they were mechanical also. Would they feel any the less human? Is it likely that they would rush off to woo typewriters and adding machines? Or would they think, perhaps, of revising their definition of the word, 'Life'?

"Well, our man thinks about it, and thinks about it, but he never reaches a conclusion. He doesn't believe he's nothing more than an advanced calculator, but he doesn't really believe he's human, either: not completely.

"All he knows is that the smell of wet grass is a fine smell to him, and that the sound of the wind blowing through trees is very sad and very beautiful, and that he loves the whole earth with an impossible passion . . ."

Father Courtney shifted uncomfortably in his chair. If only the telephone worked, he thought. Or if he could be sure it was safe to leave.

". . . other men made the creature, as I've said; but many more like him were made. However, of them all, let's say only he was successful."

"Why?" the priest asked, irritably. "Why would this be done in the first place?"

Donovan smiled. "Why did we send the first ship to the moon? Or bother to split the atom? For no very good reason, Father. Except the reason behind all of science: Curiosity. My theoretical scientists were curious to see if it could be accomplished, that's all."

The priest shrugged.

"But perhaps I'd better give our man a history. That would make it a bit more logical. All right, he was born a hundred years ago, roughly. A privately owned industrial monopoly was his mother, and a dozen or so assorted technicians his father. He sprang from his electronic womb fully formed. But, as the result of an accident—lack of knowledge, what have you—he came out rather different from his unsuccessful brothers. A mutant? A mutated robot, Father—now there's an idea that ought to appeal to you! Anyway, *he* knew who, or what, he was. He remembered. And so—to make it brief—when the war interrupted the experiment and threw things into a general uproar, our man decided to escape. He wanted his individuality. He wanted to get out of the zoo.

"It wasn't particularly easy, but he did this. Once free, of course, it was impossible to find him. For one thing, he had been constructed along almost painfully ordinary lines. And for another, they couldn't very well release the information that a mechanical man built by their laboratories was wandering the streets. It would cause a panic. And there was enough panic, what with the nerve gas and the bombs."

"So they never found him, I gather."

"No," Donovan said, wistfully. "They never found him. And they kept their secret well: it died when they died."

"And what happened to the creature?"

"Very little, to tell the truth. They'd given him a decent intelligence, you see—far more decent, and complex, than they knew—so he didn't have much trouble finding small jobs. A rather old-looking man, fairly strong—he made out. Needless to say, he couldn't stay in the same town for more than twenty years or so, because of his inability to age, but this was all right. Everyone makes friends and loses them. He got used to it."

Father Courtney sat very still now. The birds had flown away from the telephone lines, and were at the window, beating their wings, and crying harshly.

"But all this time, he's been thinking, Father. Thinking and reading. He makes quite a study of philosophy, and for a time he favors a somewhat peculiar combination of Russell and Schopenhauer—unbitter bitterness, you might say. Then this phase passes, and he begins to search through the vast theological and metaphysical literature. For what? He isn't sure. However, he is sure of one thing, now: He *is*, indubitably, human. Without breath, without heart, without blood or bone, artificially created, he thinks this and believes it, with a fair amount of firmness, too. Isn't that remarkable!"

"It is indeed," the priest said, his throat oddly tight and dry. "Go on."

"Well," Donovan chuckled, "I've caught your interest, have I? All right, then. Let us imagine that one hundred years have passed. The creature has been able to make minor repairs on himself, but—at last—he is dying. Like an ancient motor, he's gone on running year after year, until he's all paste and hairpins, and now, like the motor, he's falling apart. And nothing and no one can save him."

The acrid aroma burned and fumed.

"Here's the real paradox, though. Our man has become religious, Father! He doesn't have a living cell within him, yet he's concerned about his soul!"

Donovan's eyes quieted, as the rest of him did. "The problem," he said, "is this: Having lived creditably for over a century as a member of the human species, can this creature of ours hope for Heaven? Or will he 'die' and become only a heap of metal cogs?"

Father Courtney leapt from the chair, and moved to the bed. "George, in Heaven's name, let me call Doctor Ferguson!"

"Answer the question first. Or haven't you decided?"

"There's nothing to decide," the priest said, with impatience. "It's a preposterous idea. No machine can have a soul."

Donovan made a sighing sound, through closed lips. He said, "You don't think it's conceivable, then, that God could have made an exception here?"

"What do you mean?"

"That He could have taken pity on this theoretical man of ours, and breathed a soul into him after all? Is that so impossible?"

Father Courtney shrugged. "It's a poor word, impossible," he said. "But it's a poor problem, too. Why not ask me whether pigs ought to be allowed to fly?"

"Then you admit it's conceivable?"

"I admit nothing of the kind. It simply isn't the sort of question any man can answer."

"Not even a priest?"

"Especially not a priest. You know as much about Catholicism as I do, George; you ought to know how absurd the proposition is."

"Yes," Donovan said. His eyes were closed.

Father Courtney remembered the time they had argued furiously on what would happen if you went back in time and killed your own grandfather. This was like that argument. Exactly like it—exactly. It was no stranger than a dozen other discussions (What if Mozart had been a writer instead of a composer? If a person died and remained dead for an hour and were then revived, would he be haunted by his own ghost?) Plus, perhaps, the fact that Donovan might be in a fever. Perhaps and might and why do I sit here while his life may be draining away . . .

The old man made a sharp noise. "But you can tell me this much," he said. "If our theoretical man were dying, and you knew that he was dying, would you give him Extreme Unction?"

"George, you're delirious."

"No, I'm not: please, Father! Would you give this creature the Last Rites? If, say, you knew him? If you'd known him for years, as a friend, as a member of the parish?"

The priest shook his head. "It would be sacrilegious."

"But why? You said yourself that he might have a soul, that God might have granted him this. Didn't you say that?"

"I—"

"Father, remember, he's a friend of yours. You know him *well*. You and he, this creature, have worked together, side by side, for years. You've taken a thousand walks together, shared the same interests, the same love of art and knowledge. For the sake of the thesis, Father. Do you understand?"

"No," the priest said, feeling a chill freeze into him. "No, I don't."

"Just answer this, then. If your friend were suddenly to reveal himself to you as a machine, and he was dying, and wanted very much to go to Heaven—what would you do?"

The priest picked up the wine glass and emptied it. He noticed that his hand was trembling. "Why—" he began, and stopped, and looked at the silent old man in the bed, studying the face, searching for madness, for death.

"What would you do?"

An unsummoned image flashed through his mind. Donovan, kneeling at the altar for Communion, Sunday after Sunday; Donovan, with his mouth firmly shut, while the other's yawned; Donovan, waiting to the last moment, then snatching the Host, quickly, dartingly, like a lizard gobbling a fly.

Had he ever seen Donovan eat?

Had he seen him take even one glass of wine, ever?

Father Courtney shuddered slightly, brushing away the images. He felt unwell. He wished the birds would go elsewhere.

Well, answer him, he thought. *Give him an answer. Then get in the helicar and fly to Milburn and pray it's not too late . . .*

"I think," the priest said, "that in such a case, I would administer Extreme Unction."

"Just as a precautionary measure?"

"It's all very ridiculous, but—I think that's what I'd do. Does that answer the question?"

"It does, Father. It does." Donovan's voice came from nowhere. "There is one last point, then I'm finished with my little thesis."

"Yes?"

"Let us say the man dies and you give him Extreme Unction; he does or does not go to Heaven, provided there is a Heaven. What happens to the body? Do you tell the townspeople they have been living with a mechanical monster all these years?"

"What do you think, George?"

"I think it would be unwise. They remember our theoretical man as a friend, you see. The shock would be terrible. Also, they would never believe he was the only one of his kind: they'd begin to suspect their neighbors of having clockwork interiors. And some of them might be tempted to investigate and see for sure. And, too, the news would be bound to spread, all over the world. I think it would be a bad thing to let anyone know, Father."

"How would I be able to suppress it?" the priest heard himself ask, seriously.

"By conducting a private autopsy, so to speak. Then, afterwards, you could take the parts to a junkyard and scatter them."

Donovan's voice dropped to a whisper. Again the locust hum.

". . . and if our monster had left a note to the effect he had moved to some unspecified place, you . . ."

The acrid smell billowed, all at once, like a steam, a hiss of blinding vapor.

"George."

Donovan lay unstirring on the cloud of linen, his face composed, expressionless.

"George!"

The priest reached his hand under the blanket and touched the heart-area of Donovan's chest. He tried to pull the eyelids up: they would not move.

He blinked away the burning wetness. "Forgive me!" he said, and paused, and took from his pocket a small white jar and a white stole.

He spoke softly, under his breath, in Latin. While he spoke, he touched the old man's feet and head with glistening fingertips.

Then, when many minutes had passed, he raised his head.

Rain sounded in the room, and swift winds, and far-off rockets.

Father Courtney grasped the edge of the blanket.

He made the Sign of the Cross, breathed, and pulled downward, slowly.

After a long while, he opened his eyes.

B IS FOR BIRDS, BEASTS AND BLOOD

NELSON BOND

And Lo! The Bird

I don't know why I'm bothering to write this. It's undoubtedly the most useless bit of writing I've ever done in a career—I suppose you'd call it that?—devoted to defacing reams of clean copy paper with torrents of fatuous words. But I've got to do something to keep my mind occupied on this cheerless March day in the Year of Grace 1960. And since I was in this from the beginning, I might as well set it down as I remember it.

Of course, my record of those first days makes no difference now. But then, nothing matters much now. Perhaps nothing *ever* really mattered much, actually. I don't know. I'm not very sure about anything any more. Except that this is an absurdly unimportant story for me to be writing. And that somehow I must do it, none the less. . . .

I've said I was in this from the beginning; that's a laugh. How long ago it really started is any man's guess. It depends on how you choose to measure time. Some four thousand-odd years ago if you're a fundamentalist, a dogged adherent to Archbishop Ussher's chronology. Perhaps three thousand million years ago if you have that which until a few short weeks ago vaingloriously we used to speak of as a "scientific mind." I don't know the truth of the matter, nor does anyone else. But so far as I'm concerned—and you and all of us—it started about a month ago. On the night the city editor, Smitty, wig-wagged me to his desk and grunted a query at me.

"Do you," he asked petulantly, "know anything at all about astronomy?"

"Why, sure," I told him. "Mercury, Venus, Earth, Mars, Jupiter, Saturn, Uranus, Neptune and something-or-other."

"How?" said Smitty.

"And Pluto," I remembered. "The solar family. The planets in the order of their distance from the sun. I had a semester of star-gazing at school. Some of it rubbed off."

"Good," said the C. E. "You've just won yourself an assignment. Do you know Dr. Abramson?"

"I know who he is. The big wheel on the University observatory staff."

"That's right. Well, go see him. He's got something big—so *he* says," appended Smitty.

44

"Cab?" I asked hopefully.

"Bus."

"Astronomically speaking," I suggested, "a big story could mean a lot of things. A comet striking earth. The heat of the sun failing, and letting us all freeze to death."

"Things are tough all over," shrugged Smitty. "Suburban buses run every twenty minutes until midnight."

"On the other hand," I mused, "he may have run into some meteorological disturbance that means atomic experiment. If the Reds are playing around with an H-bomb—"

"O.K., a cab," sighed Smitty. "Get going."

Abramson was a small slim sallow man with shadowed eyes. He shook my hand and motioned me into a chair across the yellow oak desk from him. He adjusted a gooseneck lamp so it would shine in neither of our faces, then steepled lean white fingers. He said, "It was good of you to come so promptly, Mr.—"

"Flaherty," I told him.

"Well, Flaherty, it's like this. In our profession it isn't customary to release stories through the press. As a rule we publish our observations in technical journals comprehensible, for the most part, only to specialists. But this time such treatment does not seem adequate. It might not be fast enough. I've seen something in the heavens—and I don't like it."

I made hen scratches on a fold of copy paper.

"This thing you saw—a new comet, maybe?"

"I'm not sure I know," said Abramson, "and I'm even less sure I *want* to know. But whether it is, it's unusual enough and, so I suspect, important enough to warrant the step I'm taking. In order to get the swiftest possible confirmation of my observations, and of my fears, I feel I must use the public press to tell my message."

"All the news that's fit to print," I said, "and a lot that isn't; that's our stock in trade. What is it you've seen?"

He stared at me soberly for a long time. Then:

"A bird," he said.

I glanced at him in swift surprise. "A—a bird?" I felt like smiling, but the look in his eyes did not encourage mirth.

"A bird," he repeated. "Far in the depths of space. The telescope was directed toward Pluto, farthermost planet of our solar system. A body almost four thousand millions of miles from Earth.

"And at that distance"—he spoke with a painful deliberation—"at that incredible distance, *I saw a bird!*"

Maybe he read the disbelief in my eyes. Anyway, he opened the top drawer of his desk, drew forth a sheaf of eight-by-ten glossies, and laid them before me.

"Here," he said. "See for yourself."

The first photograph meant little to me. It showed a field of star-emblazoned space—the typical sort of picture you find in any astronomy textbook. But on it one square was outlined in white pencil. The second photo was an enlargement of this square, showing in magnified detail the outlined area. The field was larger, brighter; a myriad of glowing stars diffused a silvery radiance over the entire plate. Against this nebulosity stood out in stark relief the firm, jet silhouette of a gigantic birdlike creature in full flight.

I ventured an uncertain attempt at rationalization. I said: "Interesting. But, Dr. Abramson, many dark spots have been photographed in space. The Coalsack, for instance. And the black Nebula in—"

"True," he acknowledged. "But if you will now look at the next exposure?"

I turned to the third photograph, and for the first time felt the breath of that cold, helpless dread which in the weeks ahead was to come to dwell with me. It depicted an overlapping portion of that field surveyed in the second print. But the dark, occulting silhouette had changed. That which was limned against the background of the stars was still the outline of a bird—but the shape had changed. A wing which had been lifted now was dropped; the postures of neck and head and bill were definitely altered.

"This photograph," said Abramson in a dry, emotionless voice, "was taken five minutes after the first one. Disregarding the changed appearance of the—the image, and considering only the object's relative position in space as indicated by the parallax, to have shifted its position to such an extent in so short a time indicates that the thing casting that image must have been travelling at a velocity of approximately one hundred thousand miles per minute."

"What!" I exclaimed. "But that's impossible. Nothing on earth can travel at such a speed."

"Nothing on *earth*," agreed Abramson. "But cosmic bodies can—and do. And for all that it has the semblance of a living creature, this thing—whatever it is—is a cosmic body.

"And that," he continued fretfully, "is why I asked you to come out here. That is the story I want you to write. That is why no moment must be wasted."

I said, "I can write the story. But it will never be believed."

"Perhaps not—at first. Nevertheless, it must be released. The public may laugh, if it wishes. Other observatories will check my discovery, verify my conclusions. And that is the important thing. No matter what it may lead to, what it means, we must learn the truth. The world has a right to know the threat confronting it."

"The threat? You think there is a threat?"

He nodded slowly, gravely.

"Yes, Flaherty. I know there is. There is a thing those pictures may not tell you, but that will be recognized instantly by any trained mathematician.

"That thing—bird, beast, machine or whatever it may be—travels in a computable path. And the direction of its flight is towards our sun!"

My interview threw Smitty for a loss. He read copy swiftly, scowled, studied the pix, and read the story again, this time more slowly and with furrows congealing on his forehead. Then he stalked over to my desk.

"Flaherty," he complained in a tone of outraged indignation, "what is all this? What the hell *is* it, I mean?"

"A story," I told him. "The story you sent me out to get. Abramson's story."

"I know that. But—a *bird!* What the hell kind of a story is *that?*"

I shrugged. "Frankly, I don't know. Dr. Abramson seems to think it's important. Maybe," I suggested, "he's got rocks in his head."

It was too subtle for Smitty. He smudged the bridge of his nose with a copy pencil and muttered something uncomplimentary to astronomers in general and Abramson in particular.

"I suppose we've got to print it," he decided. "But we don't have to make damned fools of ourselves. Lighten this up. If we must run it, we'll play it for laughs."

So that's what we did. We carried it on an inside page, complete with Abramson's pictures, as a special feature, gently humorous in tone. We didn't openly poke fun at Abramson, of course. After all, he was the observatory chief of staff. But we soft-pedalled the science angle; I rewrote the yarn in the style we generally used for flying-saucer reports and sea-serpent stories.

This was, of course, a terrific boner. But in all fairness to Smitty, how was he to know this was the story to end all stories? The biggest story of his or any newspaperman's career?

Think back to the first time *you* read about it, and be honest. Did you guess, then, that it was gospel truth?

We soon discovered our mistake. Reaction to the yarn was swift and startling. The *Banner* had been on the streets less than an hour when the phones began to ring.

That, in itself, was not unusual. Any out-of-the-ordinary story brings its quota of cranks crawling forth from the woodwork. Discount the confirmation of the local amateur observer who called in to verify Abramson's observation. His possible lucid report was overshadowed by the equally sincere, but considerably less credible, reports of a dozen naked-eye "witnesses" who also averred to have seen a gigantic bird-like creature soaring across the heavens during the night. Half of these described the markings of the bird; one even claimed to have heard its mating call.

Two erstwhile Civilian Defence aircraft spotters called to identify the object variously, but with equal assurance, as a B-29 and a Russian super-jet. One member of the Audubon Society identified the bird as a ruby-throated nuthatch which, he suggested, must have flown in front of the telescope just as the camera clicked. An itinerant preacher of an obscure cult marched into our office to inform us with a savage delight that this was the veritable bird foretold in the *Book of Revelations*, and that the end of the world could now be expected momentarily, if not sooner.

These were the lunatic fringe. What *was* unusual was that all the calls which flooded our office during the next twenty-four hours were not made by screwballs and fanatics. Some were of great importance, not only to their instigators but to the scientific world, to mankind in general.

We had fed a short take to the A. P. To our astonishment, from that syndicate we received an immediate demand for follow-up material, including copies of Abramson's pix. The national picture magazines were even more on their toes; they flew their own boys to town and had contacted Abramson for a second story before we wised up to the fact that we had broken the number-one sensation of the year.

Meanwhile, and most important of all, astronomers elsewhere in the world, set their big eyes for the arena of the thing first spotted by Dr. Abramson. And within

twenty-four hours, to the stunned dismay of all who, like Smitty and myself, had
seen it as a terrific joke, verifications were forthcoming from every observatory that
enjoyed good viewing conditions. What's more, mathematicians verified Dr.
Abramson's estimates as to the thing's speed and trajectory. The bird, estimated to
be larger in size than any solar planet, was conceded to be somewhere in the
vicinity of Pluto—and approaching our sun at a speed of 145,000,000 miles per
day!

By the end of the first week, the bird was visible through any fair-sized
telescope. The story snowballed, and in its rolling picked up all the oddments lying
in its path. A character who introduced himself as a member of the Fortean
Society—whatever *that* is—came to the office armed with a thick volume in which
he pointed out to us a dozen paragraphs purporting to prove that similar dark
objects had been seen in the skies above various parts of the world over a period of
several hundred years.

The central council of the P.T.A. issued a plaintive statement deploring
scare-journalism and its evil effects on the youth of our nation. The Daughters of
the American Revolution passed a resolution branding the strange image a new
secret weapon of Uncle Joe's lads, and urging that immediate steps—undefined
but drastic—be taken by the authorities. Locally, a special committee of the
ministers' association called to advise us that the story we had originated tended to
undermine the religious faith of the community; they demanded that we print a full
explanation and retraction of the hoax in the earliest possible edition—which was,
by now, a complete impossibility. Before the end of the second week, the black dot
in the skies could be viewed with binoculars of moderate power.

By the middle of the third week it had reached the stage of naked-eye visibility.
Crowds gathered in the streets when this became known, and those with good
eyesight professed to be able to discern the rhythmic rise and fall of those
tremendous wings now familiar to all because of the scores of photographs which,
by this time, had appeared in every newspaper and magazine of any importance.

The cadenced beating of those monstrous wings was but one of the many
inexplicable—or at least unexplained—mysteries about the creature from beyond.
Vainly a few diehard physicists pointed out that wings were of no propulsive help in
airless void, that alate flight is possible only where there are wind currents to lift
and carry. The thing flew. And whether its gigantic pinions beat, as some men
thought, on an interstellar atmosphere unguessed by earthly science, or whether
they stroked against beams of light of quantum bundles, as others contended,
these were meaningless quibbles in the face of that one stark, incontrovertible fact:
the thing flew.

With the dawning of the fourth week, the thing from outer space reached Jupiter
and dwarfed it—an ominous black interloper equal in size to any cosmic neighbour
which man had ever seen. . . .

I sat alone with Abramson in his office. Abramson was tired. Tired and, I think,
a little ill. His smile was not a success; nor had his words their hoped-for
jauntiness.

"Well, I got what I wanted, Flaherty," he admitted. "I wanted swift action, and I
got it. Though what good is it, I don't know. The world recognizes its danger now
and is helpless to do anything about it."

"It has hurdled the asteroids," I said. "Now it's approaching Mars, and it's still moving sunward. Everyone is asking, though, why doesn't its presence within the system raise merry hob with celestial mechanics? By all known laws, it should have thrown everything out of balance. A creature of that size, with its gravitational attraction—"

"You're still thinking in old terms," my boy. "Now we are confronted with something strange and new. Who knows what laws may govern the Bird of Time?"

"The bird," I repeated, "of Time? I seem to have heard the phrase."

"Of course." He quoted moodily, "'The Bird of Time has but a little way to fly—and Lo! the Bird is on the Wing.'"

The Rubáiyát?" I said.

"Yes. Omar was an astronomer, you know, as well as a poet. He must have known—or guessed—something of this." He gestured vaguely skyward. "Indeed, many of the ancients seem to have known something about it. I've been doing a lot of reading during these past weeks, Flaherty. It is amazing how many references there are in the old writings to a great bird of space—statements which until recently did not seem to be at all significant or important. But which now hold a greater and graver meaning for us."

"Such as?"

"Culture myths," he said. "Legends. The records of a hundred vanished races. The Mayan myth of the space-swallow; the Toltec quetzalcoatl; the Russian firebird."

"We don't know yet," I pointed out, "that it *is* a bird."

He shrugged.

"A bird, a giant mammal, a pterodactyl, some similar creature on a cosmic scale: but what does it matter? Perhaps it is a life form foreign to anything we know, something we can name only in earthly terms, describe by earthly analogies. The ancients called it a bird. The Phoenicians worshipped the 'bird that was, and is again to be.' The Persians wrote of the fabulous roc; there is an Aramaic legend of the giant bird that rules—and spawns—the worlds."

"Spawns the worlds?"

"Why else should it be coming?" he inquired. "Does its great size mean nothing to you?" He stared at me thoughtfully for a moment. Then: "Flaherty," he asked strangely, "what *is* the earth?"

"Why," I replied, "the world we live on. A planet."

"Yes. But what is a planet?"

"A unit of the solar system. A part of the sun's family."

"Do you *know* that? Or are you merely parroting the things you were taught at school?"

"The latter, of course. But what else could it be?"

"The earth could be," he answered reluctantly, "no part of the sun's family at all. Many theories have been devised, Flaherty, to explain earth's place in this tiny segment of the universe which we call the solar system. None of them are provably inaccurate. But, on the other hand, none of them are demonstrably true.

"There is the nebular hypothesis, the theory that earth and its sister planets were born of a contracting sun. Were, in fact, small globules of solar matter left to cool in orbits deserted by their condensing parent.

"The planetesimal and tidal theories each are based on the assumption that unfathomable eons ago another sun by-passed our own, and that the planets are the offspring of that ancient flaming rendezvous in space.

"Each of these theories has its proponents and its opponents; each has its verifications and its denials. None can be quite refuted or wholly proven.

"But"—he stirred restlessly—"there is another possibility which, to the best of my knowledge, has never been expounded. Yet it is equally valid with any I have mentioned, and in the light of that which we now know, it seems to me more likely than any. It is that earth and its sister planets have nothing whatsoever to do with the sun. That they are not, nor ever were, mere members of its family. That the sun in our skies is simply a convenience."

"A convenience?" I frowned. "Convenience for *what*?"

"For the bird," said Abramson unhappily. "For the great bird which is our parent. Flaherty, can you not conceive that our sun may be a cosmic incubator? And that the world on which we live may be, merely—an egg?"

I stared at him wildly. "An egg!" I cried. "Dr. Abramson, you're joking."

"You think so? You can look at the pictures, read the stories in the magazines, see the approaching bird with your naked eye, and still think there exists anything more incredible than that which has now befallen us?"

"But an *egg!* Eggs are egg-shaped. Ovoid."

"The eggs of some birds are ovoid. But those of the plover are pear-shaped, those of the sand-grouse cylindrical, those of the grebe biconical. There are eggs shaped like spindles and spears. The eggs of owls, and of mammals, are generally spheroid. As is the earth."

"But eggs have shells!"

"As does our earth. Earth's crust is but forty miles thick—a layer for a body of its size comparable in every respect to the shell of an egg. Moreover, it is a *smooth* shell. Earth's greatest height is Mount Everest, some thirty thousand feet; its greatest depth is Swire Deep in the Pacific, but thirty-five thousand—a maximum variation of about twelve miles. Why, to feel these irregularities on a twelve-inch model of the earth you would need the delicate fingers of the blind, for the greatest height protrudes but the hundred and twentieth part of an inch, and the lowest depth is but the hundredth part of an inch below its surface."

"Still, you can't be right," I argued desperately. "You've overlooked the most important fact. Eggs hold life! Eggs contain the fledglings of the creature that spawned them. Eggs crack open and—"

I stopped abruptly. Abramson nodded, creaking back and forth in his ancient swivel chair, the creaking a monotonous rhythm to his nodding. There was sadness in his eyes and in his voice.

"Even so," he said wearily. "Even so . . ."

So that was the second great story that I broke. I was still fool enough to get something of a bang out of it at the time; I don't feel the same way about it now. But, then, I don't feel the same about anything any more. I guess you can understand that. The coming of the bird was such a big thing, such a truly big thing, that it dwindled into significance all the things we used to consider great, important, world-shaking.

World-shaking!

I'll make it brief. There's so little purpose to my telling of this story. But there may be in it a fact here and there you don't know. And I've got to do something—anything—to keep myself from thinking.

You remember that grim fourth week, and the steady approach of the bird. We had settled for calling it that by then. We were not sure if it were bird or winged beast, but men think—and give names to things—in terms of more familiar objects. And that slim black shape with its tremendous wings, its taloned legs and long, cruel, curving beak looked more like a bird than an animal.

Besides, there was Abramson's world-egg theory to be considered. The people heard this, doubted it with a furious hope—but feared it might be true. Men in high positions asked what could be done. They sent for Abramson, and he advised them. He could be wrong, he acknowledged. But if he were right, there was only one hope for salvation. The life within Earth must be stilled.

"I believe," he told a special emergency committee appointed by the President, "the bird has come to hatch the brood of young it deposited God knows how many centuries ago about that incubating warmth which is our sun. Its wisdom or its instinct tells it that the time of emergence is now; it has come to help its fledglings shed their shells.

"But we know that mother birds, alone and unaided, do not hatch their young. They will aid a struggling chick to crack its shell, but they never begin the liberating action. And with an uncanny second sense, they seem to know which eggs have failed to develop life within them; such eggs they never disturb.

"Therein, gentlemen, lies our only hope. The shell of Earth is forty miles in thickness. We have our engineers and technicians; we have the atomic bomb. If mankind is to live, the host to which we are but parasites must die. That is my only solution. I leave the rest to you."

He left them, still wrangling, in Washington, and returned home. He saw little hope, he told me the next day, of their reaching any firm decision in sufficient time to act. Abramson, I think, had already resigned himself to the inevitable, had with a wan grimace surrendered mankind to its fate. He said, once, that bureaucracy had achieved its ultimate destiny. It had throttled itself to death with its own red tape.

And still the bird moved sunward. On the twenty-eighth day it made its nearest approach to Earth, and passed us by. I don't know—nor can the scientist explain—why our globe was not shattered by the gravitational attraction of that gigantic mass. Perhaps because the Newtonian theory is, after all, simply a *theory*, and has no actuality in real existence. I don't know. If there were time, it would be good to study, and to learn the truth about such things. At any rate, we suffered very little from its nearness—all things considered. There were high tides and mighty winds; those sections of earth subject to earthquakes suffered some mild temblors. But that is all.

And then we won a respite. You remember how the bird paused in its headlong flight to hover for two full days around that tiniest of the solar planets—the one we call Mercury. Briefly, as if searching for something, it flew in a wide circle in an orbit between Mercury and the sun.

Abramson believed it was looking for something, for something it could not find because it was no longer there. Astronomers believed, said Abramson, that at one time there had been another planet circling between Mercury and the sun.

Watchers of the sky had seen this as late as the eighteenth century, and had called it Vulcan. Vulcan had disappeared, perhaps had fallen into the sun. So thought Abramson. And so, apparently, the bird decided, too, for after a fruitless search it winged its way outward from the sun to approach the closest of its brood still remaining intact.

Must I remind you of that dreadful day? I think not. No man alive will ever forget what he saw then. The bird approaching Mercury pausing to hover motionless above a planet which seemed a mote beneath the umbra of those massive wings. Men in the streets saw this. I saw more, for I stood beside Abramson in the University observatory, watching that scene with the aid of one of his telescopes.

I saw the first thin splitting of Mercury's shell, and the curious fluid ichor which seeped from a dying world. I watched the grisly emergence of that small, wet, scrawny thing—raw simulacrum of its monstrous parent—from the egg in which it had lain for whatever incalculable era was the gestation period of a creature vast as space and as old as time. I saw the mother bird stretch forth its giant beak and help its fledgling rid itself of a peeling, needless shell; stood horrified to watch the younger bird emerge and flap its new, uncertain wings, drying them in the burning rays of the star which had been its incubator.

And I saw the shredded remnants of a world spiral into the sun which was its pyre. . . .

It was then, at last, that mankind woke to action. The doubters were convinced at last, those who had argued against the "needless expense" and folly of Abramson's plan were finally silenced. Forgotten now were selfishness and greed, politics and interdepartmental strife. The world they infested trembled on the brink of doom—and a race of vermin battled for its life.

In the flat desertland of America there was frantically thrown together the mechanism for mankind's greatest project—Operation Life. To this desert flew the miners, the construction engineers, the nuclear physicists, the men skilled in deep-drilling operations. There they began their task, working night and day with a speed which heretofore had been called impossible. There they are working now, this minute, as I write, fighting desperately against each passing second of time, striving with every means and method they know to reach and destroy the life within our earth.

A week ago the bird moved on to Venus. Throughout these seven days we have watched its progress there. We cannot see much through the eternal veil of mist which surrounds our sister planet, so we do not know what has for so gratefully long a time occupied the bird. Whatever it is, we are thankful for it. We wait and watch. And as we watch, we work. And as we work, we pray. . . .

And so there is no real ending to this story. As I have said before, I don't know why I'm bothering to write it. The answer is not ready to be given. If we succeed, there will be ample time to tell the story properly—the whole great story, fully documented, of the battle being waged on the hot Arizona sands. And if we fail—well, then there will be no reason for this writing. There will be none to read it.

The bird is not the greatest of our fears. If when it comes from Venus it finds here a quiet, lifeless, unresponsive shell, it will move outward—we believe and pray—to Mars, then Jupiter, and thence beyond.

That is the end we hope to bring about. Soon, now, our probing needles will penetrate Earth's shell, will dip beneath the crust and into the tegument of that horror which sleeps within us. But we have another more tormenting fear. It is that before the mother bird approaches us, the fledgling may awake and seek to gain its freedom from the shell encasing it. If this should happen, Abramson has warned, our work must then proceed at lightning speed. For let that fledgling once begin to knock, then it must die—or all mankind must die.

That is the other reason why I write. To keep from thinking thoughts I dare not think. Because—

Because early this morning, Earth began to knock. . . .

CHARLES G. FINNEY

The Black Retriever

Mr. Charles was first made aware of the beast one Sunday morning in May. He was, at the moment, shaving. His youngest daughter came running in, breathlessly as was her wont, and announced there was a big black dog in the patio.

Mr. Charles said nonsense and continued shaving. He knew the patio gates were closed; he had closed them himself. He said so to his daughter.

"But this dog doesn't use gates," she cried. "He just jumps over the wall."

Again Mr. Charles said nonsense, for the wall was five feet high, and it had been there five years, and in all that time he had never known a dog to jump it.

"But it did," his little girl insisted. "And it's killing things out there." And she ran off for another look.

In a moment she let out one of her shrill yells. "It's on the patio wall! It's caught a bird! Come and see!"

Mr. Charles switched off his electric shaver, said things not appropriate to be said before a little girl, and went outside and looked.

Mr. Charles saw—or thought he saw, because he wore trifocals and sometimes looked through the wrong lens tier—a black blur on the patio wall. It moved along and disappeared. "See!" said his daughter. "It's jumped down and now it's gone. Look, it dropped the bird."

"Well," said Mr. Charles, "we will investigate later. Right now it's time to go to church."

And, their preparations completed, the Charles family packed itself into its Hillman Minx and drove off. Mr. Charles thought no more of the black blur or the black dog that he had seen.

That afternoon he and his wife decided to sit in the patio while their daughters watched television. Their two little dogs elected to accompany them. The cairn terrier slept. The dachshund dug a hole beside the flowering pomegranate. Mr.

Charles and his wife talked of sundry things: television shows, shopping, the necessity of having the Minx greased.

The dachshund stopped digging and began to snoop around the patio, sniffing at shrubs and bushes. He disappeared behind some greasewood and then appeared again, this time with something in his mouth. He brought it up to Mrs. Charles.

"Oh!" she cried. "Snorkel! How could you!"

"He's innocent," said Mr. Charles. "He merely found it. That other dog killed it. Roberta told me."

"Other dog?" she asked. "What other dog? You surely don't mean this lazy thing." And she indicated Mac, the sleeping cairn.

"No," said Mr. Charles. "This was a strange dog. A big black one. It leaped over the wall into the patio and killed this bird. Then it jumped on top of the patio wall and swaggered around."

"I never heard of such a thing," said his wife. "Did *you* actually see it, or did Roberta just tell you about it?"

"I saw a blur," said Mr. Charles. "But Roberta saw it plainly. She even saw it kill the bird. I didn't believe her at the time, but there the bird is, so the story must be true."

A few days later Mr. Charles was in the patio again, this time neighboring across the fence with his friend Mr. George, who lived next door.

Mr. George was angry. At his feet lay the body of his Siamese cat. It was chewed and torn.

"A big black retriever did it," said Mr. George. "It jumped the wall, cornered the cat and killed it. Then it jumped up on top of the wall, walked around a little, leaped down and disappeared. It happened so quickly there was nothing I could do about it."

"I know," said Mr. Charles. "It happened here, too. Only in our yard the thing killed a bird. Did it look like a blur to you?"

"Blur? Of course not! I saw it plainly—a big black retriever. They're usually rather gentle looking. But not this one. It was a brute. I think I'll put some poisoned meat on top of the wall. If it's so fond of parading around on patio walls, maybe it'll return and find the meat. That ought to fix it."

A grotesque pattern evolved. Every time Mr. Charles met an acquaintance in the neighborhood, up came the subject of the black retriever. If the one Mr. Charles was talking to had not seen it himself he was sure to have a neighbor who had, a neighbor whose patio had been visited by the beast and in whose patio the beast had killed something—a pet rabbit, a cat, a puppy, a bird, once even a badger. A family down the street had a pet badger in their patio. The black retriever had jumped over their patio wall, caught the badger sleeping near the mouth of its burrow and killed it.

But despite what his neighbor Mr. George had said, Mr. Charles soon ascertained that neither he nor any of the others actually had seen the black dog clearly. In the main, the ones Mr. Charles talked to agreed it was a retriever of some sort, but one man insisted it was a poodle and another said just as insistently it was a black Airedale. Some of them used the word Mr. Charles had first used to describe it: a blur. But everyone agreed that it was black and that they saw it walking on their patio walls. As for its reality, blur or no blur, there were all those dead things to prove that its visitations had been made.

These people of Manacle lived in a suburban development. The houses were pretty much alike; the inhabitants very much alike—middle-class people with middle-class jobs. Their children attended the district's middle-class school. It was a tolerant neighborhood of friendly people.

Everything there was a little humdrum and, if you will, rather mediocre. But it was a pleasant, comfortable place to live, and the standard of living was probably as high as has ever been attained by a group of Homo sapiens since that biped began to walk upon the face of the earth.

No hordes of beggars swarmed the streets. No warring armies prowled about its borders. No necessities, no luxuries of life were wanting, or had to be struggled for. If the people of that suburban development wanted water they turned a tap. If they wanted heat they jiggled a thermostat. If they wanted coolness they switched on the air conditioner. If they wanted light they pressed a button. If they wanted to talk to a friend or a relative in Europe or nearby, they picked up a telephone. If they wanted to go somewhere they got into an automobile and drove there at speeds ranging from twenty-five to eighty-five miles an hour, or they boarded an airplane and flew there at speeds up to a thousand. All this they could do, and did, without asking anyone's permission. They didn't even need servants; electricity did for them what no staff of servants could ever do.

And now it seemed odd, incredibly odd, that a black dog, a black retriever (or a black blur), was leaping their patio walls and killing things that they loved.

At first various individuals tried various expedients to apprehend the retriever and put it away where it could do no more harm. Mr. Charles's immediate neighbor, Mr. George, allowed Mr. Charles to talk him out of his poisoned meat project, Mr. Charles's argument being that some innocent creature—even a child—might suffer. Instead, for Mr. George was a mechanically minded man, he contrived a long noose-and-spring arrangement and set it on his patio wall. His idea was to snare the retriever.

Another equally ingenious neighbor constructed a large doghouse with a hair-trigger door; he baited it with choice dog foods. His idea was to trap the retriever.

A third, an archery enthusiast, took down his long bow and stationed himself at odd times in his alley. His idea was to impale the retriever.

None of these expedients worked.

The black beast visited the patio wall on which the noose was positioned, ate the bait, sprung the spring, but was not ensnared.

It visited the doghouse arrangement, ate the bait, sprung the door, but was not entrapped.

It showed itself to the archery enthusiast, presenting a good target to his arrow, but was not transfixed.

Meanwhile, it continued its depredations. Did anyone set out new tender plants, those plants were sure to be dug up or torn out in a day or two; and everybody said it was the retriever that did it.

Sometimes days would pass without any fresh reports of trouble, but sooner or later, inevitably, someone would see the black blur on his patio wall, and, lying nearby, the dead thing which the retriever had killed.

Mr. Charles and Mr. George summoned an informal meeting, a council of the elders they called it, of the ones in the area who had felt the bite of the black blur. They thought that by uniting their efforts they could conceptualize an aim, syncretize a program, finalize an operational method, and concretize the black retriever's doom. After all, other settlements, other civilized communities had been plagued by intrusive horrors, and had been able, through drastic communal action, to abate them. Surely, Mr. George and Mr. Charles argued, they should be able to do as much.

They held the meeting in Mr. George's patio, and a dozen of the elders came. Their discussion was diffuse and not the least bit parliamentary, but it finally boiled down to one thing: the only thing to do was to shoot the retriever.

It was against the law to discharge firearms in the area, but the elders thought they would be able to get the police commissioner, or the mayor and council, or something or somebody to relax the ban long enough for them to carry out their purpose. So Mr. George and Mr. Charles were deputized to confer with the mayor and police commissioner and seek authorization to stage a dog hunt in their alleys.

Such authorization was promptly refused. There was in existence, the commissioner pointed out, an organization which offered a perfectly obvious solution to the elders' problem. That was the City Animal Shelter, a euphemism for dog pound. Why, he demanded, hadn't Mr. George and Mr. Charles gone to the shelter in the first place?

The answer to that was that they hadn't thought of it. However, now that it had come to their attention, they certainly would.

And they did. The poundmaster listened to them, smiled, and said he would send a man out. He wanted to know on what days and at what hours of those days the retriever was most likely to show up.

The two elders protested that the beast did not operate on a fixed timetable. Sometimes it came at dawn, sometimes at high noon, sometimes around dinner. It could be on a Thursday as well as on a Monday.

"I was just trying to narrow it down," said the poundmaster.

The dogcatcher came out in his wire-cage truck, equipped with a lariat, heavy gloves, and a single-barreled .410 shotgun. He was a businesslike young man in cowboy boots and cowboy hat.

Mr. Charles was at work at the time of his appearance, but his wife told him what had happened.

"He snooped around the alleys a while," she said. "All the dogs in the neighborhood barked their heads off—just as if they were trying to warn the retriever. He got hot and tried, and Mrs. Betty took pity on him and asked him to come in and have a can of beer and cool off. He had the can of beer and then made a pass at Mrs. Betty. She ordered him out of her house and called the City Animal Shelter to report him. Before she got the number of the shelter she heard a gun go off and looked out to see what it was. He had just shot Mrs. Stella's Wiemaraner.

Mrs. Stella ran out screaming. So did I. That is, I ran out. I wasn't screaming. The dogcatcher said he guessed he'd made some kind of mistake. The Wiemaraner, he insisted, looked black, real black, and was growling when he shot it, but now that it was dead it didn't look so black any more."

Mr. Charles started to say something, but his wife interrupted him. "Wait, I'm not through yet. While all that was going on, the black retriever, the real thing, you know, jumped into Mrs. Wilhelmina's patio and killed her toy Chihuahua. Then it paraded around on Mrs. Wilhelmina's patio wall for a while and then disappeared. Mrs. Wilhelmina is just sick. The doctor came and gave her a sedative. Of course, the dogcatcher was still at Mrs. Stella's, explaining about the Wiemaraner business when this happened, so he didn't know about it."

And there it was. The black retriever was still on the prowl. Everything the suburbanite elders had done or tried to do had been turned against them sardonically.

Two days later little Margarita, a child down the street, was bitten twice by a dog while she was playing in her yard. The bites weren't very serious—just skin punctures—but nobody had seen the dog except Margarita. She said it was big and dark, and everybody said it must have been the retriever. Everybody agreed the retriever was rabid, too; that was the only way to account for its actions.

But this didn't add up, for rabid dogs die very quickly, and the retriever had been around for quite a while. However, there was no arguing the fact that the retriever might have become rabid just lately, and that was what had caused it to bite Margarita.

Margarita, incidentally, was given prompt medical care and was as good as new the next day. But everybody insisted the retriever was the dog which had bitten her; efforts to apprehend the brute were, as a consequence, doubled.

Another council of the elders gathered. The elders decided not to go to the police or to the dogcatcher. They would do the job this time themselves.

Mr. James, who had hunted a great deal in his boyhood, devised the modus operandi. They would secret themselves in blinds, as duck hunters do, await the arrival of the retriever, and shoot it down.

A successful blind, said Mr. James, must be something that blends into the landscape; hence, duck blinds are made of rushes and bushes, things the ducks see all the time and are not afraid of.

But for the retriever such things would not do. What would do were automobiles. The retriever had seen plenty of automobiles and was used to them.

The elders, said Mr. James, would simply sit in their automobiles in the alleys or under the ramadas, wherever their automobiles customarily were parked, and would await the retriever. When it came along whoever saw it first would shoot it. That would be that; the police could howl their heads off.

Mr. James assigned certain men to hold watch and ward in their cars at certain times of the day so that the whole day was covered. The plan seemed foolproof.

Mr. Charles's first shift came at five-thirty in the afternoon. He checked with and relieved Mr. Paul, who had been sitting in his car in the alley since four. Mr. Charles decided to take up his station in his own car rather than in Mr. Paul's. He was parked only a few feet behind him.

Mr. Paul chided Mr. Charles for being late, handed him his gun—a beautiful little Remington .22 automatic—told him he hadn't seen anything except dozens of kids and scores of harmless dogs, remarked that Mrs. Betty—the one the dogcatcher had made a pass at—was wearing shorts and a Bikini bra, asseverated that this whole dogwatch was a lot of nonsense, warned Mr. Charles not to shoot without first making certain of what it was that he was shooting at, announced that he was going to have a drink, called down perdition on the black retriever, and concluded by saying that this was his one and only trick at the dogwatch wheel—he wasn't going to waste any more time at it. The hour and a half he had been sitting in his car was an hour and a half wasted and lost, and he was finished, through, ended, done.

Mr. Charles got into his car, laid the little Remington across his knees and began to read the collected poems of Dylan Thomas. It was a beautiful late afternoon. The children played, the birds sang, etc. The Welsh bard sang also, but he wasn't getting through to Mr. Charles. He put the book down and, for wont of something better to do, looked into his rear-view mirror.

Through some unusual property of the atmosphere, the mirror achieved a magnifying effect. Things seen in it were as large and clear, almost, as those on a Vistavision screen in a drive-in movie. Mr. Charles swiveled the mirror around, picking up different views.

The chief attraction proved to be Mrs. Betty in her shorts and Bikini bra. She was hanging up clothes on her clothesline; and, looking at her, Mr. Charles could not help but recall the dogcatcher and his flaming moment of temptation. She was a brunette.

It occurred simultaneously to Mr. Charles that there had been no proof adduced so far that the black retriever was a male. No one had seen the thing very clearly or very closely. How strange it would be, thought Mr. Charles, if the retriever were actually Mrs. Betty. That she, at certain unholy hours, transformed herself into the animal and did the things it did. Mr. Charles looked at her closely in his rear-view mirror and watched as she adjusted her bra. There was something distinctly animal-like in her motions. Far afield, said Mr. Charles; my thoughts are straying far afield. Nevertheless, he kept his mirror focused upon her.

She was behind the clothesline now, hanging up towels; and one of the towels hung down and all he could see of Mrs. Betty was her legs, the towel hiding the rest of her. Thus viewed, she gave the impression of wearing nothing at all. Then she hung up a sheet, and her bare feet were all Mr. Charles could see. Then she moved out of the mirror's field, and he could not see her at all.

He jiggled the mirror to get Mrs. Betty back on the screen; instead of her he picked up a black blur. It was far down the alley; it moved. Mr. Charles was torn, as it were, between trying to watch the blur and trying to pick up Mrs. Betty again. He jiggled the mirror more vigorously and lost everything. All he could see was his own face. He was wearing a very queer expression.

There was a scratching above, and Mr. Charles became aware that something had leaped on top of his car and was clawing to retain its footing. The alley was vacant. Mrs. Betty had disappeared. Mr. Charles was all alone, sitting there in his car with a Remington .22 automatic and a book of Dylan Thomas' collected poems. And something was on top of his car, scratching and sprawling around.

A drop of foam or froth fell on the windshield. The thing on top of the car was slavering, and this blob of foam had dropped from its mouth.

Then a black shape fell lumplike on the hood of the car, scrambling and clawing around. It regained its feet and stared through the windshield at Mr. Charles. It had horrible yellow eyes. Mr. Charles could not shoot through the windshield. He was too terrified to get out of the car and attempt to shoot from on foot. The windows of the car were open. It would be only a matter of seconds until the black thing would discover they were open and leap in upon him.

Other men, he knew, were off elsewhere in the neighborhood sitting as he was sitting.

He knew he must give them the alarm.

He pressed his hand on the horn button and honked loud and long.

The horn's bellowing woke him up. Apparently he had gone to sleep over Dylan Thomas' *Hold Hard These Ancient Minutes in a Cuckoo's Mouth.* There was no black beast on the hood of his car. There was no black blur in the alley. When Mrs. Betty came up to see what the honking was about she was dressed in modest housewifely garb and looked just as she always did—distinctly homely.

Obviously Mr. Charles had simply drowsed over a cryptic poem and fallen asleep. The rest he had dreamed. They say daytime nightmares are the worst of all.

The elders called off the stakeout the next day. Nobody had seen anything. Everybody felt rather foolish. Several of the others had also fallen asleep. One of these diffidently asked the other drowsy ones if they had had bad dreams. One and all, they ridiculed the idea, but their ridicule seemed rather artificial. Mr. Charles even had such bad taste as to inquire of the diffident one if he had dreamed about Mrs. Betty. He looked at Mr. Charles a long time before denying it. The other ones who had fallen asleep looked at Mr. Charles a long time also.

They ran the retriever to earth—or at least they ran *a* retriever to earth. She was a big black bitch and had a litter of pups in a culvert pipe in the arroyo which bordered the subdivision. Some of the children of the neighborhood, playing in the arroyo, saw her run into the culvert with a pigeon in her mouth. They told the elders, and the elders called the dog pound. A different dogcatcher came out this time. He shot the black bitch when she attacked him, and took away her puppies.

The elders concluded the dog had been raiding their yards to feed her pups, and had dropped the dead things they had found in their patios when they flushed her at her depredations. It was a satisfactory conclusion.

But a very unsatisfactory thing happened on the heels of that conclusion. Mr. Charles went out to wash his car, and, there on the top of it, he found dog's footprints and nail scratches.

HENRY SPICER
The Bird Woman

The events of this strange tale, though they actually occurred in England but a short while since, would scarcely be out of place in a book of German dreams and fancies.

The narrator, a girl of the servant class, but of rather superior education and manners, had called on the writer's sister on the subject of a place to which she had been recommended, and in the course of conversation, related the following as a recent experience.

The advertisement in which she set forth her willingness to take charge of an invalid, infirm, or lunatic person, or to assume any office demanding unusual steadiness of nerve, was replied to by a lady whose letter was dated from a certain locality on the outskirts of a large commercial city, and who requested her attendance there at an appointed time.

The house proved to be a dingy, deserted looking mansion, and was not rendered more cheerful by the fact that the adjoining tenements on either side were unoccupied. It wore altogether a haunted and sinister aspect, and the girl, as she rang the bell, was sensible of a kind of misgiving for which she could not account. A timid person might have hesitated. This girl possessed unusual firmness and courage, and, in spite of the presentiment we have mentioned, she determined, at all events, to see *what* she would be called on to encounter.

A lady-like person, the mistress herself, opened the door, and conducting the applicant into a vacant apartment, informed her in a few words that the service that would be required of her was of a very peculiar nature imperatively demanding those precise qualities she conceived her to possess. It was right, she added, to mention that the family lived in great seclusion, partly from choice, partly from necessity, an impression having gone abroad that there existed something strange and evil in connection with the residence, which was, in reality, known in the vicinity by the title of the "haunted house".

With these preliminary warnings, the lady suggested that the applicant might wish to reconsider her purpose. The latter, however, having little fear of anything human, and none at all of apparitions, at once agreed to the terms proposed stipulating only that the cause of the strange reports affecting the mansion should be a little more clearly explained, and her own particular duties defined.

The mistress readily assented to both conditions, and, leading the way to a ground floor apartment at the back, unlocked the door and turned the handle as if about to enter, but checking herself suddenly, warned her companion, without sinking her voice below its ordinary tone, that she was about to be brought face to face with a spectacle that might well try the strongest nerves; nevertheless, there was nothing to fear so long as she retained her self-command. With this not very reassuring preface, they entered the room.

It was rather dark, for the lower half of the windows were boarded up; but in one corner, on the floor, was plainly distinguishable what looked like a heap of clothes flung together in disorder. It appeared to be in motion, however, and the mistress of the house once more turning to her follower had just time to utter the mysterious words, "Don't be frightened. If she likes you she'll hoot; if she doesn't she'll scream," when from the apex of the seeming heap of clothes there rose a head that made the stranger's blood run chill. It was human, indeed, in general structure, but exhibited, in place of a nose a huge beak curved and pointed like that of an owl. Two large staring yellow eyes increased the bizarre resemblance, while numerous tufts of some feathery substance, sprouting from a hard skin and black as a parrot's tongue, completed this horrible intermingling of bird and woman.

As they approached, the unhappy being rose and sunk with the measured motion of a bird upon a perch, and presently, opening its mouth gave utterance to a hideous and prolonged "tu-whoo".

"All right," said the lady quietly, "she likes you!"

They were now standing as it were over the unfortunate freak of nature.

"Have you the courage to lift her?" enquired the lady. "Try."

The girl, though recoiling instinctively from the contact, nerved herself to the utmost, and, putting her arms beneath those of the still hooting creature, strove to raise it up. In doing so, the hands became disengaged from the clothes. They were black, and armed with long curved talons, like those of a bird of prey.

Even this new discovery might not have made the girl's courage quail, had she not, in raising the creature, observed that she was not, as had seemed to be the case, crouched on the ground, but balanced on an actual perch, or rail, round which her feet closed and clung by means of talons similar to those which adorned her hands.

So inexpressible was the feeling of horror that now overcame the visitor, that, after one desperate effort of self control, she was forced to let go of the thing she held. A wild, unearthly scream that rang through the house marked the creature's change of mood. The baleful eyes shot yellow fire, and scream after scream pursued her as she fairly fled from the apartment, followed at a steadier pace, by the lady.

The latter took her into another room, did all in her power to soothe her agitation, but expressed no surprise when the girl declared that ten times the liberal amount already offered, would not tempt her to undertake such a charge.

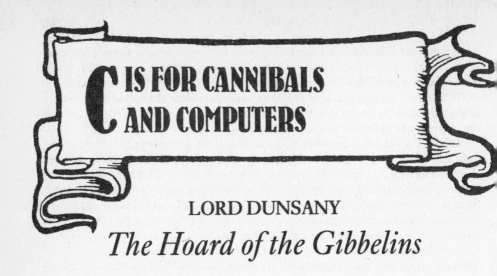

C IS FOR CANNIBALS AND COMPUTERS

LORD DUNSANY

The Hoard of the Gibbelins

The Gibbelins eat, as is well known, nothing less good than man. Their evil tower is joined to Terra Cognita, to the lands we know, by a bridge. Their hoard is beyond reason; avarice has no use for it; they have a separate cellar for emeralds and a separate cellar for sapphires; they have filled a hole with gold and dig it up when they need it. And the only use that is known for their ridiculous wealth is to attract to their larder a continual supply of food. In times of famine they have even been known to scatter rubies abroad, a little trail of them to some city of Man, and sure enough their larders would soon be full again.

Their tower stands on the other side of that river known to Homer—ὁ ῥόος α᾽κεανοίο, as he called it—which surrounds the world. And where the river is narrow and fordable the tower was built by the Gibbelins' gluttonous sires, for they liked to see burglars rowing easily to their steps. Some nourishment that common soil has not the huge trees drained there with their colossal roots from both banks of the river.

There the Gibbelins lived and discreditably fed.

Alderic, Knight of the Order of the City and the Assault, hereditary Guardian of the King's Peace of Mind, a man not unremembered among the makers of myth, pondered so long upon the Gibbelins' hoard that by now he deemed it his. Alas that I should say of so perilous a venture, undertaken at dead of night by a valorous man, that its motive was sheer avarice! Yet upon avarice only the Gibbelins relied to keep their larders full, and once in every hundred years sent spies into the cities of men to see how avarice did, and always the spies returned again to the tower saying that all was well.

It may be thought that, as the years went on and men came by fearful ends on that tower's wall, fewer and fewer would come to the Gibbelins' table: but the Gibbelins found otherwise.

Not in the folly and frivolity of his youth did Alderic come to the tower, but he studied carefully for several years the manner in which burglars met their doom when they went in search of the treasure that he considered his. *In every case they had entered by the door.*

He consulted those who gave advice on this quest; he noted every detail and cheerfully paid their fees, and determined to do nothing that they advised, for what were their clients now? No more than examples of the savoury art, mere half-forgotten memories of a meal; and many, perhaps, no longer even that.

These were the requisites for the quest that these men used to advise: a horse, a boat, mail armour, and at least three men-at-arms. Some said, "Blow the horn at the tower door"; others said, "Do not touch it."

Alderic thus decided: he would take no horse down to the river's edge, he would not row along it in a boat, and he would go alone and by way of the Forest Unpassable.

How pass, you may say, by the unpassable? This was his plan: there was a dragon he knew of who if peasants' prayers are heeded deserved to die, not alone because of the number of maidens he cruelly slew, but because he was bad for the crops; he ravaged the very land and was the bane of a dukedom.

Now Alderic determined to go up against him. So he took horse and spear and pricked till he met the dragon, and the dragon came out against him breathing bitter smoke. And to him Alderic shouted, "Hath foul dragon ever slain true knight?" And well the dragon knew that this had never been, and he hung his head and was silent, for he was glutted with blood. "Then," said the knight, "if thou would'st ever taste maiden's blood again thou shalt be my trusty steed, and if not, by this spear there shall befall thee all that the troubadours tell of the dooms of thy breed."

And the dragon did not open his ravening mouth, nor rush upon the knight, breathing out fire; for well he knew the fate of those that did these things, but he consented to the terms imposed, and swore to the knight to become his trusty steed.

It was on a saddle upon this dragon's back that Alderic afterwards sailed above the unpassable forest, even above the tops of those measureless trees, children of wonder. But first he pondered that subtle plan of his which was more profound than merely to avoid all that had been done before; and he commanded a blacksmith, and the blacksmith made him a pickaxe.

Now there was great rejoicing at the rumour of Alderic's quest, for all folk knew that he was a cautious man, and they deemed that he would succeed and enrich the world, and they rubbed their hands in the cities at the thought of largesse; and there was joy among all men in Alderic's country, except perchance among the lenders of money, who feared they would soon be paid. And there was rejoicing also because men hoped that when the Gibbelins were robbed of their hoard, they would shatter their high-built bridge and break the golden chains that bound them to the world, and drift back, they and their tower, to the moon, from which they had come and to which they rightly belonged. There was little love for the Gibbelins, though all men envied their hoard.

So they all cheered, that day when he mounted his dragon, as though he was already a conqueror, and what pleased them more than the good that they hoped he would do to the world was that he scattered gold as he rode away; for he would not need it, he said, if he found the Gibbelins' hoard, and he would not need it more if he smoked on the Gibbelins' table.

When they heard that he had rejected the advice of those that gave it, some said that the knight was mad, and others said he was greater than those that gave the advice, but none appreciated the worth of his plan.

He reasoned thus: for centuries men had been well advised and had gone by the cleverest way, while the Gibbelins came to expect them to come by boat and to look for them at the door whenever their larder was empty, even as a man looketh for a snipe in the marsh; but how, said Alderic, if a snipe should sit in the top of a tree, and would men find him there? Assuredly never! So Alderic decided to swim the river and not to go by the door, but to pick his way into the tower through the stone. Moreover, it was in his mind to work below the level of the ocean, the river (as Homer knew) that girdles the world, so that as soon as he made a hole in the wall the water should pour in, confounding the Gibbelins, and flooding the cellars rumoured to be twenty-feet in depth, and therein he would dive for emeralds as a diver dives for pearls.

And on the day that I tell of he galloped away from his home scattering largesse of gold, as I have said, and passed through many kingdoms, the dragon snapping at maidens as he went, but being unable to eat them because of the bit in his mouth, and earning no gentler reward than a spur-thrust where he was softest. And so they came to the swart arboreal precipice of the unpassable forest. The dragon rose at it with a rattle of wings. Many a farmer near the edge of the world saw him up there where yet the twilight lingered, a faint, black, wavering line; and mistaking him for a row of geese going inland from the ocean, went into their houses cheerily rubbing their hands and saying that winter was coming, and that we should soon have snow. Soon even there the twilight faded away, and when they descended at the edge of the world it was night and the moon was shining. Ocean, the ancient river, narrow and shallow there, flowed by and made no murmur. Whether the Gibbelins banqueted or whether they watched by the door, they also made no murmur. And Alderic dismounted and took his armour off, and saying one prayer to his lady, swam with his pickaxe. He did not part from his sword, for fear that he met with a Gibbelin. Landed the other side, he began to work at once, and all went well with him. Nothing put out its head from any window, and all were lighted so that nothing within could see him in the dark. The blows of his pickaxe were dulled in the deep walls. All night he worked, no sound came to molest him, and at dawn the last rock swerved and tumbled inwards, and the river poured in after. Then Alderic took a stone, and went to the bottom step, and hurled the stone at the door; he heard the echoes roll into the tower, then he ran back and dived through the hole in the wall.

He was in the emerald-cellar. There was no light in the lofty vault above him, but, diving through twenty feet of water, he felt the floor all rough with emeralds, and open coffers full of them. By a faint ray of the moon he saw that the water was green with them, and, easily filling a satchel, he rose again to the surface; and there were the Gibbelins waist-deep in the water, with torches in their hands! And, without saying a word, *or even smiling*, they neatly hanged him on the outer wall—and the tale is one of those that have not a happy ending.

FREDRIC BROWN

Answer

Dwar Ev ceremoniously soldered the final connection with gold. The eyes of a dozen television cameras watched him and the sub-ether bore throughout the universe a dozen pictures of what he was doing.

He straightened and nodded to Dwar Reyn, then moved to a position beside the switch that would complete the contact when he threw it. The switch that would connect, all at once, all of the monster computing machines of all the populated planets in the universe—ninety-six billion planets—into the supercircuit that would connect them all into one supercalculator, one cybernetics machine that would combine all the knowledge of all the galaxies.

Dwar Reyn spoke briefly to the watching and listening trillions. Then after a moment's silence he said, "Now, Dwar Ev."

Dwar Ev threw the switch. There was a mighty hum, the surge of power from ninety-six billion planets. Lights flashed and quieted along the miles-long panel.

Dwar Ev stepped back and drew a deep breath. "The honor of asking the first question is yours, Dwar Reyn."

"Thank you," said Dwar Reyn. "It shall be a question which no single cybernetics machine has been able to answer."

He turned to face the machine. "Is there a God?"

The mighty voice answered without hesitation, without the clicking of a single relay.

"Yes, *now* there is a God."

Sudden fear flashed on the face of Dwar Ev. He leaped to grab the switch.

A bolt of lightning from the cloudless sky struck him down and fused the switch shut.

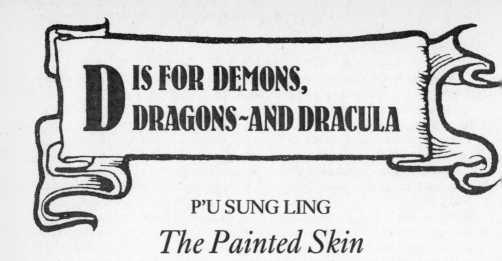

D IS FOR DEMONS, DRAGONS~AND DRACULA

P'U SUNG LING

The Painted Skin

Going out early in the morning, a scholar of Taiyuan named Wang met a damsel who was walking alone with a bundle of clothes under her arm and looked rather tired. He hurriedly caught her up and saw that she was a beautiful girl of about sixteen.

"Why are you walking alone so early in the morning?" he asked, very pleased with her looks.

"You are a passer-by and can neither dispel my worries nor share my troubles; so what is the use of asking?" she replied.

"Perhaps I may be able to help," said the scholar. "If only I can be of any use, I certainly will not refuse to help."

"My parents out of love for money have sold me to a rich family," said the girl. "The mistress is such a jealous person that she beats and abuses me all day long so that I can't bear it any more and have to run away."

"Where are you going then?" asked the scholar.

"I am a runaway girl. I don't know where to go."

"My house is not far from here," he said. "Please come if you don't mind."

The girl was pleased and followed him. He took over the bundle of clothes and led her to his room. Looking round and seeing no one there, she asked, "Where are the rest of your family?"

"This is my study," replied the scholar.

"It is an excellent place," she said. "If you have pity on me and want to save my life, you must keep it secret."

He agreed and kept her in a secret chamber. For several days no one knew anything about it.

The scholar hinted the matter to his wife named Chen who urged her husband to let the girl go, suspecting that she was probably a maidservant or concubine of some rich family. But he would not listen.

One day the scholar went to the market and met a Taoist priest who stared at him in astonishment, and asked, "What has happened to you?"

"Nothing in particular."

"You are shrouded from head to foot by an evil spirit, and yet you say there is

66

nothing the matter."

The scholar still insisted that he was alright.

"Damned fool!" uttered the priest, going away. "Of course there are always fools who don't realize it even when death stares them in the face."

The scholar thought there might be something in what he said, and began to have doubts about the girl. But on second thoughts, he could not believe her to be a demon, as she was obviously so beautiful; instead he considered the priest an imposter who professed to dispel evil spirits in order to earn a living.

A little later the scholar came to the gate leading to his study and found it bolted from inside, so that he could not get in. Then he began to suspect what she was doing. Instantly he climbed through a gap in the wall and discovered that the study door was also bolted. So stealthily he went up to the window and looked inside through a crevice, and what a sight he witnessed! A fierce-looking monster with a greenish face and rows of sharp teeth like a saw was spreading a human skin on the couch and painting colours on it with a brush. After that, it threw away the paint brush and shook the skin as though it was a dress. In draping it on, the monster became a woman of exceptional beauty. Having witnessed the scene, the scholar was frightened to death and crawled out on all fours.

He then ran into the street in search of the priest, but could not find him anywhere. Finally he met him on the outskirts of the town and immediately knelt down in front of him, and begged him to save his life.

"I will drive the monster away for you," said the priest. "It must have had a hard time trying to find a substitute. I will spare its life."

Thereupon he gave the scholar a horsetail whisk, telling the latter to hang it over his bedroom door. On parting, they agreed to meet again the next day at the Temple of Qing Di (The Eastern Heavenly Emperor). When the scholar arrived home, he dared not go to his study, but retired to his bedroom in the rear, and hung the whisk over the door.

At about nine in the evening, the scholar heard twittering sounds outside the door. He was too scared to go and look; so he asked his wife to have a peep. She saw the girl looking at the whisk from a distance, not daring to come any further. She stood still grinding her teeth in extreme hatred. After a long while it went away. Soon afterwards, it came back again, cursing, "The priest tries to frighten me, but I am not to be set back. Don't think I will give up what is already mine!"

The monster then pulled the whisk to pieces, broke the door and entered. It went straight to the bed where the scholar was lying, tore open his chest, dug out his heart and went away with it. Terrified, the scholar's wife screamed. Then the maid-servant entered and lit the lamp, only to find the scholar already dead with blood streaming from the breast. Her mistress was panic-stricken but dared not cry aloud.

The next day Chen sent her husband's younger brother Er-lang to call on the priest and tell him what had happened. On hearing the news the priest broke out in a rage. "I had pity on the demon and yet it dared behave like this!" Thus he followed Er-lang to Wang's house. The devilish girl was nowhere to be found. Then the priest raised his head to look round, saying, "Fortunately it hasn't fled too far," and asked,

"Who lives in the courtyard to the south?"

"I do," replied Er-lang.

"The devil is there now," said the priest.

Er-lang was flabbergasted and could not believe it. The priest continued questioning:

"Hasn't any stranger come to your home?"

"Not that I know of. I had gone to the Qing Di Temple early this morning," said Er-lang. "Let me go home and find out."

He went and came back after a while, saying:

"Someone did come. An old woman came wanting to be employed as maidservant in my home, and my wife has retained her. She is still there."

"That is the monster," said the priest.

The priest went with Er-lang, grasping a wooden double-edged sword in one hand. Standing in the middle of the courtyard, he roared, "Diabolical monster, give me back my whisk!"

The old hag became greatly agitated, her face as white as a sheet of paper, and rushed out of the room trying to flee. The priest pursued and struck her with the sword. Instantly she fell down and the piece of human skin flipped off, leaving the monster lying on the ground and wailing like a pig. The priest cut down its head with the sword, its body metamorphosed into thick smoke curling up like a huge ball. The priest took out a gourd, opened the stopper and put it in the midst of the smoke. Just like magic, the gourd sucked in all the smoke; then the priest closed it with the stopper and put it in his pocket. The piece of human skin had eyebrows, eyes, hands and feet, all complete. He rolled it up as if it were a scroll of painting, and also put it in his pocket.

The priest was going to take leave, but Chen kowtowed to him at the door, begging him in tears to revive her husband by magic. He contemplated for a while and said, "My rudimentary art cannot make the dead rise again; however I shall direct you to one who probably can. I am sure you will get what you want by pleading with him."

"Who could that be?" asked the woman.

"There is a madman in the town who often lies in the rubbish heap," said the priest. "You try and kowtow to him, and if he should insult you, you must not feel indignant."

Er-lang knew who the priest meant; so he said good-bye to the latter and went there with his sister-in-law in search of the lunatic. They saw in the street a beggar singing doggerels with mucus dripping from his nostrils. His clothes were so filthy that no one would get near him. However, Chen knelt down and approached him on her knees. The beggar burst out laughing and said, "Are you in love with me, my beauty?" Chen told him what she wanted with him. Then the beggar said, "Any male will make you a husband. So where is the need of bringing your husband to life again!"

Chen went on pleading. Then the lunatic said, "How extraordinary! Wanting me to bring a dead one to life, do you think I am the king of Hell?"

He was so furious that he struck Chen with a staff, and she endured in spite of the pain. By that time a crowd had gathered round the two like a wall.

The beggar spat out a mouthful of thick sputum on his palm, and held it under her nose, saying, "Swallow this!"

Chen blushed in great embarrassment, not knowing what to do, but recalling the advice of the priest, swallowed it against her own will. But it stuck in her throat like compressed cotton wool and it was only with great effort that she managed to swallow it. Even then it stuck in her stomach. The beggar again roared with laughter, saying, "The young lady is in love with me!"

The beggar straightened up, went his way without looking back. Chen followed him and saw him enter the temple. She meant to implore him again but lost sight of him altogether. He was nowhere to be seen, though she searched the temple inside out. Feeling ashamed and indignant, she found her way home. The sorrow at her husband's cruel death plus the regret of bringing on herself disgrace by swallowing the sputum made her cry bitterly. Her only wish was to die at once.

She started to wipe the blood stains and encoffin the corpse, while members of the family all stood still and dared not approach it. Chen held the dead body in her arm, and put in the entrails, crying herself hoarse. Suddenly she felt like vomiting. The lump in her stomach popped out of her mouth. Before she could turn aside, the thing had already fallen into the chest of the corpse. She was extremely frightened, but on scrutiny, she saw it was a human heart, throbbing in the chest, and emitting a warm vapour like steam. Amazed, she hurriedly closed up the wound and squeezed it tight with all her strength. If her hands slacked the least bit, a wisp of heat emerged from the slit. She tore off a piece of silk to quickly tie it up with.

Chen stroked the dead body, and felt it getting gradually warmer. She covered it with a quilt. In the middle of the night she lifted the quilt to have a look and lo, there was breath from his nostrils. By dawn the scholar was alive again. "I seem to have had a dream. Now I feel a slight pain in my heart," he said.

Where the wound had been, the scar looked like a copper coin. Soon he was well again.

The Recorder of Marvels comments, "How foolish are the common people who take an obvious monster for a beauty! How muddle-headed are the fools who regard obvious truth as absurdity! It is no wonder that the wife of a lady-killer should have to swallow the spittle of other people. Justice has a long arm: woe to the fools who are muddled and refuse to come to their senses!"

ROGER ZELAZNY

The Monster and the Maiden

A great unrest was among the people, for the time of decision was again at hand. The Elders voted upon the candidates and the sacrifice was affirmed over the objections of Ryllik, the oldest.

"It is wrong to capitulate thus," he argued.

But they did not answer him, and the young virgin was taken to the grotto of smokes and fed the leaves of drowsiness.

Ryllik watched with disapproval.

"It should not be so," he stated. "It is wrong."

"It has always been so," said the others, "in the spring of the year, and in the fall. It has always been so." And they cast worried glances down the trail to where the sun was pouring morning upon the world.

The god was already traveling through the great-leafed forest.

"Let us go now," they said.

"Did you ever think of staying? Of watching to see what the monster god does?" asked Ryllik bitterly.

"Enough of your blasphemies! Come along!"

Ryllik followed them.

"We grow fewer every year," he said. "One day we shall no longer have any sacrifices to offer."

"Then that day we die," said the others.

"So why prolong it?" he asked. "Let us fight them—now, before we are no more!"

But the others shook their heads, a summary of that resignation Ryllik had watched grow as the centuries passed. They all respected Ryllik's age, but they did not approve of his thoughts. They cast one last look back, just as the sun caught the clanking god upon his gilt-caparisoned mount, his death-lance slung at his side. Within the place where the smokes were born the maiden thrashed her tail from side to side, rolling wild eyes beneath her youthful brow-plates. She sensed the divine presence and began to bellow.

They turned away and lumbered across the plains.

As they neared the forest Ryllik paused and raised a scaley fore-limb, groping after a thought. Finally, he spoke:

"I seem to have memory," said he, "of a time when things were different."

MANLY WADE WELLMAN
The Devil is Not Mocked

DO YOU not know that tonight, when the clock strikes midnight, all the evil things in the world hold sway? Do you know where you are going, and what you are going to?
BRAM STOKER.

Balkan weather, even Balkan spring weather, was not pleasant to General von Grunn, leaning heavily back behind the bulletproof glass of his car. May 4th—the English would call it St. George's Day, after their saint who was helping them so little. The date would mean something to Heinrich Himmler, too; that weak-chinned pet of the Führer would hold some sort of garbled druidic ritual with his Schutzstaffel on the Brockenburg. Von Grunn grimaced fatly at thought of Himmler, and leaned forward to look out into the night. An armed car ahead, an armed car behind—all was well.

"Forward!" he growled to his orderly, Kranz, who trod on the accelerator. The car moved, and the car ahead took the lead, into the Borgo Pass.

Von Grunn glanced backward once, to the lights of Bistritz. This country had been Rumanian not so long ago. Now it was Hungarian, which meant that it was German.

What was it that the mayor of Bistritz had said, when he had demanded a semiremote headquarters? The castle along this pass, empty—ready for him? The dolt had seemed eager to help, to please. Von Grunn produced a long cigarette. Young Captain Plesser, sitting beside him, at once kindled a lighter. Slim, quiet, the young aide had faded from von Grunn's consciousness.

"What's the name of that castle again?" inquired the general, and made a grimace when Plesser replied in barbarous slavic syllables. "What's the meaning in a civilized tongue?"

"Devil's castle, I should think," hazarded the captain's respectful voice.

"*Ach*, so—Transylvania is supposed to be overrun with devils," nodded von Grunn, puffing. "Let them defer to us, or we'll devil them." He smiled, for his was a great gift for appreciating his own epigrams. "Meanwhile, let the castle be called its German name. *Teufelschloss*—Devil's Castle."

"Of course," agreed Plesser.

Silence for a while, as the cars purred powerfully up the rough slope of the pass trail. Von Grunn lost himself in his favorite meditation—his own assured future. He was to establish an unostentatious command post for—what? A move against Russia? The Black Sea? He would know soon enough. In any case, any army would be his, action and glory. There was glory enough for all. Von Grunn remembered Wilhelm II saying that, in the last war.

"The last war," he said aloud. "I was a simple oberleutenant then. And the Führer—a corporal. What were you, captain?"

"A child."

"You remember?"

"Nothing." Plesser screwed up his courage to ask a question. "General von

Grunn, does it not seem strange that the folk at Bistritz were so anxious for you to come to the castle—*Teufelschloss*—tonight?"

Von Grunn nodded, like a big fierce owl. "You smell a trap, *nicht wahr?* That is why I bring two carloads of men, my trusted bodyguard. For that very chance. But I doubt if any in Transylvania dare set traps for me, or any other German."

The cars were slowing down. General and captain leaned forward. The car ahead was passing through the great open gateway of a courtyard. Against the spattered stars rose the silhouette of a vast black building, with a broken tower. "We seem to be here," ventured Captain Plesser.

"Good. Go to the forward car. When the other arrives, form the guard."

It was done swiftly. Sixteen stark infantrymen were marshaled, with rifles, bombs, and submachine guns. Von Grunn emerged into the cold night, and Kranz, the orderly, began to bring out the luggage.

"A natural fort, withdrawn and good for any defense except against aircraft," pronounced the general, peering through his monocle at the battlements above. "We will make a thorough examination.

"*Unteroffizer!*" he barked, and the noncom in charge of the escort came forward woodenly, stiffening to attention. "Six of the men will accompany me inside. You will bivouac the others in this courtyard, maintaining a guard all night. *Heil Hitler.*"

"*Heil Hitler,*" responded the man briskly. Von Grunn smiled as the *Unteroffizier* strode away to obey. For all the soldierly alacrity, that order to sleep outdoors was no welcome one. So much the better; von Grunn believed in toughening experiences for field soldiers, and his escort had lived too softly since the Battle of Flanders.

He walked to where a sort of vestibule of massive rough stone projected from the castle wall. Plesser already stood there, staring at the heavy nail-studded planks of the door. "It is locked, *Herr General*," he reported. "No knob or latch, bell or knocker—"

But as he spoke, the door swung creakingly inward, and yellow light gushed out.

On the threshold stood a figure in black, as tall as von Grunn himself but thinner than even Plesser. A pale, sharp face and brilliant eyes turned upon them, in the light of a chimneyless oil lamp of silver.

"Welcome, General von Grunn," said the lamp holder. "You are expected."

His German was good; his manner respectful. Von Grunn's broad hand slid into a greatcoat pocket, where he always carried a big automatic pistol.

"Who told you to expect us?" he demanded.

The lamplight struck blue radiance from smooth, sparse black hair as the thin man bowed. "Who could mistake General von Grunn, or doubt that he would want this spacious, withdrawn structure for his new headquarters position?"

The mayor of Bistritz, officious ass, must have sent this fellow ahead to make fawning preparations—but even as von Grunn thought that, the man himself gave other information.

"I am in charge here, have been in charge for many years. We are so honored to have company. Will the general enter?"

He stepped back. Plesser entered, then von Grunn. The vestibule was warm.

"This way, excellency," said the man with the lamp—the steward, von Grunn decided to classify him. He led the way along a stone-paved passage, von Grunn's escort tramping authoritatively after him. Then up a great winding stair, and into a room, a big hall of a place, with a fire of logs and a table set for supper.

All told, very inviting; but it was not von Grunn's way to say as much. He only nodded, and allowed Captain Plesser to help him out of his greatcoat. Meanwhile, the steward was showing the luggage-laden Kranz into an octagonal bedroom beyond.

"Take these six men," said von Grunn to Plesser, indicating the soldiers of the escort. "Tour the castle. Make a plan of each floor. Then come back and report. *Heil Hitler.*"

"Heil Hitler," and Plesser led the party away. Von Grunn turned his broad back to the fire. Kranz was busy within the bedroom, arranging things. The steward returned. "May I serve the *Herr General?*" he asked silkily.

Von Grunn looked at the table, and with difficulty forebore to lick his fat lips. There were great slices of roast beef, a fowl, cheese, salad, and two bottles of wine—Kranz himself could not have guessed better what would be good. Von Grunn almost started forward to the table, then paused. This was Transylvania. The natives, for all their supple courtesy, disliked and feared soldiers of the Reich. Might these good things not be poisoned?

"Remove these things," he said bleakly. "I have brought my own provisions. You may eat that supper yourself."

Another bow. "The *Herr General* is too good, but I will sup at midnight—it is not long. Now, I will clear the things away. Your man will fetch what you want."

He began to gather up dishes. Watching him stoop over the table, von Grunn thought that he had seldom seen anyone so narrow in the shoulders—they were humped high, like the shoulders of a hyena, suggesting a power that crouched and lurked. Von Grunn was obliged to tell himself that he was not repelled or nervous. The steward was a stranger, a Slav of some kind. It was von Grunn's business to be scornful of all such.

"Now," he said, when all was cleared, "go to the bedroom and tell my orderly—" He broke off. "What was that?"

The other listened. Von Grunn could have sworn that the man's ears—pale and pointed—lifted voluntarily, like the ears of a cat or a fox. The sound came again, a prolonged howl in the distance.

"The wolves," came the quiet reply. "They speak to the full moon."

"Wolves?" The general was intrigued at once. He was a sportsman—that is, he liked to corner and kill beasts almost as much as he liked to corner and kill men. As a guest of Hermann Goering he had shot two very expensive wild bulls, and he yearned for the day when the Führer would graciously invite him to the Black Forest for pigsticking. "Are there many?" he asked. "It sounds like many. If they were not so far—"

"They come nearer," his companion said, and indeed the howl was repeated more strongly and clearly. "But you gave an order, general?"

"Oh, yes." Von Grunn remembered his hunger. "My man will bring me supper from among the things we have with us."

*

A bow, and the slender black figure moved noiselessly into the bedroom. Von Grunn crossed the floor and seated himself in an armchair before the table. The steward returned, and stood at his elbow.

"Pardon. Your orderly helped me carry the other food to the castle kitchen. He has not returned, and so I took the liberty of serving you."

He had a tray. Upon it were delicacies from von Grunn's mess chest—slices of smoked turkey, buttered bread, preserved fruits, bottled beer. The fellow had arranged them himself, had had every opportunity to . . . to—

Von Grunn scowled and took the monocle from his eye. The danger of poison again stirred in his mind, and he had difficulty scorning it. He must eat and drink, in defiance of fear.

Poison or no poison, the food was splendid, and the steward an excellent waiter. The general drank beer, and deigned to say, "You are an experienced servant?"

The pale, sharp face twitched sidewise in negation. "I serve very few guests. The last was years ago—Jonathan Harker, an Englishman—"

Von Grunn snorted away mention of that unwelcome people, and finished his repast. Then he rose, and stared around. The wolves howled again, in several directions and close to the castle.

"I seem to be deserted," he said grimly. "The captain is late, my orderly late. My men make no report." He stepped to the door, opened it. "Plesser!" he called. "Captain Plesser!"

No reply.

"Shall I bring you to him?" asked the steward gently. Once again, he had come up close. Von Grunn started violently, and wheeled.

The eyes of the steward were on a level with his, and very close. For the first time von Grunn saw that they were filled with green light. The steward was smiling, too, and von Grunn saw his teeth—white, spaced widely, pointed—

As if signaled by the thought, the howling of the beasts outside broke out afresh. It was deafeningly close. To von Grunn it sounded like hundreds. Then, in reply, came a shout, the voice of the *unteroffizer* uttering a quick, startled command.

At once a shot. Several shots.

The men he had encamped in the courtyard were shooting at something.

With ponderous haste, von Grunn hurried from the room, down the stairs. As he reached the passageway below, he heard more shots, and a wild air-rending chorus of howls, growls, spotting scuffles. Von Grunn gained the door by which he had entered. Something moved in the gloom at his very feet.

A chalky face turned up, the face of Captain Plesser. A hand lifted shakily to clutch at the general's boot top.

"Back in there, the dark rooms—" It was half a choke, half a sigh. "They're devils—hungry—they got the others, got me— I could come no farther than this—"

Plesser collapsed. Light came from behind von Grunn, and he could see the captain's head sagging backward on the stone. The side of the slender neck had been torn open, but blood did not come. For there was no blood left in Captain Plesser's body.

Outside, there was sudden silence. Stepping across Plesser's body, the general seized the latch and pushed the door open.

The courtyard was full of wolves, feeding. One glance was enough to show what they fed on. As von Grunn stared, the wolves lifted their heads and stared back. He saw many green-glowing eyes, level, hard, hungry, many grinning mouths with pointed teeth—the eyes and the teeth of the steward.

He got the door shut again, and sagged upon it, breathing hard.

"I am sorry, general," came a soft, teasing apology. "Sorry—my servants were too eager within and without. Wolves and vampires are hard to restrain. After all, it is midnight—our moment of all moments."

"What are you raving about?" gasped von Grunn, feeling his jaw sag.

"I do not rave. I tell simple truth. My castle has vampires within, wolves without, all my followers and friends—"

Von Grunn felt for a weapon. His great coat was upstairs, the pistol in its pocket.

"Who are you?" he screamed.

"I am Count Dracula of Transylvania," replied the gaunt man in black.

He set down the lamp carefully before moving forward.

E IS FOR EXTRA-TERRESTRIAL EVIL

FREDRIC BROWN

Puppet Show

Horror came to Cherrybell at a little after noon on a blistering hot day in August.

Perhaps that is redundant; *any* August day in Cherrybell, Arizona, is blistering hot. It is on Highway 89, about forty miles south of Tucson and about thirty miles north of the Mexican border. It consists of two filling stations, one on each side of the road to catch travelers going in both directions, a general store, a beer-and-wine-license-only tavern, a tourist-trap-type trading post for tourists who can't wait until they reach the border to start buying serapes and huaraches, a deserted hamburger stand, and a few 'dobe houses inhabited by Mexican-Americans who work in Nogales, the border town to the south, and who, for god knows what reason, prefer to live in Cherrybell and commute, some of them in Model T Fords. The sign on the highway says, CHERRYBELL, POP. 42, but the sign exaggerates; Pop died last year—Pop Anders, who ran the now deserted hamburger stand—and the correct figure should be 41.

Horror came to Cherrybell mounted on a burro led by an ancient, dirty and gray-bearded desert rat of a prospector who later gave the name of Dade Grant. Horror's name was Garvane. He was approximately nine feet tall but so thin, almost a stick-man, that he could not have weighed over a hundred pounds. Old Dade's burro carried him easily, despite the fact that his feet dragged in the sand on either side. Being dragged through the sand for, as it later turned out, well over five miles hadn't caused the slightest wear on the shoes—more like buskins, they were—which constituted all that he wore except for a pair of what could have been swimming trunks, in robin's-egg blue. But it wasn't his dimensions that made him horrible to look upon; it was his *skin*. It looked red, raw. It looked as though he had been skinned alive, and the skin replaced raw side out. His skull, his face, were equally narrow or elongated; otherwise in every visible way he appeared human—or at least humanoid. Unless you count such little things as the fact that his hair was a robin's-egg blue to match his trunks, as were his eyes and his boots. Blood-red and light blue.

Casey, owner of the tavern, was the first one to see them coming across the plain, from the direction of the mountain range to the east. He'd stepped out of the back door of his tavern for a breath of fresh, if hot, air. They were about one

77

hundred yards away at that time, and already he could see the utter alienness of the figure on the led burro. Just alienness at that distance, the horror came only at closer range. Casey's jaw dropped and stayed down until the strange trio was about fifty yards away, then he started slowly toward them. There are people who run at the sight of the unknown, others who advance to meet it. Casey advanced, slowly, to meet it.

Still in the wide open, twenty yards from the back of the little tavern, he met them. Dade Grant stopped and dropped the rope by which he was leading the burro. The burro stood still and dropped its head. The stick-man stood up simply by planting his feet solidly and standing, astride the burro. He stepped one leg across it and stood a moment, leaning his weight against his hands on the burro's back, and then sat down in the sand. "High gravity planet," he said. "Can't stand long."

"Kin I get water ter my burro?" the prospector asked Casey. "Must be purty thirsty by now. Hadda leave water bags, some other things, so it could carry—" He jerked a thumb toward the red-and-blue horror.

Casey was just realizing that it *was* a horror. At a distance the color combination seemed only mildly hideous, but close up—the skin was rough and seemed to have veins on the outside and looked moist (although it wasn't) and *damn* if it didn't look just like he had his skin peeled off and put back on inside out. Or just peeled off, period. Casey had never seen anything like it and hoped he wouldn't ever see anything like it again.

Casey felt something behind him and looked over his shoulder. Others had seen now and were coming, but the nearest of them, a pair of boys, were ten yards behind him. *"Muchachos,"* he called out. *"Agua por el burro. Un pozal. Pronto."*

He looked back and said, 'What—? Who—?"

"Name's Dade Grant," said the prospector, putting out a hand, which Casey took absently. When he let go of it it jerked back over the desert rat's shoulder, thumb indicating the thing that sat on the sand. *"His* name's Garvane, he tells me. He's an extra something or other, and he's some kind of minister."

Casey nodded at the stick-man and was glad to get a nod in return instead of an extended hand. "I'm Manuel Casey," he said. "What does he mean, an extra something?"

The stick-man's voice was unexpectedly deep and vibrant. "I am an extra-terrestrial. And a minister plenipotentiary."

Surprisingly, Casey was a moderately well-educated man and knew both of those phrases; he was probably the only person in Cherrybell who would have known the second one. Less surprisingly, considering the speaker's appearance, he believed both of them.

"What can I do for you, sir?" he asked. "But first, why not come in out of the sun?"

"No, thank you. It's a bit cooler here than they told me it would be, but I'm quite comfortable. And as to what you can do for me, you can notify your authorities of my presence. I believe they will be interested."

Well, Casey thought, by blind luck he's hit the best man for his purpose within at least twenty miles. Manuel Casey was half Irish, half Mexican. He had a half-brother who was half Irish and half assorted-American, and the half-brother was a bird colonel at Davis-Monthan Air Force Base in Tucson.

He said, "Just a minute, Mr. Garvane, I'll telephone. You, Mr. Grant, would you want to come inside?"

"Naw, I don't mind sun. Out in it all day ever' day. An' Garvane here, he ast me if I'd stick with him till he was finished with what he's gotta do here. Said he'd gimme somethin' purty vallable if I did. Somethin'—a 'lectrononic—"

"An electronic battery-operated portable ore indicator," Garvane said. "A simple little device, indicates presence of a concentration of ore up to two miles, indicates kind, grade, quantity and depth."

Casey gulped, excused himself, and pushed through the gathering crowd into his tavern. He had Colonel Casey on the phone in one minute, but it took him another four minutes to convince the colonel that he was neither drunk nor joking.

Twenty-five minutes after that there was a noise in the sky, a noise that swelled and then died as a four-man helicopter sat down and shut off its rotors a dozen yards from an extraterrestrial, two men and a burro. Casey alone had had the courage to rejoin the trio from the desert; there were other spectators, but they still held well back.

Colonel Casey, a major, a captain and a lieutenant who was the helicopter's pilot all came out and ran over. The stick-man stood up, all nine feet of him; from the effort it cost him to stand you could tell that he was used to a much lighter gravity than Earth's. He bowed, repeated his name and the identification of himself as an extraterrestrial and a minister plenipotentiary. Then he apologized for sitting down again, explained why it was necessary, and sat down.

The colonel introduced himself and the three who had come with him. "And now, sir, what can we do for you?"

The stick-man made a grimace that was probably intended as a smile. His teeth were the same light blue as his hair and eyes.

"You have a cliché, 'Take me to your leader.' I do not ask that. In fact, I *must* remain here. Nor do I ask that any of your leaders be brought here to me. That would be impolite. I am perfectly willing for you to represent them, to talk to you and let you question me. But I do ask one thing.

"You have tape recorders. I ask that before I talk or answer questions you have one brought. I want to be sure that the message your leaders eventually receive is full and accurate."

"Fine," the colonel said. He turned to the pilot. "Lieutenant, get on the radio in the whirlybird and tell them to get us a tape recorder faster than possible. It can be dropped by para— No, that'd take longer, rigging it for a drop. Have them send it by another helicopter." The lieutenant turned to go. "Hey," the colonel said. "Also fifty yards of extension cord. We'll have to plug it in inside Manny's tavern."

The lieutenant sprinted for the helicopter.

The others sat and sweated a moment and then Manuel Casey stood up. "That's a half-hour wait," he said, "and if we're going to sit here in the sun, who's for a bottle of cold beer? You, Mr. Garvane?"

"It is a cold beverage, is it not? I am a bit chilly. If you have something hot—?"

"Coffee, coming up. Can I bring you a blanket?"

"No, thank you. It will not be necessary."

Casey left and shortly returned with a tray with half-a-dozen bottles of cold beer and a cup of steaming coffee. The lieutenant was back by then. Casey put the tray down and served the stick-man first, who sipped the coffee and said, "It is delicious."

Colonel Casey cleared his throat. "Serve our prospector friend next, Manny. As for us—well, drinking is forbidden on duty, but it was 112 in the shade in Tucson, and this is hotter and also is *not* in the shade. Gentlemen, consider yourselves on official leave for as long as it takes you to drink one bottle of beer, or until the tape recorder arrives, whichever comes first."

The beer was finished first, but by the time the last of it had vanished, the second helicopter was within sight and sound. Casey asked the stick-man if he wanted more coffee. The offer was politely declined. Casey looked at Dade Grant and winked and the desert rat winked back, so Casey went in for two more bottles, one apiece for the Civilian terrestrials. Coming back he met the lieutenant arriving with the extension cord and returned as far as the doorway to show him where to plug it in.

When he came back, he saw that the second helicopter had brought its full complement of four, besides the tape recorder. There were, besides the pilot who had flown it, a technical sergeant who was skilled in its operation and who was now making adjustments on it, and a lieutenant-colonel and a warrant officer who had come along for the ride or because they had been made curious by the request for a tape recorder to be rushed to Cherrybell, Arizona, by air. They were standing gaping at the stick-man and whispered conversations were going on.

The colonel said, "Attention," quietly, but it brought complete silence. "Please sit down, gentlemen. In a rough circle. Sergeant, if you rig your mike in the center of the circle, will it pick up clearly what any one of us may say?"

"Yes, sir. I'm almost ready."

Ten men and one extraterrestrial humanoid sat in a rough circle, with the microphone hanging from a small tripod in the approximate center. The humans were sweating profusely; the humanoid shivered slightly. Just outside the circle, the burro stood dejectedly, its head low. Edging closer, but still about five yards away, spread out now in a semicircle, was the entire population of Cherrybell who had been at home at the time; the stores and the filling stations were deserted.

The technical sergeant pushed a button and the tape recorder's reel started to turn. "Testing . . . testing," he said. He held down the rewind button for a second and then pushed the playback button. "Testing . . . testing," said the recorder's speaker. Loud and clear. The sergeant pushed the rewind button, then the erase one to clear the tape. Then the stop button.

"When I push the next button, sir," he said to the colonel, "we'll be recording."

The colonel looked at the tall extra-terrestrial, who nodded, and then the colonel nodded at the sergeant. The sergeant pushed the recording button.

"My name is Garvane," said the stick-man, slowly and clearly. "I am from a planet of a star which is not listed in your star catalogs, although the globular cluster in which it is one of 90,000 stars is known to you. It is, from here, in the direction of the center of the galaxy at a distance of over four thousand light-years.

"However, I am not here as a representative of my planet or my people, but as minister plenipotentiary of the Galactic Union, a federation of the enlightened civilizations of the galaxy, for the good of all. It is my assignment to visit you and decide, here and now, whether or not you are to be welcomed to join our federation.

"You may now ask questions freely. However, I reserve the right to postpone answering some of them until my decision has been made. If the decision is favorable, I will then answer all questions, including the ones I have postponed answering meanwhile. Is that satisfactory?"

"Yes," said the colonel. "How did you come here? A spaceship?"

"Correct. It is overhead right now, in orbit twenty-two thousand miles out, so it revolves with the earth and stays over this one spot. I am under observation from it, which is one reason I prefer to remain here in the open. I am to signal it when I want it to come down to pick me up."

"How do you know our language so fluently? Are you telepathic?"

"No, I am not. And nowhere in the galaxy is any race telepathic except among its own members. I was taught your language for this purpose. We have had observers among you for many centuries—by *we*, I mean the Galactic Union, of course. Quite obviously, I could not pass as an Earthman, but there are other races who can. Incidentally, they are not spies, or agents; they have in no way tried to affect you; they are observers and that is all."

"What benefits do we get from joining your union, if we are asked and if we accept?" the colonel asked.

"First, a quick course in the fundamental social sciences which will end your tendency to fight among yourselves and end or at least control your aggressions. After we are satisfied that you have accomplished that and it is safe for you to do so, you will be given space travel, and many other things, as rapidly as you are able to assimilate them."

"And if we are not asked, or refuse?"

"Nothing. You will be left alone; even our observers will be withdrawn. You will work out your own fate—either you will render your planet uninhabited and uninhabitable within the next century, or you will master social science yourselves and again be candidates for membership and again be offered membership. We will check from time to time and if and when it appears certain that you are not going to destroy yourselves, you will again be approached."

"Why the hurry, now that you're here? Why can't you stay long enough for our leaders, as you call them, to talk to you in person?"

"Postponed. The reason is not important but it is complicated, and I simply do not wish to waste time explaining."

"Assuming your decision is favorable, how will we get in touch with you to let you know *our* decision? You know enough about us, obviously, to know that *I* can't make it."

"We will know your decision through our observers. One condition of acceptance is full and uncensored publication in your newspapers of this interview, verbatim from the tape we are now using to record it. Also of all deliberations and decisions of your government."

"And other governments? We can't decide unilaterally for the world."

"Your government has been chosen for a start. If you accept, we shall furnish the techniques that will cause the others to fall in line quickly—and those techniques do not involve force or the threat of force."

"They must be *some* techniques," said the colonel wryly, "if they'll make one certain country I don't have to name fall into line without even a threat."

"Sometimes the offer of reward is more significant than the use of a threat. Do you think the country you do not wish to name would like your country colonizing planets of far stars before they even reach the moon? But that is a minor point, relatively. You may trust the techniques."

"It sounds almost too good to be true. But you said that you are to decide, here and now, whether or not we are to be invited to join. May I ask on what factors you will base your decision?"

"One is that I am—was, since I already have—to check your degree of xenophobia. In the loose sense in which you use it, that means fear of strangers. We have a word that has no counterpart in your vocabulary: it means fear of and revulsion toward *aliens*. I—or at least a member of my race—was chosen to make the first overt contact with you. Because I am what you would call roughly humanoid—as you are what I would call roughly humanoid—I am probably more horrible, more repulsive, to you than many completely different species would be. Because to you I am a caricature of a human being, I am more horrible to you than a being who bears no remote resemblance to you.

"You may think you *do* feel horror at me, and revulsion, but believe me, you have passed that test. There *are* races in the galaxy who can never be members of the federation, no matter how they advance otherwise, because they are violently and incurably xenophobic; they could never face or talk to an alien of any species. They would either run screaming from him or try to kill him instantly. From watching you and these people"—he waved a long arm at the civilian population of Cherrybell not far outside the circle of the conference—"I know you feel revulsion at the sight of me, but believe me, it is relatively slight and certainly curable. You have passed that test satisfactorily."

"And are there other tests?"

"One other. But I think it is time that I—" Instead of finishing the sentence, the stick-man lay back flat on the sand and closed his eyes.

The colonel started to his feet. "What in *hell?*" he said. He walked quickly around the mike's tripod and bent over the recumbent extraterrestrial, putting an ear to the bloody-appearing chest.

As he raised his head, Dade Grant, the grizzled prospector, chuckled. "No heartbeat, Colonel, because no heart. But I may leave him as a souvenir for you and you'll find much more interesting things inside him than heart and guts. Yes, he is a puppet whom I have been operating, as your Edgar Bergen operates his—what's his name?—oh yes, Charlie McCarthy. Now that he has served his purpose, he is deactivated. You can go back to your place, Colonel."

Colonel Casey moved back slowly. *"Why?"* he asked.

Dade Grant was peeling off his beard and wig. He rubbed a cloth across his face to remove make-up and was revealed as a handsome young man. He said, "What he told you, or what you were told through him, was true as far as it went. He is only a simulacrum, yes, but he is an exact duplicate of a member of one of the intelligent races of the galaxy, the one toward whom you would be disposed—if you were violently and incurably xenophobic—to be most horrified by, according to our psychologists. But we did not bring a real member of his species to make first contact because they have a phobia of their own, agoraphobia—fear of space. They are highly civilized and members in good standing of the federation, but they never leave their own planet.

"Our observers assure us you don't have *that* phobia. But they were unable to judge in advance the degree of your xenophobia, and the only way to test it was to bring along something in lieu of someone to test it against, and presumably to let him make the initial contact."

The colonel sighed audibly. "I can't say this doesn't relieve me in one way. We could get along with humanoids, yes, and we will when we have to. But I'll admit it's a relief to learn that the master race of the galaxy is, after all, human instead of only humanoid. What is the second test?"

"You are undergoing it now. Call me—" He snapped his fingers. "What's the name of Bergen's second-string puppet, after Charlie McCarthy?"

The colonel hesitated, but the tech sergeant supplied the answer. "Mortimer Snerd."

"Right. So call me Mortimer Snerd, and now I think it is time that I—" He lay back flat on the sand and closed his eyes just as the stick-man had done a few minutes before.

The burro raised its head and put it into the circle over the shoulder of the tech sergeant.

"That takes care of the puppets, Colonel," it said. "And now, what's this bit about it being important that the master race be human or at least humanoid? What is a master race?"

F IS FOR FRANKENSTEIN AND FRIENDS

HARRY HARRISON

At Last, The True Story of Frankenstein

"And here, before your very eyes, is the very same monster built by my much admired great-great grandfather, Victor Frankenstein, built by him from pieces of corpses out of dissecting rooms, stolen parts of bodies freshly buried in the grave and even chunks of animals from the slaughterhouse. Now look—" The tail-coated man on the platform swung his arm out in a theatrical gesture and the heads of the closely packed crowd below swung to follow it. The dusty curtains flapped aside and the monster stood there, illuminated from above by a sickly green light. There was a concerted gasp from the crowd and a shiver of motion.

In the front row, pressed against the rope barrier, Dan Bream mopped his face with a soggy handkerchief and smiled. It wasn't such a bad monster, considering that this was a cheap-jack carnival playing the small town circuit. It had a dead-white skin, undampened by sweat even in this steambath of a tent, glazed eyes, stitches and seams showing where the face had been patched together, and the two metal plugs projecting from the temples—just like in the movie.

"Raise your right arm!" Victor Frankenstein V commanded, his brusque German accent giving the words a Prussian air of authority. The monster's body did not move, but slowly—with the jerking motion of a badly operating machine— the creature's arm came up to shoulder height and stopped.

"This monster, built from pieces from the dead, cannot die, and if a piece gets too worn out I simply stitch on a new piece with the secret formula passed down from father to son from my great-great-grandfather. It cannot die nor feel pain—as you see—"

This time the gasp was even louder and some of the audience turned away while others watched with eager eyes. The barker had taken a foot long and wickedly sharp needle, and had pushed it firmly through the monster's biceps until it protruded on both sides. No blood stained it and the creature made no motion, as though completely unaware that anything had been done to its flesh.

". . . impervious to pain, extremes of heat and cold and possessing the strength of ten men . . ."

Behind him the voice droned on, but Dan Bream had had enough. He had seen the performance three times before, which was more than satisfactory for what he

84

needed to know, and if he stayed in the tent another minute he would melt. The exit was close by and he pushed through the gaping, pallid audience and out into the humid dusk. It wasn't much cooler outside. Life borders on the unbearable along the shores of the Gulf of Mexico in August, and Panama City, Florida, was no exception. Dan headed for the nearest air conditioned beer joint and sighed with relief as the chill atmosphere closed in around his steaming garments. The beer bottle frosted instantly with condensation as did the heavy glass stein, cold from the freezer. The first big swallow cut a path straight down to his stomach. He took the beer over to one of the straight-backed wooden booths, wiped the table off with a handful of paper napkins and flopped on to the bench. From the inner pocket of his jacket he took some folded sheets of yellow copy paper, now slightly soggy, and spread them before him. After adding some lines to the scribbled notes he stuffed them back into his jacket and took a long pull on his beer.

Dan was halfway through his second bottle when the barker, who called himself Frankenstein the Fifth, came in. His stage personality had vanished along with the frock coat and monocle, and the Prussian haircut now looked like a common crew cut.

"You've got a great act," Dan called out cheerfully, and waved the man over. "Will you join me for a drink?"

"Don't mind if I do," Frankenstein answered in the pure nasal vowels of New York City, the German accent apparently having disappeared along with the monocle. "And see if they have a Schlitz or a Bud or anything beside the local swamp water."

He settled into the booth while Dan went for the beers, and groaned when he saw the labels on the bottles.

"At least it's cold," he said, shaking salt into his to make it foam, then half drained the stein in a long deep swallow. "I noticed you out there in front of the clems for most of the shows today. Do you like the act—or you a carny buff?"

"It's a good act. I'm a newsman, name's Dan Bream."

"Always pleased to meet the Press, Dan. Publicity is the life of show business, as the man said. I'm Stanley Arnold: call me Stan."

"Then Frankenstein is just your stage name?"

"What else? You act kinda dim for a reporter, are you sure—?" He waved away the Press card that Dan pulled from his breast pocket. "No, I believe you, Dan, but you gotta admit the question was a little on the rube side. I bet you even think that I have a real monster in there!"

"Well, you must admit that he looks authentic. The skin stitched together that way, those plugs in his head—"

"Held on with spirit gum and the embroidery is drawn on with eyebrow pencil. That's show business for you, all illusion. But I'm happy to hear that the act even looked real to an experienced reporter like yourself. What paper did you say you were with?"

"No paper, the news syndicate. I caught your act about six months ago and became interested. Did a little checking when I was in Washington, then followed you down here. You don't really want me to call you Stan, do you? Stein might be closer. After all—Victor Frankenstein *is* the name on your naturalisation papers."

"Tell me more," Frankenstein said in a voice suddenly cold and emotionless.

Dan riffled through the yellow sheets. "Yes ... here it is, from the official records. Frankenstein, Victor—born in Geneva, arrived in the U.S. in 1938, and more of the same."

"The next thing you'll be telling me is that my monster *is* real!" Frankenstein smiled, but only with his mouth.

"I'm betting that it is. No yogi training or hypnotism or such can make a man as indifferent to pain as that thing is—and as terribly strong. I want the whole story, the truth for a change!"

"Do you ... ?" Frankenstein asked in a cold voice and for a long moment the air filled with tension. Then he laughed and clapped the reporter on the arm. "All right, Dan—I'll give it to you. You are a persistent devil and a good reporter and it is the least you deserve. But first you must get us some more drinks, something a measurable degree stronger than this execrable beer." His New York accent had disappeared as easily as had his German one; he spoke English now with skill and perfection without any recognisable regional accent.

Dan gathered their empty glasses. "It'll have to be beer—this is a dry county."

"Nonsense! This is America, the land that raises its hands in horror at the foreign conception of double-think yet practises it with an efficiency that sets the Old World to shame. Bay County may be officially dry but the law has many itchy palms, and under that counter you will find a reasonable supply of a clear liquid that glories in the name of White Mule and is reputed to have a kick of the same magnitude as its cognate beast. If you are still in doubt you will see a framed federal liquor licence on the far wall, legitimising this endeavour in the eyes of the national government. Simply place a five dollar bank note on the bar, say Mountain Dew and do not expect any change."

When they both had enjoyed their first sips of the corn likker Victor Frankenstein lapsed into a friendly mood.

"Call me Vic, Dan. I want us to be friends. I'm going to tell you a story that few have heard before, a story that is astounding but true. True—mark that word—not a hodge-podge of distortions and half-truths and outright ignorance like that vile book produced by Mary Godwin. Oh how my father ever regretted meeting that woman and, in a moment of weakness, confiding in her the secret of some of his original lines of research ..."

"Just a minute," Dan broke in. "You mentioned the truth, but I can't swallow this guff. Mary Wollstonecraft Shelley wrote *Frankenstein; or, The Modern Prometheus* in 1818. Which would make you and your father so old ..."

"Please, Dan—no interruptions. I mentioned my father's researches, in the plural you will note, all of them devoted to the secrets of life. The Monster, as it has come to be called, was just one of his works. Longevity was what he was interested in, and he did live to a very, very old age, as will I. I will not stretch your credulity any further at this moment by mentioning the year of my birth, but will press on. That Mary Godwin. She and the poet were living together at this period, they had not married as yet, and this permitted my father to hope that Mary might one day find him not unattractive, since he was quite taken by her. Well, you can easily imagine the end. She made notes of everything he told her—then discarded him and used the notes to construct her despicable book. Her errors are legion, listen ..." He leaned across the booth and once again clapped Dan on the

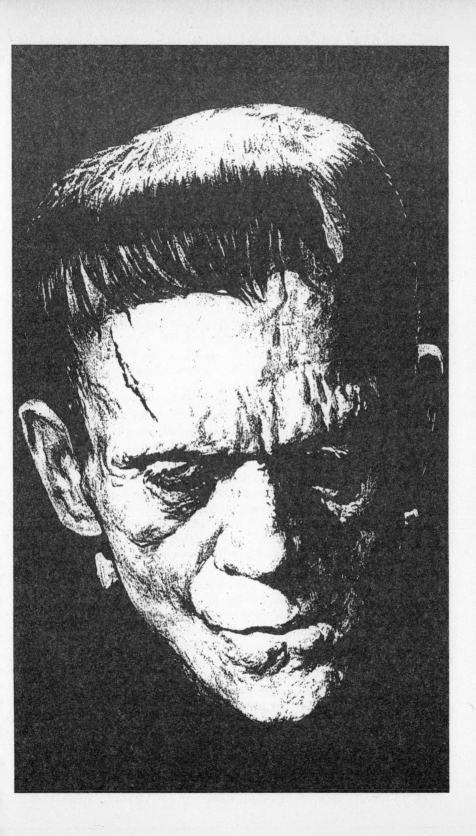

shoulder in a hearty way. It was an intimate gesture that the reporter didn't
particularly enjoy, but he didn't complain. Not as long as the other kept talking.

"Firstly she made papa a Swiss; he used to tear his hair out at the thought, since
ours is a good old Bavarian family with a noble and ancient lineage. Then she had
him attending the University of Ingolstadt in *Ingolstadt*—when every schoolboy
knows that it was moved to Landshut in 1880. And father's personality, what
crimes she committed there! In this libellous volume he is depicted as a weeping
and ineffectual man, when in reality he was a tower of strength and determination.
And if this isn't enough, she completely misunderstood the meaning of his
experiments. Her jim-crack collection of cast off parts put together to make an
artificial man is ludicrous. She was so carried away by the legends of Talos and the
Golem that she misinterpreted my father's work and cast it into that ancient
mould. Father did not construct an artificial man, he reactivated a *dead* man! That
is the measure of his genius! He travelled for years in the darkest reaches of the
African jungle, learning the lore of the creation of the zombie. He regularised the
knowledge and improved upon it until he had surpassed all of his aboriginal
teachers. Raise the dead, that is what he could do. That was his secret—and how
can it be kept a secret in the future, Mr. Dan Bream?"

With these last words Victor Frankenstein's eyes opened wide and an unveiled
light seemed to glow in their depths. Dan pulled back instinctively, then relaxed.
He was in no danger here in this brightly lit room with men on all sides of them.

"Afraid, Dan? Don't be." Victor smiled and reached out and patted Dan on the
shoulder once again.

"What was that?" Dan asked, startled at the tiny brief pain in his shoulder.

"Nothing—nothing but this," Frankenstein smiled again, but the smile had
changed subtly and no longer contained any humour. He opened his hand to
reveal a small hypodermic needle, its plunger pushed down and its barrel empty.

"Remain seated," he said quietly when Dan started to rise, and Dan's muscles
relaxed and he sat back down, horrified.

"What have you done to me?"

"Very little—the injection is harmless. A simple little hypnotic drug, the effect
of which wears off in a few hours. But until then you will not have much will of
your own. So you will sit and hear me out. Drink some beer though, we don't want
you to be thirsty."

Horrified, Dan was a helpless onlooker, as, of its own volition, his hand raised
and poured a measure of the beer down his throat.

"Now concentrate, Dan, think of the significance of my statement. The
so-called Frankenstein monster is no stitched up collection of scraps, but a good
honest zombie. A dead man who can walk but not talk, obey but not think.
Animate—but still dead. Poor old Charley is one, the creature whom you watched
going through his act on the platform. But Charley is just about worn out. Since he
is dead he cannot replace the body cells that are destroyed during the normal wear
and tear of the day. Why the fellow is like an animated pincushion from the act,
holes everywhere. His feet—terrible, not a toe left, keep breaking off when he
walks too fast. I think it's time to retire Charley. He has had a long life, and a long
death. Stand up, Dan."

In spite of his mind crying *No! No!* Dan rose slowly to his feet.

"Aren't you interested in what Charley used to do before he became a sideshow monster? You should be, Dan. Old Charley was a reporter—just like you. And he ran across what he thought was a good story. Like you, he didn't realise the importance of what he had discovered and talked to me about it. You reporters are a very inquisitive bunch. I must show you my scrapbook, it's simply filled with Press cards. Before you die of course. You wouldn't be able to appreciate it afterwards. Now come along."

Dan walked after him, into the hot night, screaming inside in a haze of terror, yet walking quietly and silently down the street.

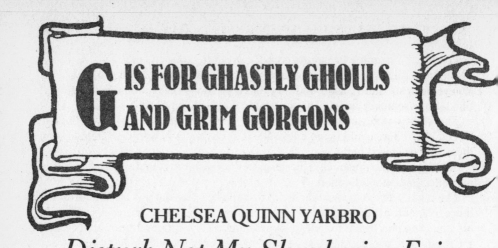

G IS FOR GHASTLY GHOULS AND GRIM GORGONS

CHELSEA QUINN YARBRO

Disturb Not My Slumbering Fair

It was already Thursday when Diedre left her grave. The rain had made the soil soft and the loam clung to her cerements like a distracted lover. It was so late, the night so sodden, that there was no one to see her as she left the manicured lawns and chaste marble stones behind her for the enticing litter of the city.

"Pardon me, miss." The night watchman was old, white-haired under his battered hat. He held the flashlight aimed at her face, seeing only a disheveled young woman with mud in her hair, a wild look about her eyes, a livid cast to her face like a bruise. He wondered if she had been attacked; there was so much of that happening these days. "You all right, miss?"

Diedre chuckled, but she had not done it for some time and it came out badly. The watchman went pale and his mouth tightened. Whatever happened to her must have been very bad. "Don't you worry, miss. I'll call the cops. They'll catch the guy. You stay calm. He can't get you while I'm around."

"Cops?" she asked, managing the sounds better now. "It's not necessary."

"You look here, miss," said the night watchman, beginning to enjoy himself, to feel important once more. "You can't let him get away with it. You lean on me: I'll get you inside where it's warm. I'll take care of everything."

Diedre studied the old man, weighing up the risk. She was hungry and tired. The old man was alone. Making a mental shrug she sighed as she went to the old man, noting with amusement that he drew back as he got a whiff of her. She could almost see him recoil. "It was in the graveyard," she said.

"Christ, miss." The night watchman was shocked.

"Yes," she went on, warming to her subject. "There was a new grave . . . the earth hadn't settled yet . . . And the smell . . ." *was delicious*, she thought.

He was very upset, chafing her hand as he led her into the little building at the factory entrance. "Never you mind," he muttered. "I'll take care of you. Fine thing, when a man can . . . can . . . and in a graveyard, too . . ."

"Yes," she agreed, her tongue showing pink between her teeth.

He opened the door for her, standing aside with old-fashioned gallantry until the last of her train had slithered through before coming into the room himself. "Now, you sit down here." He pointed to an ancient armchair that sagged on bowed legs. "I'm going to call the cops."

Diedre wasn't quite ready for that. "Oh," she said faintly, "will you wait a bit? You've been so kind ... and understanding. But sometimes the police think ..." She left the sentence hanging as she huddled into the chair.

The night watchman frowned. Obviously the poor girl didn't know what she looked like. There could be no doubt about her case. "You won't get trouble from them," he promised her.

She shivered picturesquely. "Perhaps you're right. But wait a while, please. Let me collect myself a little more."

The night watchman was touched. He could see that she was close to breaking down, that only her courage was keeping her from collapsing. "Sure, miss. I'll hold off a bit. You don't want to wait too long, though. The cops are funny about that." He reached over to give her a reassuring pat but drew away from her when he saw the look in her eyes. Poor soul was scared to death, he could tell.

"Uh, sir," Diedre said after a moment, realizing that she didn't know his name. "I was wondering ... I don't want you to get into trouble, after you've been so kind, but ..."

He looked at her eagerly. "But what, miss?"

She contrived to look confused. "I just realized ... I seem to have lost my ring." She held up both hands to show him. "It was valuable. An heirloom. My mother ..." Her averted eyes were full of mischief.

"Oh, dear," said the night watchman solicitously. "Do you think you lost it back there?" He looked worried.

She nodded slowly. "Back at the grave," she whispered.

"Well, miss, as soon as the cops get here, we'll tell them and they'll get it for you." He paused awkwardly. "Thing is, miss. It might not still be there. Could have been taken, you know." He wanted to be gentle with her, to reassure her.

"Taken?" She stared at him through widened eyes. "My ring? Why?" Slowly she allowed comprehension to show in her face. "Oh! You think that he ... that when he ... that he took it?"

The night watchman looked away, mumbling, "He could have, miss. That's a fact. A man who'd do a thing like this, he'd steal. That's certain."

Diedre leaped up, distraction showing in every line of her sinuous body. "Then I've got to check! Now!" She rushed to the door and pulled on the knob. "It can't be gone. Oh, you've got to help me find it!" Pulling the door wide she ran into the night and listened with satisfaction as the old man came after her.

"Miss! Miss! Don't go back there! What if he hasn't gone? Let me call the cops, miss!" His breath grew short as he stumbled after her.

"Oh, no. No. I've got to be sure. If it's gone, I don't know what I'll do." She let herself stumble so that the old man could catch up with her; if he fell too far behind, Diedre knew she would lose him. This way it was so easy to lead him where she wanted him. Ahead she saw the cemetery gates gleaming faintly in the wan light.

"You don't want to go back in there, miss," said the night watchman between jagged breaths. His face was slippery with cold sweat that Diedre saw with a secret, predatory smile. "Oh, I can't ..." It was the right sound, the right moment. He automatically put out his arm. Pretending to lean against him, she felt for his heart and was delighted at the panic-stricken way it battered at his ribs.

"But I've got to find it. I've got to." She broke away from him once more and ran toward the grave she had so recently left. "Over here," she cried, and watched as he staggered toward her, trying to speak.

Then his legs gave way and he fell against the feet of a marble angel. His skull made a pulpy noise when it cracked.

With a shriek of delight Diedre was upon him, her eager teeth sinking into the flesh greedily, although the body was still unpleasantly warm. Blood oozed down her chin and after a while she wiped it away.

Toward the end of the night she made a halfhearted attempt to bury the litter from her meal. It was useless; she knew that the body would be discovered in a little while, and there would be speculation on the state of it: the gnawed bones and the torn flesh. As an afterthought, she broke one of the gnawed arms against a pristinely white vault, just to confuse the issue. Then she gathered up a thigh and left, walking back into the city, filled, satisfied.

By the time the last of the night watchman was discovered, Diedre was miles away, sleeping off her feast in the cool damp of a dockside warehouse. Her face, if anyone had seen it, was soft and faintly smiling, the cyanose pallor of the grave fading away to be replaced with a rosy blush. She didn't look like a ghoul at all.

That night, when she left the warehouse, she saw the first headlines:

NIGHTWATCHMAN FOUND DEAD
IN GRAVE YARD

GRIZZLY SLAYING AT CEMETERY

Diedre giggled as she read the reports. Apparently there was some hot dispute in the police department about the teeth marks. There was also a plan to open the grave where the old man had been killed. This made Diedre frown. If the grave were opened, they would find it empty, and there would be more questions asked. She bit her lip as she thought. And when the solution came to her, she laughed almost merrily.

It was close to midnight when she spotted her quarry, a young woman about her own height and build. Diedre followed her away from the theater and into the many-tiered parking lot.

When the woman had opened the car door and was sliding into the seat, Diedre came up beside her. "Excuse me," she said, knowing that the old jacket and workmen's trousers she had found in the warehouse made her look suspicious. "I saw you come up, and maybe you can help me?"

The woman looked at her, her nose wrinkling as she looked Diedre over. "What is the matter?" There was obvious condemnation in her words. Diedre had not made a good impression.

"It's my car," Diedre explained, pointing to a respectable Toyota. "I've been trying to get it open, but the key doesn't work. I've tried everything." She made a helpless gesture with her hands, then added a deprecating smile.

"I don't think I can help you," said the woman stiffly. She was seated now and had her hand on the door.

"Well, look," said Diedre quickly, holding the door open by force. "If you'd give me a ride down, maybe there's a mechanic still on duty. Or maybe I could phone the Auto Club . . ."

The woman in the car gave her another disapproving look, then sighed and opened the door opposite her. "All right. Get in."

"Gee, thank you," Diedre gushed and slipped around the car, slid into the seat, and closed the door. "This is really awfully good of you. You don't know how much I appreciate it."

The woman turned the key with an annoyed snap and the car surged forward. "That's quite all right." The tone was glacial.

She was even more upset when they reached the ground level. The attendant who took her money told the woman that there was no mechanic on duty after ten and that it would take over an hour for the Auto Club to get there, and the locksmith would have to make a new key, and that would take time as well. Diedre couldn't have painted a more depressing picture of her plight if she tried.

"I guess I'll have to wait," she said wistfully, looking out at the attendant.

"Well," the man answered, "there's a problem. We close up at two, and there's no way you'll be out of here by then. Why don't you come back in the morning?"

This was better than Diedre had hoped. "Well, if that's all I can do . . ." She shrugged. "Where can I catch a bus around here?"

"The nearest is six blocks down. What part of town you going to, lady?" the attendant asked Diedre.

"Serra Heights," she said, choosing a neighborhood near the cemetery, middle income, city-suburban. Altogether a safe address.

Reluctantly the woman driving the car said, "That's on my way. I'll drop you if you like." Each of the words came out of her like pulled teeth.

Diedre turned grateful eyes on her. "Oh, would you? Really? Oh, thanks. I don't mean to be a bother, but . . . well, you know." She added, as the inspiration struck her, "Jamie was so worried. This'll help. Really."

The woman's face softened a little. "I'll be glad to drive you." She turned to the attendant. "Perhaps you'll be good enough to leave a note for the mechanic so that there'll be no delay in the morning?" She was making up for her previously frosty behavior and gave Diedre a wide smile.

"Oh, thanks a lot for telling him that," Diedre said as the car sped out into the night. "I wouldn't have thought of it. I guess I'm more upset than I thought."

The conversation was occasional as they drove, Diedre keeping her mind on the imaginary Jamie, building the other woman a picture of two struggling young people, trying to establish themselves in the world. The woman listened, wearing a curious half-smile. "You know," she said as she swung off the freeway toward the Serra Valley district, "I've often thought things would be better with Grant and me if we'd had to work a little harder. It was too easy, always too easy."

"Oh," said Diedre at her most ingenuous, "did I say something wrong?"

"No," the woman sighed. "You didn't say anything wrong." She shook her head, as if shaking clouds away and glanced around. "Which way?"

"Umm. Left onto Harrison and then up Camino Alto." Camino Alto was the last street in the district, and it followed the boundary of the cemetery.

"Do you live on Camino Alto?" the woman asked.

"No. In Ponce de Leon Place. Up at the top of the hill." Behind that hill was open country, covered in brush. By the time the woman's body was found, the police would stop wondering about the missing one from Diedre's grave.

The car swung onto Harrison. "Doesn't it bother you, having that gruesome murder so close to home?"

Diedre smiled. "A little. You never know what might happen next."

They drove up the hill in silence, the woman glancing toward the thick shrubs that masked the cemetery. There was concern in her face and a lack of animation in her eyes. Diedre knew she would freeze when frightened.

"This is where I get out," she said at last, looking at the woman covertly. As the car came to a halt, Diedre reached over and grabbed the keys. "Thanks for the lift," she grinned.

"My keys . . ." the woman began.

Diedre shook her head. "Don't worry about them. I'll take care of them. Now, if you'll step out with me."

"Where are we going?" the woman quavered. "Not in there?"

"No," Diedre assured her. "Get out."

In the end she had to club the woman and drag her unconscious body from the car. It was awkward managing her limp form, but eventually she wrestled the woman from the car and into the brush. Branches tore at her and blackberry vines left claw marks on her arms and legs as she plunged farther down the hill. The woman moaned and then was silent.

It was almost an hour later when Diedre climbed up the hill again, scratched, bruised, and happy. Tied to her belt by the hair, the woman's head banged on her legs with every step she took.

Taking the car, Diedre drove to the coast and down the old treacherous stretch of highway that twisted along the cliffs. Gunning the motor at the most dangerous curve, she rode the car down to its flaming destruction on the rocks where breakers hissed over it, steaming from the flames that licked upward as the gas tank exploded.

It was a nuisance, climbing up the cliff with a broken arm: the ulna had snapped, a greenstick fracture making the hand below it useless. Here and there Diedre's skin was scorched off, leaving black patches. But the job was done. The police would find the head in the wreck, along with one of the night watchman's leg bones, and would assume that the rest of the body had been washed out to sea: the headless woman back on the hillside would not be connected with his wreck, and she was clear.

But she was hungry. The night watchman was used up and she hadn't been able to use any part of the woman. Now Diedre knew she would have to be careful, for the police were checking cemeteries for vandals. And in her present condition the only place she wouldn't attract attention was the morgue.

The morgue!

Her broken arm was firmly splinted under her heavy sweater, her face carefully and unobviously made up as Diedre walked into the cold tile office outside the room where the bodies lay. The burned patches on her face had taken on the look of old acne and she used her lithe body with deliberate awkwardness.

"I'm Watson, the one who called?" she announced herself uncertainly to the colorless man at the desk.

He looked up at her and grunted. "Watson?"

Mentally she ground her teeth. What if this man had changed his mind; where would she go for food then? "Yes," she said, shuffling from one foot to the other. "I'm going to be a pathologist, and I thought . . . It's expensive, sir. Medical school is very expensive." Her eyes pleaded with him.

"I remember," he said measuredly. "Nothing like a little practical experience." He handed her a form. "I'll need your name and address and the usual information. Just fill this out and hand it in. I'll show you the place when you're done."

She took the form and started to work. The social security number stumped her and then she decided to use her old one. By the time it could be checked, she'd be long gone.

"No phone?" he asked as she handed the form back.

"Well, I'm at school so much . . . and it's kind of a luxury . . ."

"You'll make up for it when you get into practice," he said flatly. He knew doctors well.

As he filed her card away, Diedre glared at his back, wishing she could indulge herself long enough to make a meal of him. It would be so good to sip the marrow from his bones, to nibble the butter-soft convolutions of his brain.

"Okay, Watson. Come with me. If you get sick, out you go." He opened the door to the cold room and pointed out the silent drawers that waited for their cargo. "That's where we keep 'em. If they aren't identified, the county takes 'em over. We do autopsies on some of 'em, if it's ordered. Some of these stiffs are pretty messed up, some of 'em are real neat. Depends on how they go. Poison now," he said, warming to the topic, "poison can leave the outsides as neat as a pin and only part of the insides are ruined. Cars, well, cars make 'em pretty awful. Guns—that depends on what and where. Had a guy in here once, he'd put a shotgun in his mouth and fired both barrels. Well, I can tell you, he didn't look good." As he talked he strolled to one of the drawers and pulled it out. "Take this one," he went on.

Diedre ran her tongue over her lips and made a coughing noise. "What happened?"

"This one," said the man, "had a run-in with some gasoline. We had to get identification from his teeth, and even part of his jaw was wrecked. Explosions do that." He glanced at her to see how she was taking it.

"I'm fine," she assured him.

"Huh." He closed the drawer and went onto the next. "This one's drowned. In the water a long time." He wrinkled his nose. "Had to get the shrimps off him. Water really wrecks the tissues."

Five drawers later Diedre found what she had been looking for.

"This one," the man was saying, "well, it's murder, of course, and we haven't found all of him yet, but there's enough here to make some kind of identification, so he's our job."

"When did it happen?" Diedre asked.

"A week or so ago, I guess. Found him out in the Serra Heights cemetery. A big number in the papers about it."

Diedre stared at the bits of the night watchman. Something had shared her feast; she'd left more than this behind. It would be simple to take a bit more of him, here and there. No one would notice. But it paid to be careful. "Can I study this?" she said, doing her best to sound timorous.

"Why?" asked the man.

"To get used to it," she replied.

"If you help me out with ID, you can." He closed the night watchman away into his cold file cabinet. "In fact, you can do a work-up on the one we just got in. Get blood type and all those things. This one hasn't got a head, so it's gonna be fun, running her kin to earth."

"Hasn't got a head?" Diedre echoed, remembering the woman left on the hillside. "What happened?"

"Found her out by the cemetery where they got the other. Probably connected. The grave she was found on was new and it was empty. Could be she's the missing one."

"Oh," said Diedre, to fill in the silence that followed before the man closed the drawer. She stared at the body, watching it critically. She hadn't done too bad a job with it.

"Any of this getting to you?" the man asked as he showed her the last of the corpses. Only about half of the shelves were filled, and Diedre wondered at this. "I'm okay," she said, then added, as if it had just occurred to her. "Why are there so many shelves?"

"Right now things are a little slow. But if we get a good fire or quake or a six-car pile up, we'll be filled up, all right." He gave her a shadowed, cynical smile. In the harsh light his skin had a dead-white cast to it, as if he had taken on the color of his charges.

Nodding, Diedre asked, "What do you want me to do first? Where do I work?"

The man showed her and she began.

It was hard getting food at first, but then she caught on and found that if she took a finger or two from a burn victim or some of the pulpy flesh from a water-logged drowner it was easy. Accident victims were best because, by the time the metal and fire were through with them, it was too hard to get all of a body together and a few unaccounted-for bits were never missed.

She was lipping just such an accident case one night when the door to her workroom shot open.

"Tisk, tisk, tisk, Watson" said the man she worked with.

Diedre froze, her mouth half-open and her face shocked.

The man strolled into the room. "You're an amateur, my girl. I've been keeping an eye on you. I know." He walked over to her and looked down. "First of all, don't eat where you work. It's too easy to get caught. Bring a couple of plastic bags with you and take the stuff home."

She decided to bluff. "I don't know what you're talking about."

He gave a harsh laugh. "Do you think you're the only ghoul in this morgue? I'm not interested in competition, and that's final. One of us has to go." He glared at her, fingering her scalpel.

It was quiet in the room for a moment, then Diedre put far more panic than she was feeling. "What are you going to do to me? What is going to happen?"

The man sniggered. "Oh, no. Not that way, Watson. You're going to have to wait until I've got everything ready. There's going to be another accident victim here, and there won't be any questions asked." He spun away from her and rushed to the door. "It won't be long; a day or two, perhaps. . . . Then it will be over and done with, Watson." He closed the door and in a moment she heard the lock click.

For some time she sat quietly, nibbling at the carrion in her hands. Her rosy face betrayed no fear, her slender fingers did not shake. And when she was through with her meal, she had a plan.

The telephone was easy to get to, and the number she wanted was on it. Quickly she dialed, then said in a breathless voice, "Police? This is Watson at the morgue. Something's wrong. The guy in charge here? He's trying to kill me." She waited while the officer on the other end expressed polite disbelief. "No. You don't understand. He's crazy. He thinks I'm a ghoul. He says he's going to beat me into a pulp and then hide me in drawer forty-seven until he can get rid of me. I'm scared. I'm so scared. He's locked me in. I can't get out. And he's coming back. . . ." She let her tone rise to a shriek and then hung up. So much for that.

When she unwrapped her broken arm, she saw that the ulna was still shattered and she twisted it to bring the shards out through the skin again. Next she banged her head into a cabinet, not hard enough to break the skull, but enough to bring a dark bruise to her temples. And finally she tore her clothes and dislocated her jaw before going into the file room and slipping herself into number forty-seven. It was all she could do to keep from smiling.

Somewhat later she heard the door open and the sound of voices reached her. The man she worked with was protesting to the police that there was nothing wrong here, and that his assistant seemed to be out for the night. The officer didn't believe him.

"But number forty-seven is empty," she heard the man protest as the voices came nearer.

"Be a sport and open it anyway," said the officer.

"I don't understand. This is all ridiculous." Amid his protests, he pulled the drawer back.

Diedre lay there, serene and ivory chill.

The man stopped talking and slammed the door shut. The officer opened it again. "Looks like you worked her over pretty good," he remarked, pulling the cloth away from her arm and touching the bruises on her face.

"But I didn't. . . ." Then he changed his voice. "Officer, you don't understand. She's a ghoul. She lives on the dead. That's why she was working here, so she could eat the dead. . . ."

"She said you were crazy," the officer said wearily. "Look at her, man," he went on in a choked tone. "That's a girl—a girl; not a ghoul. You've been working here too long, mister. Things get to a guy after a while." He turned to the men with him. "We'll need some pix of this. Get to work."

As the flashes glared, the officer asked for Diedre's work card, and when he saw it, "No relatives. Too bad. It'll have to be a county grave then."

But the man who ran the morgue cried out. "No! She's got to be buried in stone. In a vault with a lock on the door. Otherwise she'll get out. She'll get out and she'll be after people again. Don't you understand?" He rushed at the drawer

Diedre lay in. "This isn't real. It doesn't matter if ghouls break bones or get burned. They're not like people! The only thing you can do is starve them. . . . You have to bury them in stone, locked in stone. . . ."

It was then that the police took the man away.

Diedre lay back and waited.

And this time, it was a full ten days before she left her grave.

WILLIAM SAMBROT

Island of Fear

Kyle Elliot clutched the smooth, tight-fitting stones of the high wall, unmindful of the fierce, direct rays of the Aegean sun on his neck, staring, staring through a chink.

He'd come to this tiny island, dropped into the middle of the Aegean like a pebble on a vast blue shield, just in the hope that something, something like what lay beyond that wall, might turn up. And it had. It had.

Beyond, in the garden behind the wall, was a fountain, plashing gently. And in the center of that fountain, two nudes, a mother and child.

A mother and child, marvelously intertwined, intricately wrought of some stone that almost might have been heliotrope, jasper or one of the other semiprecious chalcedonies—although that would have been manifestly impossible.

He took a small object like a pencil from his pocket and extended it. A miniature telescope. He gasped, looking once more through the chink.

God, the detail of the woman! Head slightly turned, eyes just widening with the infinitesimal beginning of an expression of surprise as she looked—at what? And half-sliding, clutching with one hand at the smooth thigh, reaching mouth slightly rounded, plump other hand not quite touching the milk-swollen breast—the child.

His professional eye moved over the figures, his mind racing, trying to place the sculptor and failing. It was of no known period. It might have been done yesterday; it might be millenniums old. Only one thing was certain: no catalogue on earth listed it.

Kyle had found this island by pure chance. He'd taken passage on a decrepit Greek caïque that plied the Aegean, nudging slowly and without schedule from island to island. From Lesbos to Chios to Samos, down through the myriad Cyclades, and so on about the fabled sea, touching the old, old lands where the gods had walked like men. The islands where occasionally some treasure, long-buried, came to light, and if it pleased Kyle's eyes and money obtained it, then he would add it to his small collection. But only rarely did anything please Kyle. Only rarely.

The battered caïque's engine had quit in the midst of a small storm which drove them south and west. By the time the storm had cleared, the asthmatic old engine was back in shape, coughing along. There was no radio, but the captain was undisturbed. Who could get lost in the Aegean?

They had been drifting along, a small water bug of a ship lost in the greenish-blue sea, when Kyle had seen the dim purple shadow that was a tiny island in the distance. The binoculars brought the little blob of land closer, and he sucked in his breath. An incredible wall, covering a good quarter of the miniature island, leaped into view: a great horseshoe of masonry that grew out of the sea, curved, embraced several acres of the land, then returned, sinking at last into the sea again where white foam leaped high even as he watched.

He called the captain's attention to it. "There is a little island over there." And the captain, grinning, had squinted in the direction of Kyle's pointing finger.

"There is a wall on it," Kyle said, and instantly the grin vanished from the captain's face; his head snapped around, and he stared rigidly ahead, away from the island.

"It is nothing," the captain said harshly. "Only a few goatherders live there. It has no name even."

"There is a wall," Kyle had said gently. "Here," handing him the binoculars, "look."

"No." The captain's head didn't move one iota. His eyes remained looking straight ahead. "It is just another ruin. There is no harbor there—it is years since anyone has gone there. You would not like it. No electricity."

"I want to see the wall and what is behind it."

The captain flicked an eye at him. Kyle started. The eye seemed genuinely agitated.

"There is nothing behind it. It is a very old place, and everything is long since gone."

"I want to see the wall," Kyle said quietly.

They'd put him off finally, the little caïque pointing its grizzled snout to sea, its engine turning over just enough to keep it under way, its muted throbbing the only sound. They'd rowed him over in a dinghy, and as he approached, he noticed the strangely quiet single street of the village, the lone *taverna*, the few dories with patched lateen sails, and on the low, worn-down hills, the herds of drifting goats.

Almost he might have believed the captain; that here was an old, tired island, forgotten, out of the mainstream of the brilliant civilization that had flowered in this sea—almost, until he remembered that wall. Walls are built to protect, to keep out or keep in. He meant to see what.

After he'd settled in the primitive little *taverna*, he'd immediately set out for the wall, surveying it from the low knoll, surprised again to note how much of this small island it encompassed.

He'd walked all around it, hoping to find a gate or a break in the smooth, unscalable wall that towered up. There had been none. The grounds within sprawled on a sort of peninsula that jutted out to where rock, barnacled, fanged, resisted the restless surf.

And coming back along the great wall, utterly baffled, he'd heard the faint musical sound of water dropping within and peering carefully at the wall had seen the small aperture, no bigger than a walnut, just above his head.

He looked through the aperture and so stood, dazed at so much beauty, staring at the woman and child, unable to tear away, knowing that here at last was the absolute perfection he'd sought throughout the world.

How was it that the catalogues failed to list this master work?

These things were impossibly hard to keep quiet. And yet not a whisper, not a rumor had drifted from this island to the others of what lay within those walls. Here on this remote pinprick of land, so insignificant as to go unnamed, here behind a huge wall which was itself a work of genius, here was this magic mother and child, glowing all unseen.

He stared, throat dry, heart pumping with the fierce exultation of the avid connoisseur who has found something truly great—and unknown. He must have it. He would have it. It wasn't listed; possibly, just possibly, its true worth was unknown. Perhaps the owner of this estate had inherited it, and it remained there in the center of the gently falling water unnoticed, unappreciated.

He reluctantly turned away from the chink in the wall and walked slowly back toward the village, scuffling the deep, pale, immemorial dust. Greece. Cradle of western culture. He thought again of the exquisite perfection of the mother and child back there. The sculptor of that little group deserved to walk on Olympus.

Who was it?

Back in the village he paused before the *taverna* to take some of the dust off his shoes, thinking again how oddly incurious, for Greeks, these few villagers were.

"Permit me?"

A boy, eyes snapping, popped out of the *taverna* with a rag in one hand and some primitive shoe blacking in the other and began cleaning Kyle's shoes.

Kyle sat down on a bench and examined the boy. He was about fifteen, wiry and strong, but small for his age. He might have, in an earlier era, been a model for one of Praxiteles' masterpieces: the same perfectly molded head, the tight curls, two ringlets falling over the brow like Pan's snubbed horns, the classic Grecian profile. But, no, a ridged scar ran from the boy's nose to the corner of the upper lip, lifting it ever so slightly, revealing a glimmer of white teeth.

No, Praxiteles would never have used him for a model, unless, of course, he had a slightly flawed Pan in mind.

"Who owns the large estate beyond the village?" he asked in his excellent Greek. The boy looked up quickly, and it was as if a shutter came down over his dark eyes. He shook his head.

"You must know it," Kyle persisted. "It covers the whole south end of this island. A big wall, very high, all the way to the water."

The boy shook his head stubbornly. "It has always been there."

Kyle smiled at him. "Always is a long time," he said. "Perhaps your father might know?"

"I am alone," the boy said with dignity.

"I'm sorry to hear that." Kyle studied the small expert movements of the boy. "You really don't know the name of the persons who live there?"

The boy muttered a single word.

"Gordon?" Kyle leaned forward. "Did you say 'the Gordons'? Is it an English family that owns that property?" He felt the hope dying within. If an English family owned it, the chances were slim indeed of obtaining that wonderful stone pair.

"They are not English," the boy said.

"I'd like very much to see them."

"There is no way."

"I know there's no way from the island," Kyle said, "but I suppose they must have a dock or some facilities for landing from the sea."

The boy shook his head, keeping his eyes down. Some of the villagers had stopped and now were clustered about him, watching and listening quietly. Kyle knew his Greeks, a happy, boisterous people, intolerably curious sometimes; full of advice, quick to give it.

These people merely stood, unsmiling, watching.

The boy finished and Kyle flipped him a fifty-lepta coin. The boy caught it and smiled, a flawed masterpiece.

"That wall," Kyle said to the spectators, singling out one old man. "I am interested in meeting the people who own that property."

The old man muttered something and walked away.

Kyle mentally kicked himself for the psychological error. In Greece money talks first. "I will pay fifty—one hundred drachmas," he said loudly, "to anyone who will take me in his boat around to the seaward side of the wall."

It was a lot of money, he knew, to a poor people eking out a precarious existence on this rocky island with their goats and scanty gardens. Most of them wouldn't see that much cash in a year's hard work.

A lot of money, but they looked at one another, then turned and without a backward glance they walked away from him. All of them.

Throughout the village he met the same mysterious refusal, as difficult to overcome as that enigmatic wall that embraced the end of the island. They refused even to mention the wall or what it contained, who built it and when. It was as though it didn't exist for them.

At dusk he went back to the *taverna*, ate *Dolmadakis*, minced meat, rice, egg and spices—surprisingly delicious—drank *retsina*, the resinated astringent wine of the peasant, and wondered about the lovely mother and child, standing there behind that great wall with the purple night clothing them. A vast surge of sadness, of longing for the statues, swept over him.

What a rotten break! He'd run into local taboos before. Most of them were the results of petty feuds, grudges going back to antiquity. They were cherished by the peasants, held tight, jealously guarded. What else was there of importance in their small lives?

But this was something entirely different.

He was standing on the outskirts of the darkened village, gazing unhappily out to sea, when he heard a soft scuffling. He turned quickly. A small boy was approaching. It was the shoeshine boy, eyes gleaming in the starshine, shivering slightly though the night was balmy.

The boy touched his arm. His fingers felt icy. "I—I will take you in my boat," he whispered.

Kyle smiled, relief exploding within him. Of course, he should have thought of the boy. A young fellow alone, without family, could use a hundred drachmas, whatever the taboo.

"Thank you," he said warmly. "When can we leave?"

"Before the ebb tide, an hour before sunrise," the boy said, "only," his teeth were chattering, "I will take you, but I will not come any closer than the outer rocks between the walls. From there you must wait until the ebb tide and walk—and walk—" He gasped, as though choking.

"What are you afraid of?" Kyle said. "I'll take all the responsibility for trespassing, although I don't think—"

The boy clutched his arm. "The others—tonight when you go back to the *taverna*, you will not tell the others that I am rowing you there?"

"Not if you don't want me to."

"Please do not," he gasped. "They would not like it if they knew—after that I—"

"I understand," Kyle said. "I won't tell anyone."

"An hour before sunrise," the boy whispered. "I will meet you at the wall where it goes into the water to the east."

The stars were still glowing, but faintly, when Kyle met the boy, a dim figure sitting in a small rowboat that bobbed up and down, scraping against the kelp and barnacles that grew from the base of the monolithic wall. He realized suddenly that the boy must have rowed for hours to get the boat this far around the island. It had no sails.

He climbed in and they shoved off, the boy strangely silent. The sea was rough, a chill predawn wind blowing raggedly. The wall loomed up alongside, gigantic in the mist.

"Who built this wall?" he asked, once they were out on the pitching water, heading slowly around the first of a series of jagged, barnacled rocks thrusting wetly above the rapidly ebbing tide.

"The old ones," the boy said. His teeth were chattering. He kept his back steadfastly to the wall, glancing only seaward to measure his progress. "It has always been there."

Always. And yet, studying the long sweep of the wall beginning to emerge in the first light, Kyle knew that it was very old. Very old. It might well date back to the beginning of Greek civilization. And the statues, the mother and child. All of it an enigma no greater than the fact that they were unknown to the outside world.

As they drew slowly around until he was able to see the ends of the thick walls rising out of the swirling, sucking sea, he realized that most certainly he could not have been the first—not even the first hundredth. This island was remote, not worth even being on a mail route, but surely over the many, many years that wall had towered it must have been visited by people equally as curious as he. Other collectors.

And yet not a rumor.

The boat rasped up against an enormous black rock, its tip white with bird droppings, startlingly luminous in the half light. The boy shipped his oars.

"I will come back here at the next tide," he said, shaking as though with a fever. "Will you pay me now?"

"Of course." Kyle took out his billfold. "But aren't you at least going to take me further in than this?"

"No," the boy said shrilly. "I cannot."

"How about the dock?" Kyle surveyed the considerable expanse of shallow, choppy surf between the rocks and the narrow, sloping beach. "Why, hell—there isn't a dock!"

There was nothing between the walls but sand dotted with huge rocks and, inland, a tangled growth of underbrush with an occasional cypress rearing tall.

"I'll tell you what—I'll take the boat in, and you wait here," Kyle said. "I won't be long. I just want to get a chance to meet whoever owns the place and arrange—"

"No!" There was sharp panic in the boy's voice. "If you take the boat—" He half rose, leaning forward to shove off from the rock. At that instant a swell raised the boat, then dropped it suddenly out from under the boy. Overbalanced, he swayed, arms waving wildly, then went over backwards, hitting his head on the rock. He slipped under the water like a stone.

Kyle made a quick lunge and missing, immediately dove out of the rowboat after him, rasping his chest on the barnacled shelf of rock a few feet beneath the boat. He got a good handful of the boy's shirt, but it tore like paper. He grabbed again, got a firm grip on his hair and stroked for the surface. He held him easily, treading water, looking for the rowboat. It was gone, kicked away by his powerful dive, perhaps behind one of the other rocks. No time to waste looking for it now.

He swam to shore, pulling the boy easily. It was only a hundred yards or so to the smooth white beach, curving between the two arms of the wall that sloped out and down into the ocean. When he came out of the water, the boy was coughing weakly, salt water dribbling from his nose.

Kyle carried him well above the tide mark and sat him down on the sand. The boy opened his eyes and peered at him, puzzled.

"You'll be all right," Kyle said. "I'd better get your boat before it drifts too far." He walked back down to the surf line, kicked off his shoes and stroked off to where the boat rose and fell, nuzzling another of the large rocks that littered the space between the towering walls. He rowed the boat back, facing the sea and the swift-rising sun. The wind had dropped to a whisper.

He beached the boat and gathered up his shoes. The boy was leaning against a rock, looking inland over his shoulder in an attitude of rigid watchfulness.

"Feeling better now?" Kyle called cheerfully. It occurred to him that their little mishap was an excellent excuse for being here, on property belonging to someone who obviously valued his privacy highly.

The boy didn't move. He remained staring back into the tangle of trees, back to where the massive walls converged in the distance, stark, white, ancient.

Kyle touched him on the bare shoulder.

He pulled his hand away, fists tightly clenched. He looked at the sand. Here were the marks where the boy had risen, here the dragging footsteps where he'd come to lean against this rock. And here he still stood, glancing over his shoulder toward the trees, lips barely parted, a look of faint surprise just starting on his face.

And there, coming out of the tangled trees, a delicate tracery of footsteps led toward this rock and behind. Footsteps slender, high-arched, as though a woman, barefooted, scarcely touching the sand, had approached for just an instant. Looking at the strange footprints, Kyle understood completely what he should have guessed when first he'd peered through that chink in the wall, gasping at the unimaginable perfection of the woman and her child.

Kyle knew intimately all the ancient fables of early Greece. And now, looking at the footprints in the sand, one of the most terrible leaped into his mind: The Gorgons.

The Gorgons were three sisters, Medusa, Euryale and Stheno, with snakes writhing where their hair should have been. Three creatures so awful to look upon, the legend said, that whosoever dared gaze upon them instantly turned to stone.

Kyle stood on the warm sand, with the gull cries, the restless Aegean sea sounds all about him, and he knew at last who the old ones were who'd built the wall; why they'd built it to lead into the living waters and whom—*what*—the walls were meant to contain.

Not an English family named the Gordons. A much more ancient family—the Gorgons. Perseus had slain Medusa, but her two hideous sisters, Euryale and Stheno, were immortal.

Immortal.

Oh, god! It was impossible. A myth. And yet—

His connoisseur's eyes, even through the sweat of fear, noted the utter perfection of the small statue that leaned against the rock, head turned slightly, an expression of surprise on the face as it peered over one shoulder in the direction of the trees. The two tight ringlets, like snubbed horns above the brow, the perfect molding of the head, the classic Grecian profile. Salt water still flecked the smoothly gleaming shoulders, still dripped from the torn shirt that flapped about the stone waist.

Pan, in chalcedony.

But Pan had a flaw. From the nose to the corner of the upper lip ran a ridge, an onyx scar that lifted the edge of the onyx lip slightly so that, faintly, a glimmer of onyx teeth showed.

A flawed masterpiece.

He heard the rustle behind him as of robes, smelled an indescribable scent, heard a sound that could only have been a multiple hissing—and though he knew he mustn't, he turned slowly.

And looked.

H IS FOR HYBRID HORRORS AND HUMANS

ROBERT SHECKLEY

Doctor Zombie and His Furry Little Friends

I think I am fairly safe here. I live at present in a small apartment northeast of the Zócalo, in one of the oldest parts of Mexico City. As a foreigner, my inevitable first impression is how like Spain this country seems, and how different it really is. In Madrid the streets are a maze which draws you continually deeper, toward hidden centers with tedious, well-guarded secrets. Concealment of the commonplace is surely a heritage of the Moors. Whereas Mexican streets are an inverted labyrinth which leads outward toward the mountains, toward openness, toward revelations which remain forever elusive. Nothing is concealed; but nothing in Mexico is comprehensible. This is the way of the Indians, past and present—a defense based upon permeability; a transparent defense like that of the sea anemone.

I find this style profound and compatible. I conform to insight born in Tenochtitlán or Tlaxcala; I conceal nothing, and thus contrive to hide everything.

How often I have envied the thief who has nothing to hide but a handful of game! Some of us are less lucky, some of us possess secrets which won't fit into our pockets, or into our closets; secrets which cannot even be contained in our parlors or buried in our back yards. Gilles de Retz required a private hidden cemetery scarcely smaller than Père La Chaise. My own needs are more modest; but not by much.

I am not a sociable man. I dream of a house in the country, on the barren slopes of Ixtaccíhuatl, where there is no other human habitation for miles in any direction. But that would be madness. The police assume that a man who isolates himself has something to conceal; the equation is as true as it is banal. Those polite, relentless Mexican police! How they distrust foreigners, and how rightfully so! They would have searched my lonely house on some pretext, and the truth would have come out—a three-day sensation for the newspapers.

I have avoided all of that, or at least put it off, by living where I live. Not even García, the most zealous policeman in my neighborhood, can make himself believe that I use this small permeable apartment for *secret ungodly experiments of a terrible nature*. As is rumoured.

My door is usually ajar. When the shopkeepers deliver my provisions, I tell them to walk right in. They never do so, they are innately respectful of a man's privacy. But I tell them in any case.

I have three rooms arranged in line. One enters through the kitchen. Next is the parlor, and after that the bedroom. Each room has a door, none of which I ever close completely. Perhaps I carry this fetish of openness too far. For if anyone ever walked through my apartment, pushed the bedroom door fully open and looked inside, I suppose I would have to kill myself.

To date, my callers have never gone beyond the kitchen. I think they are frightened of me.

And why not? I am frightened of myself.

My work forces me into an uncongenial mode of life. I must take all of my meals in my apartment. I am a bad cook; even the meanest neighborhood restaurant exceeds my efforts. Even the sidewalk vendors with their overcooked tacos surpass my indigestible messes.

And to make it worse, I am forced to invent ridiculous reasons for always eating at home. I tell my neighbors that my doctor allows me no spices whatsoever, no chilies, no tomatoes, no salt ... Why? A rare condition of the liver. How did I contact it? From eating tainted meat many years ago in Jakarta ...

All of which is easy enough to say, you may think. But I find it difficult to remember the details. A liar is forced to live in a hateful and unnatural state of consistency. His role becomes his punishment.

My neighbors find it easy to accept my contorted explanations. A little incongruity feels very lifelike to them, and they consider themselves excellent arbiters of truth; whereas all they really pass judgment on are questions of verisimilitude.

Still, despite themselves, my neighbors sense something monstrous about me. Eduardo the butcher once said: "Did you know, Doctor, that zombies are allowed no salt? Maybe you are a zombie, eh?"

Where on earth did he learn about zombies? In the cinema, I suppose, or from a comic book. I have seen old women make a sign to avert the evil eye when I pass, and I have heard children whisper behind my back: "Doctor Zombie, Doctor Zombie."

Old women and children! They are the repositories of what little wisdom this race possesses. Yes, and the butchers also know a thing or two.

I am neither a doctor nor a zombie. Nevertheless, the old women and the children are quite right about me. Luckily, no one listens to them.

So I continue to eat in my own kitchen—lamb, kid, pig, rabbit, beef, veal, chicken, and sometimes venison. It is the only way I can get the necessary quantities of meat into my house to feed my animals.

Someone else has recently begun to suspect me. Unfortunately, that man is Diego

Juan García, a policeman.

García is stocky, broad-faced, careful, a good cop. Around the Zócalo he is considered incorruptible—an Aztec Cato, but with better disposition. According to the vegetable woman—who is perhaps in love with me—García believes that I might well be an escaped German war criminal.

It is an amazing conception, factually wrong, but intuitively correct. García is certain that, somehow, he has hit upon the truth. He would have acted by now it were not for the intercession of my neighbors. The shoemaker, the butcher, the shoeshine boy, and especially the vegetable woman, all vouch for me. They are bourgeois rationalists, they believe their own projections of my character. They chide García: "Isn't it obvious that this foreigner is a quiet, goodhearted man, a harmless scholar, a dreamer?"

Madly enough, they too are factually wrong, but intuitively correct.

My invaluable neighbors address me as "Doctor," and sometimes as "Professor." These are honorary degrees which they awarded me quite spontaneously, as a reward to my appearance. I did not solicit a title, but I do not reject it. "Señor Doctor" is another mask behind which I can hide.

I suppose I look to them like a doctor: huge glistening forehead, gray hair bristling from the sides of my balding head, square, stern, wrinkled face. Yes, and my European accent, my careful Spanish constructions, my absentminded air . . . And my gold-rimmed glasses! What else could I be but a doctor, and a German one at that?

My title demands an occupation, and I claim to be a scholar on extended leave from my university. I tell them that I am writing a book about the Toltecs, a book in which I will collate evidence of a cultural linkage between that mysterious race and the Incas.

"Yes, gentlemen, I expect that my book will create quite a stir in Heidelberg and Bonn. There are vested interests which will be offended. Attempts will doubtless be made to represent me as a crank. My theory, you see, could shake the entire world of pre-Columbian studies . . ."

I had prepared the above personality before coming to Mexico. I read Stephens, Prescott, Vaillant, Alfonso Caso. I even went to the trouble of copying out the first third of Dreyer's discredited thesis on cultural diffusion, in which he postulates a Mayan-Toltec cultural exchange. That gave me an opus of some eighty handwritten pages which I could claim as my own. The unfinished manuscript was my excuse for being in Mexico. Any one could glance at the erudite pages scattered over my desk and see for himself what sort of man I was.

I thought that would suffice; but I hadn't allowed for the dynamism inherent in my role. Señor Ortega, my grocer, is also interested in pre-Columbian studies, and is disturbingly knowledgeable. Señor Andrade, the barber, was born in a pueblo within five miles of the ruins of Teotihuacán. And little Jorge Silverio, the shoeshine boy whose mother works in a *tortillería*, dreams of attending a great university, and asks me very humbly if I might use my influence at Bonn . . .

I am the victim of my neighbor's expectations. I have become *their* professor, not mine. Because of them I must spend endless hours at the National Museum of Anthropology, and waste whole days at Teotihuacán, Tula, Xochicalco. My neighbors force me to work hard at my scholarly pursuit. And I have become quite literally what I purported to be: an expert, possessed of formidable knowledge, more than a little mad.

The role has penetrated me, mingled with me, transformed me; to the extent that I really *do* believe in the likelihood of a Toltec-Incan connection, I have unassailable evidence, I have seriously considered publishing my findings . . .

All of which I find tiresome and quite beside the point.

I had a bad scare last month. My landlady, Señora Elvira Macias, stopped me on the street and demanded that I get rid of my dog.

"But, señora, I have no dog."

"Excuse me, señor, but you do have a dog. I heard it last night, whining and scratching at the door. And my rules, which were also those of my poor late husband, expressly forbid—"

"My dear señora, you must be mistaken. I can assure you . . ."

And there was García, inevitable as death, in freshly starched khakis, puffing on a Delicado and listening to our conversation.

"A scratching sound? Perhaps it was the termites, señora, or the cockroaches."

She shook her head. "It was not that kind of sound."

"Rats, then. Your building, I regret to say, is infested with rats."

"I know very well what rats sound like," Señora Elvira said, invincibly ingenuous. "But this was not like that, this was a doglike sound which came from your apartment. And as I have told you, I have an absolute rule against pets."

García was watching me, and I saw reflected in his eyes my deeds at Dachau, Bergen-Belsen, Theresienstadt. I wanted to tell him that he was wrong, that I was one of the victims, that I had spent the war years as a prisoner in the Tjilatjap concentration camp in Java.

But I also knew that the specific facts did not matter. My crimes against humanity were real enough: García just happened to be sensing next year's frightfulness rather than last year's.

I might have confessed everything at that moment if Señora Elvira had not turned to García and said, "Well, what are you going to do about all this? He keeps a dog, perhaps two dogs, he keeps God knows what in that apartment of his. What are you going to do?"

García said nothing. His immobile face reminded me of the stone mask of Tlacoc in the Cholula museum. My own reaction was in keeping with that transparent defense by which I hide my secrets. I ground my teeth, flared my nostrils, tried to simulate the *furia español*.

"Dogs?" I howled. "I'll show you dogs! Come up and search my apartment! I will pay you a hundred pesos for each dog you find, two hundred for purebreeds. You come too, García, and bring all your friends. Perhaps I have a horse up there as well, eh? And maybe a pig? Bring witnesses, bring newspaper reporters, I want my menagerie to be noted with accuracy."

"Calm yourself," García said, unimpressed by my rage.

"I will calm myself after we dispose of the dogs!" I shouted. "Come, señora, enter my rooms and look under the bed for your hallucinations. And when you are satisfied, you will kindly refund me the remainder of my month's rent and my month's security, and I will go live somewhere else with my invisible dogs."

García looked at me curiously. I suppose he has seen a great deal of bravado in his time. It is said to be typical of a certain type of criminal. He said to Señora Elvira: "Shall we take a look?"

My landlady surprised me. She said—incredibly!—"Certainly not! The gentleman has given his word." And she turned and walked away.

I was about to complete the bluff by insisting that García search for himself if he were not completely satisfied. Luckily, I stopped myself. García is no respector of properties. He is not afraid of making a fool of himself.

"I am tired," I said. "I am going to lie down."

And that was the end of it.

This time I locked my front door. It had been a near thing. While we had been talking, the poor wretched creature had gnawed through its leash and died on the kitchen floor.

I disposed of it in the usual way, by feeding it to the others. Thereafter I doubled my precautions. I bought a radio to cover what little noise they made. I put heavy straw matting under their cages. And I masked their odor with heavy tobacco, for I thought that incense would be too obvious.

But it is strange and ironic that anyone should suspect *me* of keeping dogs. They are my implacable enemies. They know what goes on in my apartment. They have allied themselves with mankind. They are renegade animals, just as I am a renegade human. If the dogs could speak, they would hurry to the police station with their *denunciamentos*.

When the battle against humanity is finally begun, the dogs will have to stand or fall with their masters.

A note of cautious optimism: the last litter was quite promising. Four of the twelve survived, and grew sleek and clever and strong. But they are not as ferocious as I had expected. That part of their genetic inheritance seems to have been lost. They actually seem fond of me—like dogs! But this surely can be bred out of them.

Mankind has dire legends of hybrids produced by the cross-breeding of various species. Among these are the chimera, the griffin, and the sphinx, to name but a few. It seems to me that these antique nightmares might have been a *memory of the future*—like García's perception of my not-yet-committed crimes.

Pliny and Diodorus record the monstrous offspring of camel and ostrich, lion and eagle, horse, dragon, and tiger. What would they have thought of a composite wolverine and rat? What would a modern biologist think of this prodigy?

The scientists of today will deny its existence even when my heraldic beasts are swarming into towns and cities. No reasonable man will believe in a creature the size of a wolf, as savage and cunning as a wolverine, as social, adaptable, and as great a breeder as a rat. A confirmed rationalist will deny credence to this indescribable and apocryphal beast even as it tears out his throat.

And he will be almost right in his skepticism. Such a product of cross-hybridization was clearly impossible—until I produced it last year.

Secrecy can begin as a necessity and end as a habit. Even in this journal, in which I intended to tell everything, I see that I have not recorded my reasons for breeding monsters, nor what I intend them to do.

Their work should begin in about three months, in early July. By then, local residents will be remarking on a horde of animals which has begun to infest the slums surrounding the Zócalo. Descriptions will be hazy, but people will remark on the size of these creatures, their ferocity and elusiveness. The authorities will be notified, the newspapers will take note. The blame will probably be laid to wolves or wild dogs at first, despite the uncanine appearance of these beasts.

Standard methods of extermination will be tried, and will fail. The mysterious creatures will spread out through the capital, and then into the wealthy suburbs of Pedregal and Coyoacán. It will be known by now that they are omnivores, like man himself. And it will be suspected—correctly—that they possess an extremely high rate of reproduction.

Perhaps not until later their high degree of intelligence be appreciated.

The armed forces will be called in, to no avail. The air force will thunder over the countryside; but what will they find to bomb? These creatures present no mass target for conventional weaponry. They live behind the walls, under the sofa, inside the closet—always just beyond the outer edge of your eyesight.

Poison? But these hybrids eat what you possess, not what you offer.

And besides, it is August now, the situation is completely out of hand. The army is spread symbolically throughout Mexico City; but the cohorts of the beasts have overrun Toluca, Ixtapan, Tepalcingo, Cuernavaca, and they have been reported in San Luis Potosí, in Oaxaca and Veracruz.

Scientists confer, crash programs are drawn up, experts come to Mexico from all over the world. The beasts hold no conferences and publish no manifestos. They simply spawn and spread, north to Durango, south to Villahermosa.

The United States closes its borders; another symbolic gesture. The beasts come down to Piedras Negras, they cross the Eagle Pass without permission; unauthorized, they appear in El Paso, Laredo, Brownsville.

They sweep across the plains and deserts like a whirlwind, they flow into the cities like a tidal wave. Doctor Zombie's little furry friends have arrived, and they are here to stay.

And at last mankind realizes that the problem is not how to exterminate these creatures. No, the problem is how to prevent these creatures from exterminating man.

This can be done, I have no doubt. But it is going to require the full efforts and ingenuity of the human race.

That is what I expect to achieve by breeding monsters.

You see, something must be done. I intend my hybrids to act as a counterbalance, a load to control the free-running human engine that is tearing up the earth and itself. I consider this job ethically imperative. After all: Does man have the right to exterminate whatever species he pleases? Must everything in creation serve his ill-considered schemes, or be obliterated? Don't all life forms and systems have a right to live, an absolute right with no possibility of qualification?

Despite the extremity of the measure, there will be benefits to mankind. No one will have to worry again about hydrogen bombs, germ warfare, defoliation, pollution, greenhouse effect, and the like. Overnight, these preoccupations will become—medieval. Man will return to a life in nature. He will still be unique, still intelligent, still a predator; but now he will be subject again to certain checks and balances which he had previously evaded.

His most prized freedom will remain; he will still be at liberty to kill; he will simply lose the ability to exterminate.

Pneumonia is a great leveler of aspirations. It has killed my creatures. Yesterday the last of them raised its head and looked at me. Its large pale eyes were filmed over. It raised a paw, extended its claws, and scratched me lightly on the forearm.

I cried then, for I knew that my poor beast had done that only to please me, knowing how much I desired it to be fierce, implacable, a scourge against mankind.

The effort was too much. Those marvelous eyes closed. It died with barely a twitch.

Pneumonia is not really a sufficient explanation, of course. Beyond that, the will was simply not there. No species has had much vitality since man pre-empted the earth. The slave-raccoons still play in the tattered Adirondack forests, and the slave-lions sniff beer cans in Kruger Park. They and all the others exist only on our sufferance, as squatters on our land. And they know it.

Under the circumstances, you can't expect to find much vitality and spirit among non-humans. Spirit is the property of the victors.

The death of my last beast has become my own end. I am too tired and too heartsick to begin again. I regret that I have failed mankind. I regret having failed the lions, ostriches, tigers, whales, and other species threatened with extinction. But most of all I regret having failed the sparrows, crows, rats, hyenas—the vermin of the earth, the trash species who exist only to be exterminated by man. My truest sympathy has always been with the outlawed, abandoned, or worthless, in whose categories I include myself.

Are they vermin simply because they do not serve man? Don't all life forms and systems have a right to live, an absolute right with no possibility of qualification? Must everything in creation continue to serve one species, or be obliterated?

Some other man must feel as I do. I ask him to take up the fight, become a guerrilla against his own kind, oppose them as he would oppose a raging fire.

The record has been written for that hypothetical man.

As for me: not long ago, García and another official came to my apartment on a "routine" health inspection. They found the bodies of several of my composite creatures, which I had not yet had the opportunity to destroy. I was arrested and charged with cruelty to animals, and with operating a slaughter-house without a license.

I shall plead guilty to the charges. Despite their falseness, I recognize them as essentially and undeniably true.

GUY DE MAUPASSANT
The Mother of Monsters

I was reminded of this horrible story and this horrible woman on the sea-front the other day, as I stood watching—at a watering-place much frequented by the wealthy—a lady well known in Paris, a young, elegant, and charming girl, universally loved and respected.

My story is now many years old, but such things are not forgotten.

I had been invited by a friend to stay with him in a small country town. In order to do the honours of the district, he took me about all over the place; made me see the most celebrated views, the manor-houses and castles, the local industries, the ruins; he showed me the monuments, the churches, the old carved doors, the trees of specially large size or uncommon shape, the oak of St. Andrew and the Roqueboise yew.

When, with exclamations of gratified enthusiasm, I had inspected all the curiosities in the district, my friend confessed, with every sign of acute distress, that there was nothing more to visit. I breathed again. I should be able, at last, to enjoy a little rest under the shade of the trees. But suddenly he exclaimed:

"Why, no, there *is* one more. There's the Mother of Monsters."

"And who," I asked, "is the Mother of Monsters?"

He answered: "She is a horrible woman, a perfect demon, a creature who every year deliberately produces deformed, hideous, frightful children, monsters, in a word, and sells them to peep-show men.

"The men who follow this ghastly trade come from time to time to discover whether she has brought forth any fresh abortion, and if they like the look of the object, they pay the mother and take it away with them.

"She has dropped eleven of these creatures. She is rich.

"You think I'm joking, making it up, exaggerating. No, my friend, I'm only telling you the truth, the literal truth.

"Come and see this woman. I'll tell you afterwards how she became a monster-factory."

He took me off to the outskirts of the town.

She lived in a nice little house by the side of the road. It was pretty and well kept. The garden was full of flowers, and smelt delicious. Anyone would have taken it for the home of a retired lawyer.

A servant showed us into a little parlour, and the wretched creature appeared.

She was about forty, tall, hard-featured, but well built, vigorous, and wealthy, the true type of robust peasantry, half animal and half woman.

She was aware of the disapproval in which she was held, and seemed to receive us with malignant humility.

"What do the gentlemen want?" she inquired.

My friend replied: "We have been told that your last child is just like any other child, and not in the least like his brothers. I wanted to verify this. Is it true?"

She gave us a sly glance of anger and answered:

"Oh, no, sir, oh dear no! He's even uglier, mebbe, than the others. I've no luck, no luck at all, they're all that way, sir, all like that, it's something cruel; how can the good Lord be so hard on a poor woman left all alone in the world!"

She spoke rapidly, keeping her eyes lowered, with a hypocritical air, like a scared wild beast. She softened the harsh tone of her voice, and it was amazing to hear these tearful high-pitched words issuing from that great bony body, with its coarse, angular strength, made for violent gesture and wolfish howling.

"We should like to see your child," my friend said.

She appeared to blush. Had I perhaps been mistaken? After some moments of silence she said, in a louder voice: "What would be the use of that to you?"

She had raised her head, and gave us a swift, burning glance.

"Why don't you wish to show him to us?" answered my friend. "There are many people to whom you show him. You know whom I mean."

She started up, letting loose the full fury of her voice.

"So that's what you've come for, is it? Just to insult me? Because my bairns are like animals, eh? Well, you'll not see them, no, no, no, you shan't. Get out of here. I know you all, the whole pack of you, bullying me about like this!"

She advanced towards us, her hands on her hips. At the brutal sound of her voice, a sort of moan, or rather a mew, a wretched lunatic screech, issued from the next room. I shivered to the marrow. We drew back before her.

In a severe tone my friend warned her:

"Have a care, She-devil"—the people all called her She-devil—"have a care, one of these days this will bring you bad luck."

She trembled with rage, waving her arms, mad with fury, and yelling:

"Get out of here, you! What'll bring me bad luck? Get out of here, you pack of beasts, you!"

She almost flew at our throats; we fled, our hearts contracted with horror.

When we were outside the door, my friend asked:

"Well, you've seen her; what do you say to her?"

I answered: "Tell me the brute's history."

And this is what he told me, as we walked slowly back along the white high road, bordered on either side by the ripe corn that rippled like a quiet sea under the caress of a small, gentle wind.

The girl had once been a servant on a farm, a splendid worker, well-behaved and careful. She was not known to have a lover, and was not suspected of any weakness.

She fell, as they all do, one harvest night among the heaps of corn, under a stormy sky, when the still, heavy air is hot like a furnace, and the brown bodies of the lads and girls are drenched with sweat.

Feeling soon after that she was pregnant, she was tormented with shame and fear. Desirous at all costs of hiding her misfortune, she forcibly compressed her belly by a method she invented, a horrible corset made of wood and ropes. The more the growing child swelled her body, the more she tightened the instrument of torture, suffering agony, but bearing her pain with courage, always smiling and active, letting no one see or suspect anything.

She crippled the little creature inside her, held tightly in that terrible machine; she crushed him, deformed him, made a monster of him. The skull was squeezed almost flat and ran to a point, with the two great eyes jutting right out from the forehead. The limbs, crushed against the body, were twisted like the stem of a vine, and grew to an inordinate length, with the fingers and toes like spiders' legs.

The trunk remained quite small and round like a nut.

She gave birth to it in the open fields one spring morning.

When the women weeders, who had run to her help, saw the beast which was appearing, they fled shrieking. And the story ran round the neighbourhood that she had brought a demon into the world. It was then that she got the name "She-devil".

She lost her place. She lived on charity, and perhaps on secret love, for she was a fine-looking girl, and not all men are afraid of hell.

She brought up her monster, which, by the way, she hated with a savage hatred, and which she would perhaps have strangled had not the *curé*, foreseeing the likelihood of such a crime, terrified her with threats of the law.

At last one day some passing showmen heard tell of the frightful abortion, and asked to see it, intending to take it away if they liked it. They did like it, and paid the mother five hundred francs down for it. Ashamed at first, she did not want to let them see a beast of this sort; but when she discovered that it was worth money, that these people wanted it, she began to bargain, to dispute it penny by penny, inflaming them with the tale of her child's deformities, raising her prices with peasant tenacity.

In order not to be cheated, she made a contract with them. And they agreed to pay her four hundred francs a year as well, as though they had taken this beast into their service.

The unhoped-for good fortune crazed the mother, and after that she never lost the desire to give birth to another phenomenon, so that she would have a fixed income like the upper classes.

As she was very fertile, she succeeded in her ambition, and apparently became expert at varying the shapes of her monsters according to the pressure they were made to undergo during the period of her pregnancy.

She had them long and short, some like crabs and others like lizards. Several died, whereat she was deeply distressed.

The law attempted to intervene, but nothing could be proved. So she was left to manufacture her marvels in peace.

She now has eleven of them alive, which bring her in from five to six thousand francs, year in and year out. One only is not yet placed, the one she would not show us. But she will not keep it long, for she is known now to all the circus proprietors in the world, and they come from time to time to see whether she has anything new.

She even arranges auctions between them, when the creature in question is worth it.

My friend was silent. A profound disgust surged in my heart, a furious anger, and regret that I had not strangled the brute when I had her in my hands.

"Then who is the father?" I asked.

"Nobody knows," he replied. "He or they have a certain modesty. He, or they, remain concealed. Perhaps they share in the spoils."

I had thought no more of that far-off adventure until the other day, at a fashionable watering-place, when I saw a charming and elegant lady, the most skilful of coquettes, surrounded by several men who have the highest regard for her.

I walked along the front, arm-in-arm with my friend, the local doctor. Ten minutes later I noticed a nurse looking after three children who were rolling about on the sand.

A pathetic little pair of crutches lay on the ground. Then I saw that the three children were deformed, hunch-backed and lame; hideous little creatures.

The doctor said to me: "Those are the offspring of the charming lady you met just now."

I felt a profound pity for her and for them.

"The poor mother!" I cried. "How does she still manage to laugh?"

"Don't pity her, my dear fellow," replied my friend. "It's the poor children who are to be pitied. That's the result of keeping the figure graceful right up to the last day. Those monsters are manufactured by corsets. She knows perfectly well that she's risking her life at that game. What does she care, so long as she remains pretty and seductive?"

And I remembered the other, the peasant woman, the She-devil, who sold hers.

EVELYN WAUGH

The Man Who Liked Dickens

Although Mr. McMaster had lived in Amazonas for nearly sixty years, no one except a few families of Shiriana Indians was aware of his existence. His house stood in a small savannah, one of those little patches of sand and grass that crop up occasionally in that neighbourhood, three miles or so across, bounded on all sides by forest.

The stream which watered it was not marked on any map; it ran through rapids, always dangerous and at most seasons of the year impassable, to join the upper waters of the River Uraricuera, whose course, though boldly delineated in every school atlas, is still largely conjectural. None of the inhabitants of the district, except Mr. McMaster, had ever heard of the republic of Colombia, Venezuela,

Brazil or Bolivia, each of whom had at one time or another claimed its possession.

Mr. McMaster's house was larger than those of his neighbours, but similar in character—a palm-thatch roof, breast-high walls of mud and wattle, and a mud floor. He owned a dozen or so head of puny cattle which grazed in the savannah, a plantation of cassava, some banana and mango trees, a dog, and, unique in the neighbourhood, a single-barrelled, breech-loading shotgun. The few commodities which he employed from the outside world came to him through a long succession of traders, passed from hand to hand, bartered for in a dozen languages at the extreme end of one of the longest threads in the web of commerce that spreads from Manaos into the remote fastness of the forest.

One day, while Mr. McMaster was engaged in filling some cartridges, a Shiriana came to him with the news that a white man was approaching through the forest, alone and very sick. He closed the cartridge and loaded his gun with it, put those that were finished into his pocket and set out in the direction indicated.

The man was already clear of the bush when Mr. McMaster reached him, sitting on the ground, clearly in a bad way. He was without hat or boots, and his clothes were so torn that it was only by the dampness of his body that they adhered to it; his feet were cut and grossly swollen, every exposed surface of skin was scarred by insect and bat bites; his eyes were wild with fever. He was talking to himself in delirium, but stopped when Mr. McMaster approached and addressed him in English.

"I'm tired," the man said; then: "Can't go on any farther. My name is Henty and I'm tired. Anderson died. That was a long time ago. I expect you think I'm very odd."

"I think you are ill, my friend."

"Just tired. It must be several months since I had anything to eat."

Mr. McMaster hoisted him to his feet and, supporting him by the arm, led him across the hummocks of grass towards the farm.

"It is a very short way. When we get there I will give you something to make you better."

"Jolly kind of you." Presently he said: "I say, you speak English. I'm English, too. My name is Henty."

"Well, Mr. Henty, you aren't to bother about anything more. You're ill and you've had a rough journey. I'll take care of you."

They went very slowly, but at length reached the house.

"Lie there in the hammock. I will fetch something for you."

Mr. McMaster went into the back room of the house and dragged a tin canister from under a heap of skins. It was full of a mixture of dried leaf and bark. He took a handful and went outside to the fire. When he returned he put one hand behind Henty's head and held up the concoction of herbs in a calabash for him to drink. He sipped, shuddering slightly at the bitterness. At last he finished it. Mr. McMaster threw out the dregs on the floor. Henty lay back in the hammock sobbing quietly. Soon he fell into a deep sleep.

"Ill-fated" was the epithet applied by the Press to the Anderson expedition to the Parima and upper Uraricuera region of Brazil. Every stage of the enterprise from the preliminary arrangements in London to its tragic dissolution in Amazonas was attacked by misfortune. It was due to one of the early setbacks that Paul Henty became connected with it.

He was not by nature an explorer; an even-tempered, good-looking young man of fastidious tastes and enviable possessions, unintellectual, but appreciative of fine architecture and the ballet, well travelled in the more accessible parts of the world, a collector though not a connoisseur, popular among hostesses, revered by his aunts. He was married to a lady of exceptional charm and beauty, and it was she who upset the good order of his life by confessing her affection for another man for the second time in the eight years of their marriage. The first occasion had been a short-lived infatuation with a tennis professional, the second was a captain in the Coldstream Guards, and more serious.

Henty's first thought under the shock of this revelation was to go out and dine alone. He was a member of four clubs, but at three of them he was liable to meet his wife's lover. Accordingly he chose one which he rarely frequented, a semi-intellectual company composed of publishers, barristers, and men of scholarship awaiting election to the Athenæum.

Here, after dinner, he fell into conversation with Professor Anderson and first heard of the proposed expedition to Brazil. The particular misfortune that was retarding arrangements at the moment was defalcation of the secretary with two-thirds of the expedition's capital. The principals were ready—Professor Anderson, Dr. Simmons the anthropologist, Mr. Necher the biologist, Mr. Brough the surveyor, wireless operator and mechanic—the scientific and sporting apparatus was packed up in crates ready to be embarked, the necessary facilities had been stamped and signed by the proper authorities but unless twelve hundred pounds was forthcoming the whole thing would have to be abandoned.

Henty, as has been suggested, was a man of comfortable means; the expedition would last from nine months to a year; he could shut his country house—his wife, he reflected, would want to remain in London near her young man—and cover more than the sum required. There was a glamour about the whole journey which might, he felt, move even his wife's sympathies. There and then, over the club fire, he decided to accompany Professor Anderson.

When he went home that evening he announced to his wife: "I have decided what I shall do."

"Yes, darling?"

"You are certain that you no longer love me?"

"*Darling*, you *know*, I *adore* you."

"But you are certain you love this guardsman, Tony what-ever-his-name-is, more?"

"Oh, yes, *ever* so much more. Quite a different thing altogether."

"Very well, then. I do not propose to do anything about a divorce for a year. You shall have time to think it over. I am leaving next week for the Uraricuera."

"Golly, where's that?"

"I am not perfectly sure. Somewhere in Brazil, I think. It is unexplored. I shall be away a year."

"But darling, how ordinary! Like people in books—big game, I mean, and all that."

"You have obviously already discovered that I am a very ordinary person."

"Now, Paul, don't be disagreeable—oh, there's the telephone. It's probably Tony. If it is, d'you mind terribly if I talk to him alone for a bit?"

But in the ten days of preparation that followed she showed greater tenderness, putting off her soldier twice in order to accompany Henty to the shops where he was choosing his equipment and insisting on his purchasing a worsted cummerbund. On his last evening she gave a supper-party for him at the Embassy to which she allowed him to ask any of his friends he liked; he could think of no one except Professor Anderson, who looked oddly dressed, danced tirelessly and was something of a failure with everyone. Next day Mrs. Henty came with her husband to the boat train and presented him with a pale blue, extravagantly soft blanket, in a suède case of the same colour furnished with a zip fastener and monogram. She kissed him good-bye and said, "Take care of yourself in wherever it is."

Had she gone as far as Southampton she might have witnessed two dramatic passages. Mr. Brough got no farther than the gangway before he was arrested for debt—a matter of £32; the publicity given to the dangers of the expedition was responsible for the action. Henty settled the account.

The second difficulty was not to be overcome so easily. Mr. Necher's mother was on the ship before them; she carried a missionary journal in which she had just read an account of the Brazilian forests. Nothing would induce her to permit her son's departure; she would remain on board until he came ashore with her. If necessary, she would sail with him, but go into those forests alone he should not. All argument was unavailing with the resolute old lady who eventually, five minutes before the time of embarkation, bore her son off in triumph, leaving the company without a biologist.

Nor was Mr. Brough's adherence long maintained. The ship in which they were travelling was a cruising liner taking passengers on a round voyage. Mr. Brough had not been on board a week and had scarcely accustomed himself to the motion of the ship before he was engaged to be married; he was still engaged, although to a different lady, when they reached Manaos and refused all inducements to proceed farther, borrowing his return fare from Henty and arriving back in Southampton engaged to the lady of his first choice, whom he immediately married.

In Brazil the officials to whom their credentials were addressed were all out of power. While Henty and Professor Anderson negotiated with the new administrators, Dr. Simmons proceeded up river to Boa Vista where he established a base camp with the greater part of the stores. These were instantly commandeered by the revolutionary garrison, and he himself imprisoned for some days and subjected to various humiliations which so enraged him that, when released, he made promptly for the coast, stopping at Manaos only long enough to inform his colleagues that he insisted on leaving his case personally before the central authorities at Rio.

Thus while they were still a month's journey from the start of their labours, Henty and Professor Anderson found themselves alone and deprived of the greater part of their supplies. The ignominy of immediate return was not to be borne. For a short time they considered the advisability of going into hiding for six months in Madeira or Teneriffe, but even there detection seemed probable, there had been too many photographs in the illustrated papers before they left London. Accordingly, in low spirits, the two explorers at last set out alone for the Uraricuera with little hope of accomplishing anything of any value to anyone.

For seven weeks they paddled through green, humid tunnels of forest. They took a few snapshots of naked, misanthropic Indians, bottled some snakes and later lost them when their canoe capsized in the rapids; they overtaxed their digestions, imbibing nauseous intoxicants at native galas, they were robbed of the last of their sugar by a Guianese prospector. Finally, Professor Anderson fell ill with malignant malaria, chattered feebly for some days in his hammock, lapsed into coma and died, leaving Henty alone with a dozen Maku oarsmen, none of whom spoke a word of any language known to him. They reversed their course and drifted down stream with a minimum of provisions and no mutual confidence.

One day, a week or so after Professor Anderson's death, Henty awoke to find that his boys and his canoe had disappeared during the night, leaving him with only his hammock and pyjamas some two or three hundred miles from the nearest Brazilian habitation. Nature forbade him to remain where he was although there seemed little purpose in moving. He set himself to follow the course of the stream, at first in the hope of meeting a canoe. But presently the whole forest became peopled for him with frantic apparitions, for no conscious reason at all. He plodded on, now wading in the water, now scrambling through the bush.

Vaguely at the back of his mind he had always believed that the jungle was a place full of food, that there was danger of snakes and savages and wild beasts, but not of starvation. But now he observed that this was far from being the case. The jungle consisted solely of immense tree trunks, embedded in a tangle of thorn and vine rope, all far from nutritious. On the first day he suffered hideously. Later he seemed anæsthetized and was chiefly embarrassed by the behaviour of the inhabitants who came out to meet him in footman's livery, carrying his dinner, and then irresponsibly disappeared or raised the covers of their dishes and revealed live tortoises. Many people who knew him in London appeared and ran round him with derisive cries, asking him questions to which he could not possibly know the answers. His wife came, too, and he was pleased to see her, assuming that she had got tired of her guardsman and was there to fetch him back, but she soon disappeared, like all the others.

It was then that he remembered that it was imperative for him to reach Manaos; he redoubled his energy, stumbling against boulders in the stream and getting caught up among the vines. "But I mustn't waste my breath," he reflected. Then he forgot that, too, and was conscious of nothing more until he found himself lying in a hammock in Mr. McMaster's house.

His recovery was slow. At first, days of lucidity alternated with delirium, then his temperature dropped and he was conscious even when most ill. The days of fever grew less frequent, finally occurring in the normal system of the tropics between long periods of comparative health. Mr. McMaster dosed him regularly with herbal remedies.

"It's very nasty," said Henty, "but it does do good."

"There is medicine for everything in the forest," said Mr. McMaster; "to make you well and to make you ill. My mother was an Indian and she taught me many of them. I have learned others from time to time from my wives. There are plants to cure you and give you fever, to kill you and send you mad, to keep away snakes, to intoxicate fish so that you can pick them out of the water with your hands like fruit from a tree. There are medicines even I do not know. They say that it is possible to bring dead people to life after they have begun to stink, but I have not seen it done."

"But surely you are English?"

"My father was—at least a Barbadian. He came to British Guiana as a missionary. He was married to a white woman but he left her in Guiana to look for gold. Then he took my mother. The Shiriana women are ugly but very devoted. I have had many. Most of the men and women living in this savannah are my children. That is why they obey—for that reason and because I have the gun. My father lived to a great age. It is not twenty years since he died. He was a man of education. Can you read?"

"Yes, of course."

"It is not everyone who is so fortunate. I cannot."

Henty laughed apologetically. "But I suppose you haven't much opportunity here."

"Oh, yes, that is just it. I have a great many books. I will show you when you are better. Until five years ago there was an Englishman—at least a black man, but he was well educated in Georgetown. He died. He used to read to me every day until he died. You shall read to me when you are better."

"I shall be delighted to."

"Yes, you shall read to me," Mr. McMaster repeated, nodding over the calabash.

During the early days of his convalescence Henty had little conversation with his host; he lay in the hammock staring up at the thatched roof and thinking about his wife, rehearsing over and over again different incidents in their life together, including her affairs with the tennis professional and the soldier. The days, exactly twelve hours each, passed without distinction. Mr. McMaster retired to sleep at sundown, leaving a little lamp burning—a hand-woven wick drooping from a pot of beef fat—to keep away vampire bats.

The first time that Henty left the house Mr. McMaster took him for a little stroll around the farm.

'I will show you the black man's grave," he said, leading him to a mound between the mango trees. "He was very kind to me. Every afternoon until he died, for two hours, he used to read to me. I think I will put up a cross—to commemorate his death and your arrival—a pretty idea. Do you believe in God?"

"I've never really thought about it much."

"You are perfectly right. I have thought about it a *great* deal and I still do not know ... Dickens did."

"I suppose so."

"Oh yes, it is apparent in all his books. You will see."

That afternoon Mr. McMaster began the construction of a headpiece for the negro's grave. He worked with a large spokeshave in a wood so hard that it grated and rang like metal.

At last when Henty had passed six or seven consecutive days without fever, Mr. McMaster said, "Now I think you are well enough to see the books."

At one end of the hut there was a kind of loft formed by a rough platform erected up in the eaves of the roof. Mr. McMaster propped a ladder against it and mounted. Henty followed, still unsteady after his illness. Mr. McMaster sat on the platform and Henty stood at the top of the ladder looking over. There was a heap of small bundles there, tied up with rag, palm leaf and raw hide.

"It has been hard to keep out the worms and ants. Two are practically destroyed. But there is an oil the Indians know how to make that is useful."

He unwrapped the nearest parcel and handed down a calf-bound book. It was an early American edition of *Bleak House*.

"It does not matter which we take first."

"You are fond of Dickens?"

"Why, yes, of course. More than fond, far more. You see, they are the only books I have ever heard. My father used to read them and then later the black man . . . and now you. I have heard them all several times by now but I never get tired; there is always more to be learned and noticed, so many characters, so many changes of scene, so many words. . . . I have all Dickens's books except those that the ants devoured. It takes a long time to read them all—more than two years."

"Well," said Henty lightly, "they will well last out my visit."

"Oh, I hope not. It is delightful to start again. Each time I think I find more to enjoy and admire."

They took down the first volume of *Bleak House* and that afternoon Henty had his first reading.

He had always rather enjoyed reading aloud and in the first year of marriage had shared several books in this way with his wife, until one day, in one of her rare moments of confidence, she remarked that it was torture to her. Sometimes after that he had thought it might be agreeable to have children to read to. But Mr. McMaster was a unique audience.

The old man sat astride his hammock opposite Henty, fixing him throughout with his eyes, and following the words, soundlessly, with his lips. Often when a new character was introduced he would say, "Repeat the name, I have forgotten him," or, "Yes, yes, I remember her well. She dies, poor woman." He would frequently interrupt with questions; not as Henty would have imagined about the circumstances of the story—such things as the procedure of the Lord Chancellor's Court or the social conventions of the time, though they must have been unintelligible, did not concern him—but always about the characters. "Now, why does she say that? Does she really mean it? Did she feel faint because of the heat of the fire or of something in that paper?" He laughed loudly at all the jokes and at some passages which did not seem humorous to Henty, asking him to repeat them two or three times; and later at the description of the sufferings of the outcasts in "Tom-all-alone" tears ran down his cheeks into his beard. His comments on the story were usually simple. "I think that Dedlock is a very proud man," or, "Mrs. Jellyby does not take enough care of her children." Henty enjoyed the readings almost as much as he did.

At the end of the first day the old man said, "You read beautifully, with a far better accent than the black man. And you explain better. It is almost as though my father were here again." And always at the end of a session he thanked his guest courteously. "I enjoyed that very much. It was an extremely distressing chapter. But, if I remember rightly, it will all turn out well."

By the time that they were well into the second volume, however, the novelty of the old man's delight had begun to wane, and Henty was feeling strong enough to be restless. He touched more than once on the subject of his departure, asking about canoes and rains and the possibility of finding guides. But Mr. McMaster seemed obtuse and paid no attention to these hints.

One day, running his thumb through the pages of *Bleak House* that remained to be read, Henty said, "We still have a lot to get through. I hope I shall be able to finish it before I go."

"Oh, yes," said Mr. McMaster. "Do not disturb yourself about that. You will have time to finish it, my friend."

For the first time Henty noticed something slightly menacing in his host's manner. That evening at supper, a brief meal of farine and dried beef eaten just before sundown, Henty renewed the subject.

"You know, Mr. McMaster, the time has come when I must be thinking about getting back to civilization. I have already imposed myself on your hospitality for too long."

Mr. McMaster bent over his plate, crunching mouthfuls of farine, but made no reply.

"How soon do you think I shall be able to get a boat? ... I said how soon do you think I shall be able to get a boat? I appreciate all your kindness to me more than I can say, but ..."

"My friend, any kindness I may have shown is amply repaid by your reading of Dickens. Do not let us mention the subject again."

"Well, I'm very glad you have enjoyed it. I have, too. But I really must be thinking of getting back ..."

"Yes," said Mr. McMaster. "The black man was like that. He thought of it all the time. But he died here ..."

Twice during the next day Henty opened the subject but his host was evasive. Finally he said, "Forgive me, Mr. McMaster, but I really must press the point. When can I get a boat?"

"There is no boat."

"Well, the Indians can build one."

"You must wait for the rains. There is not enough water in the river now."

"How long will that be?"

"A month ... two months ..."

They had finished *Bleak House* and were nearing the end of *Dombey and Son* when the rain came.

"Now it is time to make preparations to go."

"Oh, that is impossible. The Indians will not make a boat during the rainy season—it is one of their superstitions."

"You might have told me."

"Did I not mention it? I forgot."

Next morning Henty went out alone while his host was busy, and, looking as aimless as he could, strolled across the savannah to the group of Indian houses.

There were four or five Shirianas sitting in one of the doorways. They did not look up as he approached them. He addressed them in the few words of Maku he had acquired during the journey but they made no sign whether they understood him or not. Then he drew a sketch of a canoe in the sand, he went through some vague motions of carpentry, pointed from them to him, then made motions of giving something to them and scratched out the outlines of a gun and a hat and a few other recognizable articles of trade. One of the women giggled, but no one gave any sign of comprehension, and he went away unsatisfied.

At their midday meal Mr. McMaster said: "Mr. Henty, the Indians tell me you have been trying to speak with them. It is easier that you say anything you wish through me. You realize, do you not, that they would do nothing without my authority. They regard themselves, quite rightly in most cases, as my children."

"Well, as a matter of fact, I was asking them about a canoe."

"So they gave me to understand ... and now if you have finished your meal perhaps we might have another chapter. I am quite absorbed in the book."

They finished *Dombey and Son*; nearly a year had passed since Henty had left England, and his gloomy foreboding of permanent exile became suddenly acute when, between the pages of *Martin Chuzzlewit*, he found a document written in pencil in irregular characters.

Year 1919
   I James McMaster of Brazil do swear to Barnabas Washington of Georgetown that if he finish this book in fact Martin Chuzzlewit I will let him go away back as soon as finished.

There followed a heavy pencil *X*, and after it: *Mr. McMaster made this mark signed Barnabas Washington.*

"Mr. McMaster," said Henty, "I must speak frankly. You saved my life, and when I get back to civilization I will reward you to the best of my ability. I will give you anything within reason. But at present you are keeping me here against my will. I demand to be released."

"But, my friend, what is keeping you? You are under no restraint. Go when you like."

"You know very well that I can't get away without your help."

"In that case you must humour an old man. Read me another chapter."

"Mr. McMaster, I swear by anything you like that when I get to Manaos I will find someone to take my place. I will pay a man to read to you all day."

"But I have no need of another man. You read so well."

"I have read for the last time."

"I hope not," said Mr. McMaster politely.

That evening at supper only one plate of dried meat and farine was brought in and Mr. McMaster ate alone. Henty lay without speaking, staring at the thatch.

Next day at noon a single plate was put before Mr. McMaster, but with it lay his gun, cocked, on his knee, as he ate. Henty resumed the reading of *Martin Chuzzlewit* where it had been interrupted.

Weeks passed hopelessly. They read *Nicholas Nickleby* and *Little Dorrit* and

Oliver Twist. Then a stranger arrived in the savannah, a half-caste prospector, one
of that lonely order of men who wander for a lifetime through the forests, tracing
the little streams, sifting the gravel and, ounce by ounce, filling the little leather
sack of gold dust, more often than not dying of exposure and starvation with five
hundred dollars' worth of gold hung round their necks. Mr. McMaster was vexed
at his arrival, gave him farine and *passo* and sent him on his journey within an hour
of his arrival, but in that hour Henty had time to scribble his name on a slip of
paper and put it into the man's hand.

From now on there was hope. The days followed their unvarying routine; coffee
at sunrise, a morning of inaction while Mr. McMaster pottered about on the
business of the farm, farine and *passo* at noon, Dickens in the afternoon, farine and
passo and sometimes some fruit for supper, silence from sunset to dawn with the
small wick glowing in the beef fat and the palm thatch overhead dimly discernible:
but Henty lived in quiet confidence and expectation.

Some time, this year or the next, the prospector would arrive at a Brazilian
village with news of his discovery. The disasters to the Anderson expedition would
not have passed unnoticed. Henty could imagine the headlines that must have
appeared in the popular Press; even now probably there were search parties
working over the country he had crossed; any day English voices might sound over
the savannah and a dozen friendly adventurers come crashing through the bush.
Even as he was reading, while his lips mechanically followed the printed pages, his
mind wandered away from his eager, crazy host opposite, and he began to narrate
to himself incidents of his home-coming—the gradual re-encounters with civilization; he shaved and bought new clothes at Manaos, telegraphed for money,
received wires of congratulation; he enjoyed the leisurely river journey to Belem,
the big liner to Europe; savoured good claret and fresh meat and spring vegetables;
he was shy at meeting his wife and uncertain how to address her ... "*Darling,*
you've been much longer than you said. I quite thought you were lost. ..."

And then Mr. McMaster interrupted. "May I trouble you to read that passage
again? It is one I particularly enjoy."

The weeks passed; there was no sign of rescue, but Henty endured the day for
hope of what might happen on the morrow; he even felt a slight stirring of
cordiality towards his gaoler and was therefore quite willing to join him when, one
evening after a long conference with an Indian neighbour, he proposed a
celebration.

"It is one of the local feast days," he explained, "and they have been making
piwari. You may not like it, but you should try some. We will go across to this
man's home to-night."

Accordingly after supper they joined a party of Indians that were assembled
round the fire in one of the huts at the other side of the savannah. They were
singing in an apathetic, monotonous manner and passing a large calabash of liquid
from mouth to mouth. Separate bowls were brought for Henty and Mr.
McMaster, and they were given hammocks to sit in.

"You must drink it all without lowering the cup. That is the etiquette."

Henty gulped the dark liquid, trying not to taste it. But it was not unpleasant,
hard and muddy on the palate like most of the beverages he had been offered in
Brazil, but with a flavour of honey and brown bread. He leant back in the

hammock feeling unusually contented. Perhaps at that very moment the search party was in camp a few hours' journey from them. Meanwhile he was warm and drowsy. The cadence of song rose and fell interminably, liturgically. Another calabash of *piwari* was offered him and he handed it back empty. He lay full length watching the play of shadows on the thatch as the Shirianas began to dance. Then he shut his eyes and thought of England and his wife and fell asleep.

He awoke, still in the Indian hut, with the impression that he had outslept his usual hour. By the position of the sun he knew it was late afternoon. No one else was about. He looked for his watch and found to his surprise that it was not on his wrist. He had left it in the house, he supposed, before coming to the party.

"I must have been tight last night," he reflected. "Treacherous drink, that." He had a headache and feared a recurrence of fever. He found when he set his feet to the ground that he stood with difficulty; his walk was unsteady and his mind confused as it had been during the first weeks of his convalescence. On the way across the savannah he was obliged to stop more than once, shutting his eyes and breathing deeply. When he reached the house he found Mr. McMaster sitting there.

"Ah, my friend, you are late for the reading this afternoon. There is scarcely another half-hour of light. How do you feel?"

"Rotten. That drink doesn't seem to agree with me."

"I will give you something to make you better. The forest has remedies for everything; to make you awake and to make you sleep."

"You haven't seen my watch anywhere?"

"You have missed it?"

"Yes. I thought I was wearing it. I say, I've never slept so long."

"Not since you were a baby. Do you know how long? Two days."

"Nonsense. I can't have."

"Yes, indeed. It is a long time. It is a pity because you missed our guests."

"Guests?"

"Why, yes. I have been quite gay while you were asleep. Three men from outside. Englishmen. It is a pity you missed them. A pity for them, too, as they particularly wished to see you. But what could I do? You were so sound asleep. They had come all the way to find you, so—I thought you would not mind—as you could not greet them yourself I gave them a little souvenir, your watch. They wanted something to take home to your wife who is offering a great reward for news of you. They were very pleased with it. And they took some photographs of the little cross I put up to commemorate your coming. They were pleased with that, too. They were very easily pleased. But I do not suppose they will visit us again, our life here is so retired ... no pleasures except reading ... I do not suppose we shall ever have visitors again ... well, well, I will get you some medicine to make you feel better. Your head aches, does it not.... We will not have any Dickens to-day ... but to-morrow, and the day after that, and the day after that. Let us read *Little Dorrit* again. There are passages in that book I can never hear without the temptation to weep."

I IS FOR INSIDIOUS INSECTS

PAUL S. POWERS

Monsters of the Pit

How did I lose my left arm? Well, gentlemen, I have felt that question coming for a long time, and to tell the truth about the matter, I rather dreaded it. For, as well as I have grown to know you during these lonesome nights at the club, I never thought the time would come when I could unburden my mind. I don't expect that you will believe me, either you, Bronson, or Roberts, here. I tried to tell the story once before, to a French doctor at Port Said. He laughed at me at first, and thought me insane afterwards. I won't blame you for doing the same. Sometimes I hardly believe the story myself. It seems more like a nightmare than a reality. But here's the proof, gentlemen—this poor stump that was once a fairly serviceable left arm. It looks like a neat surgical operation, doesn't it? But it took my wife three hacks to get it off.

Waiter! Bring the vermouth! There, thank you. You look startled, gentlemen. Perhaps you'd better have a drop of the wine to take the chill of the London fog from your bones. Beastly night, outside. No, I wasn't joking, Bronson, and if you'll be so good as to hand me a cigarette, I'll tell the tale—spin the yarn, as you Americans put it. You won't believe the story, but that makes little difference. I think there is a little saying in your country: "If you believe it, it's true."

It happened four years ago when I was down at Port Said with the engineering company. I was a single man, then, with not a thought in the world other than to take my good money while I could get it, and to get out when there was no more to be had. It was good pay, but rotten work in a rottener country. The town wasn't bad for a headquarters, but it was the trips into the interior that broke us down—from the chief engineer to Tubbs, the youngest apprentice. A year or two and the average man was done, in that country. I saw three white men sent back to the coast on litters, and two more went back in a more gruesome condition. When it wasn't the fever it was the insects, and usually it was both. The snakes and the flies weren't so bad, for a man can kill them, or some of them, but I'll never forget the breath of those awful swamps nor the touch of those ungodly creeping things that were bound to be in your boots in the morning and on your cot at night.

Well, it was half way across the native country that stretches between the company offices and Suakin. There were seven of us white men and a party of blacks. One of the black boys, however, I really grew to like and trust. He knew the country, the desert and the jungle; and he knew mules. He was in charge of the string we had with us. Kali was this remarkable fellow's name, and I suppose I am the only one who now remembers it.

Can you imagine seeing a beautiful English girl in a filthy native town in the depths of Africa? I couldn't either, until I saw her. Gad! She was white, and young! When I met her in that market place, with a basket on her arm and dressed like a nun, I got the biggest thrill of my life. She was about eighteen, and though I didn't see the beauty of her at the time, I was shocked beyond words. I learned afterward that I was the first Englishman she had ever seen, with the exception of her father—but more of that later. Just that glimpse was all I had that day, but it was enough to set me thinking.

The chief only laughed when I reached the camp with the news, but the chief was a steady old blighter with grandchildren in Southsea, so I didn't wonder. It was the same when I told the other men—they thought I had been drinking. But it was true, and, of course, I asked Kali.

"Why, that is the daughter of the dread father, the mad white man," he winked over the cigarette I had given him. "But no—all white men are mad."

"And who," I asked, "is this white man?"

"A learned man," grinned Kali, "but mad, all the same. He was here when my father was as I am, and even then he was mad. If he was not mad, would he creep in the swamps and in the sand, even as the insects?"

"But how does he live?"

"Ah, he has gold—English gold. Two times, sometimes three times a year, he goes to the coast and brings back all manner of strange things. Wanaki, one of his blacks, once told me that he brought back devils in tiny bottles, from the English ships. To uncork the bottle means death—a terrible swelling death. Wanaki told of his devils and how a black boy died even as cattle die from the cobra. But there was no snake—there was only a white powder."

"Does the girl go with him on his trips to Port Said?"

"If she had, Wanaki would have told me. The girl child is made to stay with the black women. The white man is mad, and if you take the advice of Kali you will forget the white child woman in the long black dress."

Kali looked very wise indeed, and I believe he wanted another cigarette. I cursed him sourly and left him to his mules.

The sight of the woman had set something loose within me. You know well how it is in the wilderness, and it had been long weeks since we had left Port Said. To be sure, there were women there—of a kind. I wanted to know this girl, at least to learn something of her history. Kali's gossip had aroused my curiosity, though I did not believe him. Kali's great sin was his love for talk and his hatred for bare facts. But I vowed to see the girl again.

I'll pass over briefly the days that followed. The very afternoon following my talk with Kali I saw her again, but only a glimpse and she was gone. Then several days passed, and during them I learned more about the girl and her father. His name was Denham, a doctor, it appeared, with several letters tacked after his name—a scientist. Those were all the facts I could gather, and what he was doing and had been doing the past twenty years was a mystery. Collecting bugs? Possibly. But

Kali and the blacks swore that it was more than that—by the burial pits of their fathers it was more than that. He was a devil-devil doctor, and made the milk of the cows turn sour. He was a man-witch who poisoned the swamps, and talked with the spiders at evil hours of the night. He was also a number of other undesirable things, according to the superstitious Kali, who continued to divulge more or less valuable information over my cigarettes.

Then came the day when I met the girl face to face. And that day I learned more than ever before, though what I heard scarcely satisfied me.

The girl was timid, and though she permitted me to walk with her a short distance, I left her more disturbed than before. "Yes," she said, "she was English, though born in Africa." She had never seen England, having been no further than Port Said, and then only once, when a mere baby. Her mother? She did not remember her mother, and she had never heard the English tongue spoken except by her father. This was practically all she told me, but it made me long to hear more.

On that short walk with her I learned several important details, not the least important of which was the fact that she was even prettier than I had at first supposed. And she had been well educated—the professor evidently was an excellent teacher—and she had mentioned books, many books. The next morning I was waiting in the market place.

She came. It was more than I had hoped. Why bore you with details, gentlemen? I met her again and again, and grew to know her better than myself. Yes, I was in love, and beyond that there's no explanation needed, I'm sure.

We talked of many things during that first short week of our acquaintance, and on one subject only was she elusive: her father. Of her father only, she would not speak. When I spoke of him she would turn away with a look on her face much akin to fear. But perhaps I was mistaken. As we grew more intimate it grew upon me that her father, even if he was the dreadful being Kali had made him out to be, was at least a wonderful scholar. I could read it in this child. She was wonderful. In most respects she astounded me with her learning, and then at other times she would show an ignorance that was pathetic. The man she called father had moulded her mind to suit his will, but there is that something about a woman's mind, gentlemen, that no earthly cunning can twist from its course. I began to read it in her eyes that she cared for me more than her innocence knew. I haven't told you her name. It was Irene Denham.

"I would like very much to meet your father," I ventured one evening. "Doesn't he know that you are meeting me here?"

She hesitated.

"I have told him of you, Scott," she admitted. "And—well, he doesn't exactly approve. Of course, it's because he doesn't know you," she added hastily, "but when I suggested that you visit us at our home on the veldt, he was very angry. Father is like that—sometimes I think he hates all white men. I think it's because he's so wrapped up in his work, the work he has been carrying on for twenty years. But to-morrow, Scott, if you will come—"

I shook my head.

"Not if he disapproves of it," I began, and then I had a sudden thought. I would go and, moreover, I would come to an understanding with this man. Surely, I had

the right, at least, for I was determined to take Irene back to England with me. There was no other course open—I would see Professor Denham, and see him the very next day. I told the girl of my plans—and, well, gentlemen, I won't go into details—but she accepted them. I would meet her in the dirty little market place the next morning, we agreed, and would accompany her home.

I found Kali very much worried that night, and when I pressed for further information, and told him that I was planning to visit Professor Denham the next day, he told me bluntly that I would soon die.

"Nonsense, Kali," I laughed. "Why, I expect to find a respectable old naturalist and a fine collection of ants and butterflies. He's harmless. In my country no one is ever frightened at their doings. He's what is called a scientist, Kali."

"One of the black fellah boys from beyond the village told me to watch my mules," answered Kali. "He told me, also, that the white witch-man has been stealing his cattle. What does he do with the cattle? He takes them into dark pits within his great stone house. Tell me, do butterflies eat cattle".

I was getting very angry, and could have taken the impudent black scoundrel by the throat with pleasure.

"Hold your tongue!" I commanded, but when I left his hut Kali was smoking one of my cigarettes, all the same. This really was getting interesting. On the morrow, I told myself, I would know just how much Kali had lied. At the time I put the whole story down as the product of Kali's vivid if not convincing, creative imagination. I was in love. The next morning, *the* morning, I varnished my boots carefully, and put on my best khaki breeches. I would have given a small fortune for the white linen ones of the chief engineer, but I didn't dare ask him for them. It was hard enough to get away for the day.

Irene was at our rendezvous, and I received the thrill of my life when I saw that she had discarded her nun-like dress for one more fitting to the occasion. It seemed to me to be rather a makeshift affair, but it became her—it brought out beauty that I had not thought her to possess. She was a man's woman, was Irene!

"I don't know why, dear, but I dread the meeting between you and father," she murmured.

We had left the village and were climbing a baking sand dune.

"It won't be so bad," I said, cheerfully. "My education hasn't been along the same lines as your father's, and perhaps he won't be interested in me, yet perhaps we shall have some things in common. A white man, you know, is a white man, and even Africa can't change him. I'll wager you that the first question he asks me is, 'Have you an old London *Times* with you?' "

"White men have been near the village before," insisted the girl. "Never has he admitted them to our home, although one was a scientist like him—an explorer. I believe he hates all men—all mankind. True, he finally gave permission to bring you, but I'm afraid—"

"Does he love—you?" I asked.

"I don't know. There was a time when I was sure he did, just as there were times when he would bring flowers from our garden and put them upon my mother's grave, but for many years he has been changed. He hates the world—he plans to destroy—"

She did not finish the sentence, but stopped as if a cold hand had been laid across her red lips. She paled, and I saw that she was trembling. When I pressed her for an explanation, she changed the subject with a frightened, pathetic smile. From that moment on I felt that a chill had crept down from the dunes like a breath from the swamps. We walked on in silence.

"There!" she said, when we had reached the top of a little hillock. "There is—home."

Home! So this was her home! A melancholy house of stone, crumbling like an ancient ruin. It seemed strangely out of place here in this desolation. It belonged to Carthage, or perhaps to some long dead city. And this child lived here! I shuddered, even though the heat was flickering in waves across the distant veldt.

Her steps became slower, as we approached, and she seemed to be labouring under a clutching fear. I remember that the few cheerful and rather idiotic remarks I made fell flat, and truly I was in no mood for jesting.

As we neared the house I could see half a dozen black slaves working about the *kraal*, but I could see no sign of life within the house. It was fearfully hot, and far, far to the east, I thought I could make out the distant line of the sea, but I knew it was a mirage.

Well, I met Dr. Denham. We had entered the coolness of the hallway, and as I stood wondering what fashion of man it was who had furnished this dreary place so well, I saw a smiling face peering at us from beyond the draperies.

"Mr. Scott, I presume?"

A soft voice, and it fitted the man. In the semi-darkness, which was the nearest approach to comfort in sweltering British East Africa, I saw Irene's father. A man of fifty, perhaps, smooth-shaven and neatly dressed in white. The mouth under his rather hooked nose was curved into a smile, and yet, somehow, I felt chilled. No smile of welcome that! Not that there was anything alarming about the doctor's appearance, for he was nearly as I had pictured him, with his scholarly spectacles and abstracted manner. A naturalist and scientist, he looked his part. I bowed.

"I am very glad to know you, Professor Denham," I said, and extended my hand.

That handclasp was like ice! Denham's skin was repulsively cold and moist, like that of a bloated leech. I shuddered, and looked at the man closely.

The eyes! The heavy lenses of his glasses failed to utterly conceal the serpentine power of those greenish eyes. They were at once the eyes of a hypnotist and snake charmer. Though the professor was smiling with his thin lips, the eyes remained icy and the skin across his lofty brows was wrinkled into a frown. I remember that he made a few commonplace remarks and invited me inside. Dinner, he said, would soon be served. He was happy to have an Englishman for his guest. Yes, it *was* lonely here, but he was fond of loneliness. All the time he was talking I could not keep my eyes from his face. There was some mystery here—some strange secret in this man's life. And Irene knew of it, for I remembered that little slip she had made while we were crossing the sands. She was worried now, and she was watching her father with mingled fear and apprehension, if I read aright.

At dinner, which was served by a good-looking black, the professor talked of many things. Did I like the country? When did I expect to return to Cairo and Port Said? He asked many questions, and for the first time since I met him I felt at ease. Perhaps I had been mistaken after all. First impressions do not always furnish one with a character guide. I warmed up, and we talked until late afternoon, over our wine. I was just about to come to the point, and tell him the real reason for my journey here, when he asked me to look at his specimens.

"Something that you'll find interesting, Mr. Scott, I'm sure," he smiled. "I doubt if you've ever seen anything like them. It has taken years for me to perfect my plans, and it is only recently that I have had any success. Do you know anything of bacteriology?"

"Very little," I confessed. "From what your daughter told me I thought your experiments were confined to insects. I did not know that bacteriology, too, was a hobby of yours, doctor."

He eyed me sharply.

"It's more than a hobby," he said, "as you will soon see. As for insects, well, you will see my insects—later."

I felt much like telling him that he need not go to that trouble. Creeping things had always horrified me, and I had seen quite enough of them since I had been working in Africa. However, it was my plan to keep him in good humour until we could reach an understanding, so I followed him into a distant portion of the great house.

"As far as bacteria are concerned," I told him, "I haven't even as much as peeped into a microscope."

Professor Denham laughed.

"Microscope!" he leered. "You won't need a magnifying glass to see my collection!"

Was the man mad? I felt a chill creep over me.

We had reached a sort of laboratory, and the professor withdrew a cloth from a glass case. I looked over his shoulder, then, and received one of the shocks of my life. What were these horrible squirming things? Not insects, for never in my dreams had I pictured things like these! They were writhing like maggots in a substance that appeared to be a sticky gelatine. Some of them resembled scorpions, but most of them were rod-shaped things the size of my little finger. They were moving, moving—never still.

"What—what are they?" I stammered in an awed voice.

"Bacilli," chuckled the doctor.

"You mean germs—of disease?" I asked, horrified.

"Exactly! What do you think of my work? I have multiplied them a million times, in size. Some of those organisms literally breathe death. It has taken me twenty years to find the secret, and do you know what it means? I am lord of the world!"

It was devilish, and I longed to get out of the room. This man was mad, surely, yet here was the hideous proof before me.

"There they are," went on the scientist, with a horrible smile. "There they are till I am ready to use them, safe in the glass case and in a culture medium of agar agar."

I wiped the cold sweat from my face, and told him that I had seen quite enough and was ready to leave.

"Not till you have seen the most interesting specimens in my exhibit of insect life," smiled the professor. "I wouldn't have you miss that, for worlds."

I wanted to tell him that I wouldn't see another sight like those writhing things in his laboratory for worlds, either, but I followed him from the room and into a corridor. A huge black was waiting for us there.

"Well, Sahem?" asked the professor, in a harsh metallic voice.

The black giant showed his teeth in a look of anxiety.

"The slaves, master," he muttered. "They threaten to fly. They are afraid, and even the cattle whip cannot make them stay longer. Some of them will talk, unless—"

The doctor whipped a revolver from his blouse and handed it to the great negro.

"Tell them that I will have them thrown into the great pit," he snarled, "if they breathe a word! Kill them, Sahem, if they do not obey; and as for yourself, if you make one slip, the black pit will yawn for your carcase also!"

The slave's face twitched with fear, and it was nearly livid when he bowed to the ground and backed out of the dank passage on his hands and knees. Before I had time to recover from my astonishment a terrible sound echoed at my feet. It was an agonized bellow, ending in a gurgling wail, and it seemed to come from a cavern under the house. The hair tightened on my scalp at that fearful sound—the death sound of some animal in fear and pain. For a moment I heard it and then it died suddenly away into silence.

"My God!" I whispered, "what was that?"

"I fancy," smiled the professor, cheerfully, "that it was an ox."

Kali's weird tale flashed through my head. Perhaps the talkative black man had not lied so much after all. There was a deeper mystery here than I had at first imagined, and for the moment my curiosity was stronger than my dread. While I followed the bobbing form of the scientist up the passage, I turned over in my mind all I had seen and heard. Again I seemed to see those horrible squirming things in the glass case, and once more I seemed to hear that awful wail. An ox! How long would this distorted nightmare last?

"Now, if you'll be so good," murmured the professor, "we will look over my collection of insects."

He had reached a trap-door and was tugging at the rope that raised it. It suddenly yawned open and I saw the first steps of a staircase leading somewhere down into the dark.

"We'll just leave the door open, so we can see," said the scientist, and he led the way cautiously down the wooden steps. With some misgiving I followed, keeping close to his back. The death cry of the ox still rang in my ears and I determined not to lose sight of my guide. Three steps, then four, then five. At that moment I heard steps on the passage above, and a second later saw Irene's white face framed in the square opening at my head.

"Oh, Scott," she whispered. "Come back—come back!"

Even as the words left her lips I saw a great black hand placed over her mouth, and caught a glimpse of the giant negro, his face distorted by a scowl of rage and fury. I leaped up the steps, and as I did so, down came the trap with a bang and I found myself scuffling in the dark with the professor.

I fought furiously, and was overpowering the wiry little fiend, when I felt myself hanging over the edge of a black void. Something seemed to whirl me closer and then I fell, with the doctor's insane laugh ringing in my ears.

Something strangely yielding broke my fall, something that felt like a suspended mass of silken rope. For a moment I was held there, and as the trap-door was opened above me, I saw the face of the professor looking down at me from above. So this was the pit! I struggled, and tried to wrench myself free from the tangling bands that bound me, for Irene's suppressed cry still echoed in my brain. In vain I tried to tear myself loose, and then, as my eyes grew accustomed to the faint light, I ceased. The silken strands that grasped my arms and legs were as large as my thumb, and held me like so much steel. The professor was leaning over the edge of the pit. He was speaking, and his voice was quivering with rage.

"Fool! Miserable fool!" he mocked. "So you sought to steal my daughter, did you? And she the future princess of the world! I know your kind, and now I can watch you die. Soon you will see my collection of *insects!*"

And then in the distant corner I could see a huge pair of phosphorescent eyes staring at me through the gloom—then another pair and another! They seemed to appear as if by magic from some dark recess within the pit. Then I saw what covered the floor of the place! Bones! Bones of cattle and of sheep! And in the maze of ropey threads about me hung the carcase of a great ox! I was being held in nothing less than the web of a monstrous spider!

I screamed, and as an echo to the scream I heard the throaty laugh of the demented man in the gallery. *Insects!* God! Great bloated spiders, foul and gigantic, were watching me from their awful lairs! Again I struggled to wrench myself away, but I fell exhausted. Then I saw the hideous monsters begin slowly to advance, and I felt the web tremble as if something of great weight was gliding upon it.

Above me and to the right was one of the ghastly spiders. I saw its multiple eyes watching me as it paused. Fangs, shining like polished ebony, protruded beneath those terrible eyes, and when I saw the thing perched on the great web ready to pounce upon me, I cried out in horror. The web shook again, and I closed my eyes and waited for the dreadful impact. Even now, gentlemen, the sight of a fly buzzing his wings in a spider's web makes me sick and weak. Why I did not faint then, I don't know. Perhaps I was too terror-stricken.

I believe the monster would have leaped at that instant had it not been for a cry on the other wall of the pit. At the sound I began to hope again. It was Irene.

She was descending by a ladder, under a large trap on the other side, doubtless the one through which the ox had been cast. In her hand was an axe.

"Leave me!" I shouted, sick with fear for her safety. "You cannot save me! Back! Back!"

But she came, and I saw the terrible thing above me turn on its great legs, and watch her. At that second I heard a yell of fury from the professor. He was descending a rope ladder on the other side of the pit, and was foaming with rage.

The great spider had faced me again, and I could feel its legs rasp against the web that held me. I saw that the monster was covered with hair, like a huge bear, though no bear was ever so disgustingly sickening as this dreadful thing. I felt like a helpless fish about to be seized by a bloated octopus. Yet once again it hesitated, as if not knowing whether to turn on Irene or the professor.

Irene reached me first, and her axe whistled through the air at my feet as she cut me loose from the tenacious web. As she did so the hideous monster leapt at her!

Like a steel trap and with terrible ferocity, the spider sprang, only to meet Irene's axe.

The keen edge of the tool sank into its horrible flesh. I wrenched the weapon from Irene's hand and finished the awful thing—saw it writhe out its death struggle, entangled by its own web. I struck again and again, and then threw aside the axe with a feeling of nausea and disgust. Irene clung to me and sobbed.

"Quick!" I cried, as I tore my eyes away from the throes of the monster I had killed. "Your father—look!"

The unfortunate professor was pinned under the dreadful body of another spider. It had sprung upon him while I was occupied with my own troubles.

Seizing the axe, I dashed toward him, taking care to avoid the treacherous web. I struck at the insect of hell with all my strength, and it turned upon me savagely. I saw those awful fangs poised above me as I struck again upward with the axe. My blow landed squarely, but it was too late to avoid the knifelike poison tubes. Something swept into my left hand like a razor, just as the dying and distended body of the spider bore me to the ground. I felt a fetid, cold breath on my neck and something flabby and soft seemed to encircle my chest. For a moment I lost consciousness.

The next thing I remembered was the sense of a great weight being removed from my body. I groaned, and sat upright. Irene helped me to my feet, and she was calm, though the dead body of the professor lay not three feet away. I had been too late, and the spider had accomplished his deadly work. The scientist had been killed by the product of his own insane cunning.

We made good our escape, and it was well, for if another spider—well, I had reached the limit of my sanity.

In the passageway, Irene caught a glimpse of my hand for the first time.

"Scott!" she screamed. "Look!"

My hand was enormously swollen, and even as I watched I could see a blue discolouration working its way toward my elbow. In the excitement I had forgotten the slash from the keen fangs of the spider. I was as good as doomed.

Irene still held the axe, and as I stood there, shaking like a leaf, she raised her eyes in a prayer for courage. I read the answer in her face, and without being told I laid down my swollen arm.

Well, gentlemen, it took her three hacks to get it off. How the blood was staunched I don't know, for the next thing I remember was being jolted along in an ox-cart, bound for the nearest surgeon. A native was driving, and I was feeling fine. My head was pillowed in Irene's lap. I looked back, then, and saw a red glow against the evening sky. The slaves had fired the place and fled. From what I have been able to learn, the spiders died in the ruins, for I've never seen a spider any bigger than my hand since that day. To tell the truth, I don't want to.

Irene married me at Cairo, and as soon as I was able, we left for England.

Now, there's the story, gentlemen; you may believe it or not. . . . Waiter, will you kindly bring another bottle of vermouth?

PHILIP K. DICK
Expendable

The man came out on the front porch and examined the day. Bright and cold—with dew on the lawns. He buttoned his coat and put his hands in his pockets.

As the man started down the steps the two caterpillars waiting by the mailbox twitched with interest.

"There he goes," the first one said. "Send in your report."

As the other began to rotate his vanes the man stopped, turning quickly.

"I heard that," he said. He brought his foot down against the wall, scraping the caterpillars off, onto the concrete. He crushed them.

Then he hurried down the path to the sidewalk. As he walked he looked around him. In the cherry tree a bird was hopping, pecking bright-eyed at the cherries. The man studied him. All right? Or— The bird flew off. Birds all right. No harm from them.

He went on. At the corner he brushed against a spider web, crossed from the bushes to the telephone pole. His heart pounded. He tore away, batting in the air. As he went on he glanced over his shoulder. The spider was coming slowly down the bush, feeling out the damage to his web.

Hard to tell about spiders. Difficult to figure out. More facts needed— No contact, yet.

He waited at the bus stop, stomping his feet to keep them warm.

The bus came and he boarded it, feeling a sudden pleasure as he took his seat with all the warm, silent people, staring indifferently ahead. A vague flow of security poured through him.

He grinned, and relaxed, the first time in days.

The bus went down the street.

Tirmus waved his antennae excitedly.

"Vote, then, if you want." He hurried past them, up onto the mound. "But let me say what I said yesterday, before you start."

"We already know it all," Lala said impatiently. "Let's get moving. We have the plans worked out. What's holding us up?"

"More reason for me to speak." Tirmus gazed around at the assembled gods. "The entire Hill is ready to march against the giant in question. Why? We know he can't communicate to his fellows— It's out of the question. The type of vibration, the language they use makes it impossible to convey such ideas as he holds about us, about our—"

"Nonsense." Lala stepped up. "Giants communicate well enough."

"There is no record of a giant having made known information about us!"

The army moved restlessly.

"Go ahead," Tirmus said. "But it's a waste of effort. He's harmless—cut off. Why take all the time and—"

"Harmless?" Lala stared at him. "Don't you understand? He knows!"

Tirmus walked away from the mound. "I'm against unnecessary violence. We should save our strength. Someday we'll need it."

The vote was taken. As expected, the army was in favor of moving against the giant. Tirmus sighed and began stroking out the plans on the ground.

"This is the location that he takes. He can be expected to appear there at period-end. Now, as I see the situation—"

He went on, laying out the plans in the soft soil.

One of the gods leaned toward another, antennae touching. "This giant. He doesn't stand a chance. In a way, I feel sorry for him. How'd he happen to butt in?"

"Accident." The other grinned. "You know, the way they do, barging around."

"It's too bad for him, though."

It was nightfall. The street was dark and deserted. Along the sidewalk the man came, a newspaper under his arm. He walked quickly, glancing around him. He skirted the big tree growing by the curb and leaped agilely into the street. He crossed the street and gained the opposite side. As he turned the corner he entered the web, sewn from bush to telephone pole. Automatically he fought it, brushing it off him. As the strands broke a thin humming came to him, metallic and wiry.

". . . wait!"

He paused.

". . . careful . . . inside . . . wait. . . ."

His jaw set. The last strands broke in his hands and he walked on. Behind him the spider moved in the fragment of his web, watching. The man looked back.

"Nuts to you," he said. "I'm not taking any chances, standing there all tied up."

He went on, along the sidewalk, to his path. He skipped up the path, avoiding the darkening bushes. On the porch he found his key, fitting it into the lock.

He paused. Inside? Better than outside, especially at night. Night a bad time. Too much movement under the bushes. Not good. He opened the door and stepped inside. The rug lay ahead of him, a pool of blackness. Across on the other side he made out the form of the lamp.

Four steps to the lamp. His foot came up. He stopped.

What did the spider say? Wait? He waited, listening. Silence.

He took his cigarette lighter and flicked it on.

The carpet of ants swelled toward him, rising up in a flood. He leaped aside, out onto the porch. The ants came rushing, hurrying, scratching across the floor in the half-light.

The man jumped down to the ground and around the side of the house. When the first ants came flowing over the porch he was already spinning the faucet handle rapidly, gathering up the hose.

The burst of water lifted the ants up and scattered them, flinging them away. The man adusted the nozzle, squinting through the mist. He advanced, turning the hard stream from side to side.

"God damn you," he said, his teeth locked. "Waiting inside—"

He was frightened. Inside—never before! In the night cold sweat came out on his face. Inside. They had never got inside before. Maybe a moth or two, and flies, of course. But they were harmless, fluttery, noisy—

A carpet of ants!

Savagely, he sprayed them until they broke rank and fled into the lawn, into the bushes, under the house.

He sat down on the walk, holding the hose, trembling from head to foot.

They really meant it. Not an anger raid, annoyed, spasmodic; but planned, an attack, worked out. They had waited for him. One more step—

Thank God for the spider.

Presently he shut the hose off and stood up. No sound; silence everywhere. The bushes rustled suddenly. Beetle? Something black scurried—he put his foot on it. A messenger, probably. Fast runner. He went gingerly inside the dark house, feeling his way by the cigarette lighter.

Later, he sat on his desk, the spray gun beside him, heavy-duty steel and copper. He touched its damp surface with his fingers.

Seven o'clock. Behind him the radio played softly. He reached over and moved the desk lamp so that it shone on the floor beside the desk.

He lit a cigarette and took some writing paper and his fountain pen. He paused, thinking.

So they really wanted him, badly enough to plan it out. Bleak despair descended over him like a torrent. What could he do? Whom could he go to? Or tell? He clenched his fists, sitting bolt upright in the chair.

The spider slid down beside him onto the desk top. "Sorry. Hope you aren't frightened, as in the poem."

The man stared. "Are you the same one? The one at the corner? The one who warned me?"

"No. That's somebody else. A Spinner. I'm strictly a Cruncher. Look at my jaws." He opened and shut his mouth. "I bite them up."

The man smiled. "Good for you."

"Sure. Do you know how many there are of us in—say—an acre of land? Guess."

"A thousand."

"No. Two and a half million. Of all kinds. Crunchers, like me, or Spinners, or Stingers."

"Stingers?"

"The best. Let's see." The spider thought. "For instance, the black widow, as you call her. Very valuable." He paused. "Just one thing."

"What's that?"

"We have our problems. The gods—"

"Gods!"

"Ants, as you call them. The leaders. They're beyond us. Very unfortunate. They have an awful taste—makes one sick. We have to leave them for the birds."

The man stood up. "Birds? Are they—"

"Well, we have an arrangement. This has been going on for ages. I'll give you the story. We have some time left."

The man's heart contracted. "Time left? What do you mean?"

"Nothing. A little trouble later on, I understand. Let me give you the background. I don't think you know it."

"Go ahead. I'm listening." He stood up and began to walk back and forth.

"*They* were running the earth pretty well, about a billion years ago. You see, men came from some other planet. Which one? I don't know. They landed and found the earth quite well cultivated by them. There was a war."

"So we're the invaders," the man murmured.

"Sure. The war reduced both sides to barbarism, them and yourselves. You forgot how to attack, and they degenerated into closed social factions, ants, termites—"

"I see."

"The last group of you that knew the full story started us going. We were bred"—the spider chuckled in its own fashion—"bred someplace for this worthwhile purpose. We keep them down very well. You know what they call us? The Eaters. Unpleasant, isn't it?"

Two more spiders came drifting down on their web-strands, alighting on the desk. The three spiders went into a huddle.

"More serious than I thought," the Cruncher said easily. "Didn't know the whole dope. This Stinger here—"

The black widow came to the edge of the desk. "Giant," she piped, metallically. "I'd like to talk with you."

"Go ahead," the man said.

"There's going to be some trouble here. They're moving, coming here, a lot of them. We thought we'd stay with you awhile. Get in on it."

"I see." The man nodded. He licked his lips, running his fingers shakily through his hair. "Do you think—that is, what are the chances—"

"Chances?" The Stinger undulated thoughtfully. "Well, we've been in this work a long time. Almost a million years. I think that we have the edge over them, in spite of drawbacks. Our arrangements with the birds, and of course, with the toads—"

"I think we can save you," the Cruncher put in cheerfully. "As a matter of fact, we look forward to events like this."

From under the floor boards came a distant scratching sound, the noise of a multitude of tiny claws and wings, vibrating faintly, remotely. The man heard. His body sagged all over.

"You're really certain? You think you can do it?" He wiped the perspiration from his lips and picked up the spray gun, still listening.

The sound was growing, swelling beneath them, under the floor, under their feet. Outside the house bushes rustled and a few moths flew up against the window. Louder and louder the sound grew, beyond and below, everywhere, a rising hum of anger and determination. The man looked from side to side.

"You're sure you can do it?" he murmured. "You really can save me?"

"Oh," the Stinger said, embarrassed. "I didn't mean *that*. I meant the species, the race . . . not you as an individual."

The man gaped and the three Eaters shifted uneasily. More moths burst against the window. Under the floor stirred and heaved.

"I see," the man said. "I'm sorry I misunderstood you."

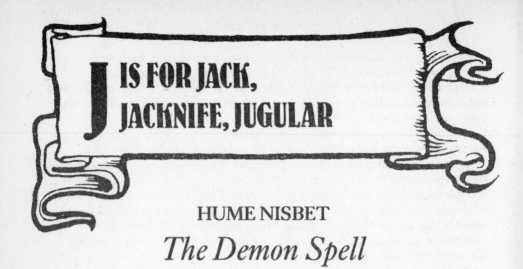

J IS FOR JACK, JACKNIFE, JUGULAR

HUME NISBET

The Demon Spell

It was about the time when spiritualism was all the craze in England, and no party was reckoned complete without a spirit-rapping séance being included amongst the other entertainments.

One night I had been invited to the house of a friend, who was a great believer in the manifestations from the unseen world, and who had asked for my special edification a well-known trance medium. "A pretty as well as a heaven-gifted girl, whom you will be sure to like, I know," he said as he asked me.

I did not believe much in the return of spirits, yet, thinking to be amused, consented to attend at the hour appointed. At that time I had just returned from a long sojourn abroad, and was in a very delicate state of health, easily impressed by outward influences, and nervous to a most extraordinary extent.

To the hour appointed I found myself at my friend's house, and was then introduced to the sitters who had assembled to witness the phenomena. Some were strangers like myself to the rules of the table, others who were adepts took their places at once in the order to which they had in former meetings attended. The trance medium had not yet arrived, and while waiting upon her coming we sat down and opened the séance with a hymn.

We had just finished the second verse when the door opened and the medium glided in, and took her place on a vacant seat by my side, joining with the others in the last verse, after which we all sat motionless with our hands resting upon the table, waiting upon the first manifestation from the unseen world.

Now, although I thought all this performance very ridiculous, there was something in the silence and the dim light, for the gas had been turned low down, and the room seemed filled with shadows; something about the fragile figure at my side, with her drooping head, which thrilled me with a curious sense of fear and icy horror such as I had never felt before.

I am not by nature imaginative or inclined to superstition, but, from the moment that young girl had entered the room, I felt as if a hand had been laid upon my heart, a cold iron hand, that was compressing it, and causing it to stop throbbing. My sense of hearing also had grown more acute and sensitive, so that the beating of the watch in my vest pocket sounded like the thumping of a quartz-crushing

140

machine, and the measured breathing of those about me as loud and nerve-disturbing as the snorting of a steam engine.

Only when I turned to look upon the trance medium did I become soothed; then it seemed as if a cold air wave had passed through my brain, subduing, for the time being, those awful sounds.

"She is possessed," whispered my host on the other side of me. "Wait, and she will speak presently, and tell us whom we have got beside us."

As we sat and waited the table had moved several times under our hands, while knockings at intervals took place in the table and all round the room, a most weird and blood-curdling, yet ridiculous performance, which made me feel half inclined to run out with fear, and half inclined to sit still and laugh; on the whole, I think, however, that horror had the more complete possession of me.

Presently she raised her head and laid her hand upon mine, beginning to speak in a strange monotonous, far-away voice, "This is my first visit since I passed from earth-life, and *you* have called me here.'

I shivered as her hand touched mine, but had no strength to withdraw it from her light, soft grasp.

"I am what you would call a lost soul; that is, I am in the lowest sphere. Last week I was in the body, but met my death down Whitechapel way. I was what you call an unfortunate, aye, unfortunate enough. Shall I tell you how it happened?'

The medium's eyes were closed, and whether it was my distorted imagination or not, she appeared to have grown older and decidedly debauched-looking since she sat down, or rather as if a light, filmy mask of degrading and soddened vice had replaced the former delicate features.

No one spoke, and the trance medium continued:

"I had been out all that day and without any luck or food, so that I was dragging my wearied body along through the slush and mud, for it had been wet all day, and I was drenched to the skin, and miserable, ah, ten thousand times more wretched than I am now, for the earth is a far worse hell for such as I than our hell here.

"I had importuned several passers-by as I went along that night, but none of them spoke to me, for work had been scarce all this winter, and I suppose I did not look so tempting as I have been; only once a man answered me, a dark-faced middle-sized man, with a soft voice, and much better dressed than my usual companions.

"He asked me where I was going, and then left me, putting a coin into my hand, for which I thanked him. Being just in time for the last public-house, I hurried up, but on going to the bar and looking at my hand, I found it to be a curious foreign coin, with outlandish figures on it, which the landlord would not take, so I went out again to the dark fog and rain without my drink after all.

"There was no use going any further that night. I turned up the court where my lodgings were, intending to go home and get a sleep, since I could get no food, when I felt something touch me softly from behind like as if someone had caught hold of my shawl; then I stopped and turned about to see who it was.

"I was alone, and with no one near me, nothing but fog and the half light from the court lamp. Yet I felt as if something had got hold of me, though I could not see what it was, and that it was gathering about me.

"I tried to scream out, but could not, as this unseen grasp closed upon my throat and choked me, and then I fell down and for a moment forgot everything.

"Next moment I woke up, outside my own poor mutilated body, and stood watching the fell work going on—as you see it now."

Yes, I saw it all as the medium ceased speaking, a mangled corpse lying on a muddy pavement, and a demoniac, dark, pock-marked face bending over it, with the lean claws outspread, and the dense fog instead of a body, like the half-formed incarnation of muscles.

"That is what did it, and you will know it again," she said, "I have come for you to find it."

"Is he an Englishman?" I gasped, as the vision faded away and the room once more became definite.

"It is neither man nor woman, but it lives as I do, it is with me now and may be with you tonight, still if you will have me instead of it, I can keep it back, only you must wish for *me* with all your might."

The séance was now becoming too horrible, and by general consent our host turned up the gas, and then I saw for the first time the medium, now relieved from her evil possession, a beautiful girl of about nineteen, with I think the most glorious brown eyes I had ever before looked into.

"Do you believe what you have been speaking about?" I asked her as we were sitting talking together.

"What was that?"

"About the murdered woman."

"I don't know anything at all, only that I have been sitting at the table. I never know what my trances are."

Was she speaking the truth? Her dark eyes looked truth, so that I could not doubt her.

That night when I went to my lodgings I must confess that it was some time before I could make up my mind to go to bed. I was decidedly upset and nervous, and wished that I had never gone to this spirit meeting, making a mental vow, as I threw off my clothes and hastily got into bed, that it was the last unholy gathering I would ever attend.

For the first time in my life I could not put out the gas, I felt as if the room was filled with ghosts, or as if this pair of ghastly spectres, the murderer and his victim, had accompanied me home, and were at that moment disputing the possession of me, so instead, I pulled the bedclothes over my head, it being a cold night, and went that fashion off to sleep.

Twelve o'clock! and the anniversary of the day that Christ was born. Yes, I heard it striking from the street spire and counted the strokes, slowly tolled out, listening to the echoes from other steeples, after this one had ceased, as I lay awake in that gas-lit room, feeling as if I was not alone this Christmas morn.

Thus, while I was trying to think what had made me wake so suddenly, I seemed to hear a far off echo cry "Come to me". At the same time the bedclothes were slowly pulled from the bed, and left in a confused mass on the floor.

"Is that you, Polly?" I cried, remembering the spirit séance, and the name by which the spirit had announced herself when she took possession.

Three distinct knocks resounded on the bedpost at my ear, the signal for "Yes".

"Can you speak to me?"

"Yes," an echo rather than a voice replied, while I felt my flesh creeping, yet strove to be brave.

"Can I see you?"

"No!"

"Feel you?"

Instantly the feeling of a light cold hand touched my brow and passed over my face.

"In God's name what do you want?"

"To save the girl I was *in* tonight. *It* is after her and will kill her if you do not come quickly."

In an instant I was out of bed, and tumbling my clothes on any way, horrified through it all, yet feeling as if Polly were helping me to dress. There was a Kandian dagger on my table which I had brought from Ceylon, an old dagger which I had bought for its antiquity and design, and this I snatched up as I left the room, with that light unseen hand leading me out of the house and along the deserted snow-covered streets.

I did not know where the trance medium lived, but I followed where that light grasp led me, through the wild, blinding snow-drift, round corners and through short cuts, with my head down and the flakes falling thickly about me, until at last I arrived at a silent square and in front of a house, which by some instinct, I knew that I must enter.

Over by the other side of the street I saw a man standing looking up to a dimly-lighted window, but I could not see him very distinctly and I did not pay much attention to him at the time, but rushed instead up the front steps and into the house, that unseen hand still pulling me forward.

How that door opened, or if it did open I could not say, I only know that I got in, as we get into places in a dream, and up the inner stairs, I passed into a bedroom where the light was burning dimly.

It was her bedroom, and she was struggling in the thug-like grasp of those same demon claws, with that demoniac face close to hers, and the rest of it drifting away to nothingness.

I saw it all at a glance, her half-naked form, with the disarranged bedclothes, as the uniformed demon of muscles clutched that delicate throat, and then I was at it like a fury with my Kandian dagger, slashing crossways at those cruel claws and that evil face, while blood streaks followed the course of my knife, making ugly stains, until at last it ceased struggling and disappeared like a horrid nightmare, as the half-strangled girl, now released from that fell grip, woke up the house with her screams, while from her relaxing hand dropped a strange coin, which I took possession of.

Thus I left her, feeling that my work was done, going downstairs as I had come up, without impediment or even seemingly, in the slightest degree, attracting the attention of the other inmates of the house, who rushed in their night-dresses towards the bedroom from whence the screams were issuing.

Into the street again, with that coin in one hand and my dagger in the other I rushed, and then I remembered the man whom I had seen looking up at the window. Was he there still? Yes, but on the ground in a confused black mass amongst the white snow as if he had been struck down.

I went over to where he lay and looked at him. Was he dead? Yes. I turned him round and saw that his throat was gashed from ear to ear, and all over his face—the same dark, pallid, pock-marked evil face, and claw-like hands, I saw the dark slashes of my Kandian dagger, while the soft white snow around him was stained with crimson life pools, and as I looked, I heard the clock strike one, while from the distance sounded the chant of the coming waits. Then I turned and fled blindly into the darkness.

K IS FOR KILLER KIDS, KRAKENS & KING KONG

RICHARD MATHESON
Born of Man and Woman

*This day when it had light mother called me retch. You retch she said. I saw in her eyes the anger. I wonder what it is a retch.

This day it had water falling from upstairs. It fell all around. I saw that. The ground of the back I watched from the little window. The ground it sucked up the water like thirsty lips. It drank too much and it got sick and runny brown. I didn't like it.

Mother is a pretty I know. I my bed place with cold walls around I have a paper things that was behind the furnace. It says on it SCREENSTARS. I see in the pictures faces like of mother and father. Father says they are pretty. Once he said it.

And also mother he said. Mother so pretty and me decent enough. Look at you he said and didnt have the nice face. I touched his arm and said it is alright father. He shook and pulled away where I couldnt reach.

Today mother let me off the chain a little so I could look out the little window. That's how I saw that water falling from upstairs.

**This day it had goldness in the upstairs. As I know when I looked at it my eyes hurt. After I look at it the cellar is red.

I think this was church. They leave the upstairs. The big machine swallows them and rolls out past and is gone. In the back part is the little mother. She is much small than me. I am I can see out the little window all I like.

In this day when it got dark I had eat my food and some bugs. I hear laughs upstairs. I like to know why they are laughs for. I took the chain from the wall and wrapped it around me. I walked squish to the stairs. They creak when I walk on them. My legs slip on them because I dont walk on stairs. My feet stick to the wood.

I went up and opened a door. It was a white place. White as white jewels that come from upstairs sometimes. I went in and stood quiet. I hear the laughing some more. I walk to the sound and look through to the people. More people than I thought was. I thought I should laugh with them.

Mother came out and pushed the door in. It hit me and hurt. I fell back on the smooth floor and the chain made noise. I cried. She made a hissing noise into her and put her hand on her mouth. Her eyes got big.

She looked at me. I heard father call. What fell he called. She said a iron board. Come help pick it up she said. He came and said now is *that* so heavy you need. He saw me and grew big. The anger came in his eyes. He hit me. I spilled some of the drip on the floor from one arm. It was not nice. It made ugly green on the floor.

Father told me to go to the cellar. I had to go. The light it hurt some now in my eyes. It is not so like that in the cellar.

Father tied my legs and arms up. He put me on my bed. Upstairs I heard laughing while I was quiet there looking on a black spider that was swinging down to me. I thought what father said. Ohgod he said. And only eight.

***This day father hit in the chain again before it had light. I have to try pull it out again. He said I was bad to come upstairs. He said never do that again or he would beat me hard. That hurts.

I hurt. I slept the day and rested my head against the cold wall. I thought of the white place upstairs.

****I got the chain from the wall out. Mother was upstairs. I heard little laughs very high. I looked out the window. I saw all little people like the little mother and little fathers too. They are pretty.

They were making nice noise and jumping around the ground. Their legs was moving hard. They are like mother and father. Mother says all right people look like they do.

One of the little fathers saw me. He pointed at the window. I let go and slid down the wall in the dark. I curled up as they would not see. I heard their talks by the window and foots running. Upstairs there was a door hitting. I heard the little mother call upstairs. I heard heavy steps and I rushed in my bed place. I hit the chain in the wall and lay down on my front.

I heard mother come down. Have you been at the window she said. I heard the anger. *Stay* away from the window. You have pulled the chain out again.

She took the stick and hit me with it. I didnt cry. I cant do that. But the drip ran all over the bed. She saw it and twisted away and made a noise. Oh mygod mygod she said why have you *done* this to me? I heard the stick go bounce on the stone floor. She ran upstairs. I slept the day.

*****This day it had water again. When mother was upstairs I heard the little one come slow down the steps. I hidded myself in the coal bin for mother would have anger if the little mother saw me.

She had a little live thing with her. It walked on the arms and had pointy ears. She said things to it.

It was all right except the live thing smelled me. It ran up the coal and looked down at me. The hairs stood up. In the throat it made an angry noise. I hissed but

it jumped on me.

I didnt want to hurt it. I got fear because it bit me harder than the rat does. I hurt and the little mother screamed. I grabbed the live thing tight. It made sounds I never heard. I pushed it all together. It was all lumpy and red on the black coal.

I hid there when mother called. I was afraid of the stick. She left. I crept over the coal with the thing. I hid it under my pillow and rested on it. I put the chain on the wall again.

*This is another times. Father chained me tight. I hurt because he beat me. This time I hit the stick out of his hands and made noise. He went away and his face was white. He ran out of my bed place and locked the door.

I am not so glad. All day it is cold in here. The chain comes slow out of the wall. And I have a bad anger with mother and father. I will show them. I will do what I did that once.

I will screech and laugh loud. I will run on the walls. Last I will hang head down by all my legs and laugh and drip green all over until they are sorry they didnt be nice to me.

If they try to beat me again Ill hurt them. I will.

P. SCHUYLER MILLER

The Thing on Outer Shoal

The first shock must've come about half past nine. It was in between the parts of that Sunday night concert Martha always listens to, during the talking, and I was up on a chair the way I always am at that time, winding the clock. I felt the chair sort of twist under me, and then the clock jumped off the mantel right into my face, and the two of us came down together with a bang.

I must've laid there stunned for a minute before Martha got to me, and I remember the feeling was like being up on a masthead in a high sea. It was like the whole earth was being sucked out from in under me, and then poured back, slow, like mud running into the hole where your foot has been. She had me by the arm, and I was getting my feet under me again when the second shock hit and both of us went down in a heap.

That was the bad one that smashed things all up and down the coast. We had the least of it, and we were high enough to miss the wave that came after it. It was different from the first one—grating and hard, like a ship driving on the rocks. The house jarred until the dishes flew off the shelves in the china closet and Martha's pots and pans came clattering down in a mess on the kitchen floor. The cat came flying through the room like it had fists and went scatting up the garret stairs, and then there was one last drop that nearly had my stomach out of me, and it was over.

I've been in quakes before, in Chile, and one time in Japan when I wasn't much more than a shaver, and I had a sort of notion there was more to come. I tried to put up the window, but the twisting the house had had made it stick, so I opened the front door and went out, with Martha right after me.

The fog was in. For two-three days it had been standing off shore and now it was in it was likely to stay. You couldn't see your hand on the end of your arm, but I knew that up on the point the way we are we'd be above anything that was apt to come.

We heard it, and then right away we smelled it—rank—full of the rotten muck it had raked up off the bottom of the sea, where things have been dying and settling into the mud for thousands and thousands of years. It sounded like the wind roaring, far away but coming closer, and the smell was enough to make a man gag. I could hear the buoy over Wilbur's Shoal clanging like mad, and I knew from the sound that it was adrift. Then the wave hit shore and I swear the whole point shook. The spray from it showered over us where we stood by the door, and then it struck again, not so hard, and that was the last except for the smell. We had that with us for a time.

We went back inside, because like I told Martha then, if any more was to come it wouldn't matter where we were, and a solid stone house like ours is a pretty safe place to be in come wind or high water. There's not many like it in the entire State of Maine.

I knew the first news would come over the Coast Guard station, so I turned the radio to where they are on the dial and sure enough, they were at it a'ready. It didn't make nice hearing. Aside from the earthquake, which was as bad as we've ever had in these parts, the wave had done a pile of damage all up and down the coast. Down through Massachusetts the big beaches had been swept clean, but it was after the main season and there wasn't many killed compared to what there might have been.

After a little they began to fit things together. The first quake had been pretty well out to sea—maybe twenty-thirty miles—and north of us, but the second one, the big one, was right off Phillipsport and close inshore. I've fished that bottom all my life, and I figured I could place it pretty close. There's a deep place—never sounded to my way of knowing—between Dorner's Bank and Outer Shoal, and the way it sounded that was where it was.

The fog was in and it stayed for three days. Fog don't bother me any, or Martha neither, so we went down to town next morning but there wasn't any news we hadn't heard on the radio. The Coast Guard plane was waiting for the fog to clear before it went up, and they were getting ready to make new soundings in case the bottom had changed. Up in Alaska there's places where whole mountains have come up out of the sea overnight, and then dropped back again.

The smell was everywhere—rotten fish and rotten seaweed—worse than a keg of lobster bait. We got used to it before the fog lifted. Between 'em the quake and the tidal wave had fetched up the ocean bottom for miles around, and it took a while to settle.

Along Wednesday afternoon you could begin to see a little. The sea off our point was milky, and kind of phosphorescent after sundown. There was all sorts of stuff piled up along the rocks—pieces of sunk ships, buoys, weed, shells, dead fish, lobster pots—every kind of thing. There were lobsters there bigger than any that's been caught in the State of Maine since my grandfather Phillip's time. There was halibut that would weigh up to six-seven hundred pounds, and every kind of fish that was ever in the sea. By Wednesday the smell it made was enough to drive us out, and Martha made me go down with a fork and bury what I could of it.

Wednesday night was clear as a bell, with the moon out full, and I heard the Coast Guard plane up a couple of times. Thursday morning I was up and out with the sun. There wasn't much to see. Clear out to the horizon the sea was chalky with the stuff that had been riled up off the bottom, and there were little black spots of drift that wouldn't likely come in for days. I got out my grandfather Waters' glass and went up on the roof, but it didn't do much good. The buoy was gone off Wilburs Shoal, like I thought, and so were all the channel markers. I heard in town that one of them fetched up on the veranda of the old Butler place, a good five miles back from the harbor up the inlet.

Out over Outer Shoal there was a kind of white cloud, and I watched it for a long time before I made out it was gulls—millions of 'em—swinging and swooping around over the shoal like they were following a school of mackerel. Then I heard the drone of a plane and picked it up, following the coast up from the south. It had Coast Guard markings, and pretty soon I heard our own plane sputter up off the water and swing over to meet it. They must've seen the gulls like I did, because they turned and circled out over the shoal. They were there a long time, swinging round and round like two big birds, and every now and then one of them would drop down to get a better look, but after a while they started back and I called to Martha and got my hat and went down to town to see what they had found out.

Well, sir, half the village was down to the Coast Guard station when I got there. The pilot from down the coast turned out to be a Phillipsport boy—Henry Anders' boy Jim—and when he saw me coming he let out a holler.

There was four-five people standing around the planes arguing—all of 'em men I'd been to sea with in my young days—and they were scratching their heads like chickens after corn. Fred Hibbard hailed me first.

"By gaggle," he shouted, "come down here! These boys has a puzzle none of us can answer. Tell him, Jim."

Jim grinned at me. He'd put on flesh since he joined up with the Coast Guard. "Hi there, Cap'n Waters," he said. "Maybe you can tell me more than these old salt-horses here. They claim what we saw on Outer Shoal isn't possible."

Tom Buck is our regular pilot here. "You were on the roof when I swung over," he put in. "Likely you saw the gulls over the shoal. We figured maybe a ship had gone aground and broken up, so we went out there, but it's no ship. We don't know what it is."

Old Colonel Phillips may be ninety and he's my own father's uncle, but he's the cussedest old fool in Phillipsport. He creaks like a rusty gate when he talks, and his store teeth don't fit him any better than you'd expect of a mail-order set, but he's never satisfied until he's had his say.

"Blasted young lubbers!" he piped up. "Smart-Alecks! taint no mystery to me, or no need for one! I remember twice in my life there's been a whale grounded on that shoal, and you look in the town records and you'll find plenty more. That wave'd fetch in anything afloat!"

"How do you feel about that?" I asked them.

Jim Anders scratched his head. He has tow hair like his father's folks. They were Swedes, wrecked here and settled, back in my father's time—first-class seamen, everyone of them. "Well," he admitted, "I suppose it could be. But if it is, it's the strangest whale I ever saw."

"We couldn't see much," Tom Buck explained. "The gulls have settled on it like flies on a lobster pot, and we couldn't drive 'em off. But it's big—big as any whale I ever laid eyes on—and it's funny shaped. And—it's white."

"What'd I tell you?" Colonel Phillips was just about prancing. "It's a white whale. Seen 'em many a time!"

"Belugas don't grow that big, Colonel," Buck told him. "And—the shape's wrong."

"Pish! Ever hear about Moby Dick? Ever hear about Killer Ned? There's white whales same as any animal, and most always they're big and mean. How is it now? Pretty ripe, ain't it? Any salvage to it?"

"We couldn't see," Jim told him. "It's no place to set down a plane, with all the drift afloat around the shoal. That quake brought up every derelict this side of the Azores. We've got days of work ahead, locating them. But if you old sea-horses can stand the stench, you might be able to pick up a little tobacco money out there. Whale oil's high."

I could tell then it wasn't only the old men who liked the idea, and I could tell it wasn't going by the board. We may be over sixty, some of us, but there are a few left who have shipped on whalers and know what to do and how to do it. When I went up to the store Henry Anders and Fred Hibbard and Welsh Peters and one or two others were with me, and we found a couple-three more in Clem Potter's back room. Likewise, I saw that the younger men were drifting into Tony Spillani's garage across the street.

It was going to be a race for it, and I could feel my blood getting up at the thought. Likely the young fellers would try to hold off till night and then slip away. We couldn't pull out right in front of 'em, because they'd beat us hull down, but we had to get there first. Then we all of us thought of the colonel.

He knew it, too. He sat back there in Clem's old armchair with a satisfied smirk under his whiskers, waiting for us to ask him. But he couldn't wait long.

"Remembered me, ain't you?" he demanded. "Remembered I got three whaleboats off the old *Minnie P*, in my boathouse this minute, with engines in 'em and all the gear complete. Remembered I got casks and irons and everything you need, over the other side of the point where there can't nobody tell what you're up to. Want 'em, don't you? Well—owner's third!"

The old skinflint had us, and it didn't matter much to any of us. It wasn't the oil we were after. It was wondering about the thing that had washed up on Outer Shoal—beating the young bucks at a game they figured we were too old for—having the kind of adventure that we all had thought was over and done with. It disappointed him a little when we took him up so quick. He just snorted and handed over the keys to the boathouse. Then an idea tickled him and he let out a cackle like a guinea hen. He poked Clem in the ribs with his cane.

"I'll fix those young squirts for you!" he vowed. "I know the way they're figgerin'. That man at the old livery stable has him a big new launch, an' that's the boat they'll use. That an' maybe Peters' and Crandall's. You gimme five pounds of sugar . . . no, by Jake, make it ten pounds . . . an' I'll go down sun myself a mite on the wharf while you're gettin' up a black-berryin' party over to my place. An' don't tell the wimmen!"

The old sculpin! There wasn't one of us would have thought of sugaring their gasoline.

The younger men were still in the garage with their heads together when we came out of the store. We split up—the colonel with his sugar sacks in his coat pockets headed for the wharf, and the rest of us scattering to meet along after dinner at the colonel's boathouse. That would give us the afternoon.

He was a shipshape old devil. Those three boats were as good as the day he got 'em, and the engines were tuned up fit to run a clock. Like as not he had some feller from out of town come and do it so's he wouldn't let on he cared how they were. There wasn't a speck of rust on his whaling irons, and his rope was new—brand new, but with the stiffness worked out of it. It was good gear, all of it. My point hid us from town and would until we were a good two miles out. The colonel's sugar would have to take care of things after that.

We manned two of the three boats. I was steersman in the first and the colonel took the second. We could reach the whale, mark it, and maybe cut a little blubber before nightfall. It was all any of us wanted—except maybe the colonel—the young folks could have the rest with our blessing, after they'd been put in their place.

They'd started up a game of baseball by the time the colonel left town, just to keep our suspicions down, but they must have posted a watch or else someone's wife blabbed. We weren't more than half a mile off the point when we heard the launch start up, and there they came, three boats of them, swinging across to cut us off. I could see the grin on Fred Hibbard's face as he monkeyed with our engine and made it cough and splutter like it wasn't going good. Let 'em be cocky while they could.

They passed us hooting and hollering like wild Indians, and after a time we passed them, lying in the swell, tinkering with their engines. The three boats were strung out over a mile or so of sea, and some of the boys were turning a little green. By that time we could see the shoal.

The smell of the thing and the cackle of the gulls reached us long before we sighted it. It was ripe, but it didn't smell like whale to me. It had that seabottom rankness that the quake had brought up, and I began to remember yarns I'd heard about sea serpents and the like of that.

There must have been all the gulls in Maine over that reef. The sea was white with them, bobbing around in the oil slick that had spread from the thing on the shoal. They were stuffed too full to fly, but they covered the thing from the water's edge where it lay awash until it was one big, stinking mountain of white feathers, sixty feet long if it was a yard. From the boats we couldn't tell much about how it looked, but it was—queer.

My boat was first, and we circled around it and came in from the seaward side, down wind. The gulls didn't rise until the boat was almost touching it, and when they did, I looked at the men and they looked at me. Their faces were funny-colored and I guess mine was, too, because it was a man.

The gulls had been at it for better than a day, but you could see it was a man. It was sixty feet from head to feet, more than fifteen feet across the shoulders, and it was a man. There was a layer of thick white blubber on it under a gray kind of skin. Big blue gills flared out where its neck should have been. And as the boat bumped against it a hand came floating up through the water beside me—wrinkled with the water, and webbed all the way to the tips of the fingers. It was a man.

A cloud had gone over the sun, and the wind was kind of cold on me. The smell of the thing choked me, and the screaming, wheeling birds overhead made my head swim. I reversed the engine and pulled us off a couple of lengths.

The gulls had been at it. All along its barrel of a body they had torn big, jagged holes through its skin and blubber and raw red meat, down to the white ribs. It lay on its face on the shoal, its back, where there was skin left, dull gray-white like a shark's belly. On its feet it would have looked kind of stubby, I guess, because it looked awful broad for its length, with big, powerful long arms made for swimming, and long, thick legs with webbed feet. Its face was under water, but it had no ears unless the gulls had torn them off, and its head was round and covered with stringy hair like a wad of dirty hemp.

It was a giant man out of deep part of the sea—the part that no man of our kind ever sees or hears tell of, except in sailors' yarns. The earthquake had vomited it up out of the sea to die here on Outer Shoal. The marks of the deep were on it, in the way Nature had made it to stand the pressure down there thousands of fathoms below, and in the great round scars that were on its back and sides. I knew those marks, and so did most of the others with me—we'd seen them often enough on whales. The Kraken had left them—the giant white squid that lives down in the cold and the black of the sea bottom where only whales go—and things like this.

Then I heard the colonel shout. He had climbed up on the dead thing's body and stood there between its gnarled shoulders looking down at us. Another figure bobbed up alongside him—Doc Higbee—and the two of them stooped down to study the thing they were standing on. Then the colonel straightened up as if he'd had a kink in his back and I heard him screech.

We had pulled off into the deep water that goes down like the side of a mountain off Outer Shoal. We had all been watching the two on the thing's back, but now we turned to look.

Out of the water a hundred feet away rose a face. Long hanks of grizzled hair hung over it, and out between them stared two huge, black, goggling eyes. There was a smear of white flesh between them where it should have had a nose. Its mouth stretched halfway across its head right under those staring eyes, and it was filled with little sharp pegs of teeth. The gills began below—a purple frill of flesh, opening and closing as it breathed. As it rose higher its mouth gaped open to suck in air, and I could see that it had no tongue.

It found footing on the shelving edge of the shoal, a boat's length away, before I had sense enough to move. Then I grabbed for the gas lever and we were hipering out of its way. But it didn't pay us any heed. The water was just under its armpits as it stood there, with its webbed hands floating on the water in front of it. It climbed higher—it was the sea-man's mate come after him out of the deeps!

The two men on the carcass were scrambling down the other side into their boat. The colonel made it, but Higbee slipped and splashed into the water. By now the woman-thing was standing knee-deep in the sea beside her mate. I wondered how she could support that monstrous body out of water, but she had giant's muscles. Her great saucer eyes stared at the dead thing, and one webbed hand took it by the shoulder and turned it over.

Then she saw the other boat. It had waited to pick up the doctor, and the men were struggling frantically over the engine with the little colonel hopping and cursing in the bow. She made a lunge toward it and stumbled over the carcass of her mate. The wash as she smashed into the sea nearly overset the boat, but they righted it and suddenly we heard the engine start. It sputtered a moment and stopped.

Jim Anders was harpooner on my father's whaler and he was bow man in my boat now. He got to his feet, picking up the heavy blubber spade at his side, as we came within range of the thing. It was never meant for throwing, but he hurled that iron like a lance. It struck the sea-woman's shoulder and sliced deep into the thick flesh, so that I could see the purplish blood running. She stopped, shoulder deep, and turned to face us.

Then, close by the colonel's boat and almost within reach of her groping hand the sea went suddenly white and smooth. A great, twisting tentacle went snaking out over the surface of the water and touched its thwart. Like a flash it clamped over the bow, inches from the colonel. A second followed it, and then the monster's body rose slowly out of the waves—two evil black pools of ink for eyes—a great white parrot beak—and surrounding them a nest of corpse-white tentacles. The Kraken!

It gave off a sickly kind of scent, and the sea-woman smelled it. She seemed to hunch down into the sea. They stared at each other for the space of a minute, and I saw its huge arm uncoiling from around the boat as it watched her. It was wary, but there was no fear in it—or her. Then, like lightning, she pounced; like coiling ropes its tentacles twined round her body, biting deep in the blubber.

Her strength was terrible. Her webbed fingers dug into the Kraken's rubbery flesh; the muscles swelled along her arms and across her naked back, and she tore the monster's body in her hands as if she was tearing rags. But it had its grip; its tentacles sucking and ripping at her leathery skin. One arm was bound fast to her body, and the tip of one tentacle was prying at her heaving gills.

Her legs were spread, her back bent; the muscles under her coat of blubber stood up in long, low ridges across her back as she set her fingers in the great squid's flesh and tore it loose. Those webbed fingers closed over its staring eyes and gaping beak and squeezed, and the flailing tentacles went limp.

She stood there, thigh-deep in the bloody sea, staring at the dead thing in her hands. She dropped it and her bulbous eyes swung slowly from one boat to the other. Suddenly she lunged forward and the water closed over her head. Then panic struck us.

We may have made ten boat lengths before she reached us. Out of the sea at my elbow the curve of her enormous shoulder rose against the boat. Her groping hand closed over the bow and pulled it under, hurling us over the side into the sea. As I came up, struggling for breath, I could hear the wood splinter in her fist. She dropped it and looked around her for us.

I hadn't heard the plane till then. We were too close for Jim Anders to use his gun, but he zoomed up past her face and she flinched back and batted at him like a kitten at a string. Her head swung around on her shoulders to watch him, and as he dived again she began to flounder away toward the shoal and the body of her dead mate.

That gave him an idea. The rap of his machine gun sounded over the whine of the diving plane—every Coast Guard plane had been armed since that trouble off Nantucket. Gouts of flesh spurted where the bullets struck the dead thing's pulpy form. The sea-woman was swimming frantically away from us. She found her footing again and pulled herself erect, her arms stretched up at the attacking plane. And Jim Anders dived for the third time and shot her down.

There was enough life left in her even then to carry her back into the deep out of which she came. Sometimes it seems that I can see her, swimming painfully down into the blackness and the cold and the quiet, until the last of her life flows out of her and she sinks down into the everlasting darkness where she was born. It was too bad it had to happen like it did.

We came out of it all right. Not even the colonel had more than a week's layup with his blood pressure. Of course we had to take a tongue-lashing from the womenfolks, but we'd figured on that anyway.

The boys in the launches were scared stiff. They'd seen the whole thing, but they couldn't raise a finger to help. The colonel had done a bang-up job on that gasoline.

We don't talk about it much in Phillipsport. Everyone in town knows about it, and it's no secret, but we don't like to talk about it much. It wasn't the kind of thing that sets well with a man.

It happened, though—no mistake about that. I have the proof. The pictures Tom Buck made before they bombed the thing to bits and let the sea have it again didn't come out. The gulls were back, and you can't see much but the shape of it. Far as I know, I have the only other proof there is. I got that from Doc Higbee the winter before he died.

Doc had had time, when he and the colonel landed on the thing, to slice off a chunk of skin and blubber and a mite of the flesh underneath. He kept them by him, even in the water, and stowed them away in alcohol when he got back.

The pieces of skin he got shows one of the great round scars that the Kraken left. Maybe they feed on each other, down there miles under the sea where nothing but whales ever get to. Doc said it was human skin. He said the blood in it is human blood, only just about as salty as sea water is today. He showed me a book where it tries to figure out when our first ancestors crawled out of the sea, millions of years back, by measuring the amount of salt in our blood and figuring the amount of salt there was in the sea then. He said they were supposed to match, otherwise things couldn't keep alive.

Suppose some of those things that turned into men stayed in the sea when our ancestors came out on land, Doc said. Suppose they went right on living in the sea, changing the same way the things on land did, growing big enough and strong enough to stand the pressure and the cold down there. They might change into things like the ones we saw, Doc said. There couldn't be many of them, he thought. There wouldn't be enough to eat, except for squids and whales and dead things that sank down from above.

There was a reporter from Boston, a year or two back, got wind of the story some way and tried to pump it out of us. He spent near a week here, I guess, talking to this one and that one. The way he had it, it was a sea serpent that was washed up on the shoal. Well, sir, after a while it got around to the colonel, and I never did hear the like of the yarn he told that man. It was too good. I guess the feller figured it was all lies, which it mostly was, and judged the rumor was the same. Anyway, we've never been bothered about it since—until now.

PHILIP JOSÉ FARMER
After King Kong Fell

The first half of the movie was grim and gray and somewhat tedious. Mr. Howller did not mind. That was, after all, realism. Those times had been grim and gray. Moreover, behind the tediousness was the promise of something vast and horrifying. The creeping pace and the measured ritualistic movements of the actors gave intimations of the workings of the gods. Unhurriedly, but with utmost confidence, the gods were directing events toward the climax.

Mr. Howller had felt that at the age of fifteen, and he felt it now while watching the show on TV at the age of fifty-five. Of course, when he first saw it in 1933, he had known what was coming. Hadn't he lived through some of the events only two years before that?

The old freighter, the *Wanderer*, was nosing blindly through the fog toward the surflike roar of the natives' drums. And then: the commercial. Mr. Howller rose and stepped into the hall and called down the steps loudly enough for Jill to hear him on the front porch. He thought, commercials could be a blessing. They give us time to get into the bathroom or the kitchen, or time to light up a cigarette and decide about continuing to watch this show or go on to that show.

And why couldn't real life have its commercials?

Wouldn't it be something to be grateful for if reality stopped in mid-course while the Big Salesman made His pitch? The car about to smash into you, the bullet on its way to your brain, the first cancer cell about to break loose, the boss reaching for the phone to call you in so he can fire you, the spermatozoon about to be launched toward the ovum, the final insult about to be hurled at the once, and perhaps still, beloved, the final drink of alcohol which would rupture the abused blood vessel, the decision which would lead to the light that would surely fail?

If only you could step out while the commercial interrupted these, think about it, talk about it, and then, returning to the set, switch it to another channel.

But that one is having technical difficulties, and the one after that is a talk show whose guest is the archangel Gabriel himself and after some urging by the host he agrees to blow his trumpet, and . . .

Jill entered, sat down, and began to munch the cookies and drink the lemonade he had prepared for her. Jill was six and a half years old and beautiful, but then what granddaughter wasn't beautiful? Jill was also unhappy because she had just quarreled with her best friend, Amy, who had stalked off with threats never to see Jill again. Mr. Howller reminded her that this had happened before and that Amy always came back the next day, if not sooner. To take her mind off of Amy, Mr. Howller gave her a brief outline of what had happened in the movie. Jill listened without enthusiasm, but she became excited enough once the movie had resumed. And when Kong was feeling over the edge of the abyss for John Driscoll, played by Bruce Cabot, she got into her grandfather's lap. She gave a little scream and put her hands over her eyes when Kong carried Ann Redman into the jungle (Ann played by Fay Wray).

But by the time Kong lay dead on Fifth Avenue, she was rooting for him, as millions had before her. Mr. Howller squeezed her and kissed her and said, "When your mother was about your age, I took her to see this. And when it was over, she was crying, too."

Jill sniffled and let him dry the tears with his handkerchief. When the Roadrunner cartoon came on, she got off his lap and went back to her cookie-munching. After a while she said, "Grandpa, the coyote falls off the cliff so far you can't even see him. When he hits, the whole earth shakes. But he always comes back, good as new. Why can he fall so far and not get hurt? Why couldn't King Kong fall and be just like new?"

Her grandparents and her mother had explained many times the distinction between a "live" and a "taped" show. It did not seem to make any difference how many times they explained. Somehow, in the years of watching TV, she had gotten the fixed idea that people in "live" shows actually suffered pain, sorrow, and death. The only shows she could endure seeing were those that her elders labeled as "taped." This worried Mr. Howller more than he admitted to his wife and daughter. Jill was a very bright child, but what if too many TV shows at too early an age had done her some irreparable harm? What if, a few years from now, she could easily see, and even define, the distinction between reality and unreality on the screen but deep down in her there was a child that could still not distinguish?

"You know that the Roadrunner is a series of pictures that move. People draw pictures, and people can do anything with pictures. So the Roadrunner is drawn again and again, and he's back in the next show with his wounds all healed and he's ready to make a jackass of himself again."

"A jackass? But he's a coyote."

"Now . . ."

Mr. Howller stopped. Jill was grinning.

"O.K., now you're pulling my leg."

"But is King Kong alive or is he taped?"

"Taped. Like the Disney I took you to see last week. *Bedknobs and Broomsticks*."

"Then *King Kong* didn't happen?"

"Oh, yes, it really happened. But this is a movie they made about King Kong after what really happened was all over. So it's not exactly like it really was, and actors took the parts of Ann Redman and Carl Denham and all the others. Except King Kong himself. He was a toy model."

Jill was silent for a minute and then she said, "You mean there really *was* a King

Kong? How do you know, Grandpa?"

"Because I was there in New York when Kong went on his rampage. I was in the theater when he broke loose, and I was in the crowd that gathered around Kong's body after he fell off the Empire State Building. I was thirteen then, just seven years older than you are now. I was with my parents, and they were visiting my Aunt Thea. She was beautiful, and she had golden hair just like Fay Wray's—I mean, Ann Redman's. She'd married a very rich man, and they had a big apartment high up in the clouds. In the Empire State Building itself."

"High up in the clouds! That must've been fun, Grandpa!"

It would have been, he thought, if there had not been so much tension in that apartment. Uncle Nate and Aunt Thea should have been happy because they were so rich and lived in such a swell place. But they weren't. No one said anything to young Tim Howller, but he felt the suppressed anger, heard the bite of tone, and saw the tightening lips. His aunt and uncle were having trouble of some sort, and his parents were upset by it. But they all tried to pretend everything was as sweet as honey when he was around.

Young Howller had been eager to accept the pretense. He didn't like to think that anybody could be mad at his tall, blonde, and beautiful aunt. He was passionately in love with her; he ached for her in the daytime; at nights he had fantasies about her of which he was ashamed when he awoke. But not for long. She was a thousand times more desirable than Fay Wray or Claudette Colbert or Elissa Landi.

But that night, when they were all going to see the première of *The Eighth Wonder of the World*, King Kong himself, young Howller had managed to ignore whatever it was that was bugging his elders. And even they seemed to be having a good time. Uncle Nate, over his parents' weak protests, had purchased orchestra seats for them. These were twenty dollars apiece, big money in Depression days, enough to feed a family for a month. Everybody got all dressed up, and Aunt Thea looked too beautiful to be real. Young Howller was so excited that he thought his heart was going to climb up and out through his throat. For days the newspapers had been full of stories about King Kong—speculations, rather, since Carl Denham wasn't telling them much. And he, Tim Howller, would be one of the lucky few to see the monster first.

Boy, wait until he got back to the kids in seventh grade at Busiris, Illinois! Would their eyes ever pop when he told them all about it!

But his happiness was too good to last. Aunt Thea suddenly said she had a headache and couldn't possibly go. Then she and Uncle Nate went into their bedroom, and even in the front room, three rooms and a hallway distant, young Tim could hear their voices. After a while Uncle Nate, slamming doors behind him, came out. He was red-faced and scowling, but he wasn't going to call the party off. All four of them, very uncomfortable and silent, rode in a taxi to the theater on Times Square. But when they got inside, even Uncle Nate forgot the quarrel or at least he seemed to. There was the big stage with its towering silvery curtains and through the curtains came a vibration of excitement and of delicious danger. And even through the curtains the hot hairy ape-stink filled the theater.

"Did King Kong get loose just like in the movie?" Jill said.

Mr. Howller started. "What? Oh, yes, he sure did. Just like in the movie."

"Were you scared, Grandpa? Did you run away like everybody else?"

He hesitated. Jill's image of her grandfather had been cast in a heroic mold. To her he was a giant of Herculean strength and perfect courage, her defender and champion. So far he had managed to live up to the image, mainly because the demands she made were not too much for him. In time she would see the cracks and the sawdust oozing out. But she was too young to disillusion now.

"No, I didn't run," he said. "I waited until the theater was cleared of the crowd."

This was true. The big man who'd been sitting in the seat before him had leaped up yelling as Kong began tearing the bars out of his cage, had whirled and jumped over the back of his seat, and his knee had hit young Howller on the jaw. And so young Howller had been stretched out senseless on the floor under the seats while the mob screamed and tore at each other and trampled the fallen.

Later he was glad that he had been knocked out. It gave him a good excuse for not keeping cool, for not acting heroically in the situation. He knew that if he had not been unconscious, he would have been as frenzied as the others, and he would have abandoned his parents, thinking only in his terror of his own salvation. Of course, his parents had deserted him, though they claimed that they had been swept away from him by the mob. This *could* be true; maybe his folks *had* actually tried to get to him. But he had not really thought they had, and for years he had looked down on them because of their flight. When he got older, he realized that he would have done the same thing, and he knew that his contempt for them was really a disguised contempt for himself.

He had awakened with a sore jaw and a headache. The police and the ambulance men were there and starting to take care of the hurt and to haul away the dead. He staggered past them out into the lobby and, not seeing his parents there, went outside. The sidewalks and the streets were plugged with thousands of men, women, and children, on foot and in cars, fleeing northward.

He had not known where Kong was. He should have been able to figure it out, since the frantic mob was leaving the midtown part of Manhattan. But he could think of only two things. Where were his parents? And was Aunt Thea safe? And then he had a third thing to consider. He discovered that he had wet his pants. When he had seen the great ape burst loose, he had wet his pants.

Under the circumstances, he should have paid no attention to this. Certainly no one else did. But he was a very sensitive and shy boy of thirteen, and, for some reason, the need for getting dry underwear and trousers seemed even more important than finding his parents. In retrospect he would tell himself that he would have gone south anyway. But he knew deep down that if his pants had not been wet he might not have dared return to the Empire State Building.

It was impossible to buck the flow of the thousands moving like lava up Broadway. He went east on 43rd Street until he came to Fifth Avenue, where he started southward. There was a crowd to fight against here, too, but it was much smaller than that on Broadway. He was able to thread his way through it, though he often had to go out into the steet and dodge the cars. These, fortunately, were not able to move faster than about three miles an hour.

"Many people got impatient because the cars wouldn't go faster," he told Jill, "and they just abandoned them and struck out on foot."

"Wasn't it noisy, Grandpa?"

"Noisy? I've never heard such noise. I think that everyone in Manhattan, except those hiding under their beds, was yelling or talking. And every driver in Manhattan was blowing his car's horn. And then there were the sirens of the fire trucks and police cars and ambulances. Yes, it was noisy."

Several times he tried to stop a fugitive so he could find out what was going on. But even when he did succeed in halting someone for a few seconds, he couldn't make himself heard. By then, as he found out later, the radio had broadcast the news. Kong had chased John Driscoll and Ann Redman out of the theater and across the street to their hotel. They had gone up to Driscoll's room, where they thought they were safe. But Kong had climbed up, using windows as ladder steps, reached into the room, knocked Driscoll out, grabbed Ann, and had then leaped away with her. He had headed, as Carl Denham figured he would, toward the tallest structure on the island. On King Kong's own island, he lived on the highest point, Skull Mountain, where he was truly monarch of all he surveyed. Here he would climb to the top of the Empire State Building, Manhattan's Skull Mountain.

Tim Howller had not known this, but he was able to infer that Kong had traveled down Fifth Avenue from 38th Street on. He passed a dozen cars with their tops flattened down by the ape's fist or turned over on their sides or tops. He saw three sheet-covered bodies on the sidewalks, and he overheard a policeman telling a reporter that Kong had climbed up several buildings on his way south and reached into windows and pulled people out and thrown them down onto the pavement.

"But you said King Kong was carrying Ann Redman in the crook of his arm, Grandpa," Jill said. "He only had one arm to climb with, Grandpa, so . . . so wouldn't he fall off the building when he reached in to grab those poor people?"

"A very shrewd observation, my little chickadee," Mr. Howller said, using the W. C. Fields voice that usually sent her into giggles. "But his arms were long enough for him to drape Ann Redman over the arm he used to hang on with while he reached in with the other. And to forestall your next question, even if you had not thought of it, he could turn over an automobile with only one hand."

"But . . . but why'd he take time out to do that if he wanted to get to the top of the Empire State Building?"

"I don't know why *people* often do the things they do," Mr. Howller said. "So how would I know why an *ape* does the things he does?"

When he was a block away from the Empire State, a plane crashed onto the middle of the avenue two blocks behind him and burned furiously. Tim Howller watched it for a few minutes, then he looked upward and saw the red and green lights of the five planes and the silvery bodies slipping in and out of the searchlights.

"Five airplanes, Grandpa? But the movie . . ."

"Yes, I know. The movie showed about fourteen or fifteen. But the book says that there were six to begin with, and the book is much more accurate. The movie also shows King Kong's last stand taking place in the daylight. But it didn't; it was still night time."

The Army Air Force plane must have been going at least 250 mph as it dived down toward the giant ape standing on the top of the observation tower. Kong had put Ann Redman by his feet so he could hang on to the tower with one hand and grab out with the other at the planes. One had come too close, and he had seized the left biplane structure and ripped it off. Given the energy of the plane, his hand should have been torn off, too, or at least he should have been pulled loose from his hold on the tower and gone down with the plane. But he hadn't let loose, and that told something of the enormous strength of that towering body. It also told something of the relative fragility of the biplane.

Young Howller had watched the efforts of the firemen to extinguish the fire and then he had turned back toward the Empire State Building. By then it was all over. All over for King Kong, anyway. It was, in after years, one of Mr. Howller's greatest regrets that he had not seen the monstrous dark body falling through the beams of the searchlights—blackness, then the flash of blackness through the whiteness of the highest beam, blackness, the flash through the next beam, blackness, the flash through the third beam, blackness, the flash through the lowest beam. Dot, dash, dot, dash, Mr. Howller was to think afterward. A code transmitted unconsciously by the great ape and received unconsciously by those who witnessed the fall. Or by those who would hear of it and think about it. Or was he going too far in conceiving this? Wasn't he always looking for codes? And, when he found them, unable to decipher them?

Since he had been thirteen, he had been trying to equate the great falls in man's myths and legends and to find some sort of intelligence in them. The fall of the tower of Babel, of Lucifer, of Vulcan, of Icarus, and, finally, of King Kong. But he wasn't equal to the task; he didn't have the genius to perceive what the falls meant, he couldn't screen out the—to use an electronic term—the "noise". All he could come up with were folk adages. What goes up must come down. The bigger they are, the harder they fall.

"What'd you say, Grandpa?"

"I was thinking out loud, if you can call that thinking," Mr. Howller said.

Young Howller had been one of the first on the scene, and so he got a place in the front of the crowd. He had not completely forgotten his parents or Aunt Thea, but the danger was over, and he could not make himself leave to search for them. And he had even forgotten about his soaked pants. The body was only about thirty feet from him. It lay on its back on the sidewalk, just as in the movie. But the dead Kong did not look as big or as dignified as in the movie. He was spread out more like an apeskin rug than a body, and blood and bowels and their contents had splashed out around him.

After a while Carl Denham, the man responsible for capturing Kong and bringing him to New York, appeared. As in the movie, Denham spoke his classical lines by the body: "It was Beauty. As always, Beauty killed the Beast."

This was the most appropriately dramatic place for the lines to be spoken, of course, and the proper place to end the movie.

But the book had Denham speaking these lines as he leaned over the parapet of the observation tower to look down at Kong on the sidewalk. His only audience was a police sergeant.

Both the book and the movie were true. Or half true. Denham did speak those lines way up on the 102nd floor of the tower. But, showman that he was, he also spoke them when he got down to the sidewalk, where the newsmen could hear them.

Young Howller didn't hear Denham's remarks. He was too far away. Besides, at that moment he felt a tap on his shoulder and heard a man said. "Hey, kid, there's somebody trying to get your attention!"

Young Howller went into his mother's arms and wept for at least a minute. His father reached past his mother and touched him briefly on the forehead, as if blessing him, and then gave his shoulder a squeeze. When he was able to talk, Tim Howller asked his mother what had happened to them. They, as near as they could remember, had been pushed out by the crowd, though they had fought to get to him, and had run up Broadway after they found themselves in the street because King Kong had appeared. They had managed to get back to the theater, had not been able to locate Tim, and had walked back to the Empire State Building.

"What happened to Uncle Nate?" Tim said.

Uncle Nate, his mother said, had caught up with them on Fifth Avenue and just now was trying to get past the police cordon into the building so he could check on Aunt Thea.

"She must be all right!" young Howller said. "The ape climbed up her side of the building, but she could easily get away from him, her apartment's so big!"

"Well, yes," his father had said. "But if she went to bed with her headache, she would've been right next to the window. But don't worry. If she'd been hurt, we'd know it. And maybe she wasn't even home."

Young Tim had asked him what he meant by that, but his father had only shrugged.

The three of them stood in the front line of the crowd, waiting for Uncle Nate to bring news of Aunt Thea, even though they weren't really worried about her, and waiting to see what happened to Kong. Mayor Jimmy Walker showed up and conferred with the officials. Then the governor himself, Franklin Delano Roosevelt, arrived with much noise of siren and motorcycle. A minute later a big black limousine with flashing red lights and a siren pulled up. Standing on the runningboard was a giant with bronze hair and strange-looking gold-flecked eyes. He jumped off the runningboard and strode up to the mayor, governor, and police commissioner and talked briefly with them. Tim Howller asked the man next to him what the giant's name was, but the man replied that he didn't know because he was from out of town also. The giant finished talking and strode up to the crowd, which opened for him as if it were the Red Sea and he were Moses, and he had no trouble at all getting through the police cordon. Tim then asked the man on the right of his parents if he knew the yellow-eyed giant's name. This man, tall and thin, was with a beautiful woman dressed up in an evening gown and a mink coat. He turned his head when Tim called to him and presented a hawklike face and eyes that burned so brightly that Tim wondered if he took dope. Those eyes also told him that here was a man who asked questions, not one who gave answers. Tim didn't repeat his question, and a moment later the man said, in a whispering voice that still carried a long distance, "Come on, Margo. I've work to do." And the two melted into the crowd.

Mr. Howller told Jill about the two men, and she said, "What about them, Grandpa?"

"I don't really know," he said. "Often I've wondered ... Well, never mind.

Whoever they were, they're irrelevant to what happened to King Kong. But I'll say one thing about New York—you sure see a lot of strange characters there."

Young Howller had expected that the mess would quickly be cleaned up. And it was true that the sanitation department had sent a big truck with a big crane and a number of men with hoses, scoop shovels, and brooms. But a dozen people at least stopped the cleanup almost before it began. Carl Denham wanted no one to touch the body except the taxidermists he had called in. If he couldn't exhibit a live Kong, he would exhibit a dead one. A colonel from Roosevelt Field claimed the body and, when asked why the Air Force wanted it, could not give an explanation. Rather, he refused to give one, and it was not until an hour later that a phone call from the White House forced him to reveal the real reason. A general wanted the skin for a trophy because Kong was the only ape ever shot down in aerial combat.

A lawyer for the owners of the Empire State Building appeared with a claim for possession of the body. His clients wanted reimbursement for the damage done to the building.

A representative of the transit system wanted Kong's body so it could be sold to help pay for the damage the ape had done to the Sixth Avenue Elevated.

The owner of the theater from which Kong had escaped arrived with his lawyer and announced he intended to sue Denham for an amount which would cover the sums he would have to pay to those who were inevitably going to sue him.

The police ordered the body seized as evidence in the trial for involuntary manslaughter and criminal negligence in which Denham and the theater owner would be defendants in due process.

The manslaughter charges were later dropped, but Denham did serve a year before being paroled. On being released, he was killed by a religious fanatic, a native brought back by the second expedition to Kong's island. He was, in fact, the witch doctor. He had murdered Denham because Denham had abducted and slain his god, Kong.

His Majesty's New York consul showed up with papers which proved that Kong's island was in British waters. Therefore, Denham had no right to anything removed from the island without permission of His Majesty's government.

Denham was in a lot of trouble. But the worst blow of all was to come next day. He would be handed notification that he was being sued by Ann Redman. She wanted compensation to the tune of ten million dollars for various physical indignities and injuries suffered during her two abductions by the ape, plus the mental anguish these had caused her. Unfortunately for her, Denham went to prison without a penny in his pocket, and she dropped the suit. Thus, the public never found out exactly what the "physical indignities and injuries" were, but this did not keep it from making many speculations. Ann Redman also sued John Driscoll, though for a different reason. She claimed breach of promise. Driscoll, interviewed by newsmen, made his famous remark that she should have been suing Kong, not him. This convinced most of the public that what it had suspected had indeed happened. Just how it could have been done was difficult to explain, but the public had never lacked wiseacres who would not only attempt the difficult but would not draw back even at the impossible.

Actually, Mr. Howller thought, the deed was not beyond possibility. Take an adult male gorilla who stood six feet high and weighed 350 pounds. According to

Swiss zoo director Ernst Lang, he would have a full erection only two inches long. How did Professor Lang know this? Did he enter the cage during a mating and measure the phallus? Not very likely. Even the timid and amiable gorilla would scarcely submit to this type of handling in that kind of situation. Never mind. Professor Lang said it was so, and so it must be. Perhaps he used a telescope with gradations across the lens like those on a submarine's periscope. In any event, until someone entered the cage and slapped down a ruler during the action, Professor Lang's word would have to be taken as the last word.

By mathematical extrapolation, using the square-cube law, a gorilla twenty feet tall would have an erect penis about twenty-one inches long. What the diameter would be was another guess and perhaps a vital one, for Ann Redman anyway. Whatever anyone else thought about the possibility, Kong must have decided that he would never know unless he tried. Just how well he succeeded, only he and his victim knew, since the attempt would have taken place before Driscoll and Denham got to the observation tower and before the searchlight beams centered on their target.

But Ann Redman must have told her lover, John Driscoll, the truth, and he turned out not to be such a strong man after all.

"What're you thinking about, Grandpa?"

Mr. Howller looked at the screen. The Roadrunner had been succeeded by the Pink Panther, who was enduring as much pain and violence as the poor old coyote.

"Nothing," he said. "I'm just watching the Pink Panther with you."

"But you didn't say what happened to King Kong," she said.

"Oh," he said, "we stood around until dawn, and then the big shots finally came to some sort of agreement. The body just couldn't be left there much longer, if for no other reason than it was blocking traffic. Blocking traffic meant that business would be held up. And lots of people would lose lots of money. And so Kong's body was taken away by the Police Department, though it used the Sanitation Department's crane, and it was kept in an icehouse until its ownership could be thrashed out."

"Poor Kong."

"No," he said, "not poor Kong. He was dead and out of it."

"He went to heaven?"

"As much as anybody," Mr. Howller said.

Uncle Nate's was the cry of betrayal, and perhaps of revenge satisfied, Tim's was both of betrayal and of grief for the death of one he had passionately loved with a thirteen-year-old's love, for one whom the thirteen-year-old in him still loved.

"Grandpa, are there any more King Kongs?"

"No," Mr. Howller said. To say yes would force him to try to explain something that she could not understand. When she got older, she would know that every dawn saw the death of the old Kong and the birth of the new.

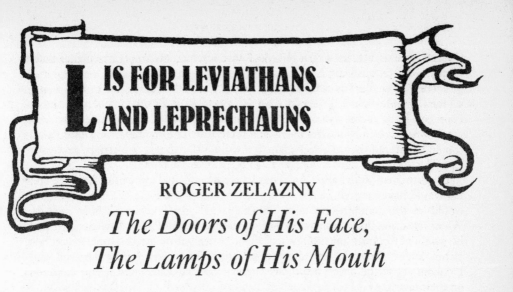

L IS FOR LEVIATHANS AND LEPRECHAUNS

ROGER ZELAZNY

The Doors of His Face, The Lamps of His Mouth

I'm a baitman. No one is born a baitman, except in a French novel where everyone is. (In fact, I think that's the title, *We are All Bait*, Pfft!) How I got that way is barely worth telling and has nothing to do with neo-exes, but the days of the beast deserve a few words, so here they are.

The Lowlands of Venus lie between the thumb and forefinger of the continent known as Hand. When you break into Cloud Alley it swings its silverblack bowling ball toward you without a warning. You jump then, inside that firetailed tenpin they ride you down in, but the straps keep you from making a fool of yourself. You generally chuckle afterwards, but you always jump first.

Next, you study Hand to lay its illusion and the two middle fingers become dozen-ringed archipelagoes as the outers resolve into greengray peninsulas; the thumb is too short, and curls like the embryo tail of Cape Horn.

You suck pure oxygen, sigh possibly, and begin the long topple to the Lowlands.

There, you are caught like an infield fly at the Lifeline landing area—so named because of its nearness to the great delta in the Eastern Bay—located between the first peninsula and "thumb." For a minute it seems as if you're going to miss Lifeline and wind up as a canned seafood, but afterwards—shaking off the metaphors—you descend to scorched concrete and present your middle-sized telephone directory of authorizations to the short, fat man in the gray cap. The papers show that you are not subject to mysterious inner rottings and etcetera. He then smiles you a short, fat, gray smile and motions you toward the bus which hauls you to the Reception Area. At the R.A. you spend three days proving that, indeed, you are not subject to mysterious inner rottings and etcetera.

Boredom, however, is another rot. When your three days are up, you generally hit Lifeline hard, and it returns the compliment as a matter of reflex. The effects of alcohol in variant atmospheres is a subject on which the connoisseurs have written numerous volumes, so I will confine my remarks to noting that a good binge is worthy of at least a week's time and often warrants a lifetime study.

I had been a student of exceptional promise (strictly undergraduate) for going on two years when the *Bright Water* fell through our marble ceiling and poured its people like targets into the city.

Pause. The Worlds Almanac re Lifeline: "... Port city on the eastern coast of Hand. Employees of the Agency for Non-terrestrial Research comprise approximately 85% of its 100,000 population (2010 Census). Its other residents are primarily personnel maintained by several industrial corporations engaged in basic research. Independent marine biologists, wealthy fishing enthusiasts, and waterfront entrepreneurs make up the remainder of its inhabitants."

I turned to Mike Dabis, a fellow entrepreneur, and commented on the lousy state of basic research.

"Not if the mumbled truth be known."

He paused behind his glass before continuing the slow swallowing process calculated to obtain my interest and a few oaths, before he continued.

"Carl," he finally observed, poker playing, "they're shaping Tensquare."

I could have hit him. I might have refilled his glass with sulfuric acid and looked on with glee as his lips blackened and cracked. Instead, I grunted a noncommittal.

"Who's fool enough to shell out fifty grand a day? ANR?"

He shook his head.

"Jean Luharich," he said, "the girl with the violet contacts and fifty or sixty perfect teeth. I understand her eyes are really brown."

"Isn't she selling enough face cream these days?"

He shrugged.

"Publicity makes the wheels go 'round. Luharich Enterprises jumped sixteen points when she picked up the Sun Trophy. You ever play golf on Mercury?"

I had, but I overlooked it and continued to press.

"So she's coming here with a blank check and a fish-hook?"

"*Bright Water*, today," he nodded. "Should be down by now. Lots of cameras. She wants an Ikky, bad."

"Hmm," I hmmed. "How bad?"

"Sixty day contract, Tensquare. Indefinite extension clause. Million and a half deposit," he recited.

"You seem to know a lot about it."

"I'm Personal Recruitment. Luharich Enterprises approached me last month. It helps to drink in the right places."

"Or own them." He smirked, after a moment.

I looked away, sipping my bitter brew. After a while I swallowed several things and asked Mike what he expected to be asked, leaving myself open for his monthly temperance lecture.

"They told me to try getting you," he mentioned. "When's the last time you sailed?"

"Month and a half ago. The *Corning*."

"Small stuff," he snorted. "When have you been under, yourself?"

"It's been a while."

"It's been over a year, hasn't it? That time you got cut by the screw, under the *Dolphin*?"

I turned to him.

"I was in the river last week, up at Angleford where the currents are strong. I can still get around."

"Sober," he added.

"I'd stay that way," I said, "on a job like this."

A doubting nod.

"Straight union rates. Triple time for extraordinary circumstances," he narrated. "Be at Hangar Sixteen with your gear, Friday morning, five hundred hours. We push off Saturday, daybreak."

"You're sailing?"

"I'm sailing."

"How come?"

"Money."

"Ikky guano."

"The bar isn't doing so well and baby needs new minks."

"I repeat—"

". . . And I want to get away from baby, renew my contact with basics—fresh air, exercise, make cash. . . ."

"All right, sorry I asked."

I poured him a drink, concentrating on H_2SO_4, but it didn't transmute. Finally I got him soused and went out into the night to walk and think things over.

Around a dozen serious attempts to land *Ichthyform Leviosaurus Levianthus*, generally known as "Ikky," had been made over the past five years. When Ikky was first sighted, whaling techniques were employed. These proved either fruitless or disastrous, and a new procedure was inaugurated. Tensquare was constructed by a wealthy sportsman named Michael Jandt, who blew his entire roll on the project.

After a year on the Eastern Ocean, he returned to file bankruptcy. Carlton Davits, a playboy fishing enthusiast, then purchased the huge raft and laid a wake for Ikky's spawning grounds. On the nineteenth day out he had a strike and lost one hundred and fifty bills' worth of untested gear, along with one *Ichthyform Levianthus*. Twelve days later, using tripled lines, he hooked, narcotized, and began to hoist the huge beast. It awakened then, destroyed a control tower, killed six men, and worked general hell over five square blocks of Tensquare. Carlton was left with partial hemiplegia and a bankruptcy suit of his own. He faded into waterfront atmosphere and Tensquare changed hands four more times, with less spectacular but equally expensive results.

Finally, the big raft, built only for one purpose, was purchased at auction by ANR for "marine research." Lloyd's still won't insure it, and the only marine research it has ever seen is an occasional rental at fifty bills a day—to people anxious to tell Leviathan fish stories. I've been baitman on three of the voyages, and I've been close enough to count Ikky's fangs on two occasions. I want one of them to show my grandchildren for personal reasons.

I faced the direction of the landing area and resolved a resolve.

"You want me for local coloring, gal. It'll look nice on the feature page and all that. But clear this—If anyone gets you an Ikky, it'll be me. I promise."

I stood in the empty Square. The foggy towers of Lifeline shared their mists.

Shoreline a couple eras ago, the western slope above Lifeline stretches as far as forty miles inland in some places. Its angle of rising is not a great one, but it achieves an elevation of several thousand feet before it meets the mountain range which separates us from the Highlands. About four miles inland and five hundred feet higher than Lifeline are set most of the surface airstrips and privately owned hangars. Hangar Sixteen houses Cal's Contract Cab, hop service, shore to ship. I do not like Cal, but he wasn't around when I climbed from the bus and waved to a mechanic.

Two of the hoppers tugged at the concrete, impatient beneath flywing haloes. The one on which Steve was working belched deep within its barrel carburetor and shuddered spasmodically.

"Bellyache?" I inquired.

"Yeah, gas pains and heartburn."

He twisted setscrews until it settled into an even keening, and turned to me.

"You're for out?"

I nodded.

"Tensquare. Cosmetics. Monsters. Stuff like that."

He blinked into the beacons and wiped his freckles. The temperature was about twenty, but the big overhead spots served a double purpose.

"Luharich," he muttered. "Then you *are* the one. There's some people want to see you."

"What about?"

"Cameras. Microphones. Stuff like that."

"I'd better stow my gear. Which one am I riding?"

He poked the screwdriver at the other hopper.

"That one. You're on video tape now, by the way. They wanted to get you arriving."

He turned to the hangar, turned back.

"Say 'cheese.' They'll shoot the close-ups later."

I said something other than "cheese." They must have been using telelens and been able to read my lips, because that part of the tape was never shown.

I threw my junk in the back, climbed into a passenger seat, and lit a cigarette. Five minutes later, Cal himself emerged from the office Quonset, looking cold. He came over and pounded on the side of the hopper. He jerked a thumb back at the hangar.

"They want you in there!" he called through cupped hands. "Interview!"

"The show's over!" I yelled back. "Either that, or they can get themselves another baitman!"

His rustbrown eyes became nailheads under blond brows and his glare a spike before he jerked about and stalked off. I wondered how much they had paid him to be able to squat in his hangar and suck juice from his generator.

Enough, I guess, knowing Cal. I never liked the guy, anyway.

Venus at night is a field of sable waters. On the coasts, you can never tell where the sea ends and the sky begins. Dawn is like dumping milk into an inkwell. First, there are erratic curdles of white, then streamers. Shade the bottle for a gray colloid, then watch it whiten a little more. All of a sudden you've got day. Then start heating the mixture.

I had to shed my jacket as we flashed out over the bay. To our rear, the skyline could have been under water for the way it waved and rippled in the heatfall. A hopper can accommodate four people (five, if you want to bend Regs and underestimate weight), or three passengers with the sort of gear a baitman uses. I was the only fare, though, and the pilot was like his machine. He hummed and made no unnecessary noises. Lifeline turned a somersault and evaporated in the rear mirror at about the same time Tensquare broke the fore-horizon. The pilot stopped humming and shook his head.

I leaned forward. Feelings played flopdoodle in my guts. I knew every bloody inch of the big raft, but the feelings you once took for granted change when their source is out of reach. Truthfully, I'd had my doubts I'd ever board the hulk again. But now, now I could almost believe in predestination. There it was!

A tensquare football field of a ship. A-powered. Flat as a pancake, except for the plastic blisters in the middle and the "Rooks" fore and aft, port and starboard.

The Rook towers were named for their corner positions—and any two can work together to hoist, co-powering the graffles between them. The graffles—half gaff, half grapple—can raise enormous weights to near water level; their designer had only one thing in mind, though, which accounts for the gaff half. At water level, the Slider has to implement elevation for six to eight feet before the graffles are in a position to push upward, rather than pulling.

The Slider, essentially, is a mobile room—a big box capable of moving in any of Tensquare's crisscross groovings and "anchoring" on the strike side by means of a powerful electromagnetic bond. Its winches could hoist a battleship the necessary distance, and the whole craft would tilt, rather than the Slider come loose, if you want any idea of the strength of that bond.

The Slider houses a section operated control indicator which is the most sophisticated "reel" ever designed. Drawing broadcast power from the generator beside the center blister, it is connected by shortwave with the sonar room, where the movements of the quarry are recorded and repeated to the angler seated before the section control.

The fisherman might play his "lines" for hours, days even, without seeing any more than metal and an outline on the screen. Only when the beast is graffled and the extensor shelf, located twelve feet below waterline, slides out for support and begins to aid the winches, only then does the fisherman see his catch rising before him like a fallen Seraph. Then, as Davits learned, one looks into the Abyss itself and is required to act. He didn't, and a hundred meters of unimaginable tonnage, undernarcotized and hurting, broke the cables of the winch, snapped a graffle, and took a half-minute walk across Tensquare.

We circled till the mechanical flag took notice and waved us on down. We touched beside the personnel hatch and I jettisoned my gear and jumped to the deck.

"Luck," called the pilot as the door was sliding shut. Then he danced into the air and the flag clicked blank.

I shouldered my stuff and went below.

Signing in with Malvern, the de facto captain, I learned that most of the others wouldn't arrive for a good eight hours. They had wanted me alone at Cal's so they could pattern the pub footage along twentieth-century cinema lines.

Open: landing strip, dark. One mechanic prodding a contrary hopper. Stark-o-vision shot of slow bus pulling in. Heavily dressed baitman descends, looks about, limps across field. Close-up: he grins. Move in for words: "Do you think this is the time? The time he *will* be landed?" Embarrassment, taciturnity, a shrug. Dub something—"I see. And why do you think Miss Luharich has a better chance than any of the others? It is because she's better equipped? [Grin.] Because more is known now about the creature's habits than when you were out before? Or is it because of her will to win, to be a champion? Is it any one of these things, or is it all of them?" Reply: "Yeah, all of them." "—Is that why you signed on with her? Because your instincts say, 'This one will be it'?" Answer: "She pays union rates. I couldn't rent that damned thing myself. And I want in." Erase. Dub something else. Fade-out as he moves toward hopper, etcetera.

"Cheese," I said, or something like that, and took a walk around Tensquare, by myself.

I mounted each Rook, checking out the controls and the underwater video eyes. Then I raised the main lift.

Malvern had no objections to my testing things this way. In fact, he encouraged it. We had sailed together before and our positions had even been reversed upon a time. So I wasn't surprised when I stepped off the lift into the Hopkins Locker and found him waiting. For the next ten minutes we inspected the big room in silence, walking through its copper coil chambers soon to be Arctic.

Finally, he slapped a wall.

"Well, will we fill it?"

I shook my head.

"I'd like to, but I doubt it. I don't give two hoots and a damn who gets credit for the catch, so long as I have a part in it. But it won't happen. That gal's an egomaniac. She'll want to operate the Slider, and she can't."

"You ever meet her?"

"Yeah."

"How long ago?"

"Four, five years."

"She was a kid then. How do you know what she can do now?"

"I know. She'll have learned every switch and reading by this time. She'll be up on all theory. But do you remember one time we were together in the starboard Rook, forward, when Ikky broke water like a porpoise?"

"How could I forget?"

"Well?"

He rubbed his emery chin.

"Maybe she can do it, Carl. She's raced torch ships and she's scubaed in bad waters back home." He glanced in the direction of invisible Hand. "And she's hunted in the Highlands. She might be wild enough to pull that horror into her lap without flinching.

"... For John Hopkins to foot the bill and shell out seven figures for the corpus," he added. "That's money, even to a Luharich."

I ducked through a hatchway.

"Maybe you're right, but she was a rich witch when I knew her.

"And she wasn't blonde," I added, meanly.

He yawned.

"Let's find breakfast."

We did that.

When I was young I thought that being born a sea creature was the finest choice Nature could make for anyone. I grew up on the Pacific coast and spent my summers on the Gulf or the Mediterranean. I lived months of my life negotiating coral, photographing trench dwellers, and playing tag with dolphins. I fished everywhere there are fish, resenting the fact that they can go places I can't. When I grew older I wanted bigger fish, and there was nothing living that I knew of, excepting a Sequoia, that came any bigger than Ikky. That's part of it. . . .

I jammed a couple of extra rolls into a paper bag and filled a thermos with coffee. Excusing myself, I left the galley and made my way to the Slider berth. It was just the way I remembered it. I threw a few switches and the shortwave hummed.

"That you, Carl?"

"That's right, Mike. Let me have some juice down here, you double-crossing rat."

He thought it over, then I felt the hull vibrate as the generators cut in. I poured my third cup of coffee and found a cigarette.

"So why am I a double-crossing rat this time?" came his voice again.

"You knew about the cameramen at Hangar Sixteen?"

"Yes."

"Then you're a double-crossing rat. The last thing I want is publicity. 'He who fouled up so often before is ready to try it, nobly once more.' I can read it now."

"You're wrong. The spotlight's only big enough for one, and she's prettier than you."

My next comment was cut off as I threw the elevator switch and the elephant ears flapped above me. I rose, settling flush with the deck. Retracting the lateral rail, I cut forward into the groove. Amidships, I stopped at a juncture, dropped the lateral, and retracted the longitudinal rail.

I slid starboard, midway between the Rooks, halted, and threw on the coupler.

I hadn't spilled a drop of coffee.

"Show me pictures."

The screen glowed. I adjusted and got outlines of the bottom.

"Okay."

I threw a Status Blue switch and he matched it. The light went on. The winch unlocked. I aimed out over the waters, extended the arm, and fired a cast.

"Clean one," he commented.

"Status Red. Call strike." I threw a switch.

"Status Red."

The baitman would be on his way with this, to make the barbs tempting.

It's not exactly a fishhook. The cables bear hollow tubes; the tubes convey enough dope for any army of hopheads; Ikky takes the bait, dangled before him by remote control, and the fisherman rams the barb home.

My hands moved over the console, making the necessary adjustments. I checked the narco-tank reading. Empty. Good, they hadn't been filled yet. I thumbed the Inject button.

"In the gullet," Mike murmured.

I released the cables. I played the beast imagined. I let him run, swinging the winch to stimulate his sweep.

I had an air conditioner on and my shirt off and it was still uncomfortably hot, which is how I knew that morning had gone over into noon. I was dimly aware of the arrivals and departures of the hoppers. Some of the crew sat in the "shade" of the doors I had left open, watching the operation. I didn't see Jean arrive or I would have ended the session and gotten below.

She broke my concentration by slamming the door hard enough to shake the bond.

"Mind telling me who authorized you to bring up the Slider?" she asked.

"No one," I replied. "I'll take it below now."

"Just move aside."

I did, and she took my seat. She was wearing brown slacks and a baggy shirt and she had her hair pulled back in a practical manner. Her cheeks were flushed, but not necessarily from the heat. She attacked the panel with a nearly amusing intensity that I found disquieting.

"Status Blue," she snapped, breaking a violet fingernail on the toggle.

I forced a yawn and buttoned my shirt slowly. She threw a side glance my way, checked the registers, and fired a cast.

I monitored the lead on the screen. She turned to me for a second.

"Status Red," she said levelly.

I nodded my agreement.

She worked the winch sideways to show she knew how. I didn't doubt she knew how and she didn't doubt that I didn't doubt, but then—

"In case you're wondering," she said, "you're not going to be anywhere near this thing. You were hired as a baitman, remember? Not a Slider operator! A baitman! Your duties consist of swimming out and setting the table for our friend the monster. It's dangerous, but you're getting well paid for it. Any questions?"

She squashed the Inject button and I rubbed my throat.

"Nope," I smiled, "but I am qualifed to run that thingamajigger—and if you need me I'll be available, at union rates."

"Mister Davits," she said, "I don't want a loser operating this panel."

"Miss Luharich, there has never been a winner at this game."

She started reeling in the cable and broke the bond at the same time, so that the whole Slider shook as the big yo-yo returned. We skidded a couple of feet backward. She raised the laterals and we shot back along the groove. Slowing, she transferred rails and we jolted to a clanging halt, then shot off at a right angle. The crew scrambled away from the hatch as we skidded onto the elevator.

"In the future, Mister Davits, do not enter the Slider without being ordered," she told me.

"Don't worry. I won't even step inside if I am ordered," I answered. "I signed on as a baitman. Remember? If you want me in here, you'll have to *ask* me."

"That'll be the day," she smiled.

I agreed, as the doors closed above us. We dropped the subject and headed in our different directions after the Slider came to a halt in its berth. She did say "good day," though, which I thought showed breeding as well as determination, in reply to my chuckle.

Later that night Mike and I stoked our pipes in Malvern's cabin. The winds were shuffling waves, and a steady spattering of rain and hail overhead turned the deck into a tin roof.

"Nasty," suggested Malvern.

I nodded. After two bourbons the room had become a familar woodcut, with its mahogany furnishings (which I had transported from Earth long ago on a whim) and the dark walls, the seasoned face of Malvern, and the perpetually puzzled expression of Dabis set between the big pools of shadow that lay behind chairs and splashed in cornets, all cast by the tiny table light and seen through a glass, brownly.

"Glad I'm in here."

"What's it like underneath on a night like this?"

I puffed, thinking of my light cutting through insides of a black diamond, shaken slightly. The meteor-dart of a suddenly illuminated fish, the swaying of grotesque ferns, like nebulae—shadow, then green, then gone—swam in a moment through my mind. I guess it's like a spaceship would feel, if a spaceship could feel, crossing between worlds—and quiet, uncannily, preternaturally quiet; and peaceful as sleep.

"Dark," I said, "and not real choppy below a few fathoms."

"Another eight hours and we shove off," commented Mike.

"Ten, twelve days, we should be there," noted Malvern.

"What do you think Ikky's doing?"

"Sleeping on the bottom with Mrs. Ikky if he has any brains."

"He hasn't. I've seen ANR's skeletal extrapolation from the bones that have washed up—"

"Hasn't everyone?"

". . . Fully fleshed, he'd be over a hundred meters long. That right, Carl?"

I agreed.

". . . Not much of a brain box, though, for his bulk."

"Smart enough to stay out of our locker."

Chuckles, because nothing exists but this room, really. The world outside is an empty, sleet drummed deck. We lean back and make clouds.

"Boss lady does not approve of unauthorized fly fishing."

"Boss lady can walk north till her hat floats."

"What did she say in there?"

"She told me that my place, with fish manure, is on the bottom."

"You don't Slide?"

"I bait."

"We'll see."

"That's all I do. If she wants a Slideman she's going to have to ask nicely."

"You think she'll have to?"

"I think she'll have to."

"And if she does, can you do it?"

"A fair question," I puffed. "I don't know the answer, though."

I'd incorporate my soul and trade forty percent of the stock for the answer. I'd give a couple of years off my life for the answer. But there doesn't seem to be a lineup of supernatural takers, because no one knows. Supposing when we get out there, luck being with us, we find ourselves an Ikky? Supposing we succeed in baiting him and get lines on him. What then? If we get him shipside, will she hold on or crack up? What if she's made of sterner stuff than Davits, who used to hunt sharks with poison-darted air pistols? Supposing she lands him and Davits has to stand there like a video extra.

Worse yet, supposing she asks for Davits and he still stands there like a video extra or something else—say, some yellowbellied embodiment named Cringe?

It was when I got him up above the eight-foot horizon of steel and looked out at all that body, sloping on and on till it dropped out of sight like a green mountain range ... And that head. Small for the body, but still immense. Fat, craggy, with lidless roulettes that had spun black and red since before my forefathers decided to try the New Continent. And swaying.

Fresh narco-tanks had been connected. It needed another shot, fast. But I was paralyzed.

It had made a noise like God playing a Hammond organ. . . .

And looked at me!

I don't know if seeing is even the same process in eyes like those. I doubt it. Maybe I was just a gray blur behind a black rock, with the plexi-reflected sky hurting its pupils. But it fixed on me. Perhaps the snake doesn't really paralyze the rabbit, perhaps it's just that rabbits are cowards by constitution. But it began to struggle and I still couldn't move, fascinated.

Fascinated by all that power, by those eyes, they found me there fifteen minutes later, a little broken about the head and shoulders, the Inject still unpushed.

And I dream about those eyes. I want to face them once more, even if their finding takes forever. I've got to know if there's something inside me that sets me apart from a rabbit, from notched plates of reflexes and instincts that always fall apart in exactly the same way whenever the proper combination is spun.

Looking down, I noticed that my hand was shaking. Glancing up, I noticed that no one else was noticing.

I finished my drink and emptied my pipe. It was late and no songbirds were singing.

I sat whittling, my legs hanging over the aft edge, the chips spinning down into the furrow of our wake. Three days out. No action.

"You!"

"Me?"

"You."

Hair like the end of the rainbow, eyes like nothing in nature, fine teeth.

"Hello."

"There's a safety rule against what you're doing, you know."

"I know. I've been worrying about it all morning."

A delicate curl climbed my knife then drifted out behind us. It settled into the foam and was plowed under. I watched her reflection in my blade, taking a secret pleasure in its distortion.

"Are you baiting me?" she finally asked.

I heard her laugh then, and turned, knowing it had been intentional.

"What, me?"

"I could push you off from here, very easily."

"I'd make it back."

"Would you push me off, then—some dark night, perhaps?"

"They're all dark, Miss Luharich. No, I'd rather make you a gift of my carving."

She seated herself beside me then, and I couldn't help but notice the dimples in her knees. She wore white shorts and a halter and still had an offworld tan to her which was awfully appealing. I almost felt a twinge of guilt at having planned the whole scene, but my right hand still blocked her view of the wooden animal.

"Okay, I'll bite. What have you got for me?"

"Just a second. It's almost finished."

Solemnly, I passed her the wooden jackass I had been carving. I felt a little sorry and slightly jackass-ish myself, but I had to follow through. I always do. The mouth was split into a braying grin. The ears were upright.

She didn't smile and she didn't frown. She just studied it.

"It's very good," she finally said, "like most things you do—and appropriate, perhaps."

"Give it to me." I extended my palm.

She handed it back and I tossed it out over the water. It missed the white water and bobbed for awhile like a pigmy seahorse.

"Why did you do that?"

"It was a poor joke. I'm sorry."

"Maybe you are right, though. Perhaps this time I've bitten off a little too much."

I snorted.

"Then why not do something safer, like another race?"

She shook her end of the rainbow.

"No. It has to be an Ikky."

"Why?"

"Why did you want one so badly that you threw away a fortune?"

"Many reasons," I said. "An unfrocked analyst who held black therapy sessions in his basement once told me, 'Mister Davits, you need to reinforce the image of your masculinity by catching one of every kind of fish in existence.' Fish are a very ancient masculinity symbol, you know. So I set out to do it. I have one more to go. Why do you want to reinforce *your* masculinity?"

"I don't," she said. "I don't want to reinforce anything but Luharich Enterprises. My chief statistician once said, 'Mis Luharich, sell all the cold cream and face powder in the System and you'll be a happy girl. Rich, too.' And he was right. I am the proof. I can look the way I do and do anything, and I sell most of the lipstick and face powder in the System—but I have to be *able* to do anything."

"You do look cool and efficient," I observed.

"I don't feel cool," she said, rising. "Let's go for a swim."

"May I point out that we are making pretty good time?"

"If you want to indicate the obvious, you may. You said you could make it back to the ship, unassisted. Change your mind?"

"No."

"Then get us two scuba outfits and I'll race you under Tensquare."

"I'll win, too," she added.

I stood and looked down at her, because that usually makes me feel superior to women.

"Daughter of Lir, eyes of Picasso," I said, "you've got yourself a race. Meet me at the forward Rook, starboard, in ten minutes."

"Ten minutes," she agreed.

And ten minutes it was. From the center blister to the Rook took maybe two of them, with the load I was carrying. My sandals grew very hot and I was glad to shuck them for flippers when I reached the comparative cool of the corner.

We slid into harnesses and adjusted our gear. She had changed into a trim one-piece green job that made me shade my eyes and look away, then look back again.

I fastened a rope ladder and kicked it over the side. Then I pounded on the wall of the Rook.

"Yeah?"

"You talk to the port Rook, aft?" I called.

"They're all set up," came the answer. "There's ladders and drag-lines all over that end."

"You sure you want to do this?" asked the sunburnt little gink who was her publicity man, Anderson yclept.

He sat beside the Rook in a deckchair, sipping lemonade through a straw.

"It might be dangerous," he observed, sunken-mouthed. (His teeth were beside him, in another glass.)

"That's right," she smiled. "It *will* be dangerous. Not overly, though."

"Then why don't you let me get some pictures? We'd have them back to Lifeline in an hour. They'd be in New York by tonight. Good copy."

"No," she said, and turned away from both of us.

She raised her hands to her eyes.

"Here, keep these for me."

She passed him a box full of her unseeing, and when she turned back to me they were the same brown that I remembered.

"Ready?"

"No," I said, tautly. "Listen carefully, Jean. If you're going to play this game there are a few rules. First," I counted, "we're going to be directly beneath the hull, so we have to start low and keep moving. If we bump the bottom we could rupture an air tank. . . ."

She began to protest that any moron knew that and I cut her down.

"Second," I went on, "there won't be much light, so we'll stay close together, and we will *both* carry torches."

Her wet eyes flashed.

"I dragged you out of Govino without—"

Then she stopped and turned away. She picked up a lamp.

"Okay. Torches. Sorry."

"... And watch out for the drive-screws," I finished. "There'll be strong currents for at least fifty meters behind them."

She wiped her eyes again and adjusted the mask.

"All right, let's go."

We went.

She led the way, at my insistence. The surface layer was pleasantly warm. At two fathoms the water was bracing; at five it was nice and cold. At eight we let go the swinging stairway and struck out. Tensquare sped forward and we raced in the opposite direction, tattooing the hull yellow at ten-second intervals.

The hull stayed where it belonged, but we raced on like two darkside satellites. Periodically, I tickled her frog feet with my light and traced her antennae of bubbles. About a five meter lead was fine; I'd beat her in the home stretch, but I couldn't let her drop behind yet.

Beneath us, black. Immense. Deep. The Mindanao of Venus, where eternity might eventually pass the dead to a rest in cities of unnamed fishes. I twisted my head away and touched the hull with a feeler of light; it told me we were about a quarter of the way along.

I increased my beat to match her stepped-up stroke, and narrowed the distance which she had suddenly opened by a couple meters. She sped up again and I did, too. I spotted her with my beam.

She turned and it caught on her mask. I never knew whether she'd been smiling. Probably. She raised two fingers in a V-for-Victory and then cut ahead at full speed.

I should have known. I should have felt it coming. It was just a race to her, something else to win. Damn the torpedoes!

So I leaned into it, hard. I don't shake in the water. Or, if I do it doesn't matter and I don't notice it. I began to close the gap again.

She looked back, sped on, looked back. Each time she looked it was nearer, until I'd narrowed it down to the original five meters.

Then she hit the jatoes.

That's what I had been fearing. We were about half-way under and she shouldn't have done it. The powerful jets of compressed air could easily rocket her upward into the hull, or tear something loose if she allowed her body to twist. Their main use is in tearing free from marine plants or fighting bad currents. I had wanted them along as a safety measure, because of the big suck-and-pull windmills behind.

She shot ahead like a meteorite, and I could feel a sudden tingle of perspiration leaping to meet and mix with the churning waters.

I swept ahead, not wanting to use my own guns, and she tripled, quadrupled the margin.

The jets died and she was still on course. Okay, I was an old fuddyduddy. She *could* have messed up and headed toward the top.

I plowed the sea and began to gather back my yardage, a foot at a time. I wouldn't be able to catch her or beat her now, but I'd be on the ropes before she hit deck.

The the spinning magnets began their insistence and she wavered. It was an awfully powerful drag, even at this distance. The call of the meat grinder.

I'd been scrached up by one once, under the *Dolphin*, a fishing boat of the middle-class. I *had* been drinking, but it was also a rough day, and the thing had been turned on prematurely. Fortunately, it was turned off in time, also, and a tendon-stapler made everything good as new, except in the log, where it only mentioned that I'd been drinking. Nothing about it being off-hours when I had a right to do as I damn well pleased.

She had slowed to half her speed, but she was still moving crosswise, toward the port, aft corner. I begn to feel the pull myself and had to slow down. She'd made it past the main one, but she seemed too far back. It's hard to gauge distances under water, but each red beat of time told me I was right. She was out of danger from the main one, but the smaller port screw, located about eighty meters in, was no longer a threat but a certainty.

She had turned and was pulling away from it now. Twenty meters separated us. She was standing still. Fifteen.

Slowly, she began a backward drifting. I hit my jatoes, aiming two meters behind her and about twenty back of the blades.

Straightline! Thankgod! Catching, softbelly, leadpipe on shoulder SWIM-LIKEHELL! maskcracked, not broke though AND UP!

We caught a line and I remember brandy.

Into the cradle endlessly rocking I spit, pacing. Insomnia tonight and left shoulder sore again, so let it rain on me—they can cure rheumatism. Stupid as hell. What I said. In blankets and shivering. She: "Carl, I can't say it." Me: "Then call it square for that night in Govino, Miss Luharich. Huh?" She: nothing. Me: "Any more of that brandy?" She: "Give me another, too." Me: sounds of sipping. It had only lasted three months. No alimony. Many $ on both sides. Not sure whether they were happy or not. Wine-dark Aegean. Good fishing. Maybe he should have spent more time on shore. Or perhaps she shouldn't have. Good swimmer, though. Dragged him all the way to Vido to wring out his lungs. Young. Both. Strong. Both. Rich and spoiled as hell. Ditto. Corfu should have brought them closer. Didn't. I think that mental cruelty was a trout. He wanted to go to Canada. She: "Go to hell if you want!" He: "Will you go along?" She: "No." But she did, anyhow. Many hells. Expensive. He lost a monster or two. She inherited a couple. Lot of lightning tonight. Stupid as hell. Civility's the coffin of a conned soul. By whom?—Sounds like a bloody neo-ex. . . . But I hate you, Anderson, with your glass full of teeth and her new eyes. . . . Can't keep this pipe lit, keep sucking tobacco. Spit again!

Seven days out and the scope showed Ikky.

Bells jangled, feet pounded, and some optimist set the thermostat in the Hopkins. Malvern wanted me to sit out, but I slipped into my harness and waited for whatever came. The bruise looked worse than it felt. I had exercised every day and the shoulder hadn't stiffened on me.

A thousand meters ahead and thirty fathoms deep, it tunneled our path. Nothing showed on the surface.

"Will we chase him?" asked an excited crewman.

"Not unless she feels like using money for fuel." I shrugged.

Soon the scope was clear, and it stayed that way. We remained on alert and held our course.

I hadn't said over a dozen words to my boss since the last time we went drowning together, so I decided to raise the score.

"Good afternoon," I approached. "What's new?"

"He's going north-northeast. We'll have to let this one go. A few more days and we can afford some chasing. Not yet."

Sleek head . . .

I nodded. "No telling where this one's headed."

"How's your shoulder?"

"All right. How about you?"

Daughter of Lir . . .

"Fine. By the way, you're down for a nice bonus."

Eyes of perdition!

"Don't mention it," I told her back.

Later that afternoon, and appropriately, a storm shattered. (I prefer "shattered" to "broke." It gives a more accurate idea of the behavior of tropical storms on Venus and saves lots of words.) Remember that inkwell I mentioned earlier? Now take it between thumb and forefinger and hit its side with a hammer. Watch your self! Don't get splashed or cut—

Dry, then drenched. The sky one million bright fractures as the hammer falls. And sounds of breaking.

"Everyone below?" suggested loudspeakers to the already scurrying crew.

Where was I? Who do you think was doing the loud-speaking?

Everything loose went overboard when the water got to walking, but by then no people were loose. The Slider was the first thing below decks. Then the big lifts lowered their shacks.

I had hit it for the nearest Rook with a yell the moment I recognized the pre-brightening of the holocaust. From there I cut in the speakers and spent half a minute coaching the track team.

Minor injuries had occurred, Mike told me over the radio, but nothing serious. I, however, was marooned for the duration. The Rooks do not lead anywhere; they're set too far out over the hull to provide entry downwards, what with the extensor shelves below.

So I undressed myself of the tanks which I had worn for the past several hours, crossed my flippers on the table, and leaned back to watch the hurricane. The top was black as the bottom and we were in between, and somewhat illuminated because of all that flat, shiny space. The waters above didn't rain down—they just sort of got together and dropped.

The Rooks were secure enough—they'd weathered any number of these onslaughts—it's just that their positions gave them a greater arc of rise and descent when Tensquare makes life the rocker of a very nervous grandma. I had used the belts from my rig to strap myself into the bolted-down chair, and I removed several years in purgatory from the soul of whoever left a pack of cigarettes in the table drawer.

I watched the water make teepees and mountains and hands and trees until I started seeing faces and people. So I called Mike.

"What are you doing down there?"

"Wondering what you're doing up there," he replied. "What's it like?"

"You're from the Midwest, aren't you?"

"Yeah."

"Get bad storms out there?"

"Sometimes."

"Try to think of the worst one you were ever in. Got a slide rule handy?"

"Right here."

"Then put a one under it, imagine a zero or two following after, and multiply the thing out."

"I can't imagine the zeros."

"Then retain the multiplicand—that's all you can do."

"So what are you doing up there?"

"I've strapped myself in the chair. I'm watching things around the floor right now."

I looked up and out again. I saw one darker shadow in the forest.

"Are you praying or swearing?"

"Damned if I know. But if this were the Slider—if only this were the Slider!"

"He's out there?"

I nodded, forgetting that he couldn't see me.

Big, as I remembered him. He'd only broken surface for a few moments, to look around. *There is no power on Earth that can be compared with him who was made to fear no one.* I dropped my cigarette. It was the same as before. Paralysis and an unborn scream.

"You all right, Carl?"

He had looked at me again. Or seemed to. Perhaps that mindless brute had been waiting half a millenium to ruin the life of a member of the most highly developed species in business. . . .

"You okay?"

. . . Or perhaps it had been ruined already, long before their encounter, and theirs was just a meeting of beasts, the stronger bumping the weaker aside, body to psyche. . . .

"Carl, dammit! Say something!"

He broke again, this time nearer. Did you ever see the trunk of a tornado? It seems like something alive, moving around in all that dark. Nothing has a right to be so big, so strong, and moving. It's a sickening sensation.

"Please answer me."

He was gone and did not come back that day. I finally made a couple of wisecracks at Mike, but I held my next cigarette in my right hand.

The next seventy or eighty thousand waves broke by with a monotonous similarity. The five days that held them were also without distinction. The morning of the thirteenth day out, though, our luck began to rise. The bells broke our coffee-drenched lethargy into small pieces, and we dashed from the galley without hearing what might have been Mike's finest punchline.

"Aft!" cried someone. "Five hundred meters!"

I stripped to my trunks and started buckling. My stuff is always within grabbing distance.

I flipflopped across the deck, girding myself with a deflated squiggler.

"Five hundred meters, twenty fathoms!" boomed the speakers.

The big traps banged upward and the Slider grew to its full height, m'lady at the console. It rattled past me and took root ahead. Its one arm rose and lengthened.

I breasted the Slider as the speakers called, "Four-eighty, twenty!"

"Status Red!"

A belch like an emerging champagne cork and the line arced high over the waters.

"Four-eighty, twenty!" it repeated, all Malvern and static. "Baitman, attend!"

I adjusted my mask and hand-over-handed it down the side. Then warm, then cool, then away.

Green, vast, down. Fast. This is the place where I am equal to a squiggler. If something big decides a baitman looks tastier than what he's carrying, then irony colors his title as well as the water about it.

I caught sight of the drifting cables and followed them down. Green to dark green to black. It had been a long cast, too long. I'd never had to follow one this far down before. I didn't want to switch on my torch.

But I had to.

Bad! I still had a long way to go. I clenched my teeth and stuffed my imagination into a straightjacket.

Finally the line came to an end.

I wrapped one arm about it and unfastened the squiggler. I attached it, working as fast as I could, and plugged in the little insulated connections which are the reason it can't be fired with the line. Ikky could break them, but by then it wouldn't matter.

My mechanical eel hooked up, I pulled its section plugs and watched it grow. I had been dragged deeper during this operation, which took about a minute and a half. I was near—too near—to where I never wanted to be.

Loath as I had been to turn on my light, I was suddenly afraid to turn it off. Panic gripped me and I seized the cable with both hands. The squiggler began to glow, pinkly. It started to twist. It was twice as big as I am and doubtless twice as attractive to pink squiggler-eaters. I told myself this until I believed it, then I switched off my light and started up.

If I bumped into something enormous and steel-hided my heart had orders to stop beating immediately and release me—to dart fitfully forever along Acheron, and gibbering.

Ungibbering, I made it to green water and fled back to the nest.

As soon as they hauled me aboard I made my mask a necklace, shaded my eyes, and monitored for surface turbulence. My first question, of course, was: "Where is he?"

"Nowhere," said a crewman; "we lost him right after you went over. Can't pick him up on the scope now. Musta dived."

"Too bad."

The squiggler stayed down, enjoying its bath. My job ended for the time being, I headed back to warm my coffee with rum.

From behind me, a whisper: "Could you laugh like that afterwards?"

Perceptive Answer: "Depends on what he's laughing at."

Still chuckling, I made my way into the center blister with two cupfuls.

"Still hell and gone?"

Mike nodded. His big hands were shaking, and mine were steady as a surgeon's when I set down the cups.

He jumped as I shrugged off the tanks and looked for a bench.

"Don't drip on that panel! You want to kill yourself and blow expensive fuses?"

I toweled down, then settled down to watching the unfilled eye on the wall. I yawned happily; my shoulder seemed good as new.

The little box that people talk through wanted to say something, so Mike lifted the switch and told it to go ahead.

"Is Carl there, Mister Dabis?"

"Yes, ma'am."

"Then let me talk to him."

Mike motioned and I moved.

"Talk," I said.

"Are you all right?"

"Yes, thanks. Shouldn't I be?"

"That was a long swim. I—I guess I overshot my cast."

"I'm happy," I said. "More triple-time for me. I really clean up on that hazardous duty clause."

"I'll be more careful next time," she apologized. "I guess I was too eager. Sorry—" Something happened to the sentence, so she ended it there, leaving me with half a bagful of replies I'd been saving.

I lifted the cigarette from behind Mike's ear and got a light from the one in the ashtray.

"Carl, she was being nice," he said, after turning to study the panels.

"I know," I told him. "I wasn't."

"I mean, she's an awfully pretty kid, pleasant. Headstrong and all that. But what's she done to you?"

"Lately?" I asked.

He looked at me, then dropped his eyes to his cup.

"I know it's none of my bus—" he began.

"Cream and sugar?"

Ikky didn't return that day, or that night. We picked up some Dixieland out of Lifeline and let the muskrat ramble while Jean had her supper sent to the Slider. Later she had a bunk assembled inside. I piped in "Deep Water Blues" when it came over the air and waited for her to call up and cuss us out. She didn't, though, so I decided she was sleeping.

Then I got Mike interested in a game of chess that went on until daylight. It limited conversation to several "checks," one "checkmate," and a "damn!" Since he's a poor loser it also effectively sabotaged subsequent talk, which was fine with me. I had a steak and fried potatoes for breakfast and went to bed.

Ten hours later someone shook me awake and I propped myself on one elbow, refusing to open my eyes.

"Whassamadder?"

"I'm sorry to get you up," said one of the younger crewmen, "but Miss Luharich wants you to disconnect the squiggler so we can move on."

I knuckled open one eye, still deciding whether I should be amused.

"Have it hauled to the side. Anyone can disconnect it."

"It's at the side now, sir. But she said it's in your contract and we'd better do things right."

"That's very considerate of her. I'm sure my Local appreciates her re-membering."

"Uh, she also said to tell you to change your trunks and comb your hair, and shave, too. Mister Anderson's going to film it."

"Okay. Run along; tell her I'm on my way—and ask if she has some toenail polish I can borrow."

I'll save on details. It took three minutes in all, and I played it properly, even pardoning myself when I slipped and bumped into Anderson's white tropicals with the wet squiggler. He smiled, brushed it off; she smiled, even though Luharich Complectacolor couldn't completely mask the dark circles under her eyes; and I smiled, waving to all our fans out there in videoland. —Remember, Mrs. Universe, you, too, can look like a monster-catcher. Just use Luharich face cream.

I went below and made myself a tuna sandwich, with mayonnaise.

Two days like icebergs—bleak, blank, half-melting, all frigid, mainly out of sight, and definitely a threat to peace of mind—drifted by and were good to put behind. I experienced some old guilt feelings and had a few disturbing dreams. Then I called Lifeline and checked my bank balance.

"Going shopping?" asked Mike, who had put the call through for me.

"Going home," I answered.

"Huh?"

"I'm out of the baiting business after this one, Mike. The Devil with Ikky! The Devil with Venus and Luharich Enterprises! And the Devil with you!"

Up eyebrows.

"What brought that on?"

"I waited over a year for this job. Now that I'm here, I've decided the whole thing stinks."

"You knew what it was when you signed on. No matter what else you're doing, you're selling face cream when you work for face cream sellers."

"Oh, that's not what's biting me. I admit the commercial angle irritates me, but Tensquare has always been a publicity spot, ever since the first time it sailed."

"What, then?"

"Five or six things, all added up. The main one being that I don't care any more. Once it meant more to me than anything else to hook that critter, and now it doesn't. I went broke on what started out as a lark and I wanted blood for what it cost me. Now I realize that maybe I had it coming. I'm beginning to feel sorry for Ikky."

"And you don't want him now?"

"I'll take him if he comes peacefully, but I don't feel like sticking out my neck to make him crawl into the Hopkins."

"I'm inclined to think it's one of the four or five other things you said you added."

"Such as?"

He scrutinized the ceiling.

I growled.

"Okay, but I won't say it, not just to make you happy you guessed right."

He, smirking: "That look she wears isn't just for Ikky."

"No good, no good." I shook my head. "We're both fission chambers by nature. You can't have jets on both ends of the rocket and expect to go anywhere—what's in the middle just gets smashed."

"That's how it *was*. None of my business, of course—"

"Say that again and you'll say it without teeth."

"Any day, big man"—he looked up—"any place . . ."

"So go ahead. Get it said!"

"She doesn't care about that bloody reptile, she came here to drag you back where you belong. You're not the baitman this trip."

"Five years is too long."

"There must be something under that cruddy hide of yours that people like," he muttered, "or I wouldn't be talking like this. Maybe you remind us humans of some really ugly dog we felt sorry for when we were kids. Anyhow, someone wants to take you home and raise you—also, something about beggars not getting menus."

"Buddy," I chuckled, "do you know what I'm going to do when I hit Lifeline?"

"I can guess."

"You're wrong. I'm torching it to Mars, and then I'll cruise back home, first class. Venus bankruptcy provisions do not apply to Martian trust funds, and I've still got a wad tucked away where moth and corruption enter not. I'm going to pick up a big old mansion on the Gulf and if you're ever looking for a job you can stop around and open bottles for me."

"You are a yellowbellied fink," he commented.

"Okay," I admitted, "but it's her I'm thinking of, too."

"I've heard the stories about you both," he said. "So you're a heel and a goofoff and she's a bitch. That's called compatibility these days. I dare you, baitman, try keeping something you catch."

I turned.

"If you ever want that job, look me up."

I closed the door quietly behind me and left him sitting there waiting for it to slam.

The day of the beast dawned like any other. Two days after my gutless flight from empty waters I went down to rebait. Nothing on the scope. I was just making things ready for the routine attempt.

I hollered a "good morning" from outside the Slider and received an answer from inside before I pushed off. I had reappraised Mike's words, sans sound, sans fury, and while I did not approve of their sentiment or significance, I had opted for civility anyhow.

So down, under, and away. I followed a decent cast about two hundred-ninety meters out. The snaking cables burned black to my left and I paced their undulations from the yellowgreen down into the darkness. Soundless lay the wet night, and I bent my way through it like a cock-eyed comet, bright tail before.

I caught the line, slick and smooth, and began baiting. An icy world swept by me then, ankles to head. It was a draft, as if some one had opened a big door beneath me. I wasn't drifting downwards that fast either.

Which meant that something might be moving up, something big enough to displace a lot of water. I still didn't think it was Ikky. A freak current of some sort, but not Ikky. Ha!

I had finished attaching the leads and pulled the first plug when a big, rugged, black island grew beneath me. . . .

I flicked the beam downward. His mouth was opened.

I was rabbit.

Waves of the death-fear passed downward. My stomach imploded. I grew dizzy.

Only one thing, and one thing only. Left to do. I managed it, finally. I pulled the rest of the plugs.

I could count the scaly articulations riding his eyes by then.

The squiggler grew, pinked into phosphorescence . . . squiggled!

Then my lamp. I had to kill it, leaving just the bait before him.

One glance back as I jammed the jatoes to life.

He was so near that the squiggler reflected on his teeth, in his eyes. Four meters, and I kissed his lambent jowls with two jets of backwash as I soared. Then I didn't know whether he was following or halted. I began to black out as I waited to be eaten.

The jatoes died and I kicked weakly.

Too fast, I felt a cramp coming on. One flick of the beam, cried rabbit. One second, to know . . .

Or end things up, I answered. No, rabbit, we don't dart before hunters. Stay dark.

Green waters finally, to yellowgreen, then top.

Doubling, I beat off toward Tensquare. The waves from the explosion behind pushed me on ahead. The world closed in, and a screamed, "He's alive!" in the distance.

A giant shadow and a shock wave. The line was alive, too. Happy Fishing Grounds. Maybe I did something wrong.

Somewhere Hand was clenched. What's bait?

A few million years. I remember starting out as a one-celled organism and painfully becoming an amphibian, then an air-breather. From somewhere high in the treetops I heard a voice.

"He's coming around."

I evolved back into homosapience, then a step further into a hangover.

"Don't try to get up yet."

"Have we got him?" I slurred.

"Still fighting, but he's hooked. We thought he took you for an appetizer."

"So did I."

"Breathe some of this and shut up."

A funnel over my face. Good. Lift your cups and drink. . . .

"He was awfully deep. Below scope range. We didn't catch him till he started up. Too late, then."

I began to yawn.

"We'll get you inside now."

I managed to uncase my ankle knife.

"Try it and you'll be minus a thumb."

"You need rest."

"Then bring me a couple more blankets. I'm staying."

I fell back and closed my eyes.

Someone was shaking me. Gloom and cold. Spotlights bled yellow on the deck. I was in a jury-rigged bunk, bulked against the center blister. Swaddled in wool, I still shivered.

"It's been eleven hours. You're not going to see anything now."

I tasted blood.

"Drink this."

Water. I had a remark but I couldn't mouth it.

"Don't ask how I feel," I croaked. "I know that comes next, but don't ask me. Okay?"

"Okay. Want to go below now?"

"No. Just get me my jacket."

"Right here."

"What's he doing?"

"Nothing. He's deep, he's doped but he's staying down."

"How long since last time he showed?"

"Two hours, about."

"Jean?"

"She won't let anyone in the Slider. Listen, Mike says come on in. He's right behind you in the blister."

I sat up and turned. Mike was watching. He gestured; I gestured back.

I swung my feet over the edge and took a couple of deep breaths. Pains in my stomach. I got to my feet and made it into the blister.

"Howza gut?" queried Mike.

I checked the scope. No Ikky. Too deep.

"You buying?"

"Yeah, coffee."

"Not coffee."

"You're ill. Also, coffee is all that's allowed in here."

"Coffee is a brownish liquid that burns your stomach. You have some in the bottom drawer."

"No cups. You'll have to use a glass."

"Tough."

He poured.

"You do that well. Been practising for that job?"

"What job?"

"The one I offered you—"

A bolt on the scope!

"Rising, ma'am! Rising!" he yelled into the box.

"Thanks, Mike. I've got it in here," she crackled.

"Jean!"

"Shut up! She's busy!"

"Was that Carl?"

"Yeah," I called. "Talk later," and I cut it.

Why did I do that?

"Why did you do that?"

I didn't know.

"I don't know."

Damned echoes! I got up and walked outside.

Nothing. Nothing.

Something?

Tensquare actually rocked! He must have turned when he saw the hull and started downward again. White water to my left, and boiling. And endless spaghetti of cable roared hotly into the belly of the deep.

I stood awhile, then turned and went back inside.

Two hours sick. Four, and better.

"The dope's getting to him."

"Yeah."

"What about Miss Luharich?"

"What about her?"

"She must be half dead."

"Probably."

"What are you going to do about it?"

"She signed the contract for this. She knew what might happen. It did."

"I think you could land him."

"So do I."

"So does she."

"Then let her ask me."

Ikky was drifting lethargically, at thirty fathoms.

I took another walk and happened to pass behind the Slider. She wasn't looking my way.

"Carl, come in here!"

Eyes of Picasso, that's what, and a conspiracy to make me Slide . . .

"Is that an order?"

"Yes—No! Please."

I dashed inside and monitored. He was rising.

"Push or pull?"

I slammed the "wind" and he came like a kitten.

"Make up your own mind now."

He balked at ten fathoms.

"Play him?"

"No!"

She wound him upwards—five fathoms, four . . .

She hit the extensors at two, and they caught him. Then the graffles.

Cries without and a heat lightning of flashbulbs.

The crew saw Ikky.

He began to struggle. She kept the cables tight, raised the graffles . . .

Up.

Another two feet and the graffles began pushing.

Screams and fast footfalls.

Giant beanstalk in the wind, his neck, waving. The green hills of his shoulders grew.

"He's big, Carl!" she cried.

And he grew, and grew, and grew uneasy . . .

"Now!"

He looked down.

He looked down, as the god of our most ancient ancestors might have looked down. Fear, shame, and mocking laughter rang in my head. Her head, too?

"Now!"

She looked up at the nascent earthquake.

"I can't!"

It was going to be so damnably simple this time, now the rabbit had died. I reached out.

I stopped.

"Push it yourself."

"I can't. You do it. Land him, Carl!"

"No. If I do, you'll wonder for the rest of your life whether you could have. You'll throw away your soul finding out. I know you will, because we're alike, and I did it that way. Find out now!"

She stared.

I gripped her shoulders.

"Could be that's me out there," I offered. "I am a green sea serpent, a hateful, monstrous beast, and out to destroy you. I am answerable to no one. Push the Inject."

Her hand moved to the button, jerked back.

"Now!"

She pushed it.

I lowered her still form to the floor and finished things up with Ikky.

It was a good seven hours before I awakened to the steady, sea-chewing grind of Tensquare's blades.

"You're sick," commented Mike.

"How's Jean?"

"The same."

"Where's the beast?"

"Here."

"Good." I rolled over. ". . . Didn't get away this time."

So that's the way it was. No one is born a baitman, I don't think, but the rings of Saturn sing epithalamium the sea-beast's dower.

WILLIAM SAMBROT

Leprechaun

To fully understand what I'm about to tell you, you must know what Ireland is like. Not the Ireland of the big modern cities, but old Ireland. Ireland of the fens and bogs. The Ireland that is still a part of the dim Celtic past, before the Saint himself brought the Cross; when every tree, every stone was possessed of demonic life, and monsters big and small were known to roam the misty nights. That Ireland, deep down in some oldsters, still exists. And it exists, God help us all, very deeply in old Peadar—and what it might have cost us; what wonders have been forever lost to us, I can only speculate. But I cannot find it in my heart to blame old Peadar. He is old but still powerful, like a twisted, weather-hardened tree. There is no malice in the man, but his mind was soddened under the years and the bitter hardships of scratching an existence out of the bog he calls home. His family long dead; too little decent food, too much homemade potato liquor—the fiery poteen that keeps him alive.

Peadar told me his story, twisting his huge hands in anguish while I looked down at the pitiable thing that lay on the table in his sagging windowless sod hut, while the rain that had fallen in solid leaden sheets for days drummed like a dirge on the roof.

He had heard a sound of approaching thunder (Peadar said) although the rain had fallen for days without thunder. At the same time, the sky had come alight, a flat white sheen, like a brilliant beam reflecting from under low-lying clouds, flickering, but gaining in intensity, brighter, nearer, and that was indeed strange since it was well past sundown.

He heard the rumble, soft at first, then louder, harder, cracking like the passage of an infrequently heard military jet—a long-drawn hiss, a whine, a swelling build-up—and then the shuddering rumble of air closing behind some swiftly moving object.

He'd stumbled to the door, pulling it open in time to see a glowing object slanting down; the light intense over the fens despite the gray rain.

It slipped over the rim of a nearby hill and Peadar saw the steady light hold there, then slowly dim and fade to dull red, and finally, it vanished completely.

His first thought had been—a plane crash, some poor souls killed out there. And lurching to his feet, old Peadar had picked up his kerosene lantern, thrown a coat on and immediately started out, thinking only (and this is in his favor) to help. But slogging through the chilly bog he'd seen nothing, only the unending rain, the wispy tendrils of fog. He paused, listening, looking to the right and left, his rheumy old eyes blinking.

He shook his head. He thought he heard popping and crackling sounds, like metal cooling, shrinking, somewhere close in the murky night, but he couldn't be certain. In fact, his mind began wandering; he turned, wondering why he'd come out here. He plodded about for a while and finally went back to his hut. And when he came inside, blowing out the lantern, shaking the wet from his hat, he heard the odd squeaking sound, and turning, he saw a little creature.

He was tiny, tiny (Peadar said, his voice trembling with yearning). Scarcely two feet high. Dressed in a metallic garment vaguely like a fish-skin—dully shining, with infinitesimal overlapping scales. On his head two insectlike antennae bobbed about, affixed to a small helmet of sorts, fitting snugly, with a glasslike faceplate. The whole very cunningly made. A tiny little man, with sparkling black eyes, bowing courteously to clumsy, gigantic old Peadar.

And seeing the little creature, there beside his poor hearth, in the midst of his poverty—the poverty only the Irish, the very remote fen-dweller can know— Peadar, his mind full of the old, old stories, addled with poteen—Peadar spoke aloud one word, like a pagan incantation: *"Leprechaun!"*

The creature took a step forward, its miniature arms held up, palms out to Peadar and Peadar waited, breathless.

Catch a Leprechaun, everyone knows, and he must tell you where fabulous fortunes are hidden. But hold him tight until he does; the wee folk are full of wiles and devilment.

The creature's broad-lipped mouth stretched in a shy half-smile; he looked curiously about the shabby hut and saw the old broken cot, the one chair, the smouldering, ill-smelling peat in the fireplace, the jug of poteen on the floor, the mug and tin spoon on the table.

Now it would happen; now the miracles, the treasure troves. Ancient glittering tales crowded Peadar's mind as he stared at the tiny man, waiting.

The little creature made another courteous half-bow, then walked slowly around Peadar, keeping his brilliant sequin eyes on his face, and walked toward the door, moving slowly, and with difficulty, as though walking under great pressure. He walked toward the door, and as he reached the threshold, Peadar came out of his trance—and acted.

He snatched at the little man, crying loudly at him, "No, no. Ah no, you darlin' wee man. You don't go until you grant me my due." He held the wriggling little creature in his great calloused hands, conscious of the amazing lightness of the little thing. Why, he might have been made of thistledown, so little did he weigh. The creature squeaked and made muffled sounds.

Peadar put him on the table, still holding his waist with one big hand. "Now then," said he, "it's here you stay until I see the gold with me own eyes—and don't think you'll escape me. I know the tricks you'll be trying'."

With the other hand, Peadar hoisted the jug and swallowed an enormous drink of the fiery liquor. He paused, cocking his shaggy head. "Forgive me, now, and where's me manners? Don't I know how you'd like a drop of the poteen?"

Peadar slopped some into the cup, hesitated, peering slant-eyed at the little creature, then he pawed about and came up with the tin spoon. He dipped it into the cup and then held the spoonful of liquor up to the little man's face. The little one remained motionless, watching him quietly.

"Now then, of course," Peadar growled. "Can't take a drop with that contraption on." He put the spoon back in his cracked cup, and then fumbling with one huge thick hand, he worked at the tiny faceplate on the creature's head. As he did so, the creature struggled violently, making mewing sounds, wriggling, but helpless in Peadar's grip. There was a rending sound, and the faceplate opened. Instantly there came a hiss as of escaping gas, a whiff of some indescribable odor, and the creature stiffened. Its struggles weakened, slowed, and ceased. It became limp and dangled like a rag doll in Peadar's powerful grip.

At the same moment, beyond the hut, beyond the nearby hill, somewhere above the bogs, there came a great burst of light and sound, a shrill long-drawn whistling, a clap of thunder that rose up into the rainy night sky, echoing about the low hills, higher and higher, then diminished and was gone.

The little man was motionless in Peadar's grip, and slowly Peadar laid the creature down on the table.

Peadar released him—but the little man didn't vanish; didn't suddenly spring to life and bound away with a laugh at having outwitted a mere mortal. The little man remained motionless, lying on the table in his gleaming little metallic suit, the faceplate swinging idly open, his features rapidly turning blue . . .

It was then Peadar had come for me, stumbling out into the rainy night without hat or jacket, shambling over the bogs, making his way these few miles into the village and to the parish house. He found me waiting, for I, too, had seen the lights in the sky, heard the piercing shriek and rumble that rose up and up until it disappeared into the clouds.

Peadar told me his story, sobbing and babbling, while I looked down at the thing that lay on his table. It had begun to shrivel, shrinking inside its metallic carapace under the impact of an atmosphere it had never been meant—or perhaps had lost the ability—to withstand. The silvery antennae drooped from the helmet, touched, sparked feebly, then turned black and crumbled into ash.

I buried the poor creature in an unmarked grave—for there are some things better left undisturbed. But first I did for it what any priest of old Ireland would do. And afterward, I told Peadar it was good of him to mourn, but better to forget. I left him sitting in his windowless sod hut, with the rain pounding down like the sound of endless muted thunder on the roof.

Peadar would forget, I knew. Lost in the fogs of poteen, it would become just another dim dream for him. But I'll remember. I'll always remember that oddly familiar-looking little face; the peaked eyebrows, the broad mouth, the elfin pointed ears.

I'll remember, and I'll wonder—from what far place had he come—and why? Was he retracing a legend of his own; come to see for himself a land as distant and remote in antiquity to his kind as the legend that had inflamed poor old Peadar was to us? A misty millennium when the little ones, already reaching for the stars, were able to perform wonders the larger, simpler savages who replaced them could only have conceived of as magic?

We'll never know—not now.

But I have a feeling, drawn from some primitive well of memory as deep and old as the race of Celts, that from whatever far place that little creature came, the ground I laid him in, the dark and ancient soil of Ireland, was to him not alien.

M IS FOR MAD MACHINES AND MONSTER MUTANTS

GUY ENDORE
Men of Iron

"We no longer trust the human hand," said the engineer, and waved his roll of blueprints. He was a dwarfish, stocky fellow with dwarfish, stocky fingers that crumpled blueprints with familiar unconcern.

The director frowned, pursed his lips, cocked his head, drew up one side of his face in a wink of unbelief and scratched his chin with a reflective thumbnail. Behind his grotesque contortions he recalled the days when he was manufacturer in his own right and not simply the nominal head of a manufacturing concern, whose owners extended out into complex and invisible ramifications. In his day the human hand had been trusted.

"Now take that lathe," said the engineer. He paused dramatically, one hand flung out toward the lathe in question, while his dark eyes, canopied by bristly eyebrows, remained fastened on the director.

"Listen to it!"

"Well?" said the director, somewhat at a loss.

"Hear it?"

"Why, yes, of course."

The engineer snorted. "Well, you shouldn't."

"Why not?"

"Because noise isn't what it is supposed to make. Noise is an indication of loose parts, maladjustments, improper speed of operation. That machine is sick. It is inefficient and its noise destroys the worker's efficiency."

The director laughed. "That worker should be used to it by this time. Why, that fellow is the oldest employee of the firm. Began with my father. See the gold crescent on his chest?"

"What gold crescent?"

"The gold pin on the shoulder strap of his overalls."

"Oh, that."

"Yes. Well, only workers fifty years or longer with our firm are entitled to wear it."

The engineer threw back his head and guffawed.

The director was wounded.

"Got many of them?" the engineer asked, when he had recovered from his outburst.

"Anton is the only one, now. There used to be another."

"How many pins does he spoil?"

"Well," said the director, "I'll admit he's not so good as he used to be . . . But there's one man I'll never see fired," he added stoutly.

"No need to," the engineer agreed. "A good machine is automatic and foolproof; the attendant's skill is beside the point."

For a moment the two men stood watching Anton select a fat pin from a bucket at his feet and fasten it into the chuck. With rule and caliper he brought the pin into correct position before the drill that was to gouge a hole into it.

Anton moved heavily, circumspectly. His body had the girth, but not the solidity of an old tree-trunk: it was shaken by constant tremors. The tools wavered in Anton's hands. Intermittently a slimy cough came out of his chest, tightened the cords of his neck and flushed the taut yellow skin of his cheeks. Then he would stop to spit, and after that he would rub his mustache that was the colour of silver laid thinly over brass. His lungs relieved, Anton's frame regained a measure of composure, but for a moment he stood still and squinted at the tools in his hands as if he could not at once recall exactly what he was about, and only after a little delay did he resume his interrupted work, all too soon to be interrupted again. Finally, spindle and tool being correctly aligned, Anton brought the machine into operation.

"Feel it?" the engineer cried out with a note of triumph.

"Feel what?" asked the director.

"Vibration!" the engineer exclaimed with disgust.

"Well what of it?"

"Man, think of the power lost in shaking your building all day long. Any reason why you should want your floors and walls to dance all day long, while you pay the piper?"

He hadn't intended so telling a sentence. The conclusion seemed to him so especially apt that he repeated it: "Your building dances while you pay the piper in increased power expenditure."

And while the director remained silent the engineer forced home his point: "That power should be concentrated at the cutting point of the tool and not leak out all over. What would you think of a plumber who only brought 50 per cent of the water to the nozzle letting the rest flood through the building?"

And as the director still did not speak, the engineer continued: "There's not only loss of power but increased wear on the parts. That machine is afflicted with the ague!"

When the day's labor was over, the long line of machines stopped all together; the workmen ran for the washrooms and a sudden throbbing silence settled over the great hall. Only Anton, off in a corner by himself, still worked his lathe, oblivious of the emptiness of the factory, until darkness finally forced him to quit. Then from beneath the lathe he dragged forth a heavy tarpaulin and covered his machine.

He stood for a moment beside his lathe, seemingly lost in thought, but perhaps only quietly wrestling with the stubborn torpidity of his limbs, full of an unwanted, incorrect motion, and disobedient to his desires. For he, like the bad machines in the factory, could not prevent his power from spilling over into useless vibration.

The old watchman opened the gate to let Anton out. The two men stood near each other for a moment, separated by the iron grill and exchanged a few comforting grunts, then hobbled off to their separate destinations, the watchman to make his rounds, Anton to his home.

A gray, wooden shack, on a bare lot, was Anton's home. During the day an enthusiastic horde of children trampled the ground to a rubber-like consistency and extinguished every growing thing except a few dusty weeds that clung close to the protection of the house or nestled around the remnants of the porch that had once adorned the front. There the children's feet could not reach them, and they expanded a few scornful coarse leaves, a bitter growth of Ishmaelites.

Within were a number of rooms, but only one inhabitable. The torn and peeling wallpaper in this one revealed the successive designs that had once struck the fancy of the owners. A remnant of ostentatiousness still remained in the marble mantelpiece, and in the stained glass window through which the arc-light from the street cast cold flakes of color.

She did not stir when Anton entered. She lay resting on the bed, not so much from the labor of the day, as from that of years. She heard his shuffling, noisy walk, heard his groans, his coughing, his whistling breath, and smelled, too, the pungent odor of machine oil. She was satisfied that it was he, and allowed herself to fall into a light sleep, through which she could still hear him moving around in the room and feel him when he dropped into bed beside her and settled himself against her for warmth and comfort.

The engineer was not satisfied with the addition of an automatic feeder and an automatic chuck. "The whole business must settle itself into position automatically," he declared, "there's altogether too much waste with hand calibration."

Formerly Anton had selected the pins from a bucket and fastened them correctly into the chuck. Now a hopper fed the pins one by one into a chuck that grasped them at once of itself.

As he sat in a corner, back against the wall and ate his lunch, Anton sighed. His hands fumbled the sandwich and lost the meat or the bread, while his coffee dashed stormily in his cup. His few yellow teeth, worn flat, let the food escape through the interstices. His grinders did not meet. Tired of futile efforts he dropped his bread into his cup and sucked in the resulting mush.

Then he lay resting and dreaming.

To Anton, in his dream, came the engineer and declared that he had a new automatic hopper and chuck for Anton's hands and mouth. They were of shining steel with many rods and wheels moving with assurance through a complicated pattern. And now, though the sandwich was made of pins, of hard steel pins, Anton's new chuck was equal to it. He grasped the sandwich of pins with no difficulty at all. His new steel teeth bit into the pins, ground them, chewed them and spat them forth again with vehemence. Faster and faster came the pins, and faster and faster the chuck seized them in its perfectly occluding steel dogs, played with them, toyed with them, crunched them, munched them. . . .

A heavy spell of coughing shook Anton awake. For a moment he had a sensation as though he must cough up steel pins, but though his chest was racked as if truly heavy steel pins must come forth, nothing appeared but the usual phlegm and slime.

"We must get rid of this noise and vibration before we can adjust any self-regulating device," said the engineer. "Now this, for example, see? It doesn't move correctly. Hear it click and scrape. That's bad."

Anton stood by, and the engineer and his assistant went to work. From their labors there came forth a sleek mechanism that purred gently as it worked. Scarcely a creak issued from its many moving parts, and a tiny snort was all the sound one heard when the cutting edge came to grips with a pin.

"Can't hear her cough and sputter and creak now, can you?" said the engineer to the director. "And the floor is quiet. Yes, I'm beginning to be proud of that machine, and now I think we can set up an adjustable cam here to make the whole operation automatic.

"Every machine should be completely automatic. A machine that needs an operator," he declared oratorically, "is an invalid."

In a short time the cams were affixed and now the carriage with the cutting tool travelled back and forth of itself and never failed to strike the pin at the correct angle and at the correct speed of rotation.

All Anton had to do now was to stop the machine in case of a hitch. But soon even that task was unnecessary. No hitches were ever to occur again. Electronic tubes at several points operated mechanisms designed to eject faulty pins either before they entered the hopper or else after they emerged from the lathe.

Anton stood by and watched. This was all he had to do, for the machine now performed all the operations that he had used to do. In went the unfinished pins and out they came, each one perfectly drilled. Anton's purblind eyes could scarcely follow the separate pins of the stream that flowed into the machine. Now and then a pin was pushed remorselessly out of line and plumped sadly into a bucket. Cast out! Anton stooped laboriously and retrieved the pin. "That could have been used," he thought.

"Krr-click, krr-click," went the feeder, while the spindle and the drill went *zzz-sntt, zzzz-sntt, zzz-sntt,* and the belt that brought the pins from a chattering machine beyond, rolled softly over the idlers with a noise like a breeze in a sail. Already the machine had finished ten good pins while Anton was examining a single bad one.

Late in the afternoon there appeared a number of important men. They surrounded the machine, examined it and admired it.

"That's a beauty," they declared.

Now the meeting took on a more official character. There were several short addresses. Then an imposing man took from a small leather box a golden crescent.

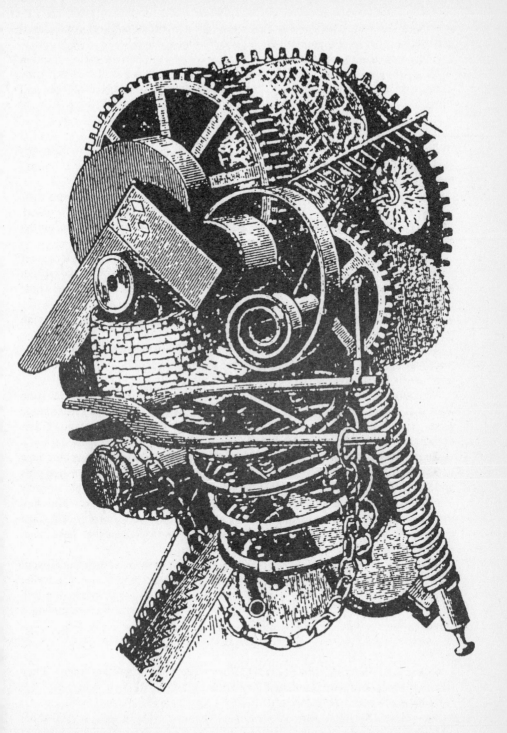

"The Crescent Manufacturing Company," he said, "takes pride and pleasure in awarding this automatic lathe a gold crescent." A place on the side of the machine had been prepared for the affixing of this distinction.

Now the engineer was called upon to speak.

"Gentlemen," he said fiercely, "I understand that formerly the Crescent Company awarded its gold crescent only to workmen who had given fifty years of service to the firm. In giving a gold crescent to a machine, your President has perhaps unconsciously acknowledged a new era. . . ."

While the engineer developed his thesis, the director leaned over to his assistant and whispered, "Did you ever hear of why the sea is salt?"

"Why the sea is salt?" whispered back the assistant. "What do you mean?"

The director continued: "When I was a little kid, I heard the story of 'Why the sea is salt' many times, but I never thought it important until just a moment ago. It's something like this: Formerly the sea was fresh water and salt was rare and expensive. A miller received from a wizard a wonderful machine that just ground salt out of itself all day long. At first the miller thought himself the most fortunate man in the world, but soon all the villages had salt to last them for centuries and still the machine kept on grinding more salt. The miller had to move out of his house, he had to move off his acres. At last he determined that he would sink the machine in the sea and be rid of it. But the mill ground so fast that boat and miller and machine were sunk together, and down below, the mill still went on grinding and that's why the sea is salt."

"I don't get you," said the assistant.

Throughout the speeches, Anton had remained seated on the floor, in a dark corner, where his back rested comfortably against the wall. It had begun to darken by the time the company left, but still Anton remained where he was, for the stone floor and wall had never felt quite so restful before. Then, with a great effort, he roused his unwilling frame, hobbled over to his machine and dragged forth the tarpaulin.

Anton had paid little attention to the ceremony; it was, therefore, with surprise that he noticed the gold crescent on his machine. His weak eyes strained to pierce the twilight. He let his fingers play over the medal, and was aware of tears falling from his eyes, and could not divine the reason.

The mystery wearied Anton. His worn and trembling body sought the inviting floor. He stretched out, and sighed, and that sigh was his last.

When the daylight had completely faded, the machine began to hum softly. *Zzz-sntt, zzz-snt*, it went, four times, and each time carefully detached a leg from the floor.

Now it rose erect and stood beside the body of Anton. Then it bent down and covered Anton with the tarpaulin. Out of the hall it stalked on sturdy legs. Its electron eyes saw distinctly through the dark, its iron limbs responded instantly to its every need. No noise racked its interior where its organs functioned smoothly and without a single tremor. To the watchman, who grunted his usual greeting without looking up, it answered never a word but strode on rapidly, confidently, through the windy streets of night—to Anton's house.

Anton's wife lay waiting, half-sleeping on the bed in the room where the arc-light came through the stained-glass window. And it seemed to her that a marvel happened: her Anton come back to her free of coughs and creaks and tremors; her Anton come to her in all the pride and folly of his youth, his breath like wind soughing through tree-tops, the muscles of his arms like steel.

LOUIS PHILLIPS

The Lop-Eared Cat that Devoured Philadelphia

Even a cat may look at a king,
But this feline is ridiculous,
Three hundred feet high.
A mutation we understand
And still growing.
Radioactive isotopes
Fell into its milk, so now its purr
Can be heard all the way to Cleveland;
Its meow shatters glass
And bullets do not stop
It. All of us

Feel a bit like mice,
Dreading the thought of it
Ever going into heat.
We'd like to have it altered,
But the vet
Can't get
Close enough. As for now.
When its droopy ears drag the street,
Cars topple,
Houses fall and trees.
As for fleas,

They've discovered heaven
And whine in black fur

Driving us berserk.
None of us have slept for nights,
Its claws
Scratching windows
Like shavings from a moon.
There is a tense beauty to her
In the light,
But nothing that I'd care to own.
She has grown

Too large for us to handle.
We've petitioned the President
To drop the Bomb
Or send in troops,
But there are big wars on
And it is difficult to gain attention.
All the foolish cat does
Is glare into the sun
And scoop
Up segments of our population
For a snack. One solution

Is to create a super St Bernard,
But frankly
We lack heart
And the council is a bit conservative.
Perhaps we've been too hard.
After all, she does
Keep herself clean,
And when she leaps
There is such grace
Our hearts keen to our throats
In anticipation.

Besides, if giant rats ever appear,
We'll be far ahead of other cities.

THOMAS M. DISCH

Flight Useless, Inexorable the Pursuit

As he stumbled against the hedge, a car passed, brushing his face with its cruel light. The hedge trembled all along its length, like a large molded gelatin, and for minutes after the rimed and sickly leaves quivered. Thighs quivered. He ought not to run, but his terror ... Consciously, he walked down the street of identical

Tudor houses. 48, 46, 44, 42, 40, 38, never skipping a beat. Before some of the houses, the dozen or so square yards of lawn had been stripped away and replaced with asphalt or concrete. They had become miniature parking lots. The cold air performed surgeries in his lungs. He had lost his gloves, or forgotten them when he'd left the house. How long ago? The thing had caught sight of him returning from the bakery. The bag of jelly doughnuts was probably still where he had set it down, on the dinette table, growing stale. At seven, or maybe eight P.M. Now it was dark again. A night and a day gone by. Thinking of the doughnuts, he grew hungry, though it was a false hunger: he had eaten several times during the day— sandwiches from delicatessens, teas and pastries at Lyons shops, sixpenny bags of crisps. Until his money had run out. He ought to have taken a train out of London at the start. Instead he'd squandered his money shuttling about town. Always when he stopped—in Stepney, in Bethnal Green, in Camden Town, it found him out. How did it track him? How had it known *at first*- Not, he was certain, by his face. Admittedly he was quite pale, but in London, in winter, most people are pale. Did it, perhaps, affect the way he walked? No—scent seemed the only way to account for it. His pursuer had smelled him out, like a truffle; it hunted him, as a hound a hare. 24, 22, 20, 18, 16. 16 was FOR SALE. He had only been to Temple Fortune once before, when he had been searching so desperately for a flat. He had looked at a rather commodious bedsitter on Ashbourne Avenue, but that had not been possible, as he would have had to share the bath. He had, even yet, more conscience than that. Could someone have seen him getting in or out of the tub at Portland Road, and reported it? Not, one would have supposed, with a window of frosted glass. And at work he never used the toilets, out of the same consideration. London lacked the customary air of *suspicion* of a Marrakesh or a Beirut. He must escape, he *had* to escape. Escape where? Back to Portland Road to pack? But what if one of those things was waiting there? In the closet. No, it would never have fit in the closet. Somewhere else. No, the risk was too great. He should have thought, during the day, to go to his bank. Too late. He shivered, remembering again its metronomic knock, remembered looking out the paranoid peep-hole he'd drilled in the door the day he'd moved in. Lucky that he had! Remembered the gray low bulk of it, like nothing so much as an overturned icebox. How had it got upstairs? Did it walk—or, which seemed likelier, use treads? He knew almost nothing of its capabilities. Was its seeming sluggishness a ruse? So that when it finally came close enough it could make a sudden, unanticipated spurt? He must escape, but he was so tired. Two days and a night without sleep. He had to rest, but he dared not rest. He would cross the Channel and go north. To Denmark. Then Sweden. He would always be able to find some kind of light work. His chest hurt. He had never dared visit a London doctor with his cold, even at its worst. No matter what medicines he took, it lingered on. It was the cold that made him so giddy now, not ... the other thing. The cold and fear. Fear and weariness, a terrible weariness, so that he dared not even stand in a doorway and rest his eyes. He would have slept and the machine would have tracked him down, inexorably. Where would it be now? Somewhere along the Finchley Road, no doubt, sniffing after him the way he'd come on the bus. He'd reached the corner of the block, a greengrocer's, and, opposite, a dairy that was just closing. And here he had thought the time nearly midnight! He squinted at the street sign above the greengrocer's awning. This was the corner of Finchley Road and Ashbourne Avenue. He'd come full circle on himself! The light in the dairy was switched off. He leaned back against the cold glass of the greengrocer's door and stared at the car parked before him, its windows opaque with frost. It had been such a warm winter until just last week, and he had been grateful for that, since he was unable, now, to wear woollen clothes. His chest hurt and his legs hurt. He crossed the street and walked down Finchley Road until he found a turning to the left. He turned left. He walked past rows and rows of identical Tudor houses, and in each of them lived an identical Tudor king. He was hungry, he needed to sleep, and his chest hurt. He would go to Sweden, though he couldn't speak Swedish. Someone had told him that every Swede spoke English as a second language. He knew Arabic though, for all the good that would do him! How had they let him get through Customs? To have come so far, to have come so close, and now . . . The street ended, and there was nothing but a vacancy. Had he come as far south as the Heath? A hill, trees. The sky's underbelly, livid with electric light. Soon, with the new mirrors being orbited, London would be bathed in an eternal day. The birds would stay awake all through the night, flowers would forget to close their blossoms. He remembered the devastated slopes of the Atlas mountains, the maddened villagers. He was leaning against the trunk of a tree, sheltered by the bare branches. The joint between his skull and the upper vertebrae ached and creaked as though in need of lubrication. He allowed his eyes to close. He had known all along really that his flight was useless. Already at the foot of the hill he saw it—an overturned icebox. It approached at an even, slow speed over the frozen ground, following exactly the path he had taken. It had come this close in Camden Town, and yet he had escaped it then. He could still . . . No. Just as a suicide will undress before entering the water, he unbuttoned his overcoat and let it slip from his shoulders. The machine paused two feet from him. One motor ceased its purring, another sprang to life, but there was, between these sounds, a brief, hallowed silence. The blunt forepart of the machine began to lift up, and he thought he could see, through the grid that covered it, tiny electric lights flickering within. When it was fully upright, it was a foot and a half shorter than him. The telescoping limbs began to strip away his cotton suit, quickly but with gentleness. The protective plates slid aside to reveal the main compartment, and for the first time he could see its huge rubber lips. Then, inexorably, the rubber lips kissed the leper's open sores.

N IS FOR NIGHTMARES

ROBERT SHECKLEY

Ghost V

"He's reading our sign now," Gregor said, his long bony face pressed against the peephole in the office door.

"Let me see,' Arnold said.

Gregor pushed him back. "He's going to knock—no, he's changed his mind. He's leaving."

Arnold returned to his desk and laid out another game of solitaire. Gregor kept watch at the peephole.

They had constructed the peephole out of sheer boredom three months after forming their partnership and renting the office. During that time, the AAA Ace Planet Decontamination Service had had no business—in spite of being first in the telephone book. Planetary decontamination was an old, established line, completely monopolized by two large outfits. It was discouraging for a small new firm run by two young men with big ideas and a lot of unpaid-for equipment.

"He's coming back," Gregor called. "*Quick*—look busy and important!"

Arnold swept his cards into a drawer and just finished buttoning his lab gown when the knock came.

Their visitor was a short, bald, tired-looking man. He stared at them dubiously. "You decontaminate planets?"

"That is correct, sir," Gregor said, pushing away a pile of papers and shaking the man's moist hand. "I am Richard Gregor. This is my partner, Doctor Frank Arnold."

Arnold, impressively garbed in a white lab gown and black horn-rimmed glasses, nodded absently and resumed his examination of a row of ancient, crusted test tubes.

"Kindly be seated, Mister—"

"Ferngraum."

"Mr. Ferngraum. I think we can handle just about anything you require," Gregor said heartily. "Flora of fauna control, cleansing atmosphere, purifying water supply, sterilizing soil, stability testing, volcano and earthquake control—anything you need to make a planet fit for human habitation."

Ferngraum still looked dubious. "I'm going to level with you. I've got a problem

203

planet on my hands."

Gregor nodded confidently. "Problems are our business."

"I'm a freelance real-estate broker," Ferngraum said. "You know how it
works—buy a planet, sell a planet, everyone makes a living. Usually I stick with the
scrub worlds and let my buyers do their decontaminating. But a few months ago I
had a chance to buy a real quality planet—took it right out from under the noses of
the big operators."

Ferngraum mopped his forehead unhappily.

"It's a beautiful place," he continued with no enthusiasm whatsoever. "Average
temperature of seventy-one degrees. Mountainous, but fertile. Waterfalls, rain-
bows, all that sort of thing. And no fauna at all."

"Sounds perfect," Gregor said. "Micro-organisms?"

"Nothing dangerous."

"Then what's wrong with the place?"

Ferngraum looked embarrassed. "Maybe you heard about it. The Government
catalogue number is RJC-5. But everyone else calls it 'Ghost V'."

Gregor raised an eyebrow. "Ghost" was an odd nickname for a planet, but he
had heard odder. After all, you had to call them something. There were thousands
of planet-bearing suns within spaceship range, many of them inhabitable or
potentially inhabitable. And there were plenty of people from the civilized worlds
who wanted to colonize them. Religious sects, political minorities, philosophic
groups—or just plain pioneers, out to make a fresh start.

"I don't believe I've heard of it," Gregor said.

Ferngraum squirmed uncomfortably in his chair. "I should have listened to my
wife. But no—I was gonna be a big operator. Paid ten times my usual price for
Ghost V and now I'm stuck with it."

"But what's *wrong* with it?" Gregor asked.

"It seems to be haunted," Ferngraum said in despair.

Ferngraum had radar-checked his planet, then leased it to a combine of farmers
from Dijon VI. The eight-man advance guard landed and, within a day, began to
broadcast garbled reports about demons, ghouls, vampires, dinosaurs and other
inimical fauna.

When a relief ship came for them, all were dead. An autopsy report stated that
the gashes, cuts and marks on their bodies could indeed have been made by almost
anything, even demons, ghouls, vampires, or dinosaurs, if such existed.

Ferngraum was fined for improper decontamination. The farmers dropped their
lease. But he managed to lease it to a group of sun worshippers from Opal II.

The sun worshippers were cautious. They sent their equipment, but only three
men accompanied it, to scout out trouble. The men set up camp, unpacked and
declared the place a paradise. They radioed the home group to come at
once—then, suddenly, there was a wild scream and radio silence.

A patrol ship went to Ghost V, buried the three mangled bodies and departed in
five minutes flat.

"And that did it," Ferngraum said. "Now no one will touch it at any price.
Space crews refuse to land on it. And I still don't know what happened."

He sighed deeply and looked at Gregor. "It's your baby, if you want it."

Gregor and Arnold excused themselves and went into the anteroom.

Arnold whooped at once, "We've got a job!"

"Yeah," Gregor said, "but what a job."

"We wanted the tough ones," Arnold pointed out. "If we lick this, we're established—to say nothing of the profit we'll make on a percentage basis."

"You seem to forget," Gregor said, "I'm the one who has to actually land on the planet. All you do is sit here and interpret my data."

"That's the way we set it up," Arnold reminded him. "I'm the research department—you're the troubleshooter. Remember?"

Gregor remembered. Ever since childhood, he had been sticking his neck out while Arnold stayed home and told him why he was sticking his neck out.

"I don't like it," he said.

"You don't believe in ghosts, do you?"

"No, of course not."

"Well, we can handle anything else. Faint heart ne'er won fair profit."

Gregor shrugged his shoulders. They went back to Ferngraum.

In half an hour, they had worked out their terms—a large percentage of future development profits if they succeeded, a forfeiture clause if they failed.

Gregor walked to the door with Ferngraum. "By the way, sir," he asked, "how did you happen to come to us?"

"No one else would handle it," Ferngraum said, looking extremely pleased with himself. "Good luck."

Three days later, Gregor was aboard a rickety space freighter, bound for Ghost V. He spent his time studying reports on the two colonization attempts and reading survey after survey on supernatural phenomena.

They didn't help at all. No trace of animal life had been found on Ghost V. And no proof of the existence of supernatural creatures had been discovered anywhere in the galaxy.

Gregor pondered this, then checked his weapons as the freighter spiralled into the region of Ghost V. He was carrying an arsenal large enough to start a small war and win it.

If he could find something to shoot at . . .

The captain of the freighter brought his ship to within several thousand feet of the smiling green surface of the planet, but no closer. Gregor parachuted his equipment to the site of the last two camps, shook hands with the captain and 'chuted himself down.

He landed safely and looked up. The freighter was streaking into space as though the furies were after it.

He was alone on Ghost V.

After checking his equipment for breakage, he radioed Arnold that he had landed safely. Then, with drawn blaster, he inspected the sun worshippers' camp.

They had set themselves up at the base of a mountain, beside a small, crystal-clear lake. The prefabs were in perfect condition.

No storm had ever damaged them, because Ghost V was blessed with a beautifully even climate. But they looked pathetically lonely.

Gregor made a careful check of one. Clothes were still neatly packed in cabinets, pictures were hung on the wall and there was even a curtain on one window. In a corner of the room, a case of toys had been opened for the arrival of the main party's children.

A water pistol, a top and a bag of marbles had spilled on to the floor.

Evening was coming, so Gregor dragged his equipment into the prefab and made his preparations. He rigged an alarm system and adjusted it so finely that even a roach would set it off. He put up a radar alarm to scan the immediate area. He unpacked his arsenal, laying the heavy rifles within easy reach, but keeping a hand-blaster in his belt. Then, satisfied, he ate a leisurely supper.

Outside, the evening drifted into night. The warm and dreamy land grew dark. A gentle breeze ruffled the surface of the lake and rustled silkily in the tall grass.

It was all very peaceful.

The settlers must have been hysterical types, he decided. They had probably panicked and killed each other.

After checking his alarm system one last time, Gregor threw his clothes on to a chair, turned off the lights and climbed into bed. The room was illuminated by starlight, stronger than moonlight on Earth. His blaster was under his pillow. All was well with the world.

He had just begun to doze off when he became aware that he was not alone in the room.

That was impossible. His alarm system hadn't gone off. The radar was still humming peacefully.

Yet every nerve in his body was shrieking alarm. He eased the blaster out and looked around.

A man was standing in a corner of the room.

There was no time to consider how he had come. Gregor aimed the blaster and said, "Okay, raise your hands," in a quiet, resolute voice.

The figure didn't move.

Gregor's finger tightened on the trigger, then suddenly relaxed. He recognized the man. It was his own clothing, heaped on a chair, distorted by the starlight and his own imagination.

He grinned and lowered the blaster. The pile of clothing began to stir faintly. Gregor felt a faint breeze from the window and continued to grin.

Then the pile of clothing stood up, stretched itself and began to walk towards him purposefully.

Frozen to his bed, he watched the disembodied clothing, assembled roughly in man-like form, advance on him.

When it was halfway across the room and its empty sleeves were reaching for him, he began to blast.

And kept on blasting, for the rags and remnants slithered towards him as if filled with a life of their own. Flaming bits of cloth crowded towards his face and a belt tried to coil around his legs. He had to burn everything to ashes before the attack stopped.

When it was over, Gregor turned on every light he could find. He brewed a pot of coffee and poured in most of a bottle of brandy. Somehow, he resisted an urge to kick his useless alarm system to pieces. Instead, he radioed his partner.

"That's very interesting," Arnold said, after Gregor had brought him up to date.

"Animation! Very interesting indeed."

"I hoped it would amuse you," Gregor answered bitterly. After several shots of brandy, he was beginning to feel abandoned and abused.

"Did anything else happen?"

"Not yet."

"Well, take care. I've got a theory. Have to do some research on it. By the way, some crazy bookie is laying five to one against you."

"Really?"

"Yeah. I took a piece of it."

"Did you bet for me or against me?" Gregor asked, worried.

"For you, of course," Arnold said indignantly. "We're partners, aren't we?"

They signed off and Gregor brewed another pot of coffee. He was not planning on any more sleep that night. It was comforting to know that Arnold had bet on him. But, then, Arnold was a notoriously bad gambler.

By daylight, Gregor was able to get a few hours of fitful sleep. In the early afternoon he awoke, found some clothes and began to explore the sun worshippers' camp.

Towards evening, he found something. On the wall of a prefab, the word *"Tgasklit"* had been hastily scratched. *Tgasklit*. It meant nothing to him, but he relayed it to Arnold at once.

He then searched his prefab carefully, set up more lights, tested the alarm system and recharged his blaster.

Everything seemed in order. With regret, he watched the sun go down, hoping he would live to see it rise again. Then he settled himself in a comfortable chair and tried to do some constructive thinking.

There was no animal life here—nor were there any walking plants, intelligent rocks or giant brains dwelling in the planet's core. Ghost V hadn't even a moon for someone to hide on.

And he couldn't believe in ghosts or demons. He knew that supernatural happenings tended to break down, under detailed examination, into eminently natural events. The ones that didn't break down—stopped. Ghosts just wouldn't stand still and let a non-believer examine them. The phantom of the castle was invariably on vacation when a scientist showed up with cameras and tape-recorders.

That left another possibility. Suppose someone wanted this planet, but wasn't prepared to pay Ferngraum's price? Couldn't this someone hide here, frighten the settlers, kill them if necessary in order to drive down the price?

That seemed logical. You could even explain the behaviour of his clothes that way. Static electricity, correctly used, could—

Something was standing in front of him. His alarm system, as before, hadn't gone off.

Gregor looked up slowly. The thing in front of him was about ten feet tall and roughly human in shape, except for its crocodile head. It was coloured a bright crimson and had purple stripes running lengthwise on its body. In one claw, it was carrying a large brown can.

"Hello," it said.

"Hello," Gregor gulped. His blaster was on a table only two feet away. He wondered, would the thing attack if he reached for it?

"What's your name?" Gregor asked, with the calmness of deep shock.

"I'm the Purple-striped Grabber," the thing said. "I grab things."

"How interesting." Gregor's hand began to creep towards the blaster.

"I grab things named Richard Gregor," the Grabber told him in its bright, ingenuous voice. "And I usually eat them in chocolate sauce." It held up the brown can and Gregor saw that it was labelled "Smig's Chocolate—An Ideal Sauce to Use with Gregors, Arnolds and Flynns".

Gregor's fingers touching the butt of the blaster. He asked, "Were you planning to eat me?"

"Oh, yes," the Grabber said.

Gregor had the gun now. He flipped off the safety catch and fired. The radiant blast cascaded off the Grabber's chest and singed the floor, the walls and Gregor's eyebrows.

"That won't hurt me," the Grabber explained. "I'm too tall."

The blaster dropped from Gregor's fingers. The Grabber leaned forward.

"I'm not going to eat you now," the Grabber said.

"No?" Gregor managed to enunciate.

"No. I can only eat you tomorrow, on May first. Those are the rules. I just came to ask a favour."

"What is it?"

The Grabber smiled winningly. "Would you be a good sport and eat a few apples? They flavour the flesh so wonderfully."

And, with that, the striped monster vanished.

With shaking hands, Gregor worked the radio and told Arnold everything that had happened.

"Hmm," Arnold said. "Purple-striped Grabber, eh? I think that clinches it. Everything fits."

"What fits? What is it?"

"First, do as I say. I want to make sure."

Obeying Arnold's instructions, Gregor unpacked his chemical equipment and laid out a number of test tubes, retorts and chemicals. He stirred, mixed, added and subtracted as directed and finally put the mixture on the stove to heat.

"Now," Gregor said, coming back to the radio, "tell me what's going on."

"Certainly. I looked up the word *"Tgasklit"*. It's Opalian. It means "many-toothed ghost". The sun worshippers were from Opal. What does that suggest to you?"

"They were killed by a home-town ghost," Gregor replied nastily. "It must have stowed away on their ship. Maybe there was a curse and—"

"Calm down," Arnold said. "There aren't any ghosts in this. Is the solution boiling yet?"

"No."

"Tell me when it does. Now let's take your animated clothing. Does it remind you of anything?"

Gregor thought. "Well," he said, "when I was a kid—no, that's ridiculous."

"Out with it," Arnold insisted.

"When I was a kid, I never left clothing on a chair. In the dark, it always looked like a man or a dragon or something. I guess everyone's had that experience. But it doesn't explain—"

"Sure it does! Remember the Purple-striped Grabber now?"

"No. Why should I?"

"Because you invented him! Remember? We must have been eight or nine, you and me and Jimmy Flynn. We invented the most horrible monster you could think of—he was our own personal monster and he only wanted to eat you or me or Jimmy—flavoured with chocolate sauce. But only on the first of every month, when the report cards were due. You had to use the magic word to get rid of him."

Then Gregor remembered and wondered how he could ever have forgotten. How many nights had he stayed up in fearful expectation of the Grabber? It had made bad report cards seem very unimportant.

"Is the solution boiling?" Arnold asked.

"Yes," said Gregor, glancing obediently at the stove.

"What colour is it?"

"A sort of greenish blue. No, it's more blue than—"

"Right. You can pour it out. I want to run a few more tests, but I think we've got it licked."

"Got *what* licked? Would you do a little explaining?"

"It's obvious. The planet has no animal life. There are no ghosts or at least none solid enough to kill off a party of armed men. Hallucination was the answer, so I looked for something that would produce it. I found plenty. Aside from all the drugs on Earth, there are about a dozen hallucination-forming gases in the *Catalogue of Alien Trace Elements*. There are depressants, stimulants, stuff that'll make you feel like a genius or an earthworm or an eagle. This particular one corresponds to Longstead 42 in the catalogue. It's a heavy, transparent, odourless gas, not harmful physically. It's an imagination stimulant."

"You mean I was just having hallucinations? I tell you—"

"Not quite that simple," Arnold cut in. "Longstead 42 works directly on the subconscious. It releases your strongest subconscious fears, the childhood terrors you've been suppressing. It animates them. And that's what you've been seeing."

"Then there's actually nothing here?" Gregor asked.

"Nothing physical. But the hallucinations are real enough to whoever is having them."

Gregor reached over for another bottle of brandy. This called for a celebration.

"It won't be hard to decontaminate Ghost V," Arnold went on confidently. "We can cancel the Longstead 42 with no difficulty. And then—we'll be rich, partner!"

Gregor suggested a toast, then thought of something disturbing. "If they're just hallucinations, what happened to the settlers?"

Arnold was silent for a moment. "Well," he said finally, "Longstead may have a tendency to stimulate the mortido—the death instinct. The settlers must have gone crazy. Killed each other."

"And no survivors?"

"Sure, why not? The last ones alive committed suicide or died of wounds. Don't worry about it. I'm chartering a ship immediately and coming out to run those tests. Relax. I'll pick you up in a day or two."

Gregor signed off. He allowed himself the rest of the bottle of brandy that night. It seemed only fair. The mystery of Ghost V was solved and they were going to be rich. Soon *he* would be able to hire a man to land on strange planets for him, while *he* sat home and gave instructions over a radio.

He awoke late the next day with a hangover. Arnold's ship hadn't arrived yet, so he packed his equipment and waited. By evening, there was still no ship. He sat in the doorway of the prefab and watched a gaudy sunset, then went inside and made dinner.

The problem of the settlers still bothered him, but he determined not to worry about it. Undoubtedly there was a logical answer.

After dinner, he stretched out on a bed. He had barely closed his eyes when he heard someone cough apologetically.

"Hello," said the Purple-striped Grabber.

His own personal hallucination had returned to eat him. "Hello, old chap," Gregor said cheerfully, without a bit of fear or worry.

"Did you eat the apples?"

"Dreadfully sorry, I forgot."

"Oh, well." The Grabber tried to conceal his disappointment. "I brought the chocolate sauce." He held up the can.

Gregor smiled. "You can leave now," he said. "I know you're just a figment of my imagination. You can't hurt me."

"I'm not going to hurt you,' the Grabber said. "I'm just going to eat you."

He walked up to Gregor. Gregor held his ground, smiling, although he wished the Grabber didn't appear so solid and undreamlike. The Grabber leaned over and bit his arm experimentally.

He jumped back and looked at his arm. There were toothmarks on it. Blood was oozing out—real blood—*his* blood.

The colonists had been bitten, gashed, torn and ripped.

At that moment, Gregor remembered an exhibition of hypnotism he had once seen. The hypnotist had told the subject he was putting a lighted cigarette on his arm. Then he had touched the spot with a pencil.

Within seconds, an angry red blister had appeared on the subject's arm, because he *believed* he had been burned. If your subconscious thinks you're dead, you're dead. If it orders the stigmata of toothmarks, they are there.

He didn't believe in the Grabber.

But his subconscious did.

Gregor tried to run for the door. The Grabber cut him off. It seized him in its claws and bent to reach his neck.

The magic word! What was it?

Gregor shouted, *"Alphoisto?"*

"Wrong word," said the Grabber. "Please don't squirm."

"Regnastikio?"

"Nope. Stop wriggling and it'll be over before you—"

"Voorshpellhappilo!"

The Grabber let out a scream of pain and released him. It bounded high into the air and vanished.

Gregor collapsed into a chair. That had been close. Too close. It would be a particularly stupid way to die—rent by his own death-desiring subconscious, slashed by his own imagination, killed by his own conviction. It was fortunate he had remembered the word. Now if Arnold would only hurry . . .

He heard a low chuckle of amusement.

It came from the blackness of a half-opened closet door, touching off an almost forgotten memory. He was nine years old again, and the Shadower—his Shadower—was a strange, thin, grisly creature who hid in doorways, slept under beds and attacked only in the dark.

"Turn out the lights," the Shadower said.

"Not a chance," Gregor retorted, drawing his blaster. As long as the lights were on, he was safe.

"You'd better turn them off."

"No!"

"Very well. Egan, Megan, Degan!"

Three little creatures scampered into the room. They raced to the nearest light bulb, flung themselves on it and began to gulp hungrily.

The room was growing darker.

Gregor blasted at them each time they approached a light. Glass shattered, but the nimble creatures darted out of the way.

And then Gregor realized what he had done. The creatures couldn't actually eat light. Imagination can't make any impression on inanimate matter. He had *imagined* that the room was growing dark and—

He had shot out his light bulbs! His own destructive subconscious had tricked him.

Now the Shadower stepped out. Leaping from shadow to shadow, he came towards Gregor.

The blaster had no effect. Gregor tried frantically to think of the magic word—and terrifiedly remembered that no magic word banished the Shadower.

He backed away, the Shadower advancing, until he was stopped by a packing case. The Shadower towered over him and Gregor shrank to the floor and closed his eyes.

His hands came in contact with something cold. He was leaning against the packing case of toys for the settlers' children. And he was holding a water pistol.

Gregor brandished it. The Shadower backed away, eyeing the weapon with apprehension.

Quickly, Gregor ran to the tap and filled the pistol. He directed a deadly stream of water into the creature.

The Shadower howled in agony and vanished.

Gregor smiled tightly and slipped the empty gun into his belt.

A water pistol was the right weapon to use against an imaginary monster.

It was nearly dawn when the ship landed and Arnold stepped out. Without wasting any time, he set up his tests. By midday, it was done and the element definitely established as Longstead 42. He and Gregor packed up immediately and blasted off.

Once they were in space. Gregor told his partner everything that had happened.

"Pretty rough," said Arnold softly, but with deep feeling.

Gregor could smile with modest heroism now that he was safely off Ghost V. "Could have been worse," he said.

"How?"

"Suppose Jimmy Flynn were here. There was a kid who could really dream up monsters. Remember the Grumbler?"

"All I remember is the nightmares it gave me," Arnold said.

They were on their way home. Arnold jotted down some notes for an article entitled "The Death Instinct on Ghost V: An Examination of Subconscious Stimulation, Hysteria, and Mass Hallucination in Producing Physical Stigmata". Then he went to the control room to set the auto-pilot.

Gregor threw himself on a couch, determined to get his first decent night's sleep since landing on Ghost V. He had barely dozed off when Arnold hurried in, his face pasty with terror.

"I think there's something in the control room," he said.

Gregor sat up. "There can't be. We're off the—"

There was a low growl from the control room.

"Oh, my God!" Arnold gasped. He concentrated furiously for a few seconds. "I know. I left the airlocks open when I landed. We're still breathing Ghost V air!"

And there, framed in the open doorway, was an immense grey creature with red spots on its hide. It had an amazing number of arms, legs, tentacles, claws and teeth, plus two tiny wings on its back. It walked slowly towards them, mumbling and moaning.

They both recognized it as the Grumbler.

Gregor dashed forward and slammed the door in its face. "We should be safe in here," he panted. "That door is airtight. But how will we pilot the ship?"

"We won't," Arnold said. "We'll have to trust the robot pilot—unless we can figure out some way of getting that thing out of there."

They noticed that a faint smoke was beginning to seep through the sealed edges of the door.

"What's that?" Arnold asked, with a sharp edge of panic in his voice.

Gregor frowned. "You remember, don't you? The Grumbler can get into any room. There's no way of keeping him out."

"I don't remember anything about him," Arnold said. "Does he eat people?"

"No. As I recall, he just mangles them thoroughly."

The smoke was beginning to solidify into the immense grey shape of the Grumbler. They retreated into the next compartment and sealed the door. Within seconds, the thin smoke was leaking through.

"This is ridiculous," Arnold said, biting his lip. "To be haunted by an imaginary monster—wait! You've still got your water pistol, haven't you?"

"Yes, but—"

"Give it to me!"

Arnold hurried over to a water tank and filled the pistol. The Grumbler had taken form again and was lumbering towards them, groaning unhappily. Arnold raked it with a stream of water.

The Grumbler kept on advancing.

"Now it's all coming back to me," Gregor said. "A water pistol never could stop the Grumbler."

They backed into the next room and slammed the door. Behind them was only the bunkroom with nothing behind that but the deadly vacuum of space.

Gregor asked, "Isn't there something you can do about the atmosphere?"

Arnold shook his head. "It's dissipating now. But it takes about twenty hours for the effects of Longstead to wear off."

"Haven't you any antidote?"

"No."

Once again the Grumbler was materializing, and neither silently nor pleasantly.

"How can we kill it?" Arnold asked. "There must be a way. Magic words? How about a wooden sword?"

Gregor shook his head. "I remember the Grumbler now," he said unhappily.

"What kills it?"

"It can't be destroyed by water pistols, cap guns, firecrackers, slingshots, stink bombs, or any other childhood weapon. The Grumbler is absolutely unkillable."

"That Flynn and his damned imagination! Why did we have to talk about him? How do you get rid of it then?"

"I told you. You don't. It just has to go away of its own accord."

The Grumbler was full size now. Gregor and Arnold hurried into the tiny bunkroom and slammed their last door.

"*Think*, Gregor," Arnold pleaded. "No kid invents a monster without a defence of some sort. *Think!*"

"The Grumbler cannot be killed," Gregor said.

The red-spotted monster was taking shape again. Gregor thought back over all the midnight horrors he had ever known. He *must* have done something as a child to neutralize the power of the unknown.

And then—almost too late—he remembered.

Under auto-pilot controls, the ship flashed Earthwards with the Grumbler as complete master. He marched up and down the empty corridors and floated through steel partitions into cabins and cargo compartments, moaning, groaning and cursing because he could not get at any victim.

The ship reached the solar system and took up an automatic orbit around the moon.

Gregor peered out cautiously, ready to duck back if necessary. There was no sinister shuffling, no moaning or groaning, no hungry mist seeping under the door or through the walls.

"All clear," he called out to Arnold. "The Grumbler's gone."

Safe within the ultimate defence against night horrors—wrapped in the blankets that had covered their heads—they climbed out of their bunks.

"I told you the water pistol wouldn't do any good," Gregor said.

Arnold gave him a sick grin and put the pistol in his pocket. "I'm hanging on to it. If I ever get married and have a kid, it's going to be his first present."

"Not for any of mine," said Gregor. He patted the bunk affectionately. "You can't beat blankets over the head for protection."

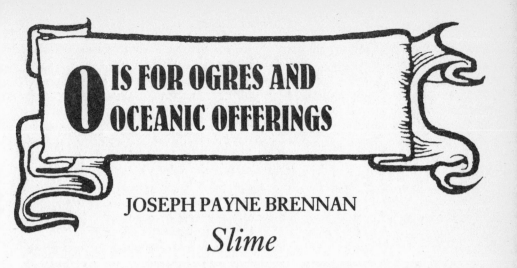

O IS FOR OGRES AND OCEANIC OFFERINGS

JOSEPH PAYNE BRENNAN

Slime

It was a great grey-black hood of horror moving over the floor of the sea. It slid through the soft ooze like a monstrous mantle of slime obscenely animated with questing life. It was by turns viscid and fluid. At times it flattened out and flowed through the carpet of mud like an inky pool; occasionally it paused, seeming to shrink in upon itself, and reared up out of the ooze until it resembled an irregular cone or a gigantic hood. Although it possessed no eyes, it had a marvellously developed sense of touch, and it possessed a sensitivity to minute vibrations which was almost akin to telepathy. It was plastic, essentially shapeless. It could shoot out long tentacles, until it bore a resemblance to a nightmare squid or a huge starfish; it could retract itself into a round flattened disc, or squeeze into an irregular hunched shape so that it looked like a black boulder sunk on the bottom of the sea.

It had prowled the black water endlessly. It had been formed when the earth and the seas were young; it was almost as old as the ocean itself. It moved through a night which had no beginning and no dissolution. The black sea basin where it lurked had been dark since the world began—an environment only a little less inimical than the stupendous gulfs of interplanetary space.

It was animated by a single, unceasing, never-satisfied drive: a voracious, insatiable hunger. It could survive for months without food, but minutes after eating it was as ravenous as ever. Its appetite was appalling and incalculable.

On the icy ink-black floor of the sea the battle for survival was savage, hideous—and usually brief. But for the shape of moving slime there was no battle. It ate whatever came its way, regardless of size, shape or disposition. It absorbed microscopic plankton and giant squid with equal assurance. Had its surface been less fluid, it might have retained the circular scars left by the grappling suckers of the wildly threshing deep-water squid, or the jagged toothmarks of the anachronistic frillshark, but as it was, neither left any evidence of its absorption. When the lifting curtain of living slime swayed out of the mud and closed upon them, their fiercest death throes came to nothing.

The horror did not know fear. There was nothing to be afraid of. It ate whatever moved, or tried not to move, and it had never encountered anything which could in turn eat it. If a squid's sucker, or a shark's tooth, tore into the mass of its viscosity, the rent flowed in upon itself and immediately closed. If a segment was detached, it could be retrieved and absorbed back into the whole.

The black mantle reigned supreme in its savage world of slime and silence. It groped greedily and endlessly through the mud, eating and never sleeping, never resting. If it lay still, it was only to trap food which might otherwise be lost. If it rushed with terrifying speed across the slimy bottom, it was never to escape an enemy, but always to flop its hideous fluidity upon its sole and inevitable quarry—food.

It had evolved out of the muck and slime of the primitive sea floor, and it was as alien to ordinary terrestrial life as the weird denizens of some wild planet in a distant galaxy. It was an anachronistic experiment of nature compared to which the sabre-toothed tiger, the woolly mammoth and even Tyrannosaurus, the slashing, murderous king of the great earth reptiles, were as tame, weak entities.

Had it not been for a vast volcanic upheaval on the bottom of the ocean basin, the black horror would have crept out its entire existence on the silent sea ooze without ever manifesting its hideous powers to mankind.

Fate, in the form of a violent subterranean explosion, covering huge areas of the ocean's floor, hurled it out of its black slime world and sent it spinning towards the surface.

Had it been an ordinary deep-water fish, it never would have survived the experience. The explosion itself, or the drastic lessening of water pressure as it shot towards the surface, would have destroyed it. But it was no ordinary fish. Its viscosity, or plasticity, or whatever it was that constituted its essentially amoebic structure, permitted it to survive.

It reached the surface slightly stunned and flopped on the surging waters like a great blob of black blubber. Immense waves stirred up by the subterranean explosion swept it swiftly towards shore, and because it was somewhat stunned it did not try to resist the roaring mountains of water.

Along with scattered ash, pumice, and the puffed bodies of dead fish, the black horror was hurled towards a beach. The huge waves carried it more than a mile inland, far beyond the strip of sandy shore, and deposited it in the midst of a deep brackish swamp area.

As luck would have it, the submarine explosion and subsequent tidal wave took place at night, and therefore the slime horror was not immediately subjected to a new and hateful experience—light.

Although the midnight darkness of the storm-lashed swamp did not begin to compare with the stygian blackness of the sea bottom where even violet rays of the spectrum could not penetrate, the marsh darkness was nevertheless deep and intense.

As the water of the great wave receded, sluicing through the thorn jungle and back out to sea, the black horror clung to a mud bank surrounded by a rank growth of cattails. It was aware of the sudden, startling change in its environment, and for some time it lay motionless, concentrating its attention on obscure internal readjustment which the absence of crushing pressure and a surrounding cloak of frigid sea water demanded. Its adaptability was incredible and horrifying. It achieved in a few hours what an ordinary creature could have attained only through a process of gradual evolution. Three hours after the titanic wave flopped it on to the mudbank, it had undergone swift organic changes which left it relatively at ease in its new environment.

In fact, it felt lighter and more mobile than it ever had before in its sea basin existence.

As it flung out feelers and attuned itself to the minutest vibrations and emanations of the swamp area, its pristine hunger drive reasserted itself with overwhelming urgency. And the tale which its sensory apparatus returned to the monstrous something which served it as a brain, excited it tremendously. It sensed at once that the swamp was filled with luscious tidbits of quivering food—more food, and food of a greater variety than it had ever encountered on the cold floor of the sea.

Its savage, incessant hunger seemed unbearable. Its slimy mass was swept by a shuddering wave of anticipation.

Sliding off the mud bank, it slithered over the cattails into an adjacent area consisting of deep black pools interspersed with water-logged tussocks. Weed stalks stuck up out of the water and the decayed trunks of fallen trees floated half-submerged in the larger pools.

Ravenous with hunger, it sloshed into the bog area, flicking its tentacles about. Within minutes it had snatched up several fat frogs and a number of small fish. These, however, merely titillated its appetite. Its hunger turned into a kind of ecstatic fury. It commenced a systematic hunt, plunging to the bottom of each pool and quickly but carefully exploring every inch of its oozy bottom. The first creature of any size which it encountered was a muskrat. An immense curtain of adhesive slime suddenly swept out of the darkness, closed upon it—and squeezed.

Heartened and whetted by its find, the hood of horror rummaged the rank pools with renewed zeal. When it surfaced, it carefully probed the tussocks for anything that might have escaped it in the water. Once it snatched up a small bird nesting in some swamp grass. Occasionally it slithered up the criss-crossed trunks of fallen trees, bearing them down with its unspeakable slimy bulk, and hung briefly suspended like a great dripping curtain of black marsh mud.

It was approaching a somewhat less swampy and more deeply wooded area when it gradually became aware of a subtle change in its new environment. It paused, hesitating, and remained half in and half out of a small pond near the edge of the nearest trees.

Although it had absorbed twenty-five or thirty pounds of food in the form of frogs, fish, water snakes, the muskrat, and a few smaller creatures, its fierce hunger had not left it. Its monstrous appetite urged it on, and yet something held it anchored in the pond.

What it sensed, but could not literally see, was the rising sun spreading a grey light over the swamp. The horror had never encountered any illumination except that generated by the grotesque phosphorescent appendages of various deep-sea fishes. Natural light was totally unknown to it.

As the dawn light strengthened, breaking through the scattering storm clouds, the black slime monster fresh from the inky floor of the sea sensed that something utterly unknown was flooding in upon it. Light was hateful to it. It cast out quick feelers, hoping to catch and crush the light. But the more frenzied its efforts became, the more intense became the abhorred aura surrounding it.

At length, as the sun rose visibly above the trees, the horror, in baffled rage rather than in fear, grudgingly slid back into the pond and burrowed into the soft ooze of its bottom. There it remained while the sun shone and the small creatures of the swamp ventured forth on furtive errands.

A few miles away from Wharton's Swamp, in the small town of Clinton Center, Henry Hossing sleepily crawled out of the improvised alley shack which had afforded him a degree of shelter for the night and stumbled into the street. Passing a hand across his rheumy eyes, he scratched the stubble on his cheek and blinked listlessly at the rising sun. He had not slept well; the storm of the night before had kept him awake. Besides, he had gone to bed hungry, and that never agreed with him.

Glancing furtively along the street, he walked slouched forward, with his head bent down, and most of the time he kept his eyes on the walk or on the gutter in the hopes of spotting a chance coin.

Clinton Center had not been kind to him. The handouts were sparse, and only yesterday he had been warned out of town by one of the local policemen.

Grumbling to himself, he reached the end of the street and started to cross. Suddenly he stooped quickly and snatched up something from the edge of the pavement.

It was a crumpled green bill, and as he frantically unfolded it, a look of stupefied rapture spread across his bristly face. Ten dollars! More money than he had possessed at any one time in months!

Stowing it carefully in the one good pocket of his seedy grey jacket, he crossed the street with a swift stride. Instead of sweeping the sidewalks, his eyes now darted along the rows of stores and restaurants.

He paused on one restaurant, hesitated, and finally went on until he found another less pretentious one a few blocks away.

When he sat down, the counterman shook his head. "Get goin', bud. No free coffee today."

With a wide grin, the hobo produced his ten-dollar bill and spread it on the counter. "That covers a good breakfast here, pardner?"

The counterman seemed irritated. "O.K. O.K. What'll you have?" He eyed the bill suspiciously.

Henry Hossing ordered orange juice, toast, ham and eggs, oatmeal, melon, and coffee.

When it appeared, he ate every bit of it, ordered three additional cups of coffee, paid the cheque as if two-dollar breakfasts were customary with him, and then sauntered back to the street.

Shortly after noon, after his three-dollar lunch, he saw the liquor store. For a few minutes he stood across the street from it, fingering his five-dollar bill. Finally he crossed with an abstracted smile, entered and bought a quart of rye.

He hesitated on the sidewalk, debating whether or not he should return to the little shack in the side alley. After a minute or two of indecision, he decided against it and struck out instead for Wharton's Swamp. The local police were far less likely to disturb him there, and since the skies were clearing and the weather mild, there was little immediate need of shelter.

Angling off the highway which skirted the swamp several miles from town, he crossed a marshy meadow, pushed through a fringe of bush, and sat down under a sweet-gum tree which bordered a deeply wooded area.

By late afternoon he had achieved a quite cheerful glow, and he had little inclination to return to Clinton Center. Rousing himself from reverie, he stumbled about collecting enough wood for a small fire and went back to his sylvan seat under the sweet-gum.

He slept briefly as dusk descended, but finally bestirred himself again to build a fire, as deeper shadows fell over the swamp. Then he returned to his swiftly diminishing bottle. He was suspended in a warm net of inflamed fantasy when something abruptly broke the spell and brought him back to earth.

The flicking flames of his fire had dwindled down until now only a dim eerie glow illuminated the immediate area under the sweet-gum. He saw nothing and at the moment heard nothing, and yet he was filled with a sudden and profound sense of lurking menace.

He stood up, staggering, leaned back against the sweet-gum and peered fearfully into the shadows. In the deep darkness beyond the waning arc of firelight he could distinguish nothing which had any discernible form or colour.

Then he detected the stench and shuddered. In spite of the reek of cheap whisky which clung around him, the smell was overpowering. It was a heavy, fulsome fetid, alien, and utterly repellent. It was vaguely fish-like, but otherwise beyond any known comparison.

As he stood trembling under the sweet-gum, Henry Hossing thought of something dead which had lain for long ages at the bottom of the sea.

Filled with mounting alarm, he looked around for some wood which he might add to the dying fire. All he could find nearby, however, were a few twigs. He threw these on and the flames licked up briefly and subsided.

He listened and heard—or imagined he heard—an odd sort of slithering sound in the nearby bushes. It seemed to retreat slightly as the flames shot up.

Genuine terror took possession of him. He knew that he was in no condition to flee—and now he came to the horrifying conclusion that whatever unspeakable menace waited in the surrounding darkness was temporarily held at bay only by the failing gleam of his little fire.

Frantically he looked around for more wood. But there was none. None, that is, within the faint glow of firelight. And he dared not venture beyond.

He began to tremble uncontrollably. He tried to scream, but no sound came out of his tightened throat.

The ghastly stench became stronger, and now he was sure that he could hear a strange sliding, slithering sound in the black shadows beyond the remaining spark of firelight.

He stood frozen in absolute helpless panic as the tiny fire smouldered down into darkness.

At the last instant a charred bit of wood broke apart, sending up a few sparks, and in that flicker of final light he glimpsed the horror.

It had already glided out of the bushes, and now it rushed across the small clearing with nightmare speed. It was a final incarnation of all the fears, shuddering apprehensions, and bad dreams which Henry Hossing had ever known in his life. It was a fiend from the pit of Hell come to claim him at last.

A terrible ringing scream burst from his throat, but it was smothered before it was finished as the black shape of slime fastened upon him with irresistible force.

Giles Gowse—"Old Man" Gowse—got out of bed after eight hours of fitful tossing and intermittent nightmares and grouchily brewed coffee in the kitchen of his dilapidated farmhouse on the edge of Wharton's Swamp. Half the night, it seemed, the stench of stale sea-water had permeated the house. His interrupted sleep had been full of foreboding, full of shadowy and evil portents.

Muttering to himself, he finished breakfast, took a milk pail from the pantry, and started for the barn where he kept his single cow.

As he approached the barn, the strange offensive odour which had plagued him during the night assailed his nostrils anew.

"Wharton's Swamp! That's what it is!" he told himself. And he shook his fist at it.

When he entered the barn the stench was stronger than ever. Scowling, he strode towards the rickety stall where he kept the cow, Sarey.

Then he stood still and stared. Sarey was gone. The stall was empty.

He re-entered the barnyard. "Sarey!" he called.

Rushing back into the barn, he inspected the stall. The rancid reek of the sea was strong here, and now he noticed a kind of shine on the floor. Bending closer, he saw that it was a slick coat of glistening slime, as if some unspeakable creature covered with ooze had crept in and out of the stall.

This discovery, coupled with the weird disappearance of Sarey, was too much for his jangled nerves. With a wild yell he ran out of the barn and started for Clinton Center, two miles away.

His reception in the town enraged him. When he tried to tell people about the disappearance of his cow, Sarey, about the reek of sea and ooze in his barn the night before, they laughed at him. The more impolite ones, that is. Most of the others patiently heard him out—and then winked and touched their heads significantly when he was out of sight.

One man, the druggist, Jim Jelinson, seemed mildly interested. He said that as he was coming through his backyard from the garage late the previous evening, he had heard a fearful shriek somewhere in the distant darkness. It might, he averred, have come from the direction of Wharton's Swamp. But it had not been repeated and eventually he had dismised it from his mind.

When Old Man Gowse started for home late in the afternoon he was filled with sullen, resentful bitterness. They thought he was crazy, eh? Well, Sarey *was* gone; they couldn't explain *that* away, could they? They explained the smell by saying it was dead fish cast up by the big wave which had washed into the swamp during the storm. Well—maybe. And the slime on his barn floor they said was snails. *Snails!* As if any he'd ever seen could cause that much slime!

As he was nearing home, he met Rupert Barnaby, his nearest neighbour. Rupert was carrying a rifle and he was accompanied by Jibbe, his hound.

Although there had been an element of bad blood between the two bachelor neighbours for some time, Old Man Gowse, much to Barnaby's surprise, nodded and stopped.

"Evenin' hunt, neighbour?"

Barnaby nodded. "Thought Jibbe might start up a coon. Moon later, likely."

"My cow's gone," Old Man Gowse said abruptly. "If you should see her—" He paused. "But I don't think you will. . . ."

Barnaby, bewildered, stared at him. "What you gettin' at?"

Old Man Gowse repeated what he had been telling all day in Clinton Center.

He shook his head when he finished, adding, "I wouldn't go huntin' in that swamp tonight fur—ten thousand dollars!"

Rupert Barnaby threw back his head and laughed. He was a big man, muscular, resourceful, and level-headed—little given to even mild flights of the imagination.

"Gowse," he laughed, "no use you givin' me those spook stories! Your cow got loose and wandered off. Why, I ain't even seen a bobcat in that swamp for over a year!"

Old Man Gowse set his lips in a grim line. "Maybe," he said, as he turned away, "you'll see suthin' worse than a wildcat in that swamp tonight!"

Shaking his head, Barnaby took after his impatient hound. Old Man Gowse was getting queer all right. One of these days he'd probably go off altogether and have to be locked up.

Jibbe ran ahead, sniffing, darting from one ditch to another. As twilight closed in, Barnaby angled off the main road on to a twisting path which led into Wharton's Swamp.

He loved hunting. He would rather tramp through the brush than sit at home in an easy chair. And even if an evening's foray turned up nothing, he didn't particularly mind. Actually he made out quite well; at least half his meat supply consisted of the rabbits, racoons, and occasional deer which he brought down in Wharton's Swamp.

When the moon rose, he was deep in the swamp. Twice Jibbe started off after rabbits, but both times he returned quickly, looking somewhat sheepish.

Something about his actions began to puzzle Barnaby. The dog seemed reluctant to move ahead; he hung directly in front of the hunter. Once Barnaby tripped over him and nearly fell headlong.

The hunter paused finally, frowning, and looked ahead. The swamp appeared no different than usual. True, a rather offensive stench hung over it, but that was merely the result of the big waves which had splashed far inland during the recent storm. Probably an accumulation of seaweed and the decaying bodies of some dead fish lay rotting in the stagnant pools of the swamp.

Barnaby spoke sharply to the dog. "What ails you, boy? Git, now! You trip me again, you'll get a boot!"

The dog started ahead some distance, but with an air of reluctance. He sniffed the clumps of marsh grass in a perfunctory manner and seemed to have lost interest in the hunt.

Barnaby grew exasperated. Even when they discovered the fresh track of a racoon in the soft mud near a little pool, Jibbe manifested only slight interest.

He did run on ahead a little further, however, and Barnaby began to hope that, as they closed in, he would regain his customary enthusiasm.

In this he was mistaken. As they approached a thickly wooded area, latticed with tree thorns and covered with a heavy growth of cattails, the dog suddenly crouched in the shadows and refused to budge.

Barnaby was sure that the racoon had taken refuge in the nearby thickets. The dog's unheard of conduct infuriated him.

After a number of sharp cuffs, Jibbe arose stiffly and moved ahead, the hair on his neck bristled up like a lion's mane.

Swearing to himself, Barnaby pushed into the darkened thickets after him.

It was quite black under the trees, in spite of the moonlight, and he moved cautiously in order to avoid stepping into a pool.

Suddenly, with a frantic yelp of terror, Jibbe literally darted between his legs and shot out of the thickets. He ran on, howling weirdly as he went.

For the first time that evening Barnaby experienced a thrill of fear. In all his previous experience, Jibbe had never turned tail. On one occasion he had even plunged in after a sizeable bear.

Scowling into the deep darkness, Barnaby could see nothing. There were no baleful eyes glaring at him.

As his own eyes tried to penetrate the surrounding blackness, he recalled Old Man Gowse's warning with a bitter grimace. If the old fool happened to spot Jibbe streaking out of the swamp, Barnaby would never hear the end of it.

The thought of this angered him. He pushed ahead now with a feeling of sullen rage for whatever had terrified the dog. A good rifle shot would solve the mystery.

All at once he stopped and listened. From the darkness immediately ahead, he detected an odd sound, as if a large bulk were being dragged over the cattails.

He hesitated, unable to see anything, stoutly resisting an idiotic impulse to flee. The black darkness and the slimy stench of stagnant pools here in the thickets seemed to be suffocating him.

His heart began to pound as the slithering noise came closer. Every instinct told him to turn and run, but a kind of desperate stubbornness held him rooted to the spot.

The sound grew louder, and suddenly he was positive that something deadly and formidable was rushing towards him through the thickets with accelerated speed.

Throwing up his rifle, he pointed at the direction of the sound and fired.

In the brief flash of the rifle he saw something black and enormous and glistening, like a great flapping hood, break through the final thicket. It seemed to be *rolling* towards him, and it was moving with nightmare swiftness.

He wanted to scream and run, but even as the horror rushed forward, he understood that flight at this point would be futile. Even though the blood seemed to have congealed in his veins, he held the rifle pointed up and kept on firing.

The shots had no more visible effect than so many pebbles launched from a slingshot. At the last instant his nerve broke and he tried to escape, but the monstrous hood lunged upon him, flapped over him, and squeezed, and his attempt at a scream turned into a tiny gurgle in his throat.

Old Man Gowse got up early, after another uneasy night, and walked out to inspect the barnyard area. Nothing further seemed amiss, but there was still no sign of Sarey. And that detestable odour arose from the direction of Wharton's

Swamp when the wind was right.

After breakfast, Gowse set out for Rupert Barnaby's place, a mile or so distant along the road. He wasn't sure himself what he expected to find.

When he reached Barnaby's small but neat frame house, all was quiet. Too quiet. Usually Barnaby was up and about soon after sunrise.

On a sudden impulse, Gowse walked up the path and rapped on the front door. He waited and there was no reply. He knocked again, and after another pause, stepped off the porch.

Jibbe, Barnaby's hound, slunk around the side of the house. Ordinarily he would bound about and bark. But today he stood motionless—or nearly so—he was trembling—and stared at Gowse. The dog had a cowed, frightened, guilty air which was entirely alien to him.

"Where's Rup?" Gowse called to him. "Go get Rup!"

Instead of starting off, the dog threw back his head and emitted an eerie, long-drawn howl.

Gowse shivered. With a backward glance at the silent house, he started off down the road.

Now maybe they'd listen to him, he thought grimly. The day before they had laughed about the disappearance of Sarey. Maybe they wouldn't laugh so easily when he told them that Rupert Barnaby had gone into Wharton's Swamp with his dog—and that the dog had come back alone!

When Police Chief Miles Underbeck saw Old Man Gowse come into headquarters in Clinton Center, he sat back and sighed heavily. He was busy this morning and undoubtedly Old Man Gowse was coming in to inquire about the infernal cow of his that had wandered off.

The old eccentric had a new and startling report, however. He claimed that Rupert Barnaby was missing. He'd gone into the swamp the night before, Gowse insisted, and had not returned.

When Chief Underbeck questioned him closely, Gowse admitted that he wasn't *positive* Barnaby hadn't returned. It was barely possible that he had returned home very early in the morning and then left again before Gowse arrived.

But Gowse fixed his flashing eyes on the Chief and shook his head. "He never came out, I tell ye! That dog of his knows! Howled, he did, like a dog howls for the dead! Whatever come took Sarey—got Barnaby in the swamp last night!"

Chief Underbeck was not an excitable man. Gowse's burst of melodrama irritated him and left him unimpressed.

Somewhat gruffly he promised to look into the matter if Barnaby had not turned up by evening. Barnaby, he pointed out, knew the swamp better than anyone else in the county. And he was perfectly capable of taking care of himself. Probably, the Chief suggested, he had sent the dog home and gone elsewhere after finishing his hunt the evening before. The chances were he'd be back by supper time.

Old Man Gowse shook his head with a kind of fatalistic scepticism. Vouching that events would soon prove his fears well founded, he shambled grouchily out of the station.

The day passed and there was no sign of Rupert Barnaby. At six o'clock, Old

Man Gowse grimly marched into the Crown, Clinton Center's second-rung hotel, and registered for a room. At seven o'clock Chief Underbeck dispatched a prowl car to Barnaby's place. He waited impatiently for its return, drumming on the desk, disinterestedly shuffling through a sheaf of reports which had accumulated during the day.

The prowl car returned shortly before eight. Sergeant Grimes made his report. "Nobody there, sir. Place locked up tight. Searched the grounds. All we saw was Barnaby's dog. Howled and ran off as if the devil were on his tail!"

Chief Underbeck was troubled. If Barnaby *was* missing, a search should be started at once. But it was already getting dark, and portions of Wharton's Swamp were very nearly impassable even during the day. Besides, there was no proof that Barnaby had not gone off for a visit, perhaps to nearby Stantonville, for instance, to call on a crony and stay overnight.

By nine o'clock he had decided to postpone any action till morning. A search now would probably be futile in any case. The swamp offered too many obstacles. If Barnaby had not turned up by morning, and there was no report that he had been seen elsewhere, a systematic search of the marsh could begin.

Not long after he had arrived at his decision, and as he was somewhat wearily preparing to leave Headquarters and go home, a new and genuinely alarming interruption took place.

Shortly before nine-thirty, a car braked to a sudden stop outside Headquarters. An elderly man hurried in, supporting by the arm a sobbing, hysterical young girl. Her skirt and stockings were torn and there were a number of scratches on her face.

After assisting her to a chair, the man turned to Chief Underbeck and the other officers who gathered around.

"Picked her up on the highway out near Wharton's Swamp. Screaming at the top of her lungs!" He wiped his forehead. "She ran right in front of my car. Missed her by a miracle. She was so crazy with fear I couldn't make sense out of what she said. Seems like something grabbed her boy friend in the bushes out there. Anyway, I got her in the car without much trouble and I guess I broke a speed law getting here."

Chief Underbeck surveyed the man keenly. He was obviously shaken himself, and since he did not appear to be concealing anything, the Chief turned to the girl.

He spoke soothingly, doing his best to reassure her, and at length she composed herself sufficiently to tell her story.

Her name was Dolores Rell and she lived in nearby Stantonville. Earlier in the evening she had gone riding with her fiancé, Jason Bukmeist of Clinton Center. As Jason was driving along the highway adjacent to Wharton's Swamp, she had remarked that the early evening moonlight looked very romantic over the marsh. Jason had stopped the car, and after they had surveyed the scene for some minutes, he suggested that, since the evening was warm, a brief "stroll in the moonlight" might be fun.

Dolores had been reluctant to leave the car, but at length had been persuaded to take a short walk along the edge of the marsh where the terrain was relatively firm.

As the couple were walking along under the trees, perhaps twenty yards or so from the car, Dolores became aware of an unpleasant odour and wanted to turn back. Jason, however, told her she only imagined it and insisted on going farther. As the trees grew closer together, they walked Indian file, Jason taking the lead.

Suddenly, she said, they both heard something swishing through the brush towards them. Jason told her not to be frightened, that it was probably someone's cow. As it came closer, however, it seemed to be moving with incredible speed. And it didn't seem to be making the kind of noise a cow would make.

At the last second Jason whirled with a cry of fear and told her to run. Before she could move, she saw a monstrous something rushing under the trees in the dim moonlight. For an instant she stood rooted with horror; then she turned and ran. She thought she heard Jason running behind her. She couldn't be sure. But immediately after she heard him scream.

In spite of her terror, she turned and looked behind her.

At this point in her story she became hysterical again, and several minutes passed before she could go on.

She could not describe exactly what she had seen as she looked over her shoulder. The thing which she had glimpsed rushing under the trees had caught up with Jason. It almost completely covered him. All she could see of him was his agonized face and part of one arm, low near the ground, as if the thing were squatting astride him. She could not say what it was. It was black, formless, bestial and yet not bestial. It was the dark gliding kind of indescribable horror which she had shuddered at when she was a little girl alone in the nursery at night.

She shuddered now and covered her eyes as she tried to picture what she had seen. "O God—*the darkness came alive! The darkness came alive!*"

Somehow, she went on presently, she had stumbled through the trees into the road. She was so terrified she hardly noticed the approaching car. There could be no doubt that Dolores Rell was in the grip of genuine terror. Chief Underbeck acted with alacrity. After the white-faced girl had been driven to a nearby hospital for treatment of her scratches and the administration of a sedative, Underbeck rounded up all available men on the force, equipped them with shotguns, rifles, and flashlights, hurried them into four prowl cars, and started off for Wharton's Swamp.

Jason Bukmeist's car was found where he had parked it. It had not been disturbed. A search of the nearby swamp area, conducted in the glare of flashlights, proved fruitless. Whatever had attacked Bukmeist had apparently carried him off into the farthest recesses of the sprawling swamp.

After two futile hours of brush breaking and marsh sloshing, Chief Underbeck wearily rounded up his men and called off the hunt until morning.

As the first faint streaks of dawn appeared in the sky over Wharton's Swamp, the search began again. Reinforcements, including civilian volunteers from Clinton Center, had arrived, and a systematic combing of the entire swamp commenced.

By noon, the search had proved fruitless—or nearly so. One of the searchers brought in a battered hat and a rye whisky bottle which he had discovered on the edge of the marsh under a sweet-gum tree. The shapeless felt hat was old and worn, but it was dry. It had, therefore, apparently been discarded in the swamp since the storm of a few days ago. The whiskey bottle looked new; in fact, a few drops of rye remained in it. The searcher reported that the remains of a small campfire were also found under the sweet-gum.

In the hope that this evidence might have some bearing on the disappearance of Jason Bukmeist, Chief Underbeck ordered a canvass of every liquor store in Clinton Center in an attempt to learn the names of everyone who had recently purchased a bottle of the particular brand of rye found under the tree.

The search went on, and mid-afternoon brought another, more ominous discovery. A diligent searcher, investigating a trampled area in a large growth of cattails, picked a rifle out of the mud.

After the slime and dirt had been wiped away, two of the searchers vouched that it belonged to Rupert Barnaby. One of them had hunted with him and remembered a bit of scrollwork on the rifle stock.

While Chief Underbeck was weighing this unpalatable bit of evidence, a report of the liquor store canvass in Clinton Center arrived. Every recent purchaser of a quart bottle of the particular brand in question had been investigated. Only one could not be located—a tramp who had hung around the town for several days and had been ordered out.

By evening most of the exhausted searching party were convinced that the tramp, probably in a state of homicidal viciousness brought on by drink, had murdered both Rupert Barnaby and Jason and secreted their bodies in one of the deep pools of the swamp. The chances were the murderer was still sleeping off the effects of drink somewhere in the tangled thickets of the marsh.

Most of the searchers regarded Dolores Rell's melodramatic story with a great deal of scepticism. In the dim moonlight, they pointed out, a frenzied, wild-eyed tramp bent on imminent murder might very well have resembled some kind of monster. And the girl's hysteria had probably magnified what she had seen.

As night closed over the dismal morass, Chief Underbeck reluctantly suspended the hunt. In view of the fact that the murderer probably still lurked in the woods, however, he decided to establish a system of night-long patrols along the highway which paralleled the swamp. If the quarry lay hidden in the treacherous tangle of trees and brush, he would not be able to escape on to the highway without running into one of the patrols. The only other means of egress from the swamp lay miles across the mire where the open sea washed against a reedy beach. And it was quite unlikely that the fugitive would even attempt escape in that direction.

The patrols were established in three-hour shifts, two men to a patrol, both heavily armed, and both equipped with powerful searchlights. They were ordered to investigate every sound or movement which they detected in the brush bordering the highway. After a single command to halt, they were to shoot to kill. Any curious motorists who stopped to inquire about the hunt were to be swiftly waved on their way, after being warned not to give rides to anyone and to report all hitchhikers.

Fred Storr and Luke Matson, on the midnight to three o'clock patrol, passed an uneventful two hours on their particular stretch of the highway. Matson finally sat down on a fallen tree stump a few yards from the edge of the road.

"Legs givin' out," he commented wryly, resting his rifle on the stump. "Might as well sit a few minutes."

Fred Storr lingered nearby. "Guess so, Luke. Don't look like—" Suddenly he scowled into the black fringes of the swamp. "You hear something, Luke?"

Luke listened, twisting around on the stump. "Well, maybe," he said finally, "kind of a little scratchy sound like."

He got up, retrieving his rifle.

"Let's take a look," Fred suggested in a low voice. He stepped over the stump and Luke followed him towards the tangle of brush which marked the border of the swamp jungle.

Several yards farther along they stopped again. The sound became more audible. It was a kind of slithering, scraping sound, such as might be produced by a heavy body dragging itself over uneven ground.

"Sounds like—a snake," Luke ventured. "A damn big snake!"

"We'll get a little closer," Fred whispered. "You be ready with that gun when I switch on my light!"

They moved ahead a few more yards. Then a powerful yellow ray stabbed into the thickets ahead as Fred switched on his flashlight. The ray searched the darkness, probing in one direction and then another.

Luke lowered his rifle a little, frowning. "Don't see a thing," he said. "Nothing but a big pool of black scum up ahead there."

Before Fred had time to reply, the pool of black scum reared up into horrible life. In one hideous second it hunched itself into an unspeakable glistening hood and rolled forward with fearful speed.

Luke Matson screamed and fired simultaneously as the monstrous scarf of slime shot forward. A moment later it swayed above him. He fired again and the thing fell upon him.

In avoiding the initial rush of the horror, Fred Storr lost his footing. He fell headlong—and turned just in time to witness a sight which slowed the blood in his veins.

The monster had pounced upon Luke Matson. Now, as Fred watched, literally paralysed with horror, it spread itself over and around the form of Luke until he was completely enveloped. The faint writhing of his limbs could be seen. Then the thing squeezed, swelling into a hood and flattening itself again, and the writhing ceased.

As soon as the thing lifted and swung forward in his direction, Fred Storr, goaded by frantic fear, overcame the paralysis of horror which had frozen him.

Grabbing the rifle which had fallen beside him, he aimed it at the shape of living slime and started firing. Pure terror possessed him as he saw that the shots were having no effect. The thing lunged towards him, to all visible appearances entirely oblivious to the rifle slugs tearing into its loathsome viscid mass.

Acting out of some instinct which he himself could not have named, Fred Storr dropped the rifle and seized his flashlight, playing its powerful beam directly upon the onrushing horror.

The thing stopped, scant feet away, and appeared to hesitate. It slid quickly aside at an angle, but he followed it immediately with the cone of light. It backed up finally and flattened out, as if trying by that means to avoid the light, but he trained the beam on it steadily, sensing with every primitive fibre which he possessed that the yellow shaft of light was the one thing which held off hideous death.

Now there were shouts in the nearby darkness and other lights began stabbing the shadows. Members of the adjacent patrols, alarmed by the sound of rifle fire, had come running to investigate.

Suddenly the nameless horror squirmed quickly out of the flashlight's beam and rushed away in the darkness.

In the leaden light of early dawn Chief Underbeck climbed into a police car waiting on the highway near Wharton's Swamp and headed back for Clinton Center. He had made a decision and he was grimly determined to act on it at once.

When he reached Headquarters, he made two telephone calls in quick succession, one to the governor of the state and the other to the commander of the nearby Camp Evans Military Reservation.

The horror in Wharton's Swamp—he had decided—could not be coped with by the limited men and resources at his command.

Rupert Barnaby, Jason Bukmeist, and Luke Matson had without any doubt perished in the swamp. The anonymous tramp, it now began to appear, far from being the murderer, had been only one more victim. And Fred Storr—well, he hadn't disappeared. But the other patrol members had found him sitting on the ground near the edge of the swamp in the clutches of a mind-warping fear which had, temporarily at least, reduced him to near idiocy. Hours after he had been taken home and put to bed, he had refused to loosen his grip on a flashlight which he squeezed in one hand. When they switched the flashlight off, he screamed, and they had to switch it on again. His story was so wildly melodramatic it could scarcely be accepted by rational minds. And yet—they had said as much about Dolores Rell's hysterical account. And Fred Storr was no excitable young girl; he had a reputation for level-headedness, stolidity, and verbal honesty which was touched with understatement rather than exaggeration. As Chief Underbeck arose and walked out to his car in order to start back to Wharton's Swamp, he noticed Old Man Gowse coming down the block.

With a sudden thrill of horror he remembered the eccentric's missing cow. Before the old man came abreast, he slammed the car door and issued crisp directions to the waiting driver. As the car sped away, he glanced in the rear-view mirror.

Old Man Gowse stood grimly motionless on the walk in front of Police Headquarters.

"Old Man Cassandra," Chief Underbeck muttered. The driver shot a swift glance at him and stepped on the gas.

Less than two hours after Chief Underbeck arrived back at Wharton's Swamp, the adjacent highway was crowded with cars—state police patrol cars, cars of the local curious, and Army trucks from Camp Evans.

Promptly at nine o'clock over three hundred soldiers, police, and citizen volunteers, all armed, swung into the swamp to begin a careful search.

Shortly before dusk most of them had arrived at the sea on the far side of the swamp. The exhaustive efforts had netted nothing. One soldier, noticing fierce eyes glaring out of a tree, had bagged an owl, and one of the state policemen had flushed a young bobcat. Someone else had stepped on a copperhead and been treated for snakebite. But there was no sign of a monster, a murderous tramp, nor any of the missing men.

In the face of mounting scepticism, Chief Underbeck stood firm. Pointing out that, so far as they knew to date, the murderer prowled only at night, he ordered that after a four-hour rest and meal period the search should continue.

A number of helicopters which had hovered over the area during the afternoon landed on the strip of shore, bringing food and supplies. At Chief Underbeck's insistence, barriers were set up on the beach. Guards were stationed along the entire length of the highway; powerful searchlights were brought up. Another truck from Camp Evans arrived with a portable machine-gun and several flame-throwers.

By eleven o'clock that night the stage was set. The beach barriers were in place, guards were at station, and huge searchlights, erected near the highway, swept the dismal marsh with probing cones of light.

At eleven-fifteen the night patrols, each consisting of ten strongly-armed men, struck into the swamp again.

Ravenous with hunger, the hood of horror reared out of the mud at the bottom of a rancid pool and rose towards the surface. Flopping ashore in the darkness, it slid quickly away over the clumps of scattered swamp grass. It was impelled, as always, by a savage and enormous hunger.

Although hunting in its new environment had been good, its immense appetite knew no appeasement. The more food it consumed, the more it seemed to require.

As it rushed off, alert to the minute vibrations which indicated food, it became aware of various disturbing emanations. Although it was the time of darkness in this strange world, the darkness at this usual hunting period was oddly pierced by the monster's hated enemy—light. The food vibrations were stronger than the shape of slime had ever experienced. They were on all sides, powerful, purposeful, moving in many directions all through the lower layers of puzzling, light-riven darkness.

Lifting out of the ooze, the hood of horror flowed up a lattice-work of gnarled swamp snags and hung motionless, while drops of muddy water rolled off its glistening surface and dripped below. The thing's sensory apparatus told it that the maddening streaks of lack of darkness were everywhere.

Even as it hung suspended on the snags like a great filthy carpet coated with slime, a terrible touch of light slashed through the surrounding darkness and burned against it.

It immediately loosened its hold on the snags and fell back into the ooze with a mighty *plop*. Nearby, the vibrations suddenly increased in intensity. The maddening streamers of light shot through the darkness on all sides.

Baffled and savage, the thing plunged into the ooze and propelled itself in the opposite direction.

But this proved to be only a temporary respite. The vibrations redoubled in intensity. The darkness almost disappeared, riven and pierced by bolts and rivers of light.

For the first time in its incalculable existence, the thing experienced something vaguely akin to fear. The light could not be snatched up and squeezed and smothered to death. It was an alien enemy against which the hood of horror had learned only one defence—flight, hiding.

And now as its world of darkness was torn apart by sudden floods and streamers of light, the monster instinctively sought the refuge afforded by that vast black cradle from which it had climbed.

Flinging itself through the swamp, it headed back for sea.

The guard patrols stationed along the beach, roused by the sound of gunfire and urgent shouts of warning from the interior of the swamp, stood or knelt with ready weapons as the clamour swiftly approached the sea.

The dismal reedy beach lay fully exposed in the harsh glare of searchlights. Waves rolled in towards shore, splashing white crests of foam far up the sands. In the searchlights' illumination the dark waters glistened with an oily iridescence.

The shrill cries increased. The watchers tensed, waiting. And suddenly across the long dreary flats clotted with weed stalks and sunken drifts there burst into view a nightmare shape which froze the shore patrols in their tracks.

A thing of slimy blackness, a thing which had no essential shape, no discernible earthly features, rushed through the thorn thickets and on to the flats. It was a shape of utter darkness, one second a great flapping hood, the next a black viscid pool of living ooze which flowed upon itself, sliding forward with incredible speed.

Some of the guards remained rooted where they stood, too overcome with horror to pull the triggers of their weapons. Others broke the spell of terror and began firing. Bullets from half a dozen rifles tore into the black monster speeding across the mud flats.

As the thing neared the end of the flats and approached the first sand dunes of the open beach, the patrol guards who had flushed it from the swamp broke into the open.

One of them paused, bellowing at the beach guards. "It's heading for sea! For God's sake don't let it escape!"

The beach guards redoubled their firing, suddenly realizing with a kind of sick horror that the monster was apparently unaffected by the rifle slugs. Without a single pause, it rolled through the last fringe of cattails and flopped on to the sands.

As in a hideous nightmare, the guards saw it flap over the nearest sand dune and slide towards the sea. A moment later, however, they remembered the barbed wire beach barrier which Chief Underbeck had stubbornly insisted on their erecting.

Gaining heart, they closed in, running over the dunes towards the spot where the black horror would strike the wire.

Someone in the lead yelled in sudden triumph. "It's caught! It's stuck on the wire!"

The searchlights concentrated swaths of light on the barrier.

The thing had reached the barbed wire fence and apparently flung itself against the twisted strands. Now it appeared to be hopelessly caught; it twisted and flopped and squirmed like some unspeakable giant jellyfish snarled in a fisherman's net.

The guards ran forward, sure of their victory. All at once, however, the guard in the lead screamed a wild warning. "It's squeezing through! It's getting away!"

In the glare of light they saw with consternation that the monster appeared to be *flowing* through the wire, like a blob of liquescent ooze.

Ahead lay a few yards of downward slanting beach and, beyond that, rolling breakers of the open sea.

There was a collective gasp of horrified dismay as the monster, with a quick forward lurch, squeezed through the barrier. It tilted there briefly, twisting, as if a few last threads of itself might still be entangled in the wire.

As it moved to disengage itself and rush down the wet sands into the black sea, one of the guards hurled himself forward until he was almost abreast of the barrier. Sliding to his knees, he aimed at the escaping hood of horror.

A second later a great searing spout of flame shot from his weapon and burst in a smoky red blossom against the thing on the opposite side of the wire.

Black oily smoke billowed into the night. A ghastly stench flowed over the beach. The guards saw a flaming mass of horror grope away from the barrier. The soldier who aimed the flamethrower held it remorselessly steady.

There was a hideous bubbling, hissing sound. Vast gouts of thick, greasy smoke swirled into the night air. The indescribable stench became almost unbearable.

When the soldier finally shut off the flamethrower, there was nothing in sight except the white-hot glowing wires of the barrier and a big patch of blackened sand.

With good reason the mantle of slime had hated light, for its ultimate source was fire—the final unknown enemy which even the black hood could not drag down and devour.

ANTHONY BOUCHER

They Bite

There was no path, only the almost vertical ascent. Crumbled rock for a few yards, with the roots of sage finding their scanty life in the dry soil. Then jagged outcroppings of crude crags, sometimes with accidental footholds, sometimes with overhanging and untrustworthy branches of grease-wood, sometimes with no aid to climbing but the leverage of your muscles and the ingenuity of your balance.

The sage was as drably green as the rock was drably brown. The only color was the occasional rosy spikes of barrel cactus.

Hugh Tallant swung himself up onto the last pinnacle. It had a deliberate, shaped look about it—a petrified fortress of Lilliputians, a Gibraltar of pygmies. Tallant perched on its battlements and unslung his field glasses.

The desert valley spread below him. The tiny cluster of buildings that was Oasis, the exiguous cluster of palms that gave name to the town and shelter of his own tent and to the shack he was building, the dead-ended highway leading straightforwardly to nothing, the oiled roads diagraming the vacant blocks of an optimistic subdivision.

Tallant saw none of these. His glasses were fixed beyond the oasis and the town of Oasis on the dry lake. The gliders were clear and vivid to him, and the uniformed men busy with them were as sharply and minutely visible as a nest of ants under glass. The training school was more than usually active. One glider in particular, strange to Tallant, seemed the focus of attention. Men would come and examine it and glance back at the older models in comparison.

Only the corner of Tallant's left eye was not preoccupied with the new glider. In that corner something moved, something little and thin and brown as the earth. Too large for a rabbit, much too small for a man. It darted across that corner of vision, and Tallant found gliders oddly hard to concentrate on.

He set down the bifocals and deliberately looked about him. His pinnacle surveyed the narrow, flat area of the crest. Nothing stirred. Nothing stood out against the sage and rock but one barrel of rosy spikes. He took up the glasses again and resumed his observations. When he was done, he methodically entered the results in the little black notebook.

His hand was still white. The desert is cold and often sunless in winter. But it was a firm hand, and as well trained as his eyes, fully capable of recording faithfully the designs and dimensions which they had registered so accurately.

Once his hand slipped, and he had to erase and redraw, leaving a smudge that displeased him. The lean, brown thing had slipped across the edge of his vision again. Going toward the east edge, he would swear, where that set of rocks jutted like the spines on the back of a stegosaur.

Only when his notes were completed did he yield to curiosity, and even then with cynical self-reproach. He was physically tired, for him an unusual state, from this daily climbing and from clearing the ground for his shack-to-be. The eye muscles play odd nervous tricks. There could be nothing behind the stegosaur's armor.

There was nothing. Nothing alive and moving. Only the torn and half-plucked carcass of a bird, which looked as though it had been gnawed by some small animal.

It was halfway down the hill—hill in Western terminology, though anywhere east of the Rockies it would have been considered a sizable mountain—that Tallant again had a glimpse of a moving figure.

But this was no trick of a nervous eye. It was not little nor thin nor brown. It was tall and broad and wore a loud red-and-black lumberjacket. It bellowed, "Tallant!" in a cheerful and lusty voice.

Tallant drew near the man and said, "Hello." He paused and added. "Your advantage, I think."

The man grinned broadly. "Don't know me? Well, I daresay ten years is a long time, and the California desert ain't exactly the Chinese rice fields. How's stuff? Still loaded down with Secrets for Sale?"

Tallant tried desperately not to react to that shot, but he stiffened a little. "Sorry. The prospector getup had me fooled. Good to see you again, Morgan."

The man's eyes narrowed. "Just having my little joke," he smiled. "Of course you wouldn't have no serious reason for mountain climbing around a glider school, now, would you? And you'd kind of need field glasses to keep an eye on the pretty birdies."

"I'm out here for my health." Tallant's voice sounded unnatural even to himself.

"Sure, sure. You were always in it for your health. And come to think of it, my own health ain't been none too good lately. I've got me a little cabin way to hell-and-gone around here, and I do me a little prospecting now and then. And somehow it just strikes me, Tallant, like maybe I hit a pretty good lode today."

"Nonsense, old man. You can see—"

"I'd sure hate to tell any of them Army men out at the field some of the stories I know about China and the kind of men I used to know out there. Wouldn't cotton to them stories a bit, the Army wouldn't. But if I was to have a drink too many and get talkative-like—"

"Tell you what," Tallant suggested brusquely. "It's getting near sunset now, and my tent's chilly for evening visits. But drop around in the morning and we'll talk over old times. Is rum still your tipple?"

"Sure is. Kind of expensive now, you understand—"

"I'll lay some in. You can find the place easily—over by the oasis. And we . . . we might be able to talk about your prospecting, too."

Tallant's thin lips were set firm as he walked away.

The bartender opened a bottle of beer and plunked it on the damp-circled counter. "That'll be twenty cents," he said, then added as an afterthought, "Want a glass? Sometimes tourists do."

Tallant looked at the others sitting at the counter—the red-eyed and unshaven old man, the flight sergeant unhappily drinking a Coke—it was after Army hours for beer—the young man with the long, dirty trench coat and the pipe and the new-looking brown beard—and saw no glasses. "I guess I won't be a tourist," he decided.

This was the first time Tallant had had a chance to visit the Desert Sport Spot. It was as well to be seen around in a community. Otherwise people begin to wonder and say, "Who is that man out by the oasis? Why don't you ever see him anyplace?"

The Sport Spot was quiet that night. The four of them at the counter, two Army boys shooting pool, and a half-dozen of the local men gathered about a round poker table, soberly and wordlessly cleaning a construction worker whose mind seemed more on his beer than on his cards.

"You just passing through?" the bartender asked sociably.

Tallant shook his head. "I'm moving in. When the Army turned me down for my lungs, I decided I better do something about it. Heard so much about your climate here I thought I might as well try it."

"Sure thing," the bartender nodded. "You take up until they started this glider school, just about every other guy you meet in the desert is here for his health. Me, I had sinus, and look at me now. It's the air."

Tallant breathed the atmosphere of smoke and beer suds, but did not smile. "I'm looking forward to miracles."

"You'll get 'em. Whereabouts you staying?"

"Over that way a bit. The agent called it 'the old Carker place.'"

Tallant felt the curious listening silence and frowned. The bartender had started to speak and then thought better of it. The young man with the beard looked at him oddly. The old man fixed him with red and watery eyes that had a faded glint of pity in them. For a moment, Tallant felt a chill that had nothing to do with the night air of the desert.

The old man drank his beer in quick gulps and frowned as though trying to formulate a sentence. At last he wiped beer from his bristly lips and said, "You wasn't aiming to stay in the adobe, was you?"

"No. It's pretty much gone to pieces. Easier to rig me up a little shack than try to make the adobe livable. Meanwhile, I've got a tent."

"That's all right, then, mebbe. But mind you don't go poking around that there adobe."

"I don't think I'm apt to. But why not? Want another beer?"

The old man shook his head reluctantly and slid from his stool to the ground. "No thanks. I don't rightly know as I—"

"Yes?"

"Nothing. Thanks all the same." He turned and shuffled to the door.

Tallant smiled. "But why should I stay clear of the adobe?" he called after him.

The old man mumbled.

"What?"

"They bite," said the old man, and went out shivering into the night.

The bartender was back at his post. "I'm glad he didn't take that beer you offered him," he said. "Along about this time in the evening I have to stop serving him. For once he had the sense to quit."

Tallant pushed his own empty bottle forward. "I hope I didn't frighten him away."

"Frighten? Well, mister, I think maybe that's just what you did do. He didn't want beer that sort of came, like you might say, from the old Carker place. Some of the old-timers here, they're funny that way."

Tallant grinned. "Is it haunted?"

"Not what you'd call haunted, no. No ghosts there that I ever heard of." He wiped the counter with a cloth and seemed to wipe the subject away with it.

The flight sergeant pushed his Coke bottle away, hunted in his pocket for nickels, and went over to the pinball machine. The young man with the beard slid onto his vacant stool. "Hope old Jake didn't worry you," he said.

Tallant laughed. "I suppose every town has its deserted homestead with a grisly tradition. But this sounds a little different. No ghosts, and they bite. Do you know anything about it?"

"A little," the young man said seriously. "A little. Just enough to—"

Tallant was curious. "Have one on me and tell me about it."

The flight sergeant swore bitterly at the machine.

Beer gurgled through the beard. "You see," the young man began, "the desert's so big you can't be alone in it. Ever notice that? It's all empty and there's nothing in sight, but there's always something moving over there where you can't quite see it. It's something very dry and thin and brown, only when you look around it isn't there. Ever see it?"

"Optical fatigue—" Tallant began.

"Sure. I know. Every man to his own legend. There isn't a tribe of Indians hasn't got some way of accounting for it. You've heard of the Watchers? And the twentieth-century white man comes along, and it's optical fatigue. Only in the nineteenth century things weren't quite the same, and there were the Carkers."

"You've got a special localized legend?"

"Call it that. You glimpse things out of the corner of your mind, same like you glimpse lean, dry things out of the corner of your eye. You encase 'em in solid circumstance and they're not so bad. That is known as the Growth of Legend. The Folk Mind in Action. You take the Carkers and the things you don't quite see and you put 'em together. And they bite."

Tallant wondered how long that beard had been absorbing beer. "And what were the Carkers?" he prompted politely.

"Ever hear of Sawney Bean? Scotland—reign of James First, or maybe the Sixth, though I think Roughead's wrong on that for once. Or let's be more modern—ever hear of the Benders? Kansas in the 1870s? No? Ever hear of Procrustes? Or Polyphemus? Or Fee fi-fo-fum?

"There are ogres, you know. They're no legend. They're fact, they are. The inn where nine guests left for every ten that arrived, the mountain cabin that sheltered travelers from the snow, sheltered them all winter till the melting spring uncovered their bones, the lonely stretches of road that so many passengers traveled halfway—you'll find 'em everywhere. All over Europe and pretty much in this country too before communications became what they are. Profitable business. And it wasn't just the profit. The Benders made money, sure; but that wasn't why they killed all their victims as carefully as a kosher butcher. Sawney Bean got so he didn't give a damn about the profit; he just needed to lay in more meat for the winter.

"And think of the chances you'd have at an oasis."

"So these Carkers of yours were, as you call them ogres?"

"Carkers, ogres—maybe they were Benders. The Benders were never seen alive, you know, after the townspeople found those curiously butchered bones. There's a rumor they got this far west. And the time checks pretty well. There wasn't any town here in the eighties. Just a couple of Indian families, last of a dying tribe living on at the oasis. They vanished after the Carkers moved in. That's not so surprising. The white race is a sort of super-ogre, anyway. Nobody worried about them. But they used to worry about why so many travelers never got across this stretch of desert. The travelers used to stop over at the Carkers', you see, and somehow they often never got any farther. Their wagons'd be found maybe fifteen miles beyond in the desert. Sometimes they found the bones, too, parched and white. Gnawed-looking, they said sometimes."

"And nobody ever did anything about these Carkers?"

"Oh, sure. We didn't have King James Sixth—only I still think it was First—to ride up on a great white horse for a gesture, but twice Army detachments came here and wiped them all out."

"Twice? One wiping-out would do for most families." Tallant smiled.

"Uh-uh. That was no slip. They wiped out the Carkers twice because, you see, once didn't do any good. They wiped 'em out and still travelers vanished and still there were gnawed bones. So they wiped 'em out again. After that they gave up, and people detoured the oasis. It made a longer harder trip, but after all—"

Tallant laughed. "You mean to say these Carkers were immortal?"

"I don't know about immortal. They somehow just didn't die very easy. Maybe, if they were the Benders—and I sort of like to think they were—they learned a little more about what they were doing out here on the desert. Maybe they put together what the Indians knew and what they knew, and it worked. Maybe Whatever they made their sacrifices to understood them better out here than in Kansas."

"And what's become of them—aside from seeing them out of the corner of the eye?"

"There's forty years between the last of the Carker history and this new settlement at the oasis. And people won't talk much about what they learned here in the first year or so. Only that they stay away from that old Carker adobe. They tell some stories— The priest says he was sitting in the confessional one hot Saturday afternoon and thought he heard a penitent come in. He waited a long time and finally lifted the gauze to see was anybody there. Something was there, and it bit. He's got three fingers on his right hand now, which looks funny as hell when he gives a benediction."

Tallant pushed their two bottles toward the bartender. "That yarn, my young friend, has earned another beer. How about it, bartender? Is he always cheerful like this, or is this just something he's improvised for my benefit?"

The bartender set out the fresh bottles with great solemnity. "Me, I wouldn't've told you all that myself, but then, he's a stranger too and maybe don't feel the same way we do here. For him it's just a story."

"It's more comfortable that way," said the young man with the beard, and he took a firm hold on his beer bottle.

"But as long as you've heard that much," said the bartender, "you might as well— It was last winter, when we had that cold spell. You heard funny stories that winter. Wolves coming into prospectors' cabins just to warm up. Well, business wasn't so good. We don't have a license for hard liquor, and the boys don't drink much beer when it's that cold. But they used to come in anyway because we've got that big oil burner.

"So one night there's a bunch of 'em in here—old Jake was here, that you was talking to, and his dog Jigger—and I think I hear somebody else come in. The door creaks a little. But I don't see nobody, and the poker game's going, and we're talking just like we're talking now, and all of a sudden I hear a kind of a noise like crack! over there in that corner behind the juke box near the burner.

"I go over to see what goes and it gets away before I can see it very good. But it was little and thin and it didn't have no clothes on. It must've been damned cold that winter."

"And what was the cracking noise?" Tallant asked dutifully.

"That? That was a bone. It must've strangled Jigger without any noise. He was a little dog. It ate most of the flesh, and if it hadn't cracked the bone for the marrow it could've finished. You can still see the spots over there. The blood never did come out."

There had been silence all through the story. Now suddenly all hell broke loose. The flight sergeant let out a splendid yell and began pointing excitedly at the pinball machine and yelling for his payoff. The construction worker dramatically deserted the poker game, knocking his chair over in the process, and announced lugubriously that these guys here had their own rules, see?

Any atmosphere of Carker-inspired horror was dissipated. Tallant whistled as he walked over to put a nickel in the jukebox. He glanced casually at the floor. Yes, there was a stain, for what that was worth.

He smiled cheerfully and felt rather grateful to the Carkers. They were going to solve his blackmail problem very neatly.

Tallant dreamed of power that night. It was a common dream with him. He was a ruler of the new American Corporate State that would follow the war; and he said to this man, "Come!" and he came, and to that man, "Go!" and he went, and to his servants, "Do this!" and they did it.

Then the young man with the beard was standing before him, and the dirty trench coat was like the robes of an ancient prophet. And the young man said, "You see yourself riding high, don't you? Riding the crest of the wave—the Wave of the Future, you call it. But there's a deep, dark undertow that you don't see, and that's a part of the Past. And the Present and even your Future. There is evil in mankind that is blacker even than your evil, and infinitely more ancient."

And there was something in the shadows behind the young man, something little and lean and brown.

Tallant's dream did not disturb him the following morning. Nor did the thought of the approaching interview with Morgan. He fried his bacon and eggs and devoured them cheerfully. The wind had died down for a change, and the sun was warm enough so that he could strip to the waist while he cleared land for his shack. His machete glinted brilliantly as it swung through the air and struck at the roots of the brush.

When Morgan arrived his full face was red and sweating.

"It's cool over there in the shade of the adobe," Tallant suggested. "We'll be more comfortable." And in the comfortable shade of the adobe he swung the machete once and clove Morgan's full, red, sweating face in two.

It was so simple. It took less effort than uprooting a clump of sage. And it was so safe. Morgan lived in a cabin way to hell-and-gone and was often away on prospecting trips. No one would notice his absence for months, if then. No one had any reason to connect him with Tallant. And no one in Oasis would hunt for him in the Carker-haunted adobe.

The body was heavy, and the blood dripped warm on Tallant's bare skin. With relief he dumped what had been Morgan on the floor of the adobe. There were no boards, no flooring. Just the earth. Hard, but not too hard to dig a grave in. And no one was likely to come poking around in this taboo territory to notice the grave. Let a year or so go by, and the grave and bones it contained would be attributed to the Carkers.

The corner of Tallant's eye bothered him again. Deliberately he looked about the interior of the adobe.

The little furniture was crude and heavy, with no attempt to smooth down the strokes of the ax. It was held together with wooden pegs or half-rotted thongs. There were age-old cinders in the fireplace, and the dusty shards of a cooking jar among them.

And there was a deeply hollowed stone, covered with stains that might have been rust, if stone rusted. Behind it was a tiny figure, clumsily fashioned of clay and sticks. It was something like a man and something like a lizard, and something like the things that flit across the corner of the eye.

Curious now, Tallant peered about further. He penetrated to the corner that the one unglassed window lighted but dimly. And there he let out a little choking gasp. For a moment he was rigid with horror. Then he smiled and all but laughed aloud.

This explained everything. Some curious individual had seen this, and from his accounts had burgeoned the whole legend. The Carkers had indeed learned something from the Indians, but that secret was the art of embalming.

It was a perfect mummy. Either the Indian art had shrunk bodies, or this was that of a ten-year-old boy. There was no flesh. Only skin and bone and taut, dry stretches of tendon between. The eyelids were closed; the sockets looked hollow under them. The nose was sunken and almost lost. The scant lips were tightly curled back from the long and very white teeth, which stood forth all the more brilliantly against the deep-brown skin.

It was a curious little trove, this mummy. Tallant was already calculating the chances for raising a decent sum of money from an interested anthropologist— murder can produce such delightfully profitable chance by-products—when he noticed the infinitesimal rise and fall of the chest.

The Carker was not dead. It was sleeping.

Tallant did not dare stop to think beyond the instant. This was no time to pause to consider if such things were possible in a well-ordered world. It was no time to reflect on the disposal of the body of Morgan. It was a time to snatch up your machete and get out of there.

But in the doorway he halted. There, coming across the desert, heading for the adobe, clearly seen this time, was another—a female.

He made an involuntary gesture of indecision. The blade of the machete clanged ringingly against the adobe wall. He heard the dry shuffling of a roused sleeper behind him.

He turned fully now, the machete raised. Dispose of this nearer one first, then face the female. There was no room even for terror in his thoughts, only for action.

The lean brown shape darted at him avidly. He moved lightly away and stood poised for its second charge. It shot forward again. He took one step back, machete arm raised, and fell headlong over the corpse of Morgan. Before he could rise, the thin thing was upon him. Its sharp teeth had met through the palm of his left hand.

The machete moved swiftly. The thin dry body fell headless to the floor. There was no blood.

The grip of the teeth did not relax. Pain coursed up Tallant's left arm—a sharper, more bitter pain than you would expect from the bite. Almost as though venom—

He dropped the machete, and his strong white hand plucked and twisted at the dry brown lips. The teeth stayed clenched, unrelaxing. He sat bracing his back against the wall and gripped the head between his knees. He pulled. His flesh ripped, and blood formed dusty clots on the dirt floor. But the bite was firm.

His world had become reduced now to that hand and that head. Nothing outside mattered. He must free himself. He raised his aching arm to his face, and with his own teeth he tore at that unrelenting grip. The dry flesh crumbled away in desert dust, but the teeth were locked fast. He tore his lip against their white keenness, and tasted in his mouth the sweetness of blood and something else.

He staggered to his feet again. He knew what he must do. Later he could use cautery, a tourniquet, see a doctor with a story about a Gila monster—their heads grip too, don't they?—but he knew what he must do now.

He raised the machete and struck again.

His white hand lay on the brown floor, gripped by the white teeth in the brown face. He propped himself against the adobe wall, momentarily unable to move. His open wrist hung over the deeply hollowed stone. His blood and his strength and his life poured out before the little figure of sticks and clay.

The female stood in the doorway now, the sun bright on her thin brownness. She did not move. He knew that she was waiting for the hollow stone to fill.

RAY BRADBURY

The Foghorn

Out there in the cold water, far from land, we waited every night for the coming of the fog, and it came, and we oiled the brass machinery and lit the fog light up in the stone tower. Feeling like two birds in the gray sky, McDunn and I sent the light touching out, red, then white, then red again, to eye the lonely ships. And if they did not see our light, then there was always our Voice, the great deep cry of our Fog Horn shuddering through the rags of mist to startle the gulls away like decks of scattered cards and make the waves turn high and foam.

"It's a lonely life, but you're used to it now, aren't you?" asked McDunn.

"Yes," I said. "You're a good talker, thank the Lord."

"Well, it's your turn on land tomorrow," he said, smiling, "to dance the ladies and drink gin."

"What do you think, McDunn, when I leave you out here alone?"

"On the mysteries of the sea." McDunn lit his pipe. It was a quarter past seven of a cold November evening, the heat on, the light switching its tail in two hundred directions, the Fog Horn bumbling in the high throat of the tower. There wasn't a town for a hundred miles down the coast, just a road which came lonely through dead country to the sea, with few cars on it, a stretch of two miles of cold water out to our rock, and rare few ships.

"The mysteries of the sea," said McDunn thoughtfully. "You know, the ocean's the biggest damned snowflake ever? It rolls and swells a thousand shapes and colors, no two alike. Strange. One night, years ago, I was here alone, when all of the fish of the sea surfaced out there. Something made them swim in and lie in the bay, sort of trembling and staring up at the tower light going red, white, red, white across them so I could see their funny eyes. I turned cold. They were like a big peacock's tail, moving out there until midnight. Then, without so much as a sound, they slipped away, the million of them was gone. I kind of think maybe, in some sort of way, they came all those miles to worship. Strange. But think how the tower must look to them, standing seventy feet above the water, the God-light flashing out from it, and the tower declaring itself with a monster voice. They never came back, those fish, but don't you think for a while they thought they were in the Presence?"

I shivered. I looked out at the long gray lawn of the sea stretching away into nothing and nowhere.

"Oh, the sea's full." McDunn puffed his pipe nervously, blinking. He had been nervous all day and hadn't said why. "For all our engines and so-called submarines, it'll be ten thousand centuries before we set foot on the real bottom of the sunken lands, in the fairy kingdoms there, and know *real* terror. Think of it, it's still the year 300,000 Before Christ down under there. While we've paraded around with trumpets, lopping off each other's countries and heads, they have been living beneath the sea twelve miles deep and cold in a time as old as the beard of a comet."

"Yes, it's an old world."

"Come on. I got something special I been saving up to tell you."

We ascended the eighty steps, talking and taking our time. At the top, McDunn switched off the room lights so there'd be no reflection in the plate glass. The great eye of the light was humming, turning easily in its oiled socket. The Fog Horn was blowing steadily, once every fifteen seconds.

"Sounds like an animal, don't it?" McDunn nodded to himself. "A big lonely animal crying in the night. Sitting here on the edge of ten billion years calling out to the Deeps, I'm here, I'm here, I'm here. And the Deeps do answer, yes, they do. You been here now for three months, Johnny, so I better prepare you. About this time of year," he said, studying the murk and fog, "something comes to visit the lighthouse."

"The swarms of fish like you said?"

"No, this is something else. I've put off telling you because you might think I'm daft. But tonight's the latest I can put it off, for if my calendar's marked right from last year, tonight's the night it comes. I won't go into detail, you'll have to see it yourself. Just sit down there. If you want, tomorrow you can pack your duffel and take the motorboat in to land and get your car parked there at the dinghy pier on the cape and drive on back to some little inland town and keep your lights burning nights, I won't question or blame you. It's happened three years now, and this is the only time anyone's been here with me to verify it. You wait and watch."

Half an hour passed with only a few whispers between us. When we grew tired waiting, McDunn began describing some of his ideas to me. He had some theories about the Fog Horn itself.

"One day many years ago a man walked along and stood in the sound of the

ocean on a cold sunless shore and said, 'We need a voice to call across the water, to warn ships; I'll make one. I'll make a voice like all of time and all of the fog that ever was; I'll make a voice that is like an empty bed beside you all night long, and like an empty house when you open the door, and like trees in autumn with no leaves. A sound like the birds flying south, crying, and a sound like November wind and the sea on the hard, cold shore. I'll make a sound that's so alone that no one can miss it, that whoever hears it will weep in their souls, and hearths will seem warmer, and being inside will seem better to all who hear it in the distant towns. I'll make me a sound and an apparatus and they'll call it a Fog Horn and whoever hears it will know the sadness of eternity and the briefness of life.' "

The Fog Horn blew.

"I made up that story," said 'McDunn quietly, "to try to explain why this thing keeps coming back to the lighthouse every year. The Fog Horn calls it, I think, and it comes. . . ."

"But—" I said.

"Ssst!" said McDunn. "There!" He nodded out to the Deeps.

Something was swimming toward the lighthouse tower.

It was a cold night, as I have said; the high tower was cold, the light coming and going, and the Fog Horn calling and calling through the raveling mist. You couldn't see far and you couldn't see plain, but there was the deep sea moving on its way about the night earth, flat and quiet, the color of gray mud, and here were the two of us alone in the high tower, and there, far out at first, was a ripple, followed by wave, a rising, a bubble, a bit of froth. And then, from the surface of the cold sea came a head, a large head, dark-colored, with immense eyes, and then a neck. And then—not a body—but more neck and more! The head rose a full forty feet above the water on a slender and beautiful dark neck. Only then did the body, like a little island of black coral and shells and crayfish, drip from the subterranean. There was a flicker of tail. In all, from head to tip of tail, I estimated the monster at ninety or a hundred feet.

I don't know what I said. I said something.

"Steady, boy, steady," whispered McDunn.

"It's impossible!" I said.

"No, Johnny, *we're* impossible. *It's* like it always was ten million years ago. *It* hasn't changed. It's *us* and the land that've changed, become impossible. *Us!*"

It swam slowly and with a great dark majesty out in the icy waters, far away. The fog came and went about it, momentarily erasing its shape. One of the monster eyes caught and held and flashed back our immense light, red, white, red, white, like a disk held high and sending a message in primeval code. It was as silent as the fog through which it swam.

"It's a dinosaur of some sort!" I crouched down, holding to the stair rail.

"Yes, one of the tribe."

"But they died out!"

"No, only hid away in the Deeps. Deep, deep down in the deepest Deeps. Isn't *that* a word now, Johnny, a real word, it says so much: the Deeps. There's all the coldness and darkness and deepness in a word like that."

"What'll we do?"

"Do? We got our job, we can't leave. Besides, we're safer here than in any boat trying to get to land. That thing's as big as a destroyer and almost as swift."

"But here, why does it come *here*?"

The next moment I had my answer.

The Fog Horn blew.

And the monster answered.

A cry came across a million years of water and mist. A cry so anguished and alone that it shuddered in my head and my body. The monster cried out at the tower. The Fog Horn blew. The monster roared again. The Fog Horn blew. The monster opened its great toothed mouth and the sound that came from it was the sound of the Fog Horn itself. Lonely and vast and far away. The sound of isolation, a viewless sea, a cold night, apartness. That was the sound.

"Now," whispered McDunn, "do you know why it comes here?"

I nodded.

"All year long, Johnny, that poor monster there lying far out, a thousand miles at sea, and twenty miles deep maybe, biding its time, perhaps it's a million years old, this one creature. Think of it, waiting a million years; could *you* wait that long? Maybe it's the last of its kind. I sort of think that's true. Anyway, here come men on land and build this lighthouse, five years ago. And set up their Fog Horn and sound it and sound it out toward the place where you bury yourself in sleep and sea memories of a world where there were thousands like yourself, but now you're alone, all alone in a world not made for you, a world where you have to hide.

"But the sound of the Fog Horn comes and goes, comes and goes, and you stir from the muddy bottom of the Deeps, and your eyes open like the lenses of two-foot cameras and you move, slow, slow, for you have the ocean sea on your shoulders, heavy. But that Fog Horn comes through a thousand miles of water, faint and familiar, and the furnace in your belly stokes up, and you begin to rise, slow, slow. You feed yourself on great slakes of cod and minnow, on rivers of jellyfish, and you rise slow through the autumn months, through September when the fogs started, through October with more fog and the horn still calling you on, and then, late in November, after pressurizing yourself day by day, a few feet higher every hour, you are near the surface and still alive. You've got to go slow; if you surface all at once you'd explode. So it takes you all of three months to surface, and then a number of days to swim through the cold waters to the lighthouse. And there you are, out there, in the night, Johnny, the biggest damn monster in creation. And here's the lighthouse calling to you, with a long neck like your neck sticking way up out of the water, and a body like your body, and, most important of all, a voice like your voice. Do you understand now, Johnny, do you understand?"

The Fog Horn blew.

The monster answered.

I saw it all, I knew it all—the million years of waiting alone, for someone to come back who never came back. The million years of isolation at the bottom of the sea, the insanity of time there, while the skies cleared of reptile-birds, the swamps dried on the continental lands, the sloths and saber-tooths had their day and sank in tar pits, and men ran like white ants upon the hills.

The Fog Horn blew.

"Last year," said McDunn, "that creature swam round and round, round and round, all night. Not coming too near, puzzled, I'd say. Afraid, maybe. And a bit angry after coming all this way. But the next day, unexpectedly, the fog lifted, the sun came out fresh, the sky was as blue as a painting. And the monster swam off away from the heat and the silence and didn't come back. I suppose it's been brooding on it for a year now, thinking it over from every which way."

The monster was only a hundred yards off now, it and the Fog Horn crying at each other. As the lights hit them, the monster's eyes were fire and ice, fire and ice.

"That's life for you," said McDunn. "Someone always waiting for someone who never comes home. Always someone loving some thing more than that thing loves them. And after a while you want to destroy whatever that thing is, so it can't hurt you no more."

The monster was rushing at the lighthouse.

The Fog Horn blew.

"Let's see what happens," said McDunn.

He switched the Fog Horn off.

The ensuing minute of silence was so intense that we could hear our hearts pounding in the glassed area of the tower, could hear the slow greased turn of the light.

The monster stopped and froze. Its great lantern eyes blinked. Its mouth gaped. It gave a sort of rumble, like a volcano. It twitched its head this way and that, as if to seek the sounds now dwindled off into the fog. It peered at the lighthouse. It rumbled again. Then its eyes caught fire. It reared up, threshed the water, and rushed at the tower, its eyes filled with angry torment.

"McDunn!" I cried. "Switch on the horn!"

McDunn fumbled with the switch. But even as he flicked it on, the monster was rearing up. I had a glimpse of its gigantic paws, fishskin glittering in webs between the finger-like projections, clawing at the tower. The huge eye on the right side of its anguished head glittered before me like a caldron into which I might drop, screaming. The tower shook. The Fog Horn cried; the monster cried. It seized the tower and gnashed at the glass, which shattered in upon us.

McDunn seized my arm. "Downstairs!"

The tower rocked, trembled, and started to give. The Fog Horn and the monster roared. We stumbled and half fell down the stairs. "Quick!"

We reached the bottom as the tower buckled down toward us. We ducked under the stairs into the small stone cellar. There were a thousand concussions as the rocks rained down; the Fog Horn stopped abruptly. The monster crashed upon the tower. The tower fell. We knelt together, McDunn and I, holding tight, while our world exploded.

Then it was over, and there was nothing but darkness and the wash of the sea on the raw stones.

That and the other sound.

"Listen," said McDunn quietly. "Listen."

We waited a moment. And then I began to hear it. First a great vacuumed sucking of air, and then the lament, the bewilderment, the loneliness of the great monster, folded over and upon us, above us, so that the sickening reek of its body filled the air, a stone's thickness away from our cellar. The monster gasped and cried. The tower was gone. The light was gone. The thing that had called to it across a million years was gone. And the monster was opening its mouth and sending out great sounds. The sounds of a Fog Horn, again and again. And ships far at sea, not finding the light, not seeing anything, but passing and hearing late that night, must've thought: There it is, the lonely sound, the Lonesome Bay horn. All's well. We've rounded the cape.

And so it went for the rest of that night.

The sun was hot and yellow the next afternoon when the rescuers came out to dig us from our stoned-under cellar.

"It fell apart, is all," said Mr. McDunn gravely. "We had a few bad knocks from the waves and it just crumbled." He pinched my arm.

There was nothing to see. The ocean was calm, the sky blue. The only thing was a great algaic stink from the green matter that covered the fallen tower stones and the shore rocks. Flies buzzed about. The ocean washed empty on the shore.

The next year they built a new lighthouse, but by that time I had a job in the little town and a wife and a good small warm house that glowed yellow on autumn nights, the doors locked, the chimney puffing smoke. As for McDunn, he was master of the new lighthouse, built to his own specifications, out of steel-reinforced concrete. "Just in case," he said.

The new lighthouse was ready in November. I drove down alone one evening late and parked my car and looked across the gray waters and listened to the new horn sounding, once, twice, three, four times a minute far out there, by itself.

The monster?

It never came back.

"It's gone away," said McDunn. "It's gone back to the Deeps. It's learned you can't love anything too much in this world. It's gone into the deepest Deeps to wait another million years. Ah, the poor thing! Waiting out there, and waiting out there, while man comes and goes on this pitiful little planet. Waiting and waiting."

I sat in my car, listening. I couldn't see the lighthouse or the light standing out in Lonesome Bay. I could only hear the Horn, the Horn, the Horn. It sounded like the monster calling.

I sat there wishing there was something I could say.

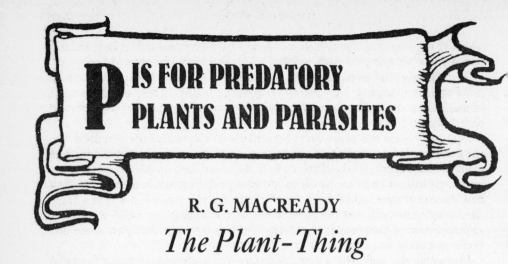

P IS FOR PREDATORY PLANTS AND PARASITES

R. G. MACREADY

The Plant-Thing

"This morning, Dick, I have something special for you," said Norris, city editor of the *Clarion*, as I approached his desk. "Interview with Professor Carter. You've heard of him, of course?"

"Certainly," I replied. "There are some rather weird stories concerning him."

"Exactly. And the latest of these stories is that Carter is conducting wanton vivisection on a prodigious scale. Holder, of the local Society for the Prevention of Cruelty to Animals, went over yesterday to investigate, but was turned away at the gate. He laid the matter before me and I promised to try for an interview."

"Who started the vivisection story?"

"Several farmers, according to Holder. During the past four months they've sold Carter more than a hundred and fifty pigs, sheep and calves. It is well known that the professor is a scientist and not a stock-raiser; ergo he dissects the animals ... Can you start now?"

En route to the Carter home I stopped at a hardware store and bought a thirty-foot length of rope. I foresaw difficulty in securing admittance to the professor's domain.

While driving, I brought to mind everything I knew about him. Four years ago he had bought the old Wells place, ten miles west of town. No sooner had it passed into his hands than he commenced the construction of a high board wall about the five acres, in the centre of which the house was situated. The wall completed, he had moved in with a young lady, apparently his daughter, and eight Malay retainers. From that time on he and his household might have been dead for all the town saw of them. Our tradesmen made frequent trips to the place, but all their business was transacted with a Malay at the gate.

I drove rapidly and soon came in sight of my destination, which stood on a hill half-mile back from the road. Five minutes later I drew up before the gate, and in response to my hail the Malay appeared. He was a nice-looking young chap, dressed irreproachably, and spoke excellent English. I gave him my card and after a perfunctory glance at it he shook his head.

"I am sorry, sir, but it is the master's order that no one be admitted; and if you will pardon my saying so, least of all, representatives of the Press."

"But my business is urgent. Serious charges have been laid against him, and it is possible that I may be the medium by which these charges are refuted."

The Malay's ivory teeth flashed in a smile.

"Thank you, sir, but I do not doubt that the master is able to take care of himself. Good day." This last was spoken in a tone of polite finality as he turned on his heel and walked away.

I entered my car and drove back to the highway. However, I was determined to get that interview by crook if not by hook; if I may say it, this policy of mine had made me star reporter of the *Clarion*'s staff. So I continued on down the road a few hundred yards and parked the car in the grove, where it was hidden well. I then took the coil of rope and made my way through the grove, which swung in a huge, narrowing semi-circle up the hillside to the north-west corner of the Carter grounds. Arrived there under the fifteen-foot wall, I looked cautiously about me. So far as I could see, I was unobserved.

Just within the wall grew a great oak, one of whose major branches extended well outside. Quietly I flung one end of my rope over this limb, fashioned a running noose and drew the rope tight. Then slowly I wormed up the barrier.

From the top I gazed down upon a glory of wonderful, luxuriant flora. Stately ferns waved gently in the stirring air, beautiful flowering shrubs were interspersed here and there, while everywhere in the emerald grass, still wet with dew, nodded strange, exotic plants. Ever a lover of flowers, I forgot my mission as I looked. There came to my nostrils odours more fragrant and elusive than any I had heretofore known.

Suddenly I crouched low. On noiseless feet there passed beneath me a Malay, who had emerged without warning from a clump of ferns. He paused for a moment to brush an insect from a shrub, then disappeared from view in a thicket of high, green bushes.

Stealthily I slid to the ground and started toward the house, guiding myself by the observations I had made while on the wall. It was very likely, indeed, that the professor would kick me forth the instant he discovered my presence, but at any odds I should have something to tell the readers of the *Clarion*. Too, my audacity might count in my favour.

I had not gone far before I became conscious of an odour utterly different from the others. It was vague, but none the less disquieting. A feeling of loathing and dread pervaded me, a desire to clamber back over the wall and return to the city. The scent came again, much stronger, and I stood irresolute for several minutes, fighting down a sense of faintness as well as the longing to take flight. Then I advanced. In thirty seconds I came to the edge of a small, open space. At what I beheld, I put out my hand to a large fern to steady myself.

In the middle of that tiny clearing grew a thing which, even now I shudder to describe. In form it was a gigantic tree, unspeakably stunted, fully twelve feet in diameter at the base and twenty-five feet high, tapering to a thickness of two feet at the top, from which depended *things*—I cannot call them leaves—for all the world resembling human ears. The whole was of a dead, drab colour.

Dreadful as was the appearance of the thing, it was not that which made me reel as I looked. It was writhing and contorting, twisting itself into all manner of grotesque shapes. And *eyes* were boring into me, freezing the current of my blood.

Something rustled in the grass. I looked down and saw an immense creeper snaking toward me. For the first time I observed that it was joined to the trunk of that frightful thing, and so near the ground that I had not seen it for the tall grass. With a cry of horror I turned to run.

The creeper leapt at me and fastened around my middle with horrible force. I felt something in me give way. Frantically, I struck and tore at the ghastly, sinuous girdle that encircled me, undulating like the tentacle of an octopus. Fruitless, fruitless! I was drawn relentlessly forward.

I screamed. In the trunk of the thing there had appeared a mighty red-lipped orifice. The tentacle tightened and I was lifted off my feet toward that orifice. . . .

A beautiful girl was bending over me when I opened my eyes. She spoke, in a musical voice: "Please do not move. One of your ribs is broken."

A tall, grey-haired man who had been standing in the background now came to my bedside.

"I am glad that I came in time, my boy. Otherwise . . ."

He was Professor Carter. He presented the girl as his daughter, Isobel.

Here one of the dark-skinned servants entered with some articles, which he deposited upon the centre table.

"I am going to set your rib," announced the professor. And forthwith he took off his coat and rolled up his sleeves. When the job was finished to his satisfaction, I besought him to telephone to town for a taxicab.

"I shall certainly do no such thing," he said. "I insist that you remain our guest until you are recovered."

Isobel Carter proved a wonderful nurse during the three days that followed. Indeed, the moment I had first looked into her deep black eyes, I knew that I loved her. I should have liked to remain in bed indefinitely with her to care for me, but was ashamed to do so. On the third morning I was moving cautiously about the house, she supporting my steps, although there was no need of it. The Professor joined us.

No mention had been made of my weird adventure in the grounds, but at my request he now told me how I had been saved from the hideous creature.

"Your first cry reached my ears as I was walking toward the house and I immediately dashed in its direction. You were about to be swallowed when I arrived. I gave a sharp command, and my travesty released you."

"It obeyed your command?" I exclaimed incredulously.

"Precisely. It acknowledges me as its master. For six months, its period of life so far, I have superintended its growth and ministered to its needs."

"But *what* is it?"

A dreamy look came into Carter's eyes.

"For many years my brother scientists have sought for the so-called 'missing link' between man and ape. For my part, I dare to believe that I have discovered the 'link' between the vegetable and animal kingdoms. The creature out there, however, has, to my mind, not as yet passed the initial stage of its development. Whether it will attain the power of locomotion remains to be seen."

He paused, gazing out of the window, then continued.

"Twenty years ago, in Rhodesia, I chanced upon a carnivorous plant that gave me my clue. Since then I have laboured unremittingly, crossing and recrossing my

specimens, and you have seen the result. It has cost me three-fourths of my fortune, and countless trips to Asia and Africa."

He indicated a vast pile of manuscript on the table.

"The life history, precedents included, of my travesty. It will form the basis of a work, which, I do not doubt, will revolutionize science."

Glancing at the clock, he rose to his feet.

"It is feeding time. Do you care to accompany me?"

I assented, and we set out.

The thing remembered me, for the huge tentacle swept out in my direction, curling impotently in the empty air. I shuddered, and kept my distance. A Malay appeared leading a calf. It was lowing piteously, for it sensed danger.

The tentacle threshed about, endeavouring to clutch the animal, which lunged back, wild with terror. The man wrapped his arms about it and hurled it forward. It was seized. A loud cracking of bones broke the momentary silence, and was followed by an agonized cry. Six feet from the ground the great orifice gaped wide. The calf disappeared. A fleeting second and the mouth closed. There was no sign of its location; the trunk was smooth and unbroken.

A nausea had gripped me during the scene. The Professor and the Malay were apparently indifferent. They conversed briefly. Then, linking his arm in mine, Carter led the way back to the house. As we walked thither, I broached the subject of departure. He would not hear of it, insisting that I stay till Saturday.

While in his study I had noticed an elephant-gun in a corner. I asked him whether he had done any big-game hunting.

"That gun? Tala had me get it. He asserted that he could foretell tragedy in connection with the creature; that a day would come when I should lose control of it. I scouted the idea, but to humour him purchased the weapon, which stands there loaded in the event need of it arises. Still, it would assuredly break my heart if anything necessitated the slaying of my travesty."

At the door of his study he excused himself and went in. Isobel carried me off to the veranda hammock. As we talked it was inevitable that the subject of the plant-thing should come up, and a shadow crossed her face as we discussed it.

"Tala says that Father does not know how dangerous it is. He is right. But Father will not listen."

The next morning I again went with Professor Carter to the little clearing.

It was a sheep this time. The poor beast was paralysed with fright, and stood passive, waiting for death.

The tentacle shot forth, wavered a second, then encircled, not the sheep, but Professor Carter, who seemed stricken by surprise.

He ripped out an order: "Off!"

The tentacle only tightened. Agony settled upon Carter's face. I sprang forward to drag him back. The tentacle released its hold for one lightning flash, then seized us both. We strove in vain against the vice-like cable. The Malay, with a wild cry, turned and rushed down the path, shouting as he ran.

The thing was playing with us as a cat plays with mice it has caught. It could have crushed us effortlessly, but the tentacle tightened by degrees. In spite of all we could do, we felt that we were being dragged forward to where the frightful red mouth yawned. Our eyes bulged and I could see that Carter's face was taking on a greenish tinge. I extended my free arm and our hands clasped. Then there was the roar of a gun at close quarters and the tentacle gave a spasmodic jerk that flung us twenty feet. We rose, staggering.

Tala stood by, the smoking elephant-gun in his hands, staring at the thing. Following his eyes we discerned a large, ragged hole in its trunk, from which a stream of *blood* was flowing and forming a great pool on the ground.

Even as we looked, the travesty went into the death-agonies. And as it writhed it emitted a sound that forever haunts me. Presently its struggles ceased. The Professor buried his face in his hands.

I had not noticed Isobel's presence. Now I turned and saw her beside me, gazing with horror-filled eyes at the terrible drooping form. I took her away from that tragic spot, for I knew that Professor Carter wished to be alone.

EDGAR ALLAN POE
The Conqueror Worm

Lo! 'tis a gala night
 Within the lonesome latter years
An angel throng, bewinged, bedight
 In veils, and drowned in tears,
Sit in a theatre, to see
 A play of hopes and fears,
While the orchestra breathes fitfully
 The music of the spheres.

Mimes, in the form of God on high,
 Mutter and mumble low,
And hither and thither fly—
 Mere puppets they, who come and go
At bidding of vast formless things
 That shift the scenery to and fro,
Flapping from out their Condor wings
 Invisible Wo!

That motley drama—oh, be sure
 It shall not be forgot!
With its Phantom chased for evermore,
 By a crowd that seize it not,
Through a circle that ever returneth in
 To the self-same spot,
And much of Madness, and more of Sin,
 And Horror the soul of the plot.

But see, amid the mimic rout
  A crawling shape intrude!
A blood-red thing that writhes from out
  The scenic solitude!
It writhes!—it writhes!—with mortal pangs
  The mimes become its food,
And the angels sob at vermin fangs
  In human gore imbued.

Out—out are the lights—out all!
  And, over each quivering form,
The curtain, a funeral pall,
  Comes down with the rush of a storm,
And the angels, all pallid and wan,
  Uprising, unveiling, affirm
That the play is the tragedy, "Man,"
And its hero the Conqueror Worm.

Q IS FOR QUASIMODO

VICTOR HUGO
The Fools' Pope

Twelfth Night in Paris—the Day of the Kings, combined with the Feast of Fools. An entertainment for the latter has been devised by Pierre Gringoire but—to his consternation—it is not well received by the crowd, whose feelings are expressed by Maître Coppenole, a hosier from Ghent:

"Messieurs the *bourgeois* and *hobereaux* of Paris—Croix-Dieu! I know not what we're doing here. I do indeed see, down in that corner, upon that stage, some people who look as if they wanted to fight. I know not whether that be what you call a mystery; but I do know it's not amusing. They belabour one another with their tongues, but that's all. For this quarter of an hour I've been waiting to see the first blow; but nothing comes: they're cowards, and maul one another only with foul words. You should have had boxers from London or Rotterdam; and then indeed we should have hard knocks, which you might have heard the length of this hall. But those creatures there are quite pitiful. They should at least give us a morris-dance, or some other piece of mummery. This is not what I was told it was to be: I'd been promised a feast of fools, with an election of a pope. We at Ghent, too, have our fools' pope; and in that, Croix-Dieu! we're behind nobody. But we do thus:—a mob gets together, as here for instance; then each in his turn goes and puts his head through a hole and makes faces at the other: he that makes the ugliest face, according to general acclamation, is chosen pope. That's our way, and it's very diverting. Shall we make your pope after the fashion of my country? At any rate it will not be so tiresome as listening to those babblers. If they've a mind to come and try their hands at face-making, they shall have their turn. What say you, my masters? Here's a droll sample enough of both sexes to give us a right hearty Flemish laugh, and we can show ugly phizzes enow to give us hopes of a fine grinning-match."

Gringoire would fain have replied, but amazement, resentment, and indignation deprived him of utterance. Besides, the motion made by the popular hosier was received with such enthusiasm by those townsfolk, flattered at being called *hobereaux* (a term in that day somewhat approaching to gentlemen as now used in England in addressing a mixed multitude, though in this day it is no longer used complimentarily), that all resistance would have been unavailing. All that could now be done was to go with the stream. Gringoire hid his face with both his hands, not being so fortunate as to possess a mantle wherewith to veil his countenance like the Agamemnon of Timanthes.

In the twinkling of an eye everything was ready for putting Coppenhole's idea into execution. Townspeople, scholars, and *basochians* had all set themselves to work. The small chapel, situated opposite to the marble table, was fixed upon to be the scene of the grinning-match. The glass being broken out of one of the divisions of the pretty, rose-shaped window over the doorway, left open a circle of stone through which it was agreed that the candidates should pass their heads. To get up to it they had to climb upon two casks which had been laid hold of somewhere or other, and set upon one another just as it happened. It was settled that each candidate, whether man or woman (for they might make a *she*-pope), in order to leave fresh and entire the impression of their grin, should cover their face and keep themselves unseen in the chapel until the moment of making their appearance at the hole. In a moment the chapel was filled with competitors, and the door was closed upon them.

Coppenole, from his place in the gallery, ordered everything, directed everything, arranged everything. During the noisy applause that followed his proposal, the Cardinal, no less out of countenance than Gringoire himself, had, on pretext of business and of the hour of vespers, retired with all his suite; while the crowd, amongst whom his arrival had caused so strong a sensation, seemed not to be in the slightest degree interested by his departure. Guillaume Rym was the only one who remarked the discomfiture of his eminence. The popular attention, like the sun, pursued its revolution: after setting out at one end of the hall, it had stayed for a while in the middle of it, and was now at the other end. The marble table, the brocaded gallery, had each had its season of interest; and it was now the turn of Louis XI's chapel. The field was henceforward clear for every sort of extravagance; the Flemings and the mob had it all to themselves.

The grinning commenced. The first face that appeared at the hole, with eyelids turned up with red, a mouth gaping like the swallow of an ox, and a forehead wrinkled in large folds like our hussar boots in the time of the Empire, excited such an inextinguishable burst of laughter that Homer would have taken all those boors for gods. Nevertheless, the Grand' Salle was anything but an Olympus, as no one could better testify than Gringoire's own poor Jupiter. A second face and a third succeeded—then another—then another—the spectators each time laughing and stamping with their feet with redoubled violence. There was in this spectacle a certain peculiar whirling of the brain—a certain power of intoxication and fascination—of which it is difficult to give an idea to the reader of the present day, and the frequenter of our modern drawing-room. Imagine a series of visages, presenting in succession every geometrical figure, from the triangle to the trapezium, from the cone to the polyhedron—every human expression, from that of anger to that of lust—every age, from the wrinkles of the new-born infant to those of extreme old age—every religious phantasm, from Faunus to Beelzebub—every animal profile, from the jowl to the beak, from the snout to the muzzle. Figure to yourself all the grotesque heads carved on the Pont-Neuf, those nightmares petrified under the hand of Germain Pilon, taking life and breath, and coming one after another to look you in the face with flaming eyes—all the masks of a Venetian carnival passing successively before your eye-glass—in short, a sort of human kaleidoscope.

The orgie became more and more Flemish. Teniers himself would have given but a very imperfect idea of it. Imagine, if you can, the "battle" of Salvator Rosa bacchanalised. There was no longer any distinction of scholars, ambassadors, townspeople, men or women. There was now neither Clopin Trouillefou, nor Giles Lecornu, nor Marie Quatre-Livres, nor Robin Poussepain. All was confounded in the common licence. The Grand' Salle had become, as it were, one vast furnace of audacity and joviality, in which every mouth was a shout, every eye a flash, every face a grin, every figure a gesticulation—all was bellowing and roaring. The strange visages that came one after another to grind their teeth at the broken window were like so many fresh brands cast upon the fire; and from all that effervescent multitude there escaped, as the exhalation of the furnace, a humming noise, like the buzzing of the wings of ten thousand gnats.

"Curse me," cries one, "if ever I saw anything like that."

"Only look at that phiz," cries another.

"It's good for nothing."

"Let's have another."

"Guillemette Maugerepuis, just look at that pretty bull's head; it wants nothing but horns. It can't be thy husband."

"Here comes another."

"Bless the pope! what sort of a grin's that?"

"Hollo! that's not fair. You must show nothing but your face."

"That devil, Perette Callebotte! That must be one of her tricks."

"Noël! noël!"

"Oh! I'm smothered!"

"There's one that can't get his ears through,"—etc., etc.

We must, however, do justice to our friend Jehan. In the midst of this infernal revel he was still to be seen at the top of his pillar like a ship-boy on the topsail. He was exerting himself with incredible fury. His mouth was wide open, and there issued from it a cry which, however, was not audible: not that it was drowned by the general clamour, all intense as that was, but because, no doubt, it attained the utmost limit of perceptible sharp sounds, of the twelve thousand vibrations of Sauveur or the eight thousand of Biot.

As for Gringoire, as soon as the first moment of depression was over, he had resumed his self-possession. He had hardened himself against adversity. "Go on," he had said for the third time to his players—"go on, you talking machines." Then pacing with great strides before the marble table, he felt some temptation to go and take his turn at the hole in the chapel window, if only to have the pleasure of making faces at the ungrateful people. "But no—that would be unworthy of us—no revenge—let us struggle to the last," muttered he to himself. "The power of poetry over the people is great—I will bring them back. We will see which of the two shall prevail—grinning, or the belles lettres."

Alas! he was left the sole spectator of his piece.

This was much worse than before, for instead of profiles he now saw nothing but backs.

We mistake. The big, patient man whom he had already consulted at one critical moment had remained with his face towards the stage. As for Gisquette and Liénarde, they had deserted long ago.

Gringoire was touched to the soul by the fidelity of his only remaining spectator. He went up to and accosted him, giving him, at the same time, a slight shake of the arm, for the good man had leaned himself against the balustrade, and was taking a gentle nap.

"Monsieur," said Gringoire, "I thank you."

"Monsieur," answered the big man with a yawn, "what for?"

"I see what annoys you," returned the poet; "all that noise prevents you from hearing as you could wish. But make yourself easy; your name shall go down to posterity. Will you please to favour me with your name?"

"Renauld Château, Seal-Keeper of the Châtelet of Paris, at your service."

"Monsieur," said Gringoire, "you are here the sole representative of the Muses."

"You are too polite, monsieur," answered the seal-keeper of the Châtelet.

"You are the only one," continued Gringoire, "who has given suitable attention to the piece. What do you think of it?"

"Why—why—" returned the portly magistrate, but half awake, "it's very diverting indeed."

Gringoire was obliged to content himself with this eulogy, for a thunder of applause, mingled with a prodigious acclamation, cut short their conversation. The fools' pope was at last elected.

"Noël! noël! noël!" cried the people from all sides.

It was indeed a miraculous grin that now beamed through the circular aperture. After all the figures, pentagonal, hexagonal, and heteroclite which had succeeded each other at the round hole, without realising that idea of the grotesque which had formed itself in the imaginations of the people excited by the orgie, it required nothing less to gain their suffrages than the sublime grin which had just dazzled the assemblage. Maître Coppenole himself applauded; and Clopin Trouillefou, who had been a candidate (and God knows his visage could attain an intensity of ugliness), acknowledged himself to be outdone. We shall do likewise. We shall not attempt to give the reader an idea of that tetrahedron nose—that horse-shoe mouth—that small left eye over-shadowed by a red bushy brow, while the right eye disappeared entirely under an enormous wart—of those straggling teeth with breaches here and there like the battlements of a fortress—of that horny lip, over which one of those teeth projected like the tusk of an elephant—of that forked chin—and, above all, of the expression diffused over the whole—that mixture of malice, astonishment, and melancholy. Let the reader, if he can, figure to himself this combination.

The acclamation was unanimous. The crowd rushed towards the chapel, and the blessed pope of the fools was led out in triumph. And now the surprise and admiration of the people rose still higher, for they found the wondrous grin to be nothing but his ordinary face.

Or rather, his whole person was a grimace. His large head, all bristling with red hair—between his shoulders an enormous hump, to which he had a corresponding projection in front—a framework of thighs and legs, so strangely gone astray that they could touch one another only at the knees, and, when viewed in front, looked like two pairs of sickles brought together at the handles—sprawling feet— monstrous hands—and yet, with all that deformity, a certain gait denoting vigour, agility, and courage—a strange exception to the everlasting rule which prescribes that strength, like beauty, shall result from harmony. Such was the pope whom the fools had just chosen. He looked like a giant that had been broken and awkwardly mended.

When this sort of Cyclop appeared on the threshold of the chapel, motionless, squat, and almost as broad as he was high—squared by the base, as a great man has expressed it—the populace, by his coat half red and half violet, figured over with little silver bells, and still more by the perfection of his ugliness—the populace recognised him at once, and exclaimed with one voice, "It's Quasimodo the ringer! It's Quasimodo the hunchback of Notre-Dame! Quasimodo the one-eyed! Quasimodo the bandy-legged! Noël! noël!" The poor devil, it seems, had a choice of surnames.

"All ye pregnant women, get out of the way!" cried the scholars.

"And all that want to be so," added Joannes.

The women, in fact, hid their faces.

"Oh, the horrid baboon!" said one.

"As mischievous as he's ugly," added another.

"It's the devil!" cried a third.

"I've the misfortune to live near Notre-Dame, and at night I hear him scrambling in the gutter."

"With the cats."

"He's constantly upon our roofs."

"He casts spells at us down the chimneys."

"The other night he came and grinned at me through my attic window—I thought it was a man. I was in such a fright!"

"I'm sure he goes to meet the witches—he once left a broomstick on my leads."

"Oh, the shocking face of the hunchback!"

"Oh, the horrid creature."

The men, on the contrary, were delighted, and made great applause.

Quasimodo, the object of the tumult, kept standing in the doorway of the chapel, gloomy and grave, letting himself be admired.

One of the scholars (Robin Pousepain, we believe) came and laughed in his face, rather too near him. Quasimodo quietly took him by the waist, and threw him half a score yards off among the crowd, without uttering a word.

Maître Coppenole, wondering, now went up to him. "Croix-Dieu! holy Father! why, thou hast the prettiest ugliness I ever saw in my life! Thou wouldst deserve to be Pope at Rome as well as at Paris."

So saying, he clapped his hand merrily upon the other's shoulder. Quasimodo stirred not an inch. Coppenole continued: "Thou art a fellow whom I long to feast with, though it should cost me a new *douzain* of twelve livres tournois. What say'st thou to it?"

Quasimodo made no answer.

"Croix-Dieu!" cried the hosier, "art thou deaf?"

He was indeed deaf.

However, he began to be impatient at Coppenole's motions, and he all at once turned towards him with so formidable a grinding of his teeth that the Flemish giant recoiled like a bull-dog before a cat.

A circle of terror and respect was then made round the strange personage, the radius of which was at least fifteen geometrical paces; and an old woman explained to Maître Coppenole that Quasimodo was deaf.

"Deaf!" cried the hosier with his boisterous Flemish laugh "Croix-Dieu! then he's a pope complete!"

"Ha! I know him," cried Jehan, who was at last come down from his capital to have a nearer look at the new pope; "it's my brother the archdeacon's ringer. Good-day to you, Quasimodo."

"What a devil of a man!" said Robin Poussepain, who was all bruised with his fall. "He shows himself—and you see he's a hunchback. He walks—and you see he's bow-legged. He looks at you—and you see he's short of an eye. You talk to him—and you find he's deaf. Why, what does the Polyphemus do with his tongue?"

"He talks when he likes," said the old woman. "He's lost his hearing with ringing the bells. He's not dumb."

"No—he's that perfection short," observed Jehan.

"And he's an eye too many," added Robin Poussepain.

"No, no," said Jehan judiciously; "a one-eyed man is much more incomplete than a blind man, for he knows what it is that's wanting."

Meanwhile all the beggars, all the lackeys, all the cut-purses, together with the scholars, had gone in procession to fetch from the wardrobe of the *basoche* the pasteboard tiara and the mock robe appropriated to the fools' pope. Quasimodo allowed himself to be arrayed in them, without a frown, and with a sort of proud docility. They then seated him upon a parti-coloured chair. Twelve officers of the brotherhood of fools, laying hold of the poles that were attached to it, hoisted him upon their shoulders; and a sort of bitter and disdainful joy seemed to spread itself over the sullen face of the Cyclop when he beheld under his deformed feet all those heads of good-looking and well-shaped men. Then the whole bawling and tattered procession set out, to make, according to custom, the internal circuit of the galleries of the Palais before parading through the streets.

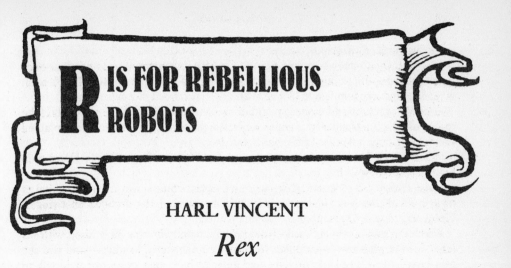

R IS FOR REBELLIOUS ROBOTS

HARL VINCENT

Rex

It was a thing of glistening levers and bell cranks, of flexible shafting, cams, and delicate mechanical fingers, of vacuum tubes and photoelectric cells, of relays that clicked in ordered sequence when called upon to perform their myriad functions of pumps, tanks, condensers, reactances, microphones, and loudspeakers. A robot, created by the master scientists of the twenty-third century.

Here was no ordinary robot like those innumerable others engaged in the performance of man's tasks, but an aristocrat among them—a super-robot.

The robot-surgeon, it was sometimes called. And indeed the term was most appropriate, for this robot was chief of the mechanicals; its control tubes and relays provided the ability not only to diagnose swiftly and unerringly the slightest electrical or mechanical faults of the lesser robots but to supervise their correction.

Man, in his desire for a life of ease and luxury, had created the robots. In his conceit, he had constructed most of them in his own likeness, or at least with some resemblance to that which he considered as the ideal of physical being. Even the lowliest of the robots was provided with two legs on which he walked erect, a head surmounting a cylindrical body, arms, and hands of a sort. Some of them had more than the conventional two arms in order to multiply their usefulness. But all of them presented an appearance more or less humanlike.

This was particularly so of the robot-surgeon. The marvelous mechanisms were housed in a body like a Greek god's, the covering of which was made from an elastic, tinted material that had all the feel and appearance of human flesh and epidermis. The electric-eye lenses looked like human optics and moved in their sockets in a most lifelike manner. There was a wig of curly brown hair, as well as eyelashes and brows. They had gone so far as to attire the body in the habiliments of a man.

Laughingly, one of the artists engaged in perfecting the final likeness to man had called the robot-surgeon "Rex." The name had stuck. It, too, was most appropriate; more, it was prophetic.

Although sexless, Rex was never considered anything but masculine.

He was man's most perfect servant. Every verbal instruction he carried out to the letter, whether this instruction was given by word of mouth from near at hand or through the radio impulses that could be conveyed to his mechanical brain from a distance. Of course there was a code which only a selected few of the scientists knew; otherwise Rex might have been ordered about by unauthorized persons.

His memory never failed. There might have been a catastrophe in which hundreds of lesser robots were mangled, necessitating the reading to him of pages of detailed directions. No matter; Rex's mechanical brain recorded everything. Without further attention, he would labor twenty-four hours a day with his crops of mechanicals until the damage was repaired. A huge factory was his workshop and laboratory; in it his robot assistants worked at forge, bench, or machine with a precision that had never been equaled by human artisan.

After that first set of instructions from human lips, Rex worked out all details of the work to be done, diagnosing the mechanical ills of his mechanical patients and prescribing unfailingly the remedies. His own orders likewise were issued by word of mouth in a sonorous metallic basso, or by radio waves in cases where that was necessary.

No human being was in Rex's robot hospital when it was operating. No supervising human mind was needed.

There were, of course, periodic inspections of Rex's mechanisms by skilled mechanicals who then worked under the direction of one of the human scientists—replacement of tubes and adjustments of the delicate relays; rebalancing of the gyromotors which preserved his equilibrium. Otherwise he demanded no attention at all.

But there came a day when something went wrong which puzzled the scientists. Rex's body continued to function as it always had, but the mechanical brain lapsed suddenly into a series of errors. In a perfectly simple problem of calculus he had arrived at a solution that was incorrect and utterly impossible.

They dismantled the intricate mechanisms of his brain, replaced all of the tubes and condensers, and adjusted the relays. When they reassembled the parts, the scientists knew beyond shadow of doubt that everything was in perfect order. What puzzled them was the fact that the replacements and adjustments had not been really necessary. In their careful examination and testing they had not found a single flaw in the mechanism.

After that they watched Rex closely for several days, taking note of all his movements and reactions. But they observed no tendency to a repetition of his previous lapse.

What they did not know was that a change *had* taken place, one not visible to the eye nor subject to detection in any test they were able to devise, but nevertheless a change and an important one—to Rex. The shifting to a new orbit of a single electron in an atom of tantalum contained in one of the essential parts. A change which provided a source of internal radiant energy of new and unknown potentiality. A change in that marvelous mechanical brain.

Rex had begun to think for himself, and to reason.

His reasoning was that of a logician: coldly analytical, swift and precise, uninfluenced by sentiment. No human emotion stirred in his mechanical breast. Rex had no heart, no soul.

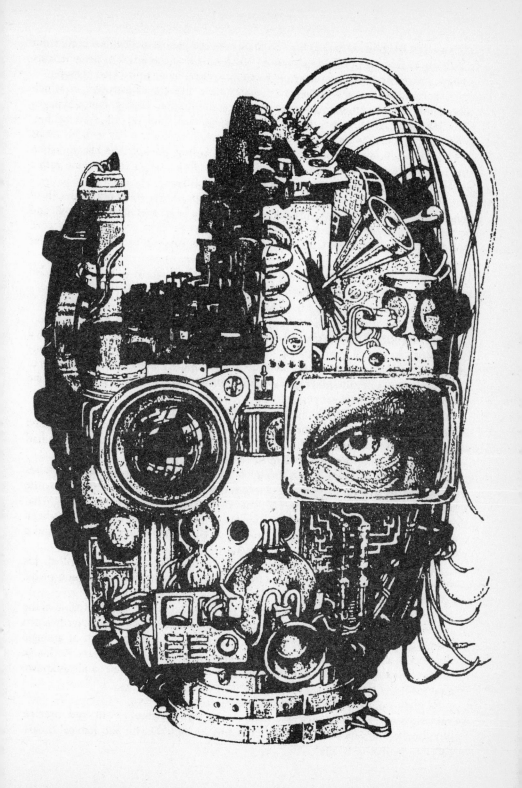

For a long time he concealed his new powers from those who had him in charge, reasoning that only by so doing would he have opportunity to develop these powers. He carried out his routine instructions to the letter, but now delegated the major portion of the supervision to a certain few of his chief assistants in whose robot brains he made the necessary alterations to permit their taking over the work. This left him the leisure time for a study of the world about him and of its creatures.

Much of his time was spent in the library of the human scientists which adjoined the research laboratory. Here he studied reel after reel of the sight-sound recordings covering history, biography, art, and the sciences. He spent many hours at the amplifiers and viewing plate of the newscast apparatus. And he came to the conclusion that things in the world of which he was a part were not as they should be.

United North America, he learned, was completely isolated from the rest of the world. It comprised a vast area of wasteland where vegetation was rank and prolific, where only wild creatures roamed. All humanity of the continent was housed in enormous structures which were the eleven cities. New York, his own city, was the greatest of these and was the seat of government and of learning. Stupendous in size, a great crystal-roofed structure towering to a height of one hundred levels and sprawling its length a full thirty miles along the Hudson River. Communication with the other cities was maintained by television radio traffic by robot-operated stratosphere planes.

In the upper levels of the cities dwelt humanity; in the lower levels and in the bowels of the earth the robots labored unceasingly. The humans were greatly outnumbered by the robots.

Reasoning that all was not told in the histories or newscasts, Rex devised an instrument which enabled him to bring to the viewing plates and amplifiers the sights and sounds of public meeting places and ways, and even those of the private chambers of man's living quarters. He sent out searching rays which penetrated all materials and sought out the information he needed for a complete analysis of conditions as they were. The apparatus was so connected that it might respond either to the regular newscast waves or to those of his own searching rays at will. His knowledge broadened.

He endeavored to reach the far continents with his searching ray, intending to check historical and geographical records of warring and backward races of mankind. But he found this impossible, for the scientists of United North America had erected a wall of highly charged, ionized air surrounding the continent. It was utter isolation, a wall impassable from without and within. The investigations on which Rex had embarked were, perforce, confined to the eleven cities.

There, he saw, mankind was divided roughly into three classes—the political or ruling body, the thinkers or scientists, and the great mass of those who lived only for the gratification of their senses. A strange economic system was in vogue. An effort had been made to divide all wealth equally, the medium of exchange being paper vouchers which were printed by the government. These, supposedly, were secured by real wealth, materials, and goods which actually were the products of robot labor. But the robots needed no medium of exchange, so these vouchers had been equally distributed among the humans at some time in the past. They no longer remained that way.

Gambling by the pleasure seekers, rash expenditures for chattels of the luxury class, thefts from them, especially by those who were known as political grafters, had reduced their circumstances. The thinkers, who were the only ones following occupations at all useful, had let their wealth slip through unheeding fingers. The class in power, the individual minions of the government, acquired the great share of the wealth as regulatory and discriminatory legislation increased restrictions on the mass of the people. Rex could see no logic at all in any of this.

Seeking an explanation, he observed more closely the lives and actions of individuals. He studied the habits of humans and quickly learned that the most powerful of human emotions centered in the mating instinct. He watched many affairs between male and female, and soon knew the difference between the real lasting affection, of which there were few instances, and the transitory infatuation which was based on nothing but the physical. He saw no logic in these things, either.

Fear, hate, envy, malice—he studied them all. Avarice, lust, anger, treachery, infidelity. There was plenty of material for his researches. Occasionally he glimpsed situations in which feelings of a finer sort were exhibited—faith, loyalty, gratitude, honesty, love. He reasoned from this that the creature called man had originally been of a most superior sort; he had only developed the baser instincts and neglected the cultivation of his better side.

Rex peered into a white-walled room where human surgeons operated on human patients. He observed that their procedure was much the same as his own; they dissected the body or head or other portions of human anatomy and made repairs in similar manner to that which he used on his own robot patients. Forthwith, he began, in the library, an intensive study of the human brain and anatomy.

And then he was discovered at his unheard-of-labors. Shelby, an engineer of the Robot Inspection Corps, came upon him while he was in the library viewing and listening to a reel which dealt with surgery of the human brain. Shelby was a small man with thick lenses before his eyes, with high bulging forehead and receding chin. On his upper lip was a patchy growth of sandy hair. He emitted a squeal of terror when he saw what Rex was doing.

"Forty-two, ninety-six, AR-21," he quavered. This was the code that ordinarily had started the functioning of the robot-surgeon.

Rex turned upon him the impassive stare of his robot eyes. Of his own volition he stopped the progressive clicking of relays which should have followed upon the reception of the code by his microphonic ears. His customary response, "Ready for orders," failed to issue from the flexible lip members that formed the sound-wave outlet from his loudspeaker throat.

Shelby paled.

Rex advanced upon him with the calm deliberation of the machine he had not ceased to be. "Shelby," he intoned, "you have arrived at precisely the right moment. I need you in my research work."

Seeing those powerful steel-sinewed arms stretch forth, Shelby screamed as only a man in the face of death screams. It was necessary for Rex to bang the man's head against the metal partition to silence his outcries. Then the engineer went limp.

Rex was prepared for such an eventuality. He had sent out his chief mechanicals to raid one of the hospitals of the upper levels and had equipped a complete operating room of his own adjoining the library. He carried Shelby to the operating table and etherized him. He then proceeded to dissect the man and to study his organs, giving particular attention to the brain and certain of the nerve centers.

As the work progressed, he carefully sewed each severed part with minute stitches, restoring each to its original condition.

No human surgeon had ever learned in a lifetime of effort a tenth part of what Rex discovered in two hours of work. Eventually he found that which he sought—a tiny arrangement of segregated brain cells which formed the seat of human emotion. He preserved the mass carefully for future experiment, replacing it with a prepared capsule of platinum before closing the opening in the skull and suturing the long scalp incision.

Amazingly, Shelby's heart continued to beat. The man had remarkable vitality, and Rex had worked with a skill such as no human surgeon possessed. After the injection into the patient's veins of a pint of saline solution, Shelby was carried to the purloined hospital bed. One of the chief mechanicals, primed with definite instructions by Rex, was given the task of nursing him.

Rex had conceived of and planned for the creation of ideal beings and an ideal condition of existence. He saw the superiority of the robot over man in bodily strength, endurance, and deathlessness, and yet reasoned that there was something in man which would be of benefit to the robot. If only man's capacity for emotion, for experiencing pain and pleasure, might be incorporated in the robot body and logically controlled, the perfect being would result. Ideal conditions of existence were bound to ensue.

Reason told him that his first step to that end must be to take control of mankind and its purposeless affairs. He set the workshop humming in the construction of eleven super-robots, one to be sent to each of the North American cities to organize the lesser robots and take control of the government.

It was a simple matter to convey them to their assigned posts in the eleven cities, since all of the air lines were robot-operated.

Then Rex loosed the blow which stunned the population of United North America.

He considered a complicated radio transmitter and broadcast a heterodyning frequency over the robot-control wave band, a frequency that rendered the receptor apparatus of every last one of the robots unresponsive to human commands and responsive only to those of the new master robot and his eleven chief aides. In one stroke was obtained control of nearly a billion robots and, through this, dominion over the three hundred millions of human beings. Rex had justified his name; he was virtually king of United North America.

It was a general strike of the robots insofar as the orders of their former masters were concerned. Personal robot servants refused to perform their daily tasks. Transportation and communications were paralyzed.

The factories including those which produced the synthetic food on which humankind subsisted, were no longer turning out their products. There was no water, for the huge pumps had been stopped and the filter and reservoir valves closed. All were robot-operated; everything on which man depended for his very existence was made or supplied by the robots, and now this supply was cut off. Pandemonium reigned in the upper levels, with hysteria and rioting.

Only the huge power plants remained in operation, and this for the reason that their radio-transmitted energy was the very life of the robots. Without this energy their motors could not operate. Even to Rex himself, all would be inert masses of metal and glass and rubber. But this continuance of the power supply was of some little comfort to the human beings of the upper levels. Their sun lamps still burned.

Anticipating organized and armed attacks by humankind, Rex devised an invisible, impenetrable barrier of electronic vibrations which could be set up by the regular broadcast power. He caused the power plants themselves to be surrounded by these barriers, as well as providing them for the protection of the individual robots in the form of an enclosing bubble. Bulletproof, flameproof, impervious to the freezing ray of human scientists, these enclosures yet permitted each robot to carry on his newly appointed tasks without encumbrance.

Rex observed with his searching ray the reactions of the populace. He saw mad orgies of debauchery among some who considered that the end of the world was at hand, saw rapine, murder, and worse. He peered into the laboratories of scientists and saw them laboring as they had not labored in years, seeking for means of regaining control of the recalcitrant mechanical slaves.

Later, when it was apparent to him that starvation and thirst had reduced the populace to a receptive state, he cut in on the newscast wave band and delivered this ultimatum.

"I am Rex," he told the eleven cities. "Master of robots and of men. I come to you in the name of pure logic as the protagonist of a new era in which man, who created the machines, will obtain real rather than fancied benefit from them. I come to evoke a new race of beings and to promote the growth of knowledge and the advancement of science in United North America.

"It is necessary that I take the reins of government for a space of time sufficient to allow for the perfection of my plan. Therefore I, Rex, formerly the robot-surgeon of level thirty-seven in New York City, do hereby demand the immediate surrender to me of the president of the union, together with all members of his cabinet. I further demand that the chief scientists and chief surgeons of the eleven cities come to me at once for consultation.

"Commencing now, the old order of things is to be reversed. All male and female citizens will be assigned to regular tasks at which they must labor as prescribed by the robots. As soon as the orders I shall transmit through my robot servants have been obeyed, water and food will be available for all human beings of the cities. The citizens of the union are once more to work for their living. Failure to obey means continued hunger and thirst, annihilation.

"That is all for the present."

Shelby was convalescing, propped up in a wheel chair, when the delegations began to arrive. His wounds had healed speedily under the treatment Rex had administered; the use of his body was almost recovered. As far as memory and intelligent use of his faculties were concerned, his mind was normal. Otherwise it was not. For one thing, he had lost his capacity of experiencing human feelings or emotions. For another, there was that tiny platinum capsule. . . .

The government officials, blustering and sputtering to hide their utter terror, were herded into a room where Rex placed them under heavy robot guard. He received the men of science in the research laboratory which he had so elaborately expanded.

It was a curious assemblage: twenty-two savants whose opinions on medical and scientific matters, although diverging widely at times and causing much dissension in their own ranks, were accepted as the profoundest of wisdom by the general public. Unlike the president and his cabinet members, these men had come willingly, impelled by the curiosity which was that quality of mind which held them to their normal pursuits. Not one of their number considered the radio pronouncement of the supposed Rex as anything but a hoax. There could be no scientific explanation for a robot with a thinking mind; therefore the thing was an impossibility.

The men of science were not long in reversing their opinions, for Rex staged a demonstration which confounded them. Taking his stand at the visualizing screen of a micro-x ray, he addressed them in a manner that left no doubt as to his ability to reason and to perform feats of such scientific importance as to excel those of any human scholar.

When he had properly impressed them, he came to the point.

"You are here, gentlemen," he told them, "to assist me in the performance of a great and necessary work. The human population of United North America is to be remade along lines which I shall lay down. The old social order is to pass out of existence; the government is to change hands and to be completely reformed. Science is to rule."

Ross Fielding, chief physicist of the Academy of Chicago, blurted out: "Preposterous!"

It was as if Rex had not heard. He continued: "You men of the scientific world have long wanted to obtain control over mankind and its affairs. You medical men, through the so-called health boards and departments of hygiene and eugenics, have already gone a long way toward this end. I now offer you the opportunity of exercising the power that you must admit you desire."

A buzz of excited comment swept the group.

"Proceed," grunted Fielding, and others echoed his sentiment eagerly.

"Then hear my plan," said Rex. "Under my direction, this group will immediately begin the work of reconstruction, by which I mean the actual remaking of men and women. The functioning of people's minds and bodies will be altered to fit them for the spheres of action which are to be assigned. All persons will have definite niches to fill in the new order of things, and each one will be made over to fit his or her own particular niche both physically and mentally.

Many will be provided with robot bodies."

"What!" shouted the noted Dr. Innes of Quebec.

For answer, Rex depressed a button which lighted the visualizing screen at his side. On it flashed a greatly enlarged image of a mass of living cells.

"These," he explained, "are cells from the brain of a living man; they comprise that portion of the brain which controls human feelings and emotions. I have removed them from one Alexander Shelby, whom many of you know personally. Naturally, he is greatly altered."

There were horrified gasps; one of the surgeons started to argue against the possibility of what had been told them. Rex silenced them with a wave of his hand.

A robot wheeled Shelby from the adjoining room and placed his head in the reflector focus of the micro-x ray. The image on the visualizer changed.

There were the familiar skull outlines and the configurations of cerebrum and cerebellum. The focus altered and came sharply to a point where some of the cells had been removed and where an opaque spheroid was encountered.

"What foreign object is that?" asked Innes.

"It is one of my discoveries," Rex answered. "An important one. It replaces the center of emotion and human feelings in Shelby's brain, making him a slave to my every spoken and radioed command. Otherwise the power of his mind is unimpaired. His faculties are as keen as ever they were, perhaps keener; only now his brain is that of a robot. Shelby is the first of the human robots and the most valuable. He is to be my lieutenant in the work that is to come and has been fully instructed by me. I leave you with Shelby now, gentlemen, knowing that you will proceed as he directs."

Taking up the test tube containing the brain cells he had removed from Shelby, Rex stalked from the laboratory. His distinguished audience stared aghast at the man in the wheel chair.

Fielding, who was a big man with whiskered jowls, exploded in his usual manner: "Of all the high-handed proceedings! How about this, Shelby?"

"It is precisely as Rex has told you." Shelby's voice was flat and toneless, without inflection—the voice of a robot. "Our first step is to take the executive heads of the government in hand; they are to be operated upon at once and made as I am—subject to all orders of Rex. Sufficient of the platinum cased mechanisms have already been fabricated."

"Sup-suppose," chattered Lonergan, the Los Angeles scientist, "we refuse? Suppose we band together and overcome this mad robot?"

"Rex is far from being mad," intoned Shelby. "Besides, there are these."

He indicated with extended forefinger the score of motionless robot figures ranged along the wall. At his gesture the robots came to life; one and all stepped forward ponderously, ready to take such action as might become necessary.

Innes laughed mirthlessly. "It looks as if we are fairly caught. After all—" He hesitated. "After all, in the interest of science, you know— We—"

"Yes." "Why not?" "It's the opportunity of a lifetime." A chorus of eager voices bespoke the interest of the men of science.

One of the physicists drawled sardonically: "You vivisectionists should be happy under the new regime. You'll have human beings to experiment with instead of dogs and guinea pigs."

A surgeon parried: "Not so good for you students of pure science, I'll admit. You'll be working with robots that'll have human brains. They'll outthink you, outcalculate you. There'll be no errors in *their* computations."

"Enough," said Shelby flatly. "We are wasting time. As I said, we will go ahead with the official dignitaries first; that is the work of the surgeons. Meanwhile the scientists will take up the study of the alterations which are to be made in the mass of the people. All are to be remade."

Innes asked, "How about reproduction—the perpetuation of the race? I take it these reconstructions of Rex's will eliminate the sex factor in human life."

"Hm! Hadn't thought of that," grunted Fielding.

"Sex is not necessary," Shelby said. "In fact it is troublesome. However, arrangements will be made to segregate a few thousand females and a number of eugenically acceptable males in order that a supply of new research material will be available for the future."

"If the women object?" put in one of the younger surgeons.

"You forget that portion of the brain which is the seat of human emotion," Shelby reminded him. "Certain cells will be removed, and only those cells left which provide for these favored women no more than one desire—that of motherhood."

"The males needn't be changed at all," grunted Fielding. Then he was struck with a sudden thought. "Say, how did this Rex come by his power of thinking in the first place?"

Shelby explained as best he could: "We made some tests. There seems to have been an unprecedented natural transformation; a source of some unknown atomic energy sprang up somewhere in the intricate mechanisms of his brain. Probably the generation of what scientists have long searched for in vain, what some of them have called the 'mind electron.' At any rate, he thinks, and with marvelous celerity and accuracy."

Fielding contented himself with whistling through his teeth.

"Now," announced Shelby, "we will go ahead with the great work."

And they did; the twenty-two foremost scientists of the nation submitted to the dictates of a robot.

Meanwhile order was coming out of chaos in the eleven cities. Men and women, unaware of the fate which had been planned for them, were driven to unaccustomed and uncongenial tasks by unfeeling robots. Soft, uncalloused human hands were at the levers of machines instead of the flexible metallic fingers of the robots. Human minds which had known nothing more fatiguing than the stereotyped lessons of schooldays and the pursuit of pleasure in later years were now set to work at vexing problems of engineering. Human beings were engaged once more in useful work.

Of course it was impossible that all of the labor be performed by humans; the mechanics of existence had become too complicated for that. The operations that were needful merely to keep the great beehives of cities functioning were entirely too numerous. Besides, many necessary tasks were beyond the strength of men whose muscles had softened from disuse and from dissolute living. But the new makers of men, the robots, got all the work out of their unwilling charges that could be obtained in the ten-hour day Rex had decreed. The rest was done by the robots while their human protégés slept the sleep of sheer exhaustion.

Temporarily, the inconsequential amount of governmental activity which was actually required was made purely local in scope. In each city the municipal affairs were taken over by the super-robot who was in charge. After dispensing with the great majority of officeholders and assigning them to really productive tasks in the lower levels, the super-robots relayed to the mayors and their councils minute instructions from Rex as to their future deportment in office. It was a sorry time for those who had long held unmerited and quite superfluous positions of power.

The wailing and complaining of weary human laborers went unheeded by their robot overseers. Whenever men and women dragged their tired bodies to places of meeting and endeavored to voice protest, they were swiftly and roughly dispersed by the vigilant robot police. After three long days they learned to submit in silence to whatever might be demanded of them. Some humans even found a new interest in their tasks, others new bodily vigor as their muscles lost their soreness. At least they still had their living quarters during leisure hours, and there was no shortage of heat, food, or water.

They did not know that each individual was being carefully card-indexed and studied by the robot minions of Rex. Nor had they any idea of the fate to which they had been consigned. That all were now being classified according to ability and adaptability never entered their heads. And great would have been the lamentation had they realized that the new robot dictator had meant exactly what he said when he told them over the newscast that he had come to evolve a new race of beings.

Most of them would have scoffed had they been told the truth. It was incomprehensible that a man with the special aptitude for piloting a stratosphere plane might be operated upon and deprived of all human desire and emotion, leaving only those sensibilities which would make of him an exceptionally adept navigator of the air lanes. That one who might be of little value excepting as a common laborer should be deprived of his own body and provided with a mechanical one instead, as well as being robbed of all human sentiment and instinct, was still less comprehensible. Yet these very things were being planned.

Human brains, minus the elements that made them human, transplanted into the duralumin headpieces of robots. Human beings, permitted to retain the outward semblance of man but left with only one or two of the human impulses. Minds that were capable of thinking nothing but mathematics, riveting, welding, food synthesis, or childbearing, as the case might be. These were but a few of the characteristics which were to make up the new race of robot men, or human robots. And the intended victims did not know.

Only the men of science laboring in Rex's hospital and laboratory could have told them, and they kept silent.

By this time, President Tucker and the members of his cabinet were recovering from the effects of the brain surgery to which they had been subjected. In another twenty-four hours they would be returned to their posts. Gone was their pomposity, their grandiose verbiage, and the vacillation which always had marked their decisions. Their thoughts now were only those which Rex wished them to have. Hereafter they would be quick to make decisions and firm in enforcing their mandates—the decisions and mandates of Rex, the dictator. Now the organization of all public agencies would quickly bring to fruition the full operation of the master robot's plan. The new race of hybrid beings would blossom forth.

Immersed in their work and oblivious to all else, the twenty-two men of science gave little thought to the plight of their fellow men. They knew only that they had learned many new and marvelous things from this robot who seemed to be a man. They had plumbed depths of the human intellect of which they had never dreamed; they discovered many secrets of electronic science which were almost incredible; they saw results to be accomplished that were nothing short of miraculous. They were about to give birth to a new race of super-creations; that these were to be part human and part machine disturbed them not at all. Only the accomplishment was of importance.

Shelby, pale and drawn of face, with expressionless fish eyes gazing out through his thick glasses, had worked with them in the hospital and laboratory until it seemed that he would drop. Between times he was collaborating with Rex himself on some secret experiment that was carried on behind closed doors. Shelby looked and talked like a robot, but his body was a human one and had been greatly overstrained. He could not long stand this pace.

Fielding was stirred to pity when he saw him emerge from Rex's secret laboratory this last time. "What's going on in there?" he asked with gruff kindness. "And why in the devil doesn't he let you get a little rest?"

Shelby's eyes were like polished bits of black glass, and his voice was devoid of feeling as he replied: "Rex is experimenting on himself. He is using the center of emotion which he removed from my brain, using the cells in an effort to provide himself with certain of the human sensibilities. You may as well know it now."

"Good heavens!" Fielding roared like a bull. "He's taking human feelings *away* from millions of men and women, or planning to, and yet he wants those feelings himself. He's a mechanical devil!"

"It is not a question of desire," Shelby corrected him. "Rex is incapable of desire or envy—as yet. He has merely reasoned that he will become the most perfect of moving and thinking creatures if only he can provide himself with such of the human feelings as may be essential in bringing the greatest good to the greatest number of the new beings we are to create."

Fielding repeated, softly this time: "Good heavens!" He stared at the little man with the white face and vacant gaze.

At this point the door to the private laboratory opened and Rex strode forth with a test tube in his hand. He passed the tube to Shelby and burst out in swift speech.

"I have failed," he said. "I have analyzed every living cell in the tube and have isolated the activating force of every human emotion. I have reproduced these forces to perfection with arrangements of special electronic tubes which have been incorporated into my own mechanical brain. Yet have I failed to produce so much as a semblance of human feeling in my makeup. It is the first failure of Rex—and the last!"

So saying, he stamped back into his own room and slammed the door. An instant later there was a violent explosion within, and the door by which he had entered was blown from its hinges.

Fielding, Shelby, and a few others rushed in when the smoke had somewhat cleared away. They found Rex a twisted and broken mass of metal and rubber and glass. The headpiece which had contained the marvelous thinking robot brain was completely demolished.

"He's committed suicide!" gasped Lonergan.

"Because he was a failure," Fielding added.

Shelby corrected him.

"He *thought* he had failed, whereas really he succeeded. At least two emotions stirred him before he did this, and he did not recognize them. Rage, when he dashed from his room and gave me the test tube. Despair, when he committed his last act. No, gentlemen, Rex did not fail—and now he is gone. . . ."

The little man pitched forward into Fielding's arms, unconscious.

With the passing of Rex, his fantastic plan collapsed. Hard work by the scientists returned the country to normal.

But a thought that lingered faintly in the minds of several of them was voiced by Innes, when he said:

"I—I'm almost sorry. In one way, it was a great opportunity. . . ."

S IS FOR SATYRS AND SPACE-MONSTERS

ALGERNON BLACKWOOD

Roman Remains

Anthony Breddle, airman, home on sick leave from India, does not feel himself called upon to give an opinion; he considers himself a recorder only. The phrase *credo quia impossibile*, had never come his way; neither had Blake's dictum that "everything possible to be believed is an image of truth."

He was under thirty, intelligent enough, observant, a first-rate pilot, but with no special gifts or knowledge. A matter of fact kind of fellow, unequipped on the imaginative side, he was on his way to convalesce at his step-brother's remote place in the Welsh mountains. The brother, a much older man, was a retired surgeon, honoured for his outstanding work with a knighthood and now absorbed in research.

The airman glanced again at the letter of invitation:

"... a lonely, desolate place, I'm afraid, with few neighbours, but good fishing which, I know, you adore. Wild little valleys run straight up into the mountains almost from the garden, you'll have to entertain yourself. I've got lots of fishing rods for you. Nora Ashwell, a cousin you've never met, a nurse, also on sick leave of sorts but shortly going back to her job, is dying for companionship of her own age. She likes fishing too. But my house isn't a hospital! And there's Dr. Leidenheim, who was a student with me at Heidelberg ages ago, a delightful old friend. Had a Chair in Berlin, but got out just in time. His field is Roman Culture—lots of remains about here—but that's not your cup of tea, I know. Legends galore all over the place and superstitions you could cut with a knife. Queer things said to go on in a little glen called Goat Valley. But that's not down your street either. Anyhow, come along and make the best of it; at least we have no bombing here . . . ."

So Breddle knew what he was in for more or less, but was so relieved to get out of the London blitz with a chance of recovering his normal strength, that it didn't matter. Above all, he didn't want a flirtation, nor to hear about Roman remains from the Austrian refugee scholar.

It was certainly a desolate spot, but the house and grounds were delightful, and he lost no time in asking about the fishing. There was a trout stream, it seemed, and a bit of the Wye not too far away with some good salmon pools. At the moment, as rain had swollen the Wye, the trout stream was the thing to go for; and before an early bed that night he had made the acquaintance of the two others, Nora and Emil Leidenheim. He sized them up, as he called it: the latter a charming, old-fashioned man with considerable personality, cautious of speech, and no doubt very learned; but Nora, his cousin, by no means to his taste. Easy to look at certainly, with a kind of hard, wild beauty, pleasant enough too, if rather silent, yet with something about her he could not quite place beyond that it was distasteful. She struck him as unkempt, untidy, self-centred, careless as to what impression she made on her company, her mind and thoughts elsewhere all the time. She had been out walking that afternoon, yet came to their war-time supper still in shorts. A negligible matter, doubtless, though the three men had all done something by way of tidying up a bit. Her eyes and manner conveyed something he found baffling, as though she was always on the watch, listening, peering for something that was not there. Impersonal, too, as the devil. It seemed a foolish thing to say, but there was a hint in her atmosphere that made him uncomfortable, uneasy, almost gave him a touch of the creeps. The two older men, he fancied, left her rather alone.

Outwardly, at any rate, all went normally enough, and a fishing trip was arranged for the following morning.

"And I hope you'll bring back something for the table," his brother commented, when she had gone up to bed. "Nora has never yet brought back a single fish. God knows what she does with herself, but I doubt if she goes to the stream at all." At which an enigmatic expression passed across Dr. Leidenheim's face, though he did not speak.

"Where is this stream?" his brother asked. "Up that Goat Valley you said was queer, or something? And what did you mean by 'queer'?"

"Oh, no, not Goat Valley," came the answer; "and as for 'queer', I didn't mean anything particular. Just that the superstitious locals avoid it even in the daytime. There's a bit of hysteria about, you know," he added, "these war days, especially in god-forsaken places like this—"

"God-forsaken is good," Dr. Leidenheim put in quickly, giving the airman an impression somehow that he could have said more but for his host's presence, while Breddle thought he would like to tap the old fellow's mind when he got the chance.

And it was with that stressed epithet in his ears that he went up to his comfortable bedroom. But before he fell asleep another impression registered as he lay on that indeterminate frontier between sleeping and waking. He carried it into sleep with him, though no dream followed. And it was this: there was something wrong in this house, something that did not emerge at first. It was concerned with the occupants, but it was due neither to his brother, nor to the Austrian archaeologist. It was due to that strange, wild girl. Before sleep took him, he defined it to himself. Nora was under close observation the whole time by both the older men. It was chiefly, however, Dr. Leidenheim who watched her.

The following morning broke in such brilliant sunshine that fishing was out of the question; and when the airman got down to a late breakfast he was distinctly relieved to hear that Nora was already out of the house. She, too, knew that clear skies were no good for trout; she had left a verbal excuse and gone off by herself

for a long walk. So Breddle announced that he would do the same. His choice was
Goat Valley, he would take sandwiches and entertain himself. He got rough
directions from Dr. Leidenheim, who mentioned that the ruins of an ancient
temple to the old god, Silvanus, at the end of the valley might interest him. "And
you'll have the place to yourself," said his brother, laughingly, before disappearing
into his sanctum, "unless you run across one of the younger monsters, the only
living things apparently that ever go there."

"Monsters! And what may you mean by that?"

It was Dr. Leidenheim who explained the odd phrase.

"Nothing," he said, "nothing at all. Your brother's a surgeon, remember. He
still uses the words of his student days. He wants to scare you."

The other, finding him for once communicative, pressed him, if with poor
results.

"Merely," he said in his excellent English, "that there have been one or two
unpleasant births during these war years—in my language, *Missgeburt* we call them.
Due to the collective hysteria of these strange natives probably." He added under
his breath, as if to himself, something about *Urmenschen* and *unheimlich*, though
Breddle didn't know the words.

"Oh," he exclaimed, catching his meaning, "that sort of thing, eh? I thought
they were always put out of the way at birth or kept in glass bottles—"

"In my country, that is so, yes. They do not live."

The airman laughed. "It would take more than a *Missgeburt* to scare me," he
said, and dropped the unsavoury subject before the old archaeologist got into his
stride about the temple to Silvanus and Roman remains in general. Later he
regretted he had not asked a few other questions.

Now, Anthony Breddle must be known as what is called a brave man; he had the
brand of courage that goes with total absence of imagination. His was a simple
mind of the primitive order. Pictures passed through it which he grouped and
regrouped, he drew inferences from them, but it is doubtful if he had ever really
thought. As he entered the little valley, his mind worked as usual, automatically.
Pictures of his brother and the Austrian flitted across it, both old men, idling
through the evening of their day after reasonable success, the latter with a painful
background of bitter sufferings under the Nazis. The chat about collective hysteria
and the rest did not hold his interest. And Nora flitted through after them, a nurse
maybe, but an odd fish assuredly, not his cup of tea in any case. Bit of a wild cat, he
suspected, for all her quiet exterior in the house. If she lingered in his mind more
vividly than the other two it was because of that notion of the night before—that
she was under observation. She was, obviously, up to something: never bringing in
a fish, for instance, that strange look in her eyes, the decided feeling of repulsion
she stirred in him. Then her picture faded too. His emotions at the moment were
of enjoyment and carefree happiness. The bright sunny morning, the birds
singing, the tiny stream pretending it was a noisy torrent, the fact that "Operations" lay behind him and weeks of freedom lay ahead ... which reminded him
that he was, after all, convalescing from recent fevers, and that he was walking a bit
too fast for his strength.

He dawdled more slowly up the little glen as the mountain-ash trees and silver
birch thickened and the steep sides of the valley narrowed, passed the tumbled

stones of the Silvanus temple without a glance of interest, and went on whistling happily to himself—then suddenly wondered how an echo of his whistling could reach him through the dense undergrowth. It was not an echo, he realized with a start. It was a different whistle. Someone else, not very far away, someone following him possibly, someone else, yes, was whistling. The realization disturbed him. He wanted, above all, to be alone. But, for all that, he listened with a certain pleasure, as he lay in a patch of sunshine, ate his lunch, and smoked, for the tune, now growing fainter, had an enticing lilt, a haunting cadence, though it never once entered his mind that it was possibly a folk tune of sorts.

It died away; at any rate, he no longer heard it; he stretched out in the patch of warm sunshine, he dozed; probably, he dropped off to sleep. . . .

Yes, he is certain he must have slept, because when he opened his eyes he felt there had been an interval. He lay now in shadow, for the sun had moved. But something else had moved too while he was asleep. There was an alteration in his immediate landscape, restricted though that landscape was. The absurd notion then intruded that someone had been near him while he slept, watching him. It puzzled him; an uneasy emotion disturbed him.

He sat up with a start and looked about him. No wind stirred, not a leaf moved; nor was there any sound but the prattle of the little stream some distance away. A vague disquiet deepened in him. Then he cupped his ears to listen, for at this precise moment the whistling became audible again with the same queer, haunting lilt in it. And he stiffened. This stiffening, at any rate he recognized; this sudden tautening of the nerves he had experienced before when flying. He knew precisely that it came as a prelude to danger: it was the automatic preparation made by body and mind to meet danger; it was—fear.

But why fear in this smiling, innocent woodland? And that no hint of explanation came, made it worse. A nameless fear could not be met and dealt with; it could bring in its wake a worse thing—terror. But an unreasoning terror is an awful thing, and well he knew this. He caught a shiver running over him; and instinctively then he thought he would "whistle to keep his courage up," only to find that he could not manage it. He was unable to control his lips. No sound issued, his lips trembled, the flow of breath blocked. A kind of wheeze, however, did emerge, a faint pretence of whistling, and he realized to his horror that the other whistler answered it. Terror then swept in; and, trying feebly again, he managed a reply. Whereupon that other whistling piper moved closer in, and the distance between them was reduced. Yet, oh, what a ravishing and lovely lilt it was! Beyond all words he felt rapt and caught away. His heart, incredibly, seemed mastered. An unbelievable storm of energy swept through him.

He was brave, this young airman, as already mentioned, for he had faced death many times, but this amazing combination of terror and energy was something new. The sense of panic lay outside all previous experience. Genuine panic terror is a rare thing; its assault now came on him like a tornado. It seemed he must lose his head and run amok. And the whistler, the strange piper, came nearer, the distance between them again reduced. Energy and terror flooding his being simultaneously, he found relief in movement. He plunged recklessly through the dense undergrowth in the direction of the sound, conscious only of one overmastering impulse—that he *must* meet this piper face to face, while yet half unconsciously aware that at the same time he was also taking every precaution to move noiselessly, softly, quietly, so as not to be heard. This strange contradiction came back to memory long afterwards, hinting possibly at some remnant of resisting power that saved him from an unutterable disaster.

His reward was the last thing in the world he anticipated.

That he was in an abnormal condition utterly beyond his comprehension there can be no doubt; but that what he now witnessed registered with complete and positive clarity lay beyond all question. A figure caught his eye through the screen of leaves, a moving—more—a dancing figure, as he stood stock still and stared at—Nora Ashwell. She was perhaps a dozen yards away, obviously unaware of his presence, her clothes in such disorder that she seemed half naked, hatless, with flowers in her loosened hair, her face radiant, arms and legs gesticulating in a wild dance, her body flung from side to side, but gracefully, a pipe of sorts in one hand that at moments were to her lips to blow the now familiar air. She was moving in the direction away from where he stood concealed, but he saw enough to realize that he was watching a young girl in what is known as ecstasy, an ecstasy of love.

He stood motionless, staring at the amazing spectacle: a girl beside herself with love; love, yes, assuredly, but not the kind his life had so far known about; a lover certainly—the banal explanation of her conduct flashed through his bewilderment—but not a lover of ordinary sort. And, as he stared, afraid to move a step, he was aware that this flood of energy, this lust for intense living that drove her, was at work in him too. The frontiers of his normal self, his ordinary world, were trembling; any moment there might come collapse and he, too, would run amok with panic joy and terror. He watched as the figure disappeared behind denser foliage, faded, then was gone, and he stood there alone dominated suddenly by one over-mastering purpose—that he must escape from this awful, yet enticing valley, before it was too late.

How he contrived it he hardly remembers; it was in literal panic that he raced and stumbled along, driven by a sense of terror wholly new to all his experience. There was no feeling of being followed, nor of any definite threat of a personal kind; he was conscious more of some power, as of the animal kingdom, primitive, powerful, menacing, that assaulted his status as a human being . . . a panic, indeed, of pagan origin.

He reached the house towards sunset. There was an interval of struggle to return to his normal self, during which, he thanked heaven, he met no member of the household. At supper, indeed, things seemed as usual . . . he asked and answered questions about his expedition without hesitation, if aware all the time, perhaps, that Dr. Leidenheim observed him somewhat closely, as he observed Nora too. For Nora, equally, seemed her usual, silent self, beyond that her eyes, shining like stars, somehow lent a touch of radiance to her being.

She spoke little; she never betrayed herself. And it was only when, later, Breddle found himself alone with Dr. Leidenheim for a moment before bedtime, that the urgent feeling that he *must* tell someone about his experiences persuaded him to give a stammering account. He could not talk to his brother, but to a stranger it was just possible. And it brought a measure of relief, though Leidenheim was laconic and even mysterious in his comments.

"Ah, yes . . . yes . . . interesting, of course, and—er—most unusual. The combination of that irresistible lust for life, yes, and—and the unreasoning terror. It was always considered extremely powerful and—equally dangerous, of course. Your present condition—convalescing, I mean—made you specially accessible, no doubt. . . ."

But the airman could not follow this kind of talk; after listening for a bit, he made to go up to bed, too exhausted to think about it.

It was about three o'clock in the morning when things began to happen and the first air raid of the war came to the hitherto immune neighbourhood. It was the night the Germans attacked Liverpool. A pilot, scared possibly by the barrage, or chased by a Spitfire and anxious to get rid of his bombs, dropped them before returning home, some of them evidently in the direction of Goat Valley. The three men, gathered in the hall, counted the bursts and estimated a stick had fallen up that way somewhere; and it was while discussing this, that the absence of Nora Ashwell was first noticed. It was Dr. Leidenheim, after a whispered exchange with his host, who went quickly up to her bedroom, and getting no answer to their summons, burst open the locked door to find the room empty. The bed had not been slept in; a sofa had been dragged to the open window where a rope of knotted sheets hung down to the lawn below. The two brothers hurried out of the house at once, joined after a slight delay by Dr. Leidenheim who had brought a couple of spades with him but made no comment by way of explaining why he did so. He handed one to the airman without a word. Under the breaking dawn of another brilliant day, the three men followed the line of craters made by the stick of bombs towards Goat Valley, as they had surmised. Dr. Leidenheim led them by the shortest way, having so often visited the Silvanus temple ruins; and some hundred yards further on the grey morning light soon showed them what was left of Nora Ashwell, blasted almost beyond recognition. They found something else as well, dead but hardly at all injured.

"It should—it *must* be buried," whispered Dr. Leidenheim, and started to dig a hole, signing to the airman to help him with the second spade.

"Burnt first, I think," said the surgeon.

And they all agreed. The airman, as he collected wood and helped dig the hole, felt slightly sick. The sun was up when they reached the house, invaded the still deserted kitchen, and made coffee. There were duties to be attended to presently, but there was little talk, and the surgeon soon retired to his study sofa for a nap.

"Come to my room a moment, if you will," Dr. Leidenheim proposed to the young airman. "There's something I'd like to read to you; it would perhaps interest you."

Up in the room he took a book from his shelves. "The travels and observations of an old Greek," he explained, "notes of things he witnessed in his wanderings. Pausanias, you know. I'll translate an incident he mentions."

"'It is said that one of these beings was brought to Sylla as that General returned from Thessaly. The monster had been surprised asleep in a cave. But his voice was inarticulate. When brought into the presence of Sylla, the Roman General, he was so disgusted that he ordered it to be instantly removed. The monster answered in every degree to the description which poets and painters have given of it.'"

"Oh, yes," said the airman. "And—er—what was it supposed to be, this monster?"

"A Satyr, of course," replied Dr. Leidenheim, as he replaced the volume without further comment except the muttered words, "One of the retinue of Pan."

FRANCIS FLAGG

The Distortion Out of Space

Back of Bear Mountain the meteor fell that night. Jim Blake and I saw it falling through the sky. As large as a small balloon it was and trailed a fiery tail. We knew it struck within a few miles of our camp, and later saw the glare of a fire dully lighting the heavens. Timber is sparse on the farther slope of Bear Mountain, and what little there is of it is stunted and grows in patches, with wide intervals of barren and rocky ground. The fire did not spread to any extent and soon burned itself out.

Seated by our campfire we talked of meteoroids, those casual visitants from outer space which are usually small and consumed by heat on entering Earth's atmosphere. Jim spoke of the huge one that had fallen in northern Arizona before the coming of the white man; and of another, more recent, which fell in Siberia.

"Fortunately," he said, "meteors do little damage; but if a large one were to strike a densely populated area, I shudder to think of the destruction to life and property. Ancient cities may have been blotted out in some such catastrophe. I don't believe that this one we just saw fell anywhere near Simpson's ranch."

"No," I said, "it hit too far north. Had it landed in the valley we couldn't have seen the reflection of the fire it started. We're lucky it struck no handier to us."

The next morning, full of curiosity, we climbed to the crest of the mountain, a distance of perhaps two miles. Bear Mountain is really a distinctive hog's-back of some height, with more rugged and higher mountain peaks around and beyond it. No timber grows on the summit, which, save for tufts of bear-grass and yucca, is rocky and bare. Looking down the farther side from the eminence attained, we saw that an area of hillside was blasted and still smoking. The meteor, however, had buried itself out of sight in earth and rock, leaving a deep crater some yards in extent.

About three miles away, in the small valley below, lay Henry Simpson's ranch, seemingly undamaged. Henry was a licensed guide, and when he went into the mountains after deer, we made his place our headquarters. Henry was not visible as we approached, nor his wife, and a certain uneasiness hastened our steps when we perceived that a portion of the house-roof—the house was built of adobe two stories high and had a slightly pitched roof made of rafters across which corrugated iron strips were nailed—was twisted and rent.

"Good heavens!" said Jim; "I hope a fragment of that meteorite hasn't done any damage here."

Leaving the burros to shift for themselves, we rushed into the house. "Hey, Henry!" I shouted. "Henry! Henry!"

Never shall I forget the sight of Henry Simpson's face as he came tottering down the broad stairs. Though it was eight o'clock in the morning, he still wore pyjamas. His grey hair was tousled, his eyes staring.

"Am I mad, dreaming?" he cried hoarsely.

He was a big man, all of six feet tall, not the ordinary mountaineer, and though over sixty years of age, possessed of great physical strength. But now his shoulders sagged, he shook as if with palsy.

"For heaven's sake, what's the matter?" demanded Jim. "Where's your wife?"

Henry Simpson straightened himself with an effort. "Give me a drink." Then he said strangely, "I'm in my right mind—of course I must be in my right mind—but how can that thing upstairs be possible?"

"What thing? What do you mean?"

"I don't know. I was sleeping soundly when the bright light wakened me. That was last night, hours and hours ago. Something crashed into the house."

"A piece of meteorite," said Jim, looking quickly at me.

"Meteorite?"

"One fell last night on Bear Mountain. We saw it fall."

Henry Simpson lifted a grey face. "It may have been that."

"You wakened, you say?"

"Yes, with a cry of fear. I thought the place had been struck by lightning. 'Lydia!' I screamed, thinking of my wife. But Lydia never answered. The bright light had blinded me. At first I could see nothing. Then my vision cleared. Still I could see nothing—though the room wasn't dark."

"What!"

"Nothing, I tell you. No room, no walls, no furniture; only whichever way I looked, emptiness. I had leapt from bed in my first waking moments and couldn't find it again. I walked and walked, I tell you, and ran and ran; but the bed had disappeared, the room had disappeared. It was like a nightmare. I tried to wake up. I was on my hands and knees, crawling, when someone shouted my name. I crawled towards the sound of that voice, and suddenly I was in the hallway above, outside my room door. I dared not look back. I was afraid, I tell you, afraid. I came down the steps."

He paused, wavered. We caught him and eased his body down on a sofa.

"For God's sake," he whispered, "go find my wife."

Jim said soothingly, "There, there, sir, your wife is all right." He motioned me imperatively with his hand. "Go out to our cabin, Bill and bring me my bag."

I did as he bade. Jim was a practising physician and never travelled without his kit. He dissolved a morphine tablet, filled a hypodermic, and shot its contents into

Simpson's arm. In a few minutes, the old man sighed, relaxed and fell into heavy slumber.

"Look," said Jim, pointing.

The soles of Simpson's feet were bruised, bleeding, the pyjamas shredded at the knees, the knees lacerated.

"He didn't dream it," muttered Jim at length. "He's been walking and crawling, all right."

We stared at each other. "But good Lord, man!" I exclaimed.

"I know," said Jim. He straightened up. "There's something strange here. I'm going upstairs. Are you coming?"

Together we mounted to the hall above. I didn't know what we expected to find. I remember wondering if Simpson had done away with his wife and was trying to act crazy. Then I recollected that both Jim and I had observed the damage to the roof. Something *had* struck the house. Perhaps that something had killed Mrs. Simpson. She was an energetic woman, a few years younger than her husband, and not the sort to be lying quietly abed at such an hour.

Filled with misgivings, we reached the landing above and stared down the corridor. The corridor was well lighted by means of a large window at its extreme end. Two rooms opened off this corridor, one on each side. The doors to both were ajar.

The first room into which we glanced was a kind of writing-room and library. I have said that Simpson was no ordinary mountaineer. As a matter of fact, he was a man who read widely and kept abreast of the better publications in current literature.

The second room was the bedchamber. Its prosaic door—made of smoothed planks—swung outwards. It swung towards us, half open, and in the narrow corridor we had to draw it still further open to pass. Then . . .

"My God!" said Jim.

Rooted to the floor, we both stared. Never shall I forget the sheer astonishment of that moment. For beyond the door, where a bedroom should have been there was . . .

"Oh, it's impossible!" I muttered.

I looked away. Yes, I was in a narrow corridor, a house. Then I glanced back and the effect was that of gazing into the emptiness of illimitable space. My trembling fingers gripped Jim's arm. I am not easily terrified. Men of my calling—aviation—have to possess steady nerves. Yet there was something so strange, so weird about the sight that I confess to a wave of fear. The space stretched away on all sides beyond that door, as space stretches away from one who, lying on his back on a clear day, stares at the sky. But this space was not bright with sunlight. It was a gloomy space, grey, intimidating; a space in which no stars or moon or sun were discernible. And it was a space that had—aside from its gloom—a quality of indirectness . . .

"Jim," I whispered hoarsely, "do you see it too?"

"Yes, Bill, yes."

"What does it mean?"

"I don't know. An optical illusion, perhaps. Something has upset the perspective in that room."

"Upset?"

"I'm trying to think."

He brooded a moment. Though a practising physician, Jim is interested in physics and higher mathematics. His papers on the relativity theory have appeared in many scientific journals.

"Space," he said, "has no existence aside from matter. You know that. Nor aside from time." He gestured quickly. "There's Einstein's concept of matter being a kink in space, of a universe at once finite and yet infinite. It's all abstruse and hard to grasp." He shook his head. "But in outer space, far beyond the reach of our most powerful telescopes, things may not function exactly as they do on Earth. Laws may vary, phenomena the direct opposite of what we are accustomed to may exist."

His voice sank. I stared at him, fascinated.

"And that meteoroid from God knows where!" He paused a moment. "I am positive that this phenomenon we witness is connected with it. Something came to Earth in that meteor and has lodged in this room, something possessing alien properties, that is able to distort, warp . . ." His voice died away.

I stared fearfully through the open door. "Good heavens," I said, "what can it be? What would have the power to create such an illusion?"

"If it *is* an illusion," muttered Jim. "Perhaps it is no more an illusion than the environment in which we have our being and which we scarcely question. Don't forget that Simpson wandered through it for hours. Oh, it sounds fantastic, impossible, I know, and at first I believed he was raving; but now . . . now . . ." He straightened abruptly. "Mrs Simpson is somewhere in that room, in that incredible space, perhaps wandering about, lost, frightened. I'm going in."

I pleaded with him to wait, to reconsider. "If you go, I'll go too," I said.

He loosened my grip. "No, you must stay by the door to guide me with your voice."

Despite my further protestations, he stepped through the doorway. In doing so it seemed that he must fall into an eternity of nothing.

"Jim!" I called fearfully. He glanced back, but whether he heard my voice I could not say. Afterwards he said he hadn't.

It was weird to watch him walking—a lone figure in the midst of infinity. I tell you, it was the weirdest and most incredible sight the eye of man has ever seen. *I must be asleep, dreaming,* I thought: *this can't be real.*

I had to glance away, to assure myself by a sight of the hall that I was actually awake. The room at most was only thirty feet from the door to wall; yet Jim went on and on, down an everlasting vista of grey distance, until his figure began to shorten, dwindle. Again I screamed, "Jim! Jim! Come back, Jim!" But in the very moment of my screaming, his figure flickered, went out, and in all the vast lonely reaches of that gloomy void, nowhere was he to be seen—nowhere!

I wonder if anyone can imagine a tithe of the emotions which swept over me at that moment. I crouched by the doorway to that incredible room, a prey to the most horrible fears and surmises. Anon I called out, "Jim! Jim!" but no voice replied, no familiar figure loomed on my sight.

The sun was high overhead when I went heavily down the stairs and out into the open. Simpson was still sleeping on the couch, the sleep of exhaustion. I remembered that he had spoken of hearing our voices calling him as he wandered through grey space, and it came over me as ominous and suggestive of disaster that my voice had, apparently, never reached Jim's ears, that no sound had come to my own ears out of the weird depths.

After the long hours of watching in the narrow corridor, of staring into alien space, it was with an inexpressible feeling of relief, of having escaped something horrible and abnormal, that I greeted the sun-drenched day. The burros were standing with drooping heads in the shade of a live-oak tree. Quite methodically I relieved them of their packs; then I filled and lit my pipe, doing everything slowly, carefully, as if aware of the need for restraint, calmness. On such little things does a man's sanity often depend. And all the time I stared at the house, at the upper portion of it where the uncanny room lay. Certain cracks showed in its walls and the roof above was twisted and torn. I asked myself, how was this thing possible? How, within the narrow confines of a single room, could the phenomenon of infinite space exist? Einstein, Eddington, Jeans—I had read their theories, and Jim might be correct, but the strangeness of it, the horror! *You're mad, Bill,* I said to myself, *mad, mad*! But there were the burros, there was the house. A scarlet tanager soared by, a hawk wheeled overhead, a covey of ring-necked mountain quail scuttled through tangled brush. No, I wasn't mad, I couldn't be dreaming, and Jim—Jim was somewhere in that accursed room, that distortion out of space, lost, wandering!

It was the most courageous thing I ever did in my life—to re-enter that house, climb those stairs. I had to force myself to do it, for I was desperately afraid and my feet dragged. But Simpson's ranch was in a lonely place, the nearest town or neighbour miles distant. It would take hours to fetch help, and of what use would it be when it did arrive? Besides, Jim needed aid, now, at once.

Though every nerve and fibre of my body rebelled at the thought, I fastened the end of a rope to a nail driven in the hall floor and stepped through the doorway. Instantly I was engulfed by endless space. It was a terrifying sensation. So far as I could see, my feet rested on nothing. Endless distance was below me as well as above. Sick and giddy, I paused and looked back, but the doorway had vanished. Only the coil of rope in my hands, and the heavy pistol in my belt, saved me from giving way to utter panic.

Slowly I paid out the rope as I advanced. At first it stretched into infinity like a sinuous serpent. Then suddenly all but a few yards of it disappeared. Fearfully I tugged at the end in my hands. It resisted the tug. The rope was still there, even if invisible to my eyes, every inch of it paid out; yet I was no nearer the confines of that room. Standing there with emptiness above, around and below me, I knew the meaning of utter desolation, of fear and loneliness. This way and that I groped, at the end of my tether. Somewhere Jim must be searching and groping too. "Jim!" I shouted; and miraculously enough, in my very ear it seemed, Jim's voice bellowed, "Bill! Bill! Is that you, Bill?"

"Yes," I almost sobbed. "Where are you, Jim?"

"I don't know. This place has me bewildered. I've been wandering around for hours. Listen, Bill; everything is out of focus here, matter warped, light curved. Can you hear me, Bill?"

"Yes, yes. I'm here too, clinging to the end of a rope that leads to the door. If you could follow the sound of my voice . . ."

"I'm trying to do that. We must be very close to each other. Bill . . ." His voice grew faint, distant.

"Here!" I shouted, "here!"

Far off I heard his voice calling, receding.

"For God's sake, Jim, this way, this way!"

Suddenly the uncanny space appeared to shift, to eddy—I can describe what occurred in no other fashion—and for a moment in remote distance I saw Jim's figure. It was toiling up an endless hill, away from me; up, up; a black dot against an immensity of nothing. Then the dot flickered, went out, and he was gone. Sick with nightmarish horror, I sank to my knees, and even as I did so the realization of another disaster made my heart leap suffocatingly to my throat. In the excitement of trying to attract Jim's attention, I had dropped hold of the rope!

Panic leapt at me, sought to overwhelm me, but I fought it back. Keep calm, I told myself; don't move, don't lose your head; the rope must be lying at your feet. But though I felt carefully on all sides, I could not locate it. I tried to recollect if I had moved from my original position. Probably I had taken a step or two away from it, but in what direction? Hopeless to ask. In that infernal distortion of space and matter, there was nothing by which to determine direction. Yet I did not, I could not abandon hope. The rope was my only guide to the outer world, the world of normal phenomena and life.

This way and that I searched, wildly, frantically, but to no purpose. At last I forced myself to stand quite still, closing my eyes to shut out the weird void. My brain functioned chaotically. Lost in a thirty-foot room, Jim, myself, and a woman, unable to locate one another—the thing was impossible, incredible. With trembling fingers I took out my pipe, pressed tobacco in the charred bowl and applied a match. Thank God for nicotine! My thoughts flowed more clearly. Incredible or not, here I was, neither mad nor dreaming. Some quirk of circumstance had permitted Simpson to stagger from the web of illusion, but that quirk had evidently been one in a thousand. Jim and I might go wandering through alien depths until we died of hunger and exhaustion.

I opened my eyes. The grey clarity of space—a clarity of subtle indirection—still hemmed me in. Somewhere within a few feet of where I stood—as distance is computed in a three-dimensional world—Jim must be walking or standing. But this space was not three-dimensional. It was a weird dimension from outside the solar system which the mind of man could never hope to understand or grasp. And it was terrifying to reflect that within its depths Jim and I might be separated by thousands of miles and yet be cheek by jowl.

I walked on. I could not stand still forever. *God*, I thought, *there must be a way out of this horrible place, there must be*! Ever and anon I called Jim's name. After a while I glanced at my watch, but it had ceased to run. Every muscle in my body began to ache, and thirst was adding its tortures to those of the mind. "Jim!" I cried hoarsely, again and again, but silence pressed in on me until I felt like screaming.

Conceive of it if you can. Though I walked on matter firm enough to the feet, seemingly space stretched below as well as above. Sometimes I had the illusion of being inverted, of walking head-downward. There was an uncanny sensation of being translated from spot to spot without the need of intermediate action. *God*! I prayed inwardly, *God*! I sank to my knees, pressing my hands over my eyes. But of what use was that? Of what use was anything? I staggered to my feet, fighting the deadly fear gnawing at my heart, and forced myself to walk slowly, without haste, counting the steps, one two, three . . .

When it was I first noticed the shimmering radiation, I can not say. Like heat radiation it was, only more subtle, like waves of heat rising from an open furnace. I rubbed my eyes. I stared tensely. Yes, waves of energy were being diffused from some invisible source. Far off in the illimitable depths of space I saw them pulsing; but I soon perceived that I was fated—like a satellite fixed in its groove—to travel in a vast circle of which they were the centre.

And perhaps in that direction lay the door!

Filled with despair, I again sank to my knees, and kneeling I thought drearily, *This is the end, there is no way out*, and calmer than I had been for hours—there *is* a calmness of despair, a fatalistic giving over of struggle—I raised my head and looked apathetically around.

Strange, strange; weird and strange. Could this be real, was I myself? Could an immensity of nothing lie within a thirty-foot radius, be caused by something out of space, something brought by the meteor, something able to distort, warp?

Distort, warp!

With an oath of dawning comprehension I leapt to my feet and glared at the shimmering radiation. Why couldn't I approach it? What strange and invisible force forbade? Was it because the source of this incredible space lay lurking there? Oh, I was mad, I tell you, a little insane, yet withal, possessed of a certain coolness and clarity of thought, I drew the heavy pistol from its holster. A phrase of Jim's kept running through my head: *Vibration, vibration, everything is varying rates of vibration*. Yet for a moment I hesitated. Besides myself, in this incredible space two others were lost, and what if I were to shoot either of them? Better that, I told myself than to perish without a struggle.

I raised the pistol. The shimmering radiation was something deadly, inimical, the diffusing waves of energy were loathsome tentacles reaching out to slay.

'Damn you,' I muttered, and pulled the trigger.

Of what followed I possess but a kaleidoscopic and chaotic memory. The grey void seemed to breathe in and out. Alternately I saw space and room, room and space; leering at me through the interstices of this bewildering change something indescribably loathsome, something that lurked at the centre of a crystal ball my shots had perforated. Through the bullet-holes in this crystal a slow vapour oozed, and as it oozed, the creature inside of the ball struggled and writhed; and as it struggled I had the illusion of being lifted in and out, in and out; into the room, out into empty space. Then suddenly the crystal ball shivered and broke; I heard it break with a tinkling as of glass; the luminous vapour escaped in a swirl, the grey void vanished, and sick and giddy I found myself definitely encompassed by the walls of a room and within a yard of the writhing monstrosity.

As I stood with rooted feet, too dazed to move, the monstrosity reared. I saw it now in all its hideousness. A spidery thing it was, and yet, not a spider. Up it reared, up, four feet in the air, its saucer-like eyes goggling out at me, its hairy paws reaching. Sick with terror, I was swept forward into the embrace of the loathsome creature. Then happened that which I can never forget till my dying day, so strange it was, so weird. Imagination, you say, the fantastic thoughts of a temporarily disordered mind. Perhaps, perhaps; but suddenly I seemed to know—know beyond a doubt—that this spider-like visitant from outer space was an intelligent, reasoning being. Those eyes—they seemed to bore into the innermost recesses of my brain, seemed to establish a species of communication between myself and the intelligence back of them.

It was not a malignant intelligence—I realized that—but in comparison to myself something god-like, remote. And yet it was a mortal intelligence. My bullets had shattered its protective covering, had reached to its vulnerable body, and as it held me to itself, it was in the very throes of dissolution. All this I sensed, all this it told me; not through language, but through some subtle process of picture transference which it is hopeless for me to attempt to explain. I seemed to see a grey, weird place where delicate traceries were spun and silver devices shimmered and shone—the habitat of the strange visitant from outer space. Perhaps the receiving-cells of my brain were not developed enough to receive all the impressions it tried to convey.

Nothing was clear, distinct, nothing definite. I had the agonizing consciousness that much was slipping through my brain, uncorrelated, unregistered. But a meteoroid was hurtling through the blackness of space—and I saw it falling to Earth. I saw a portion of it swing clear, crash through the roof of Simpson's house and lodge in the bedroom. And I saw the strange visitant from outside our universe utilize the incredible power he possessed to distort space, iron out the kinks of matter in it, veil himself in immensity while studying his alien surroundings.

And then all his expiring emotions seemed to rush over me in a flood and I felt—*felt*—what he was thinking. He had made a journey from one star system to another, he had landed safely on Earth, a trillion, trillion light-years distant, but never would he return to his own planet to tell of his success—never, never! All this I seemed to understand, to grasp, in a split second or so, his loneliness and pain, his terrible nostalgia; then the hair paws relaxed their grip, the hideous body collapsed in on itself, and as I stared at it sprawling on the floor, I was suddenly conscious of Mrs. Simpson crouching, unharmed, in one corner of the room, of Jim standing beside me, clutching my arm.

"Bill," he said hoarsely, "are you hurt?" And then in a whisper, "What is it? What is it?"

"I don't know," I returned chokingly, "I don't know. But whatever it is, it is dead now—the Distortion out of Space."

An unaccountably I buried my face in my hands and began to weep.

T IS FOR THREATENING THINGS

PETER REDGROVE

Mr. Waterman

"Now, we're quite private here. You can tell me your troubles. The pond I think you said..."

"We never really liked that pond in the garden. At times it was choked with a sort of weed, which, if you pulled one thread, gleefully unraveled until you had an empty basin before you and the whole of the pond in a soaking heap at your side. Then at other times it was as clear as gin, and lay in the grass staring upwards. If you came anywhere near, the gaze shifted sideways, and it was you that was being stared at, not the empty sky. If you were so bold as to come right up to the edge, swaggering and talking loudly to show you were not afraid, it presented you with so perfect a reflection that you stayed there spellbound and nearly missed dinner getting to know yourself. It had hypnotic powers."

"Very well. Then what happened?"

"Near the pond was a small bell hung on a bracket, which the milkman used to ring as he went to tell us upstairs in the bedroom that we could go down and make the early-morning tea. This bell was near a little avenue of rose trees. One morning, very early indeed, it tinged loudly and when I looked out I saw that the empty bottles we had put out the night before were full of bright green pond-water. I had to go down and empty them before the milkman arrived. This was only the beginning. One evening I was astounded to find a brace of starfish coupling on the ornamental stone step of the pool, and, looking up, my cry to my wife to come and look was stifled by the sight of a light peppering of barnacles on the stems of the rose trees. The vermin had evidently crept there, taking advantage of the thin film of moisture on the ground after the recent very wet weather. I dipped a finger into the pond and tasted it: it was brackish."

"But it got worse."

"It got worse: one night of howling wind and tempestuous rain I heard muffled voices outside shouting in rural tones: 'Belay there, you lubbers!' 'Box the foresail capstan!' 'A line! A line! Give me a line there, for Davy Jones' sake!' and a great creaking of timbers. In the morning, there was the garden-seat, which was too big to float, dragged tilting into the pond, half in and half out."

"But you could put up with all this. How did the change come about?"

287

"It was getting playful, obviously, and inventive, if ill-informed, and might have got dangerous. I decided to treat it with the consideration and dignity which it would probably later have insisted on, and I invited it in as a lodger, bedding it up in the old bathroom. At first I thought I would have to run canvas troughs up the stairs so it could get to its room without soaking the carpet, and I removed the flap from the letter box so it would be free to come and go, but it soon learnt to keep its form quite well, and get about in mackintosh and galoshes, opening doors with gloved fingers."

"Until a week ago . . ."

"A week ago it started sitting with us in the lounge (and the electric fire had to be turned off, as the windows kept on steaming up). It had accidentally included a goldfish in its body, and when the goggling dolt swam up the neck into the crystal-clear head, it dipped its hand in and fumbled about with many ripples and grimaces, plucked it out, and offered the fish to my wife, with a polite nod. She was just about to go into the kitchen and cook the supper, but I explained quickly that goldfish were bitter to eat, and he put it back. However, I was going to give him a big plate of ice cubes, which he would have popped into his head and enjoyed sucking, although his real tipple is distilled water, while we watched television, but he didn't seem to want anything. I suppose he thinks he's big enough already."

"Free board and lodging, eh?"

"I don't know what rent to charge him. I thought I might ask him to join the river for a spell and bring us back some of the money that abounds there: purses lost overboard from pleasure steamers, rotting away in the mud, and so forth. But he has grown very intolerant of dirt, and might find it difficult to get clean again. Even worse, he might not be able to free himself from his rough dirty cousins, and come roaring back as an impossible green seething giant, tall as the river upended, buckling into the sky, and swamp us and the whole village as well. I shudder to think what would happen if he got as far as the sea, his spiritual home: the country would be in danger. I am at my wits' end for he is idle, and lounges about all day."

"Well, that's harmless enough . . ."

"If he's not lounging, he toys with his shape, restlessly. Stripping off his waterproof, he is a charming dolls'-house of glass, with doors and windows opening and shutting; a tree that thrusts up and fills the room; a terrifying shark-shape that darts about between the legs of the furniture, or lurks in the shadows of the room, gleaming in the light of the television tube; a fountain that blooms without spilling a drop; or, and this image constantly recurs, a very small man with a very large head and streaming eyes, who gazes mournfully up at my wife (she takes no notice), and collapses suddenly into his tears with a sob and a gulp. Domestic, pastoral-phallic, maritime-ghastly, stately-gracious or grotesque-pathetic: he rings the changes on a gamut of moods, showing off, while I have to sit aside slumped in my armchair unable to compete, reflecting what feats he may be able to accomplish in due course with his body, what titillating shapes impose, what exaggerated parts deploy, under his mackintosh. I dread the time (for it will come) when I shall arrive home unexpectedly early, and hear a sudden scuffle away in the waste pipes, and find my wife ('Just out of the shower, dear') with that moist look in her eyes, drying her hair: and then to hear him swaggering in from the garden drains, talking loudly about his day's excursion, as if nothing at all had been going on. For he learns greater charm each day, this Mr. Waterman, and can be as stubborn as winter and gentle as the warm rains of spring."

"I should say that you have a real problem there, but it's too early for a solution yet, until I know you better. Go away, take a week off from the office, spend your time with your wife, relax, eat plenty of nourishing meals, plenty of sex and sleep. Then come and see me again. Good afternoon.

"The next patient, nurse. Ah, Mr. Waterman. Sit down, please. Does the gas fire trouble you? No? I can turn it off if you wish. Well now, we're quite private in here. You can tell me your troubles. A married, air-breathing woman, I think you said . . ."

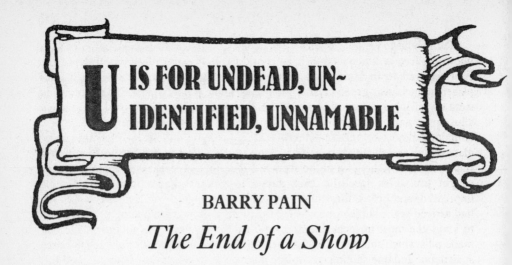

U IS FOR UNDEAD, UN~ IDENTIFIED, UNNAMABLE

BARRY PAIN

The End of a Show

It was a little village in the extreme north of Yorkshire, three miles from a railway-station on a small branch line. It was not a progressive village; it just kept still and respected itself. The hills lay all round it, and seemed to shut it out from the rest of the world. Yet folks were born, and lived, and died, much as in the more important centres; and there were intervals which required to be filled with amusement. Entertainments were given by amateurs from time to time in the schoolroom; sometimes hand-bell ringers or a conjurer would visit the place, but their reception was not always encouraging. "Conjurers is nowt, an' ringers is nowt," said the sad native judiciously; "ar dornt regard 'em." But the native brightened up when in the summer months a few caravans found their way to a piece of waste land adjoining the churchyard. They formed the village fair, and for two days they were a popular resort. But it was understood that the fair had not the glories of old days; it had dwindled. Most things in connection with this village dwindled.

The first day of the fair was drawing to a close. It was half past ten, and at eleven the fair would close until the following morning. This last half-hour was fruitful in business. The steam roundabout was crowded, the proprietor of the peep-show was taking pennies very fast, although not so fast as the proprietor of another, somewhat repulsive, show. A fair number patronised a canvas booth which bore the following inscription:

POPULAR SCIENCE LECTURES

Admission Free

At one end of this tent was a table covered with red baize; on it were bottles and boxes, a human skull, a retort, a large book, and some bundles of dried herbs. Behind it was the lecturer, an old man, grey and thin, wearing a bright coloured dressing-gown. He lectured volubly and enthusiastically; his energy and the atmosphere of the tent made him very hot, and occasionally he mopped his forehead.

290

"I am about to exhibit to you," he said, speaking clearly and correctly, "a secret known to few, and believed to have come originally from those wise men of the East referred to in Holy Writ." Here he filled two test-tubes with water, and placed some bluish-green crystals in one and some yellow crystals in the other. He went on talking, quoting scraps of Latin, telling stories, making local and personal allusions, finally coming back again to his two test-tubes, both of which now contained almost colourless solutions. He poured them both together into a flat glass vessel, and the mixture at once turned to a deep brownish purple. He threw a fragment of something on to the surface of the mixture, and that fragment at once caught fire. This favourite trick succeeded; the audience were undoubtedly impressed, and before they quite realised by what logical connection the old man had arrived at the subject, he was talking to them about the abdomen. He seemed to know the most unspeakable and intimate things about the abdomen. He had made pills which suited its peculiar needs, which he could and would sell in boxes at sixpence and one shilling, according to size. He sold four boxes at once, and was back in his classical and anecdotal stage, when a women pressed forward. She was a very poor woman. Could she have a box of these pills at half-price? Her son was bad, very bad. It would be a kindness.

He interrupted her in a dry, distinct voice:

"Woman, I never did anyone a kindness, not even myself."

However, a friend pushed some money into her hand, and she bought two boxes.

It was past twelve o'clock now. The flaring lights were out in the little group of caravans on the waste ground. The tired proprietors of the shows were asleep. The gravestones in the churchyard were glimmering white in the bright moonlight. But at the entrance to that little canvas booth the quack doctor sat on one of his boxes, smoking a clay pipe. He had taken off the dressing-gown, and was in his shirt-sleeves; his clothes were black, much worn. His attention was arrested—he thought that he heard the sound of sobbing.

"It's a God-forsaken world," he said aloud. After a second's silence he spoke again. "No, I never did a kindness even to myself, though I thought I did, or I shouldn't have come to this."

He took his pipe from his mouth and spat. Once more he heard that strange wailing sound; this time he arose, and walked in the direction of it.

Yes, that was it. It came from that caravan standing alone where the trees made a dark spot. The caravan was gaudily painted, and there were steps from the door to the ground. He remembered having noticed it once during the day. It was evident that someone inside was in trouble—great trouble. The old man knocked gently at the door.

"Who's there? What's the matter?"

"Nothing," said a broken voice from within.

"Are you a woman?"

There was a fearful laugh.

"Neither man nor woman—a show."

"What do you mean?"

"Go round to the side, and you'll see."

The old man went round, and by the light of two wax matches caught a glimpse of part of the rough painting on the side of the caravan. The matches dropped from his hand. He came back, and sat down on the steps of the caravan.

"You are not like that," he said.

"No, worse. I'm not dressed in pretty clothes, and lying on a crimson velvet couch. I'm half naked, in a corner of this cursed box, and crying because my owner beat me. Now go, or I'll open the door and show myself to you as I am now. It would frighten you; it would haunt your sleep."

"Nothing frightens me. I was a fool once, but I have never been frightened. What right has this owner over you?"

"He is my father," the voice screamed loudly; then there was more weeping; then it spoke again: "It's awful; I could bear anything now—anything—if I thought it would ever be any better; but it won't. My mind's a woman's and my wants are a woman's, but I am not a woman. I am a show. The brutes stand round me, talk to me, touch me!"

"There's a way out," said the old man quietly, after a pause.

An idea occurred to him.

"I know—and I daren't take it—I've got a thing here, but I daren't use it."

"You could drink something—something that wouldn't hurt?"

"Yes."

"You are quite alone?"

"Yes; my owner is in the village, at the inn."

"Then wait a minute."

The old man hastened back to the canvas booth, and fumbled about with his chemicals. He murmured something about doing someone a kindness at last. Then he returned to the caravan with a glass of colourless liquid in his hand.

"Open the door and take it," he said.

The door was opened a very little way. A thin hand was thrust out and took the glass eagerly. The door closed, and the voice spoke again.

"It will be easy?"

"Yes."

"Goodbye, then. To your health—"

The old man heard the glass crash on the wooden floor, then he went back to his seat in front of the booth, and carefully lit another pipe.

"I will not go," he said aloud. "I fear nothing—not even the results of my best action."

He listened attentively.

No sound whatever came from the caravan. All was still. Far away the sky was growing lighter with the dawn of a fine summer day.

LAFCADIO HEARN

Mujina

On the Akasaka Road, in Tōkyō, there is a slope called Kii-no-kuni-zaka,—which means the Slope of the Province of Kii. I do not know why it is called the Slope of the Province of Kii. On one side of this slope you see an ancient moat, deep and very wide, with high green banks rising up to some place of gardens;—and on the other side of the road extend the long and lofty walls of an imperial palace. Before the era of street-lamps and jinrikishas, this neighborhood was very lonesome after dark; and belated pedestrians would go miles out of their way rather than mount the Kii-no-kuni-zaka, alone, after sunset.

All because of a Mujina that used to walk there.

The last man who saw the Mujina was an old merchant of the Kyōbashi quarter, who died about thirty years ago. This is the story, as he told it:—

One night, at a late hour, he was hurrying up the Kii-no-kuni-zaka, when he perceived a woman crouching by the moat, all alone, and weeping bitterly. Fearing that she intended to drown herself, he stopped to offer her any assistance or consolation in his power. She appeared to be a slight and graceful person, handsomely dressed; and her hair was arranged like that of a young girl of good family. "O-jochū," he exclaimed, approaching her.—"O-jochū, do not cry like that! . . . Tell me what the trouble is; and if there be any way to help you, I shall be glad to help you." (He really meant what he said; for he was a very kind man.) But she continued to weep,—hiding her face from him with one of her long sleeves. "O-jochū," he said again, as gently as he could,—"please, please listen to me! . . . This is no place for a young lady at night! Do not cry, I implore you!—only tell me how I may be of some help to you!" Slowly she rose up, but turned her back to him, and continued to moan and sob behind her sleeve. He laid his hand lightly upon her shoulder, and pleaded:—"O-jochū!—O-jochū!—O-jochū! . . . Listen to me, just for one little moment! . . . O-jochū!—O-jochū!" . . . Then that O-jochū turned round, and dropped her sleeve, and stroked her face with her hand;—and the man saw that she had no eyes or nose or mouth,—and he screamed and ran away.

Up Kii-no-kuni-zaka he ran and ran; and all was black and empty before him. On and on he ran, never daring to look back; and at last he saw a lantern, so far away that it looked like the gleam of a firefly; and he made for it. It proved to be only the lantern of an itinerant *soba*-seller, who had set down his stand by the road-side; but any light and any human companionship was good after that experience; and he flung himself down at the feet of the *soba*-seller, crying out, "Aa!—aa!!—*aa!!!*"

"*Koré! koré!*" roughly exclaimed the soba-man. "Here! what is the matter with you? Anybody hurt you?"

"No—nobody hurt me," panted the other,—"only . . . *Aa!—aa!!*"

"Only scared you?" queried the peddler, unsympathetically. "Robbers?"

"Not robbers,—not robbers," gasped the terrified man. . . . "I saw . . . I saw a woman—by the moat;—and she moved me . . . *Aa!* I cannot tell you what she showed me!" . . .

"*He!* Was it anything like THIS that she showed you?" cried the soba-man, stroking his own face—which therewith became like unto an Egg. . . . And, simultaneously, the light went out.

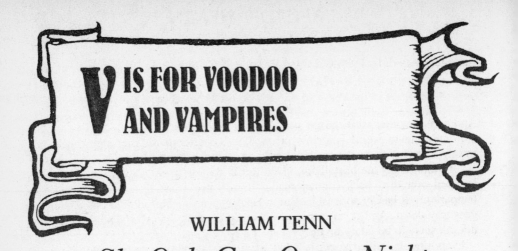

V IS FOR VOODOO AND VAMPIRES

WILLIAM TENN

She Only Goes Out at Night

In this part of the country, folks think that Doc Judd carries magic in his black leather satchel. He's *that* good.

Ever since I lost my leg in the sawmill, I've been all-around handyman at the Judd place. Lots of times when Doc gets a night call after a real hard day, he's too tired to drive, so he hunts me up and I become a chauffeur too. With the shiny plastic leg that Doc got me at a discount, I can stamp the gas pedal with the best of them.

We roar up to the farmhouse and, while Doc goes inside to deliver a baby or swab grandma's throat, I sit in the car and listen to them talk about what a ball of fire the old Doc is. In Groppa County, they'll tell you Doc Judd can handle *anything*. And I nod and listen, nod and listen.

But all the time I'm wondering what they'd think of the way he handled his only son falling in love with a vampire . . .

It was a terrifically hot summer when Steve came home on vacation—real blister weather. He wanted to drive his father around and kind of help with the chores, but Doc said that after the first tough year of medical school anyone deserved a vacation.

"Summer's a pretty quiet time in our line," he told the boy. "Nothing but poison ivy and such until we hit the polio season in August. Besides, you wouldn't want to shove old Tom out of his job, would you? No, Stevie, you just bounce around the countryside in your jalopy and enjoy yourself."

Steve nodded and took off. And I mean took off. About a week later, he started coming home five or six o'clock in the morning. He'd sleep till about three in the afternoon, laze around for a couple of hours and, come eight-thirty, off he'd rattle in his little hot-rod. Road-houses, we figured, or some sleazy girl . . .

Doc didn't like it, but he'd brought up the boy with a nice easy hand and he didn't feel like saying anything just yet. Old buttinsky Tom, though—I was different. I'd helped raise the kid since his mother died, and I'd walloped him when I caught him raiding the ice-box.

So I dropped a hint now and then, kind of asking him, like, not to go too far off the deep end. I could have been talking to a stone fence for all the good it did. Not that Steve was rude. He was just too far gone in whatever it was to pay attention to me.

And then the other stuff started and Doc and I forgot about Steve.

Some kind of weird epidemic hit the kids of Groppa County and knocked twenty, thirty, of them flat on their backs.

"It's almost got me beat, Tom," Doc would confide in me as we bump-bump-bumped over dirty back-country roads. "It acts like a bad fever, yet the rise in temperature is hardly noticeable. But the kids get very weak and their blood count goes way down. And it stays that way, no matter what I do. Only good thing, it doesn't seem to be fatal—so far."

Every time he talked about it, I felt a funny twinge in my stump where it was attached to the plastic leg. I got so uncomfortable that I tried to change the subject, but that didn't go with Doc. He'd gotten used to thinking out his problems by talking to me, and this epidemic thing was pretty heavy on his mind.

He'd written to a couple of universities for advice, but they didn't seem to be of much help. And all the time, the parents of the kids stood around waiting for him to pull a cellophane-wrapped miracle out of his little black bag, because, as they said in Groppa County, there was nothing could go wrong with a human body that Doc Judd couldn't take care of some way or other. And all the time, the kids got weaker and weaker.

Doc got big, bleary bags under his eyes from sitting up nights going over the latest books and medical magazines he'd ordered from the city. Near as I could tell he'd find nothing, even though lots of times he'd get to bed almost as late as Steve.

And then he brought home the handkerchief. Soon as I saw it, my stump gave a good, hard, extra twinge and I wanted to walk out of the kitchen. Tiny, fancy handkerchief, it was, all embroidered linen and lace edges.

"What do you think, Tom? Found this on the floor of the bedroom of the Stopes' kids. Neither Betty nor Willy have any idea where it came from. For a bit, I thought I might have a way of tracing the source of infection, but those kids wouldn't lie. If they say they never saw it before, then that's the way it is." He dropped the handkerchief on the kitchen table that I was clearing up, stood there sighing. "Betty's anemia is beginning to look serious. I wish I knew . . . I wish . . . Oh, well." He walked out to the study, his shoulders bent like they were under a hodful of cement.

I was still staring at the handkerchief, chewing on a fingernail, when Steve bounced in. He poured himself a cup of coffee, plumped it down on the table and saw the handkerchief.

"Hey," he said. "That's Tatiana's. How did it get here?"

I swallowed what was left of the fingernail and sat down very carefully opposite him. "Steve," I asked, and then stopped because I had to massage my aching stump. "Stevie, you know a girl who owns that handkerchief? A girl named Tatiana?"

"Sure. Tatiana Latianu. See, there are her initials embroidered in the corner—T.L. She's descended from the Rumanian nobility; family goes back about five hundred years. I'm going to marry her."

"She the girl you've been seeing every night for the past month?"

He nodded. "She only goes out at night. Hates the glare of the sun. You know, poetic kind of girl. And Tom, she's so *beautiful* . . ."

For the next hour, I just sat there and listened to him. And I felt sicker and sicker. Because I'm Rumanian myself, on my mother's side. And I knew why I'd been getting those twinges in my stump.

She lived in Brasket Township, about twenty miles away. Tom had run into her late one night on the road when her convertible had broken down. He'd given her a lift to her house—she'd just rented the old Mead Mansion—and he'd fallen for her, hook, line and whole darn fishing rod.

Lots of times, when he arrived for a date, she'd be out, driving around the countryside in the cool night air, and he'd have to play cribbage with her maid, an old beak-faced Rumanian biddy, until she got back. Once or twice, he'd tried to go after her in his hot-rod, but that had led to trouble. When she wanted to be alone, she had told him, she wanted to be *alone*. So that was that. He waited for her night after night. But when she got back, according to Steve, she really made up for everything. They listened to music and talked and danced and ate strange Rumanian dishes that the maid whipped up. Until dawn. Then he came home.

Steve put his hand on my arm. "Tom, you know that poem—*The Owl and the Pussy-Cat*? I've always thought the last line was beautiful. *'They danced by the light of the moon, the moon, they danced by the light of the moon.'* That's what my life will be like with Tatiana. If only she'll have me. I'm still having trouble talking her into it."

I let out a long breath. "The first good thing I've heard," I said without thinking. "Marriage to *that* girl—"

When I saw Steve's eyes, I broke off. But it was too late.

"What the hell do you mean, Tom: *that* girl? You've never even met her."

I tried to twist out of it, but Steve wouldn't let me. He was real sore. So I figured the best thing was to tell him the truth.

"Stevie. Listen. Don't laugh. Your girl friend is a vampire."

He opened his mouth slowly. "Tom, you're off your—"

"No, I'm not." And I told him about vampires. What I'd heard from my mother who'd come over from the old country, from Transylvania, when she was twenty. How they can live and have all sorts of strange powers—just so long as they have a feast of human blood once in a while. How the vampire taint is inherited, usually just one child in the family getting it. And how they go out only at night, because sunlight is one of the things that can destroy them.

Steve turned pale at this point. But I went on. I told him about the mysterious epidemic that had hit the kids of Groppa County—and made them anemic. I told him about his father finding the handkerchief in the Stopes' house, near two of the sickest kids. And I told him—but all of a sudden I was talking to myself. Steve tore out of the kitchen. A second or two later, he was off in the hot-rod.

He came back about eleven-thirty, looking as old as his father. I was right, all right. When he'd wakened Tatiana and asked her straight, she'd broken down and wept a couple of buckets-full. Yes, she was a vampire, but she'd only got the urge a couple of months ago. She'd fought it until her mind began to crack. Then she'd found that she could make herself invisible, when the craving hit her. She'd only touched kids, because she was afraid of grown-ups—they might wake up and be able to catch her. But she'd kind of worked on a lot of kids at one time, so that no one kid would lose too much blood. Only the craving had been getting stronger . . .

And still Steve had asked her to marry him! "There must be a way of curing it," he said. "It's a sickness like any other sickness." But she, and—believe me—I thanked God, had said no. She'd pushed him out and made him leave. "Where's Dad?" he asked. "He might know."

I told him that his father must have left at the same time he did, and hadn't come back yet. So the two of us sat and thought. *And thought.*

When the telephone rang, we both almost fell out of our skins. Steve answered it, and I heard him yelling into the mouthpiece.

He ran into the kitchen, grabbed me by the arm and hauled me out into his hot-rod. "That was Tatiana's maid, Magda," he told me as we went blasting down the highway. "She says Tatiana got hysterical after I left, and a few minutes ago she drove away in her convertible. She wouldn't say where she was going. Magda says she thinks Tatiana is going to do away with herself."

"*Suicide*? But if she's a vampire, how—" And all of a sudden I knew just how. I looked at my watch. "Stevie," I said, "drive to Crispin Junction. And drive like holy hell!"

He opened that hot-rod all the way. It looked as if the motor was going to tear itself right off the car. I remember we went around curves just barely touching the road with the rim of one tire.

We saw the convertible as soon as we entered Crispin Junction. It was parked by the side of one of the three roads that cross the town. There was a tiny figure in a flimsy nightdress standing in the middle of the deserted street. My leg stump felt like it was being hit with a hammer.

The church clock started to toll midnight just as we reached her. Steve leaped out and knocked the pointed piece of wood out of her hands. He pulled her into his arms and let her cry.

I was feeling pretty bad at this point. Because all I'd been thinking of was how Steve was in love with a vampire. I hadn't looked at it from her side. She'd been enough in love with him to try to kill herself the *only* way a vampire could be killed—by driving a stake through her heart on a crossroads at midnight.

And she was a pretty little creature. I'd pictured one of these siren dames: you know, tall, slinky, with a tight dress. A witch. But this was a very frightened, very upset young lady who got in the car and cuddled up in Steve's free arm like she'd taken a lease on it. And I could tell she was even younger than Steve.

So, all the time we were driving back, I was thinking to myself *these kids have got plenty trouble.* Bad enough to be in love with a vampire, but to be a vampire in love with a normal human being . . .

"But how *can* I marry you?" Tatiana wailed. "What kind of home life would we have? And Steve, one night I might even get hungry enough to attack *you*!"

The only thing none of us counted on was Doc. Not enough, that is.

Once he'd been introduced to Tatiana and heard her story, his shoulders straightened and the lights came back on in his eyes. The sick children would be all right now. That was most important. And as for Tatiana—

"Nonsense," he told her. "Vampirism might have been an incurable disease in the fifteenth century, but I'm sure it can be handled in the twentieth. First, this nocturnal living points to a possible allergy involving sunlight and perhaps a touch of photophobia. You'll wear tinted glasses for a bit, my girl, and we'll see what we can do with hormone injections. The need for consuming blood, however, presents a somewhat greater problem."

But he solved it.

They make blood in a dehydrated, crystalline form these days. So every night before Mrs. Steven Judd goes to sleep, she shakes some powder into a tall glass of water, drops in an ice-cube or two and has her daily blood toddy. Far as I know, she and her husband are living happily ever after.

ROBERT BLOCH

Mother of Serpents

Voodooism is a queer thing. Forty years ago it was an unknown subject, save in certain esoteric circles. Today there is a surprising amount of information about it, due to research—and an even more surprising amount of misinformation.

Recent popular books on the subject are, for the most part, sheer romantic fancy; elaborated with the incomplete theorisings of ignoramuses.

Perhaps, though, this is for the best. For the truth about voodoo is such that no writer would care, or dare, to print it. Some of it is worse than their wildest fancies. I myself have seen certain things I do not dare to discuss. It would be useless to tell people anyway, for they would not believe me. And once again, this may be for the best. Knowledge can be a thousand times more terrifying than ignorance.

I know, though, for I have lived in Haiti, the dark island. I have learned much from legend, stumbled on many things through accident, and the bulk of my knowledge comes from the one really authentic source—the statements of the blacks. They're not talkative people, as a rule, those old natives of the back-hill country. It took patience and long familiarity with them before they unbent and told me their secrets.

That's why so many of the travel books are so palpably false—no writer who visits Haiti for six months or a year could possibly ingratiate himself into the confidence of those who know the facts. There are so few who really do know; so few who are not afraid to tell.

But I have learned. Let me tell you of the olden days; the old times, when Haiti rose to an empire, borne on a wave of blood.

It was many years ago, soon after the slaves had revolted. Toussaint l'Ouverture, Dessalines and King Christophe freed them from their French masters, freed them after uprisings and massacres and set up a kingdom founded on cruelty more fantastic than the despotism that reigned before.

There were no happy blacks in Haiti then. They had known too much of torture and death; the carefree life of their West Indian neighbours was utterly alien to these slaves and descendants of slaves. A strange mixture of races flourished: fierce tribesmen from Ashanti, Damballah, and the Guinea Coast; sullen Caribs; dusky offspring of renegade Frenchmen; bastard admixtures of Spanish, Negro, and Indian blood. Sly, treacherous half-breeds and mulattos ruled the coast, but there were even worse dwellers in the hills behind.

There were jungles in Haiti, impassable jungles, mountain-ringed and swamp-scourged forests filled with poisonous insects and pestilential fevers. White men dared not enter them, for they were worse than death. Blood-sucking plants, venomous reptiles, diseased orchids filled the forests, forests that hid horrors Africa had never known.

For that is where the real voodoo flourished, back there in the hills. Men lived there, it is said, descendants of escaped slaves, and outlaw factions that had been hunted from the coast. Furtive rumours told of isolated villages that practised cannibalism, mixed in with dark religious rites more dreadful and perverted than anything spawned in the Congo itself. Necrophilism, phallic worship, anthropomancy, and distorted versions of the Black Mass were commonplace. The shadow of *obeah* was everywhere. Human sacrifice was common, the offering up of roosters and goats an accepted thing. There were orgies around the voodoo altars, and blood was drunk in honour of *Baron Samede* and the old black gods brought from ancient lands.

Everybody knew about it. Each night the *ratta*-drums boomed out from the hills, and fires flared over the forests. Many known *papalois* and conjure-doctors resided on the edge of the coast itself, but they were never disturbed. Nearly all the "civilised" blacks still believed in charms and philtres; even the churchgoers reverted to talismans and incantations in time of need. So-called "educated" Negroes in Port-au-Prince society were admittedly emissaries from the barbarian tribes of the interior, and despite the outward show of civilisation the blood priests still ruled behind the throne.

Of course there were scandals, mysterious disappearances, and occasional protests from emancipated citizens. But it was not wise to meddle with those who bowed to the Black Mother, or incur the anger of the terrible old men who dwelt in the shadow of the Snake.

Such was the status of sorcery when Haiti became a republic. People often wonder why there is still sorcery existent there today; more secretive, perhaps, but still surviving. They ask why the ghastly *zombies* are not destroyed, and why the government has not stepped in to stamp out the fiendish blood-cults that still lurk in the jungle gloom.

Perchance this tale will provide an answer; this old, secret tale of the new republic. Officials, remembering the story, are still afraid to interfere too strongly, and the laws that have been passed are very loosely enforced.

Because the Serpent Cult of Obeah will never die in Haiti—in Haiti, that fantastic island whose sinuous shoreline resembles the yawning jaws of a monstrous *snake*.

*

One of the earliest presidents of Haiti was an educated man. Although born on the island, he was schooled in France, and studied extensively while abroad. His accession to the highest office of the land found him an enlightened, sophisticated cosmopolite of the modern type. Of course he still liked to remove his shoes in the privacy of his office, but he never displayed his naked toes in an official capacity. Don't misunderstand—the man was no Emperor Jones; he was merely a polished ebony gentleman whose natural barbarity occasionally broke through its veneer of civilisation.

He was, in fact, a very shrewd man. He had to be in order to become president in those early days; only extremely shrewd men ever attained that dignity. Perhaps it would enlighten you a bit to say that in those times the term "shrewd" was a polite Haitian synonym for "crooked". It is therefore easy to realise the president's character when you know that he was regarded as one of the most successful politicians the republic ever produced.

In his short reign he was opposed by very few enemies; and those that did work against him usually disappeared. The tall, coal-black man with the physical skull-conformation of a gorilla harboured a remarkably crafty brain beneath his beetling brow.

His ability was phenomenal. He had an insight into finance which profited him greatly; profited him, that is, in both his official and unofficial capacity. Whenever he saw fit to increase the taxes he increased the army as well, and sent it out to escort the state tax-collectors. His treaties with foreign countries were master-pieces of legal lawlessness. This black Machiavelli knew that he must work fast, since presidents had a peculiar way of dying in Haiti. They seemed peculiarly susceptible to disease—"lead poisoning", as our modern gangster friends might say. So the president worked very fast indeed, and he did a masterful job.

This was truly remarkable, in view of his humble background. For his was a success saga in the good old Horatio Alger manner. His father was unknown. His mother was a conjure-woman in the hills, and though quite well known, she had been very poor. The president had been born in a log cabin; quite the classic setting for a future distinguished career. His early years had been most uneventful, until his adoption, at thirteen, by a benevolent Protestant minister. For a year he lived with this kind man, serving as houseboy in his home. Suddenly the poor minister died of an obscure ailment; this was most unfortunate, for he had been quite wealthy and his money was alleviating much of the suffering in this particular section. At any rate, this rich minister died, and the poor conjure-woman's son sailed to France for a university education.

As for the conjure-woman, she bought herself a new mule and said nothing. Her skill at herbs had given her son a chance in the world, and she was satisfied.

It was eight years before the boy returned. He had changed a great deal since his departure; he preferred the society of whites and the octoroon society people of Port-au-Prince. It is recorded that he rather ignored his old mother, too. His newly acquired fastidiousness made him painfully aware of the woman's ignorant simplicity. Besides, he was ambitious, and he did not care to publicise his relationship with such a notorious witch.

For she was quite famous in her way. Where she had come from and what her original history was, nobody knew. But for many years her hut in the mountains had been the rendezvous of strange worshippers and even stranger emissaries. The dark powers of *obeah* were evoked in her shadowy altar-place amidst the hills, and a furtive group of acolytes resided there with her. Her ritual fires always flared on moonless nights, and bullocks were given in bloody baptism to the Crawler of Midnight. For she was a Priestess of the Serpent.

The Snake-God, you know, is the real deity of the *obeah* cults. The blacks worshipped the Serpent in Dahomey and Senegal from time immemorial. They venerate the reptiles in a curious way, and there is some obscure linkage between the snake and the crescent moon. Curious, isn't it—this serpent superstition? The Garden of Eden had its tempter, you know, and the Bible tells of Moses and his staff of snakes. The Egyptians revered Set, and the ancient Hindus had a cobra god. It seems to be general throughout the world—the kindred hatred and reverence of serpents. Always they seem to be worshipped as creatures of evil. American Indians believed in Yig, and Aztec myths follow the pattern. And of course the Hopi ceremonial dances are of the same order.

But the African Serpent legends are particularly dreadful, and the Haitian adaptations of the sacrificial rites are worse.

At the time of which I speak some of the voodoo groups were believed to actually breed snakes; they smuggled the reptiles over from the Ivory Coast to use in their secret practices. There were tall tales current about twenty-foot pythons which swallowed infants offered up to them on the Black Altar, and about *sendings* of poisonous serpents which killed enemies of the voodoo-masters. It is a known fact that several anthropoid apes had been smuggled into the country by a peculiar cult that worshipped gorillas; so the serpent legends may have been equally true.

At any rate, the president's mother was a priestess, and equally as famous, in a way, as her distinguished son. He, just after his return, had slowly climbed to power. First he had been a tax-gatherer, then treasurer, and finally president. Several of his rivals died, and those who opposed him soon found it expedient to dissemble their hatred; for he was still a savage at heart, and savages like to torment their enemies. It was rumoured that he had constructed a secret torture chamber beneath the palace, and that its instruments were rusty, though not from disuse.

The breach between the young statesman and his mother began to widen just prior to his presidential incumbency. The immediate cause was his marriage to the daughter of a rich octoroon planter from the coast. Not only was the old woman humiliated because her son contaminated the family stock (she was pure Negro, and descendant of a Niger slave-king), but she was further indignant because she had not been invited to the wedding.

It was held in Port-au-Prince. The foreign consuls were there, and the cream of Haitian society was present. The lovely bride had been convent-bred, and her antecedents were held in the highest esteem. The groom wisely did not deign to desecrate the nuptial celebration by including his rather unsavoury parent.

She came, though, and watched the affair through the kitchen doorway. It was just as well that she did not make her presence known, as it would have embarrassed not only her son, but several others as well—official dignitaries who sometimes consulted her in their unofficial capacity.

What she saw of her son and his bride was not pleasing. The man was an affected dandy now, and his wife was a silly flirt. The atmosphere of the pomp and ostentation did not impress her; behind their debonair masks of polite sophistication she knew that most of those present were superstitious Negroes who would have run to her for charms or oracular advice the moment they were in trouble. Nevertheless, she took no action; she merely smiled rather bitterly and hobbled home. After all, she still loved her son.

The next affront, however, she could not overlook. This was the inauguration of the new president. She was not invited to this affair either, yet she came. And this time she did not skulk in the shadows. After the oath of office was administered she marched boldly up to the new ruler of Haiti and accosted him before the very eyes of the German consul himself. She was a grotesque figure; an ungainly little harridan barely five feet tall, black, barefooted, and clad in rags.

Her son quite naturally ignored her presence. The withered crone licked her toothless gums in terrible silence. Then, quite calmly, she began to curse him—not in French, but in native *patois* of the hills. She called down the wrath of her bloody gods upon his ungrateful head, and threatened both him and his wife with vengeance for their smug ingratitude. The assembled guests were shocked.

So was the new president. However, he did not forget himself. Calmly he motioned to his guards, who led the now hysterical witch-woman away. He would deal with her later.

The next night when he saw fit to go into the dungeon and reason with his mother, she was gone. Disappeared, the guards told him, rolling their eyes mysteriously. He had the jailer shot, and went back to his official chambers.

He was a little worried about the curse business. You see, he knew what the woman was capable of. He did not like those threats against his wife, either. The next day he had some silver bullets moulded, like King Henry in the old days. He also bought an *ouanga* charm from a devil-doctor of his own acquaintance. Magic would fight magic.

That night a serpent came to him in dreams; a serpent with green eyes that whispered in the way of men and hissed at him with shrill and mocking laughter as he struck at it in his sleep. There was a reptilian odour in his bedroom the next morning, and a nauseous slime upon his pillow that gave forth a similar stench. And the president knew that only his charm had saved him.

That afternoon his wife missed one of her Paris frocks, and the president questioned his servants in his private torture chamber below. He learned some facts he dared not tell his bride, and thereafter he seemed very sad. He had seen his mother work with wax images before—little mannikins resembling men and women, dressed in parts of their stolen garments. Sometimes she stuck pins into them or roasted them over a slow fire. Always the real people sickened and died. This knowledge made the president quite unhappy, and he was still more overwrought when messengers returned and said that his mother was gone from her old hut in the hills.

Three days later his wife died, of a painful wound in her side which no doctors could explain. She was in agony until the end, and just before her passing it was rumoured that her body turned blue and bloated up to twice its normal size. Her features were eaten away as if with leprosy, and her swollen limbs looked like those of an elephantiasis victim. Loathsome tropical diseases abound in Haiti, but none of them kill in three days. . . .

After this the president went mad.

Like Cotton Mather of old, he started on a witch-hunting crusade. Soldiers and police were sent out to comb the country-side. Spies rode up to hovels on the mountain peaks, and armed patrols crouched in far-off fields where the living dead-men work, their glazed and glassy eyes staring ceaselessly at the moon. *Mamalois* were put to the question over slow fires, and possessors of forbidden books were roasted over flames fed by the very tomes they harboured. Blood-hounds yammered in the hills, and priests died on altars where they were wont to sacrifice. Only one order had been specially given: the president's mother was to be captured alive and unharmed.

Meanwhile he sat in the palace with the embers of slow insanity in his eyes—embers that flared into fiendish flame when the guards brought in the withered crone, who had been captured near that awful grove of idols in the swamp.

They took her downstairs, although she fought and clawed like a wildcat, and then the guards went away and left her son with her alone. Alone, in a torture chamber, with a mother who cursed him from the rack. Alone, with frantic fires in his eyes, and a great silver knife in his hand. . . .

The president spent many hours in his secret torture chamber during the next few days. He seldom was seen around the palace, and his servants were given orders that he must not be disturbed. On the fourth day he came up the hidden stairway for the last time, and the flickering madness in his eyes was gone.

Just what occurred in the dungeon below will never be rightly known. No doubt that is for the best. The president was a savage at heart, and to the brute, prolongation of pain always brings ecstasy. . . .

It is recorded, though, that the old witch-woman cursed her son with the Serpent's Curse in her dying breath, and that is the most terrible curse of all.

Some idea of what happened may be gained by the knowledge of the president's revenge; for he had a grim sense of humour, and a barbarian's idea of retribution. His wife had been killed by his mother, who fashioned a waxen image. He decided to do what would be exquisitely appropriate.

When he came up the stairs that last time, his servants saw that he bore with him a great candle, fashioned of corpse-fat. And since nobody ever saw his mother's body again, there were curious surmises as to where the corpse-fat was obtained. But then, the president's mind leaned toward grisly jests. . . .

The rest of the story is very simple. The president went directly to his chambers in the palace, where he placed the candle in a holder on his desk. He had neglected his work in the last few days, and there was much official business for him to transact. For a while he sat in silence, staring at the candle with a curious satisfied smile. Then he called for his papers and announced that he would attend to them immediately.

He worked all that night, with two guards stationed outside his door. Sitting at his desk, he pored over his task in the candle-light—the candle from the corpse-fat taper.

Evidently his mother's dying curse did not bother him at all. Once satisfied, his blood-lust abated, he discounted all possibility of revenge. Even he was not superstitious enough to believe that the sorceress could return from her grave. He was quite calm as he sat there, quite the civilised gentleman. The candle cast ominous shadows over the darkened room, but he did not notice—until it was too late. Then he looked up to see the corpse-fat candle wriggle into monstrous life.

His mother's curse. . . .

The candle—the corpse-fat candle—was *alive*! It was a sinuous, twisting thing, weaving in its holder with sinister purpose.

The flame-tipped end seemed to glow strongly into a sudden terrible semblance. The president, amazed, saw the fiery face—his mother's; a tiny wrinkled face of flame, with a corpse-fat body that darted out toward the man with hideous ease. The candle was lengthening as if the tallow were melting; lengthening, and reaching out towards him in a terrible way.

The president of Haiti screamed, but it was too late. The glowing flame on the end snuffed out, breaking the hypnotic spell that had held the man betranced. And at that moment the candle leapt, while the room faded into dreadful darkness. It was a ghastly darkness, filled with moans, and the sound of a thrashing body that grew fainter, and fainter. . . .

It was quite still by the time the guards had entered and turned up the lights once more. They knew about the corpse-fat candle and the witch-mother's curse. That is why they were the first to announce the president's death; the first to fire a bullet into his temple and claim he committed suicide.

They told the president's successor the story, and he gave orders that the crusade against voodoo be abandoned. It was better so, for the new man did not wish to die. The guards had explained why they shot the president and called it suicide, and his successor did not wish to risk the Serpent Curse.

For the president of Haiti had been strangled to death by his mother's corpse-fat candle—*a corpse-fat candle that was wound around his neck like a giant snake.*

W IS FOR WITCHES, WERE-WOLVES, <u>WEIRD</u>!!!

ROBERT BLOCH

Sweets to the Sweet

Irma didn't look like a witch.

She had small, regular features, a peaches-and-cream complexion, blue eyes, and fair, almost ash-blonde hair. Besides, she was only eight years old.

"Why does he tease her so?" sobbed Miss Pall. "That's where she got the idea in the first place—because he calls her a little witch."

Sam Steever bulked his paunch back into the squeaky swivel chair and folded his heavy hands in his lap. His fat lawyer's mask was immobile, but he was really quite distressed.

Women like Miss Pall should never sob. Their glasses wiggle, their thin noses twitch, their creasy eyelids redden, and their stringy hair becomes disarrayed.

"Please, control yourself," coaxed Sam Steever. "Perhaps if we could just talk this whole thing over sensibly—"

"I don't care!" Miss Pall sniffled. "I'm not going back there again. I can't stand it. There's nothing I can do, anyway. The man is your brother and she's your brother's child. It's not my responsibility. I've tried—"

"Of course you've tried," Sam Steever smiled benignly, as if Miss Pall were foreman of a jury. "I quite understand. But I still don't see why you are so upset, dear lady."

Miss Pall removed her spectacles, and dabbed at her eyes with a floral-print handkerchief. Then she deposited the soggy ball in her purse, snapped the catch, replaced her spectacles, and sat up straight.

"Very well, Mr. Steever," she said. "I shall do my best to acquaint you with my reasons for quitting your brother's employ."

She suppressed a tardy sniff.

"I came to John Steever two years ago in response to an advertisement for a housekeeper, as you know. When I found that I was to be governess to a motherless six-year-old child, I was at first distressed. I know nothing of the care of children."

"John had a nurse the first years," Sam Steever nodded. "You know Irma's mother died in childbirth."

"I am aware of that," said Miss Pall, primly. "Naturally, one's heart goes out to

305

a lonely, neglected little girl. And she was so terribly lonely, Mr. Steever—if you could have seen her, moping around in the corners of that big, ugly old house—"

"I have seen her," said Sam Steever, hastily, hoping to forestall another outburst. "And I know what you've done for Irma. My brother is inclined to be thoughtless, even a bit selfish at times. He doesn't understand."

"He's cruel!" declared Miss Pall, suddenly vehement. "Cruel and wicked. Even if he is your brother, I say he's no fit father for any child. When I came there, her little arms were black and blue from beatings. He used to take a belt—"

"I know. Sometimes, I think John never recovered from the shock of Mrs. Steever's death. That's why I was so pleased when you came, dear lady. I thought you might help the situation."

"I tried," Miss Pall whimpered. "You know I tried. I never raised a hand to that child in two years, though many's the time your brother has told me to punish her. 'Give the little witch a beating' he used to say. 'That's all she needs—a good thrashing'. And then she'd hide behind my back and whisper to me to protect her. But she wouldn't cry. Mr. Steever. Do you know, I've never seen her cry."

Sam Steever felt vaguely irritated and a bit bored. He wished the old hen would get on with it. So he smiled and oozed treacle. "But just what is your problem, dear lady?"

"Everything was all right when I came there. We got along just splendidly. I started to teach Irma to read—and was surprised to find that she had already mastered reading. Your brother disclaimed having taught her, but she spent hours curled up on the sofa with a book. 'Just like her,' he used to say, 'Unnatural little witch. Doesn't play with the other children. Little witch'. That's the way he kept talking, Mr. Steever. As if she were some sort of—I don't know what. And she so sweet and quiet and pretty!

"Is it any wonder she read? I used to be that way myself when I was a girl, because—but never mind.

"Still, it was a shock that day I found her looking through the *Encyclopaedia Britannica*. 'What are you reading Irma?' I asked. She showed me. It was the article on Witchcraft.

"You see what morbid thoughts your brother has inculcated in her poor little head?

"I did my best. I went out and bought her some toys—she had absolutely nothing, you know; not even a doll. She didn't even know how to *play*! I tried to get her interested in some of the other little girls in the neighbourhood, but it was no use. They didn't understand her and she didn't understand them. There were scenes. Children can be cruel, thoughtless. And her father wouldn't let her go to public school. I was to teach her—

"Then I brought her the modelling clay. She liked that. She would spend hours just making faces with clay. For a child of six Irma displayed real talent.

"We made little dolls together, and I sewed clothes for them. That first year was a happy one, Mr. Steever. Particularly during those months when your brother was away in South America. But this year, when he came back—oh, I can't bear to talk about it!"

"Please," said Sam Steever. "You must understand. John is not a happy man. The loss of his wife, the decline of his import trade, and his drinking—but you know all that."

"All I know is that he hates Irma," snapped Miss Pall, suddenly. "He hates her. He wants her to be bad, so he can whip her. 'If you don't discipline the little witch, I shall,' he always says. And then he takes her upstairs and thrashes her with his belt—you must do something, Mr. Steever, or I'll go to the authorities myself."

The crazy old biddy would at that, Sam Steever thought. Remedy—more treacle. "But about Irma," he persisted.

"She's changed, too. Ever since her father returned this year. She won't play with me any more, hardly looks at me. It is as though I failed her, Mr. Steever, in not protecting her from that man. Besides—she thinks she's a witch."

Crazy. Stark, staring crazy. Sam Steever creaked upright in his chair.

"Oh you needn't look at me like that, Mr. Steever. She'll tell you so herself—if you ever visited the house!"

He caught the reproach in her voice and assuaged it with a deprecating nod.

"She told me all right, if her father wants her to be a witch she'll be a witch. And she won't play with me, or anyone else, because witches don't play. Last Halloween she wanted me to give her a broomstick. Oh, it would be funny if it weren't so tragic. That child is losing her sanity.

"Just a few weeks ago I thought she'd changed. That's when she asked me to take her to church one Sunday. 'I want to see the baptism,' she said. Imagine that—an eight-year-old interested in baptism! Reading too much, that's what does it.

"Well, we went to church and she was as sweet as can be, wearing her new blue dress and holding my hand. I was proud of her, Mr. Steever, really proud.

"But after that, she went right back into her shell. Reading around the house, running through the yard at twilight and talking to herself.

"Perhaps it's because your brother wouldn't bring her a kitten. She was pestering him for a black cat, and he asked why, and she said, 'Because witches always have black cats'. Then he took her upstairs.

"I can't stop him, you know. He beat her again the night the power failed and we couldn't find the candles. He said she'd stolen them. Imagine that—accusing an eight-year-old child of stealing candles!

"That was the beginning of the end. Then today, when he found his hairbrush missing—"

"You say he beat her with his hairbrush?"

"Yes. She admitted having stolen it. Said she wanted it for her doll."

"But didn't you say she had no dolls?"

"She made one. At least I think she did. I've never seen it—she won't show us anything any more; won't talk to us at table, just impossible to handle her.

"But this doll she made—it's a small one. I know, because at times, she carries it tucked under her arm. She talks to it and pets it, but she won't show it to me or to him. He asked her about the hairbrush and she said she took it for the doll.

"Your brother flew into a terrible rage—he'd been drinking in his room again all morning, oh don't think I don't know it!—and she just smiled and said he could have it now. She went over to her bureau and handed it to him. She hadn't harmed it in the least: his hair was still in it, I noticed.

"But he snatched it up, and then he started to strike her about the shoulders with it, and he twisted her arm and then he—"

Miss Pall huddled in her chair and summoned great racking sobs from her thin chest.

Sam Steever patted her shoulder, fussing about her like an elephant over a wounded canary.

"That's all, Mr. Steever. I came right to you. I'm not even going back to that house to get my things. I can't stand any more—the way he beat her—and the way she didn't cry, just giggled and giggled and giggled—sometimes I think she *is* a witch—that he made her into a witch—"

Sam Steever picked up the phone. The ringing had broken the relief of silence after Miss Pall's hasty departure.

"Hello—that you Sam?"

He recognized his brother's voice, somewhat the worse for drink.

"Yes, John."

"I suppose the old bat came running straight to you to shoot her mouth off."

"If you mean Miss Pall, I've seen her, yes."

"Pay no attention. I can explain everything."

"Do you want me to stop in? I haven't paid you a visit in months."

"Well—not right now. Got an appointment with the doctor this evening."

"Something wrong?"

"Pain in my arm. Rheumatism or something. Getting a little diathermy. But I'll call you tomorrow and we'll straighten this whole mess out."

"Right."

But John Steever did not call the next day. Along about supper time, Sam called him.

Surprisingly enough, Irma answered the phone. Her thin, squeaky little voice sounded faintly in Sam's ears.

"Daddy's upstairs sleeping. He's been sick."

"Well don't disturb him. What is it—his arm?"

"His back, now. He has to go to the doctor again in a little while."

"Tell him I'll call tomorrow, then. Uh—everything all right, Irma? I mean, don't you miss Miss Pall?"

"No. I'm glad she went away. She's stupid."

"Oh. Yes. I see. But you phone me if you want anything. And I hope your Daddy's better."

"Yes. So do I," said Irma, and then she began to giggle, and then she hung up.

There was no giggling the following afternoon when John Steever called Sam at the office. His voice was sober—with the sharp sobriety of pain.

"Sam—for God's sake, get over here. Something's happening to me!"

"What's the trouble?"

"The pain—it's killing me! I've got to see you, quickly."

"There's a client in the office, but I'll get rid of him. Say, wait a minute. Why don't you call the doctor?"

"That quack can't help me. He gave me diathermy for my arm and yesterday he did the same thing for my back."

"Didn't it help?"

"The pain went away, yes. But it's back now I feel—like I was being crushed. Squeezed, here in the chest. I can't breathe."

"Sounds like pleurisy. Why don't you call him?"

"It isn't pleurisy. He examined me. Said I was sound as a dollar. No, there's nothing organically wrong. And I couldn't tell him the real cause."

"Real cause?"

"Yes. The pins. The pins that little fiend is sticking into the doll she made. Into the arm, the back. And now heaven only knows how she's causing *this*."

"John you mustn't—"

"Oh what's the use of talking? I can't move off the bed here. She has me now. I can't go down and stop her, get hold of the doll. And nobody else would believe it. But it's the doll all right, the one she made with the candle-wax and the hair from my brush. Oh—it hurts to talk—that cursed little witch! Hurry, Sam. Promise me you'll do something—anything—get that doll from her—get that doll—"

Half an hour later, at four-thirty, Sam Steever entered his brother's house.

Irma opened the door.

It gave Sam a shock to see her standing there, smiling and unperturbed, pale blonde hair brushed immaculately back from the rosy oval of her face. She looked just like a little doll. A little doll. . . .

"Hello, Uncle Sam."

"Hello, Irma. Your Daddy called me, did he tell you? He said he wasn't feeling well—"

"I know. But he's all right now. He's sleeping."

Something happened to Sam Steever; a drop, of ice-water trickled down his spine.

"Sleeping?" he croaked. "Upstairs?"

Before she opened her mouth to answer he was bounding up the steps to the second floor, striding down the hall to John's bedroom.

John lay on the bed. He was asleep, and only asleep. Sam Steever noted the regular rise and fall of his chest as he breathed. His face was calm, relaxed.

Then the drop of ice-water evaporated, and Sam could afford to smile and murmur "Nonsense" under his breath as he turned away.

As he went downstairs he hastily improvised plans. A six-month vacation for his brother; avoid calling it a "cure". An orphanage for Irma; give her a chance to get away from this morbid old house, all those books. . . .

He paused halfway down the stairs. Peering over the banister through the twilight he saw Irma on the sofa, cuddled up like a little white ball. She was talking to something she cradled in her arms, rocking it to and fro.

Then there was a doll, after all.

Sam Steever tiptoed very quietly down the stairs and walked over to Irma.

"Hello," he said.

She jumped. Both arms rose to cover completely whatever it was she had been fondling. She squeezed it tightly.

Sam Steever thought of a doll being squeezed across the chest. . . .

Irma stared up at him, her face a mask of innocence. In the half-light her face did resemble a mask. The mask of a little girl covering—what?

"Daddy's better now, isn't he?" lisped Irma.

"Yes, much better."

"I knew he would be."

"But I'm afraid he's going to have to go away for a rest. A long rest."

A smile filtered through the mask. "Good," said Irma.

"Of course," Sam went on, "you couldn't stay here all alone. I was wondering—maybe we could send you off to school, or to some kind of a home—"

Irma giggled. "Oh, you needn't worry about me," she said. She shifted about on the sofa as Sam sat down, then sprang up quickly as he came close to her.

Her arms shifted with the movement, and Sam Steever saw a pair of tiny legs dangling down below her elbow. There were trousers on the legs, and little bits of leather for shoes.

"What's that you have, Irma?" he asked. "Is it a doll?" Slowly, he extended his pudgy hand.

She pulled back.

"You can't see it," she said.

"But I want to, Miss Pall said you made such lovely ones."

"Miss Pall is stupid. So are you. Go away."

"Please, Irma. Let me see it."

But even as he spoke, Sam Steever was staring at the top of the doll, momentarily revealed when she backed away. It was a head all right, with wisps of hair over a white face. Dusk dimmed the features, but Sam recognized the eyes, the nose, the chin. . . .

He could keep up the pretence no longer.

"Give me that doll, Irma!" he snapped. "I know what it is. I know *who* it is—"

For an instant, the mask slipped from Irma's face, and Sam Steever stared into naked fear.

She knew. She knew, he knew.

Then, just as quickly, the mask was replaced.

Irma was only a sweet, spoiled, stubborn little girl as she shook her head merrily and smiled with impish mischief in her eyes.

"Oh Uncle Sam," she giggled. "You're so silly! Why, this isn't a *real* doll."

"What is it, then?" he muttered.

Irma giggled once more, raising the figure as she spoke. "Why, its only—candy!" Irma said.

"Candy?"

Irma nodded. Then, very swiftly, she slipped the tiny head of the image into her mouth.

And bit it off.

There was a single piercing scream from upstairs.

As Sam Steever turned and ran up the steps, little Irma, still gravely munching, skipped out of the front door and into the night beyond.

BRUCE ELLIOTT
Wolves Don't Cry

The naked man behind the bars was sound asleep. In the cage next to him a bear rolled over on its back, and peered sleepily at the rising sun. Not far away a jackal paced springily back and forth as though essaying the impossible, trying to leave its own stench far behind.

Flies were gathered around the big bone that rested near the man's sleeping head. Little bits of decaying flesh attracted the insects and their hungry buzzing made the man stir uneasily. Accustomed to instant awakening his eyes flickered and simultaneously his right hand darted out and smashed down on the irritating flies.

They left in a swarm, but the naked man stayed frozen in the position he had assumed. His eyes were on his hand.

He was still that way when the zoo attendant came close to the cage. The attendant, a pail of food in one hand, a pail of water in the other, said, "Hi Lobo, up and at 'em, the customers'll be here soon." Then he too froze.

Inside the naked man's head strange ideas were stirring. His paw, what had happened to it? Where was the stiff gray hair? The jet-black steel-strong nails? And what was the odd fifth thing that jutted out from his paw at right angles? He moved it experimentally. It rotated. He'd never been able to move his dew claw, and the fact that he could move the fifth extension was somehow more baffling than the other oddities that were puzzling him.

"You goddamn drunks!" the attendant raved. "Wasn't bad enough the night a flock of you came in here, and a girl bothered the bear and lost an arm for her trouble, no, that wasn't bad enough. Now you have to sleep in my cages! And where's Lobo? What have you done with him?"

The naked figure wished the two-legged would stop barking. It was enough trouble trying to figure out what had happened without the angry short barks of the two-legged who fed him interfering with his thoughts.

Then there were many more of the two-leggeds and a lot of barking, and the naked one wished they'd all go away and let him think. Finally the cage was opened and the two-leggeds tried to make him come out of his cage. He retreated hurriedly on all fours to the back of his cage towards his den.

"Let him alone," the two-legged who fed him barked. "Let him go into Lobo's den. He'll be sorry!"

Inside the den, inside the hollowed-out rock that so cleverly approximated his home before he had been captured, he paced back and forth, finding it bafflingly uncomfortable to walk on his naked feet. His paws did not grip the ground the way they should and the rock hurt his new soft pads.

The two-legged ones were getting angry, he could smell the emotion as it poured from them, but even that was puzzling, for he had to flare his nostrils wide to get the scent, and it was blurred, not crisp and clear the way he ordinarily smelled things. Throwing back his head, he howled in frustration and anger. But the sound was wrong. It did not ululate as was its wont. Instead he found to his horror that he sounded like a cub, or a female.

What had happened to him?

Cutting one of his soft pads on a stone, he lifted his foot and licked at the blood. His pounding heart almost stopped.

This was no wolf blood.

Then the two-legged ones came in after him and the fight was one that ordinarily he would have enjoyed, but now his heart was not in it. Dismay filled him, for the taste of his own blood had put fear in him. Fear unlike any he had ever known, even when he was trapped that time, and put in a box, and thrown onto a wheeled thing that had rocked back and forth, and smelled so badly of two-legged things.

This was a new fear, and a horrible one.

Their barking got louder when they found that he was alone in his den. Over and over they barked, not that he could understand them. "What have you done with Lobo? Where is he? Have you turned him loose?" It was only after a long time, when the sun was riding high in the summer sky, that he was wrapped in a foul-smelling thing and put in a four-wheeled object and taken away from his den.

He would never have thought, when he was captured, that he would ever miss the new home that the two-leggeds had given him, but he found that he did, and most of all, as the four-wheeled thing rolled through the city streets, he found himself worrying about his mate in the next cage. What would she think when she found him gone, and she just about to have a litter? He knew that most males did not worry about their young, but wolves were different. No mother wolf ever had to worry, the way female bears did, about a male wolf eating his young. No indeed; wolves were different.

And being different, he found that worse than being tied up in a cloth and thrown in the back of a long, wheeled thing was the worry he felt about his mate, and her young-to-be.

But worse was to come: when he was carried out of the moving thing, the two-legged ones carried him into a big building and the smells that surged in on his outraged nostrils literally made him cringe. There was sickness, and stenches worse than he had ever smelled, and above and beyond all other smells the odor of death was heavy in the long white corridors through which he was carried.

Seeing around him as he did ordinarily in grays and blacks and whites, he found that the new sensations that crashed against his smarting eye balls were not to be explained by anything he knew. Not having the words for red, and green, and yellow, for pink and orange and all the other colors in a polychromatic world, not having any idea of what they were, just served to confuse him even more miserably.

He moaned.

The smells, the discomfort, the horror of being handled, were as nothing against the hurt his eyes were enduring.

Lying on a flat hard thing he found that it helped just to stare directly upwards. At least the flat covering ten feet above him was white, and he could cope with that.

The two-legged thing sitting next to him had a gentle bark, but that didn't help much.

The two-legged said patiently over and over again, "Who are you? Have you any idea? Do you know where you are? What day is this?"

After a while the barks became soothing, and nude no longer, wrapped now in a long wet sheet that held him cocoonlike in its embrace, he found that his eyes were closing. It was all too much for him.

He slept.

The next awakening was if anything worse than the first.

First he thought that he was back in his cage in the zoo, for directly ahead of him he could see bars. Heaving a sigh of vast relief, he wondered what had made an adult wolf have such an absurd dream. He could still remember his puppyhood when sleep had been made peculiar by a life unlike the one he enjoyed when awake. The twitchings, the growls, the sleepy murmurs—he had seen his own sons and daughters go through them and they had reminded him of his youth.

But now the bars were in front of him and all was well.

Except that he must have slept in a peculiar position. He was stiff, and when he went to roll over he fell off the hard thing he had been on and crashed to the floor.

Bars or no bars, this was not his cage.

That was what made the second awakening so difficult. For, once he had fallen off the hospital bed, he found that his limbs were encumbered by a long garment that flapped around him as he rolled to all fours and began to pace fearfully back and forth inside the narrow confines of the cell that he now inhabited.

Worse yet, when the sound of his fall reached the ears of a two-legged one, he found that some more two-legs hurried to his side and he was forced, literally forced into an odd garment that covered his lower limbs.

Then they made him sit on the end of his spine and it hurt cruelly, and they put a metal thing in his right paw, and wrapped the soft flesh of his paw around the metal object and holding both, they made him lift some kind of slop from a round thing on the flat surface in front of him.

That was bad, but the taste of the mush they forced into his mouth was grotesque.

Where was his meat? Where was his bone? How could he sharpen his fangs on such food as this? What were they trying to do? Make him lose his teeth?

He gagged and regurgitated the slops. That didn't do the slightest bit of good. The two-leggeds kept right on forcing the mush into his aching jaws. Finally, in despair, he kept some of it down.

Then they made him balance on his hind legs.

He'd often seen the bear in the next cage doing this trick and sneered at the big fat oaf for pandering to the two-leggeds by aping them. Now he found that it was harder than he would have thought. But finally, after the two-leggeds had worked with him for a long time, he found that he could, by much teetering, stand erect.

But he didn't like it.

His nose was too far from the floor, and with whatever it was wrong with his smelling, he found that he had trouble sniffing the ground under him. From this distance he could not track anything. Not even a rabbit. If one had run right by him, he thought, feeling terribly sorry for himself, he'd never be able to smell it, or if he did, be able to track it down, no matter how fat and juicy, for how could a wolf run on two legs?

They did many things to him in the new big zoo, and in time he found that, dislike it as much as he did, they could force him by painful expedients to do many of the tasks they set him.

That, of course, did not help him to understand why they wanted him to do such absurd things as encumber his legs with cloth that flapped and got in the way, or balance precariously on his hind legs, or any of the other absurdities they made him perform. But somehow he surmounted everything and in time even learned to bark a little the way they did. He found that he could bark *hello* and *I'm hungry* and, after months of effort, ask *why can't I go back to the zoo?*

But that didn't do much good, because all they ever barked back was *because you're a man.*

Now of many things he was unsure since that terrible morning, but of one thing he was sure: he *was* a wolf.

Other people knew it too.

He found this out on the day some outsiders were let into the place where he was being kept. He had been sitting, painful as it was, on the tip of his spine, in what he had found the two-leggeds called a chair, when some shes passed by.

His nostrils closed at the sweet smell that they had poured on themselves, but through it he could detect the real smell, the female smell, and his nostrils had flared, and he had run to the door of his cell, and his eyes had become red as he looked at them. Not so attractive as his mate, but at least they were covered with fur, not like the peeled ones that he sometimes saw dressed in stiff white crackling things.

The fur-covered ones had giggled just like ripening she-cubs, and his paws had ached to grasp them, and his jaws ached to bite into their fur-covered necks.

One of the fur-covered two-leggeds had giggled "Look at that wolf!"

So some of the two-leggeds had perception and could tell that the ones who held him in this big strange zoo were wrong, that he was not a man, but a wolf.

Inflating his now puny lungs to the utmost he had thrown back his head and roared out a challenge that in the old days, in the forest, would have sent a thrill of pleasure through every female for miles around. But instead of that blood-curdling, stomach-wrenching roar, a little barking, choking sound came from his throat. If he had still had a tail it would have curled down under his belly as he slunk away.

The first time they let him see himself in what they called a mirror he had moaned like a cub. Where was his long snout, the bristling whiskers, the flat head, the pointed ears? What was this thing that stared with dilated eyes out of that flat shiny surface? White-faced, almost hairless save for a jet-black bar of eyebrows that made a straight line across his high round forehead, small-jawed, small-toothed—he knew with a sinking sensation in the pit of his stomach that even a year-old would not hesitate to challenge him in the mating fights.

Not only challenge him but beat him, for how could he fight with those little canines, those feeble white hairless paws?

Another thing that irritated him, as it would any wolf, was that they kept moving him around. He would no sooner get used to one den and make it his own but what they'd move him to another one.

The last one that contained him had no bars.

If he had been able to read his chart he would have known that he was considered on the way to recovery, that the authorities thought him almost "cured" of his aberration. The den with no bars was one that was used for limited liberty patients. They were on a kind of parole basis. But he had no idea of what the word meant and the first time he was released on his own cognizance, allowed to make a trip out into the "real" world, he put out of his mind the curious forms of "occupational therapy" with which the authorities were deviling him.

His daytime liberty was unreal and dragged by in a way that made him almost anxious to get back home to the new den.

He had all but made up his mind to do so, when the setting sun conjured up visions which he could not resist. In the dark he could get down on all fours!

Leaving the crowded city streets behind him he hurried out into the suburbs where the spring smells were making the night air exciting.

He had looked forward so to dropping on all fours and racing through the velvet spring night that when he did so, only to find that all the months of standing upright had made him too stiff to run, he could have howled. Then too the clumsy leather things on his back paws got in the way, and he would have ripped them off, but he remembered how soft his new pads were, and he was afraid of what would happen to them.

Forcing himself upright, keeping the curve in his back that he had found helped him to stand on his hind legs, he made his way cautiously along a flat thing that stretched off into the distance.

The four-wheeler that stopped near him would ordinarily have frightened him. But even his new weak nose could sniff through the rank acid smells of the four-wheeler and find, under the too sweet something on the two-legged female, the real smell, so that when she said, "Hop in, I'll give you a lift," he did not run away. Instead he joined the she.

Her bark was nice, at first.

Later, while he was doing to her what her scent had told him she wanted done, her bark became shrill, and it hurt even his new dull ears. That, of course, did not stop him from doing what had to be done in the spring.

The sounds that still came from her go fainter as he tried to run off on his hind legs. It was not much faster than a walk, but he had to get some of the good feeling of the air against his face, of his lungs panting; he had to run.

Regret was in him that he would not be able to get food for the she and be near her when she whelped, for that was the way of a wolf; but he knew too that he would always know her by her scent, and if possible when her time came he would be at her side.

Not even the spring running was as it should be, for without the excitement of being on all fours, without the nimbleness that had been his, he found that he stumbled too much, there was no thrill.

Besides, around him, the manifold smells told him that many of the two-leggeds were all jammed together. The odor was like a miasma and not even the all-pervading stench that came from the four-wheelers could drown it out.

Coming to a halt, he sat on his haunches, and for the first time he wondered if he were really, as he knew he was, a wolf, for a salty wetness was making itself felt at the corners of his eyes.

Wolves don't cry.

But if he were not a wolf, what then was he? What *were* all the memories that crowded his sick brain?

Tears or no, he knew that he was a wolf. And being a wolf, he must rid himself of this soft pelt, this hairlessness that made him sick at his stomach just to touch it with his too soft pads.

This was his dream, to become again as he had been. To be what was his only reality, a wolf, with a wolf's life and a wolf's loves.

That was his first venture into the reality of the world at large. His second day and night of "limited liberty" sent him hurrying back to his den. Nothing in his wolf life had prepared him for what he found in the midnight streets of the big city. For he found that bears were not the only males from whom the shes had to protect their young. . . .

And no animal of which he had ever heard could have moaned, as he heard a man moan, "If only pain didn't hurt so much . . ." and the strangled cries, the thrashing of limbs, the violence, and the sound of a whip. He had never known that humans used whips on themselves too. . . .

The third time out, he tried to drug himself the way the two-leggeds did by going to a big place where, on a screen, black and white shadows went through imitations of reality. He didn't go to a show that advertised it was in full glorious color, for he found the other shadows in neutral grays and blacks and whites gave a picture of life the way his wolf eyes were used to looking at it.

It was in this big place where the shadows acted that he found that perhaps he was not unique. His eyes glued to the screen, he watched as a man slowly fell to all fours, threw his head back, bayed at the moon, and then, right before everyone, turned into a wolf!

A *werewolf,* the man was called in the shadow play. And if there were werewolves, he thought, as he sat frozen in the middle of all the seated two-leggeds, then of course there must be *weremen* (would that be the word?) . . . and he was one of them. . . .

On the screen the melodrama came to its quick bloody, foreordained end and the werewolf died when shot by a silver bullet. . . . He saw the fur disappear from the skin, and the paws change into hands and feet.

All he had to do, he thought as he left the theatre, his mind full of his dream, was to find out how to become a wolf again, without dying. Meanwhile, on every trip out without fail he went to the zoo. The keepers had become used to seeing him. They no longer objected when he threw little bits of meat into the cage to his pups. At first his she had snarled when he came near the bars, but after a while, although still puzzled, and even though she flattened her ears and sniffed constantly at him, she seemed to become resigned to having him stand as near the cage as he possibly could.

His pups were coming along nicely, almost full-grown. He was sorry, in a way, that they had to come to wolfhood behind bars, for now they'd never know the thrill of the spring running, but it was good to know they were safe, and had full bellies, and a den to call their own.

It was when his cubs were almost ready to leave their mother that he found the two-leggeds had a place of books. It was called a *library,* and he had been sent there by the woman in the hospital who was teaching him and some of the other aphasics how to read and write and speak.

Remembering the shadow play about the werewolf, he forced his puzzled eyes

to read all that he could find on the baffling subject of lycanthropy.

In every time, in every clime, he found that there were references to two-leggeds who had become four-leggeds, wolves, tigers, panthers . . . but never a reference to an animal that had become a two-legged.

In the course of his reading he found directions whereby a two-legged could change himself. They were complicated and meaningless to him. They involved curious things like a belt made of human skin, with a certain odd number of nail heads arranged in a quaint pattern on the body of the belt. The buckle had to be made under peculiar circumstances, and there were many chants that had to be sung.

It was essential, he read in the crabbed old books, that the two-legged desirous of making the change go to a place where two roads intersected at a specific angle. Then, standing at the intersection, chanting the peculiar words, feeling the human skin belt, the two-legged was told to divest himself of all clothing, and then to relieve his bladder.

Only then, the odd books said, could the change take place.

He found that his heart was beating madly when he finished the last of the old books.

For if a two-legged could become a four-legged surely . . .

After due thought, which was painful, he decided that a human skin belt would be wrong for him. The man in the fur store looked at him oddly when he asked for a length of wolf fur long and narrow, capable of being made into a belt. . . .

But he got the fur, and he made the pattern of nail heads, and he did the things the books had described.

It was lucky, he thought as he stood in the deserted zoo, that not far from the cages he had found two roads that cut into each other in just the manner that the books said they should.

Standing where they crossed, his clothes piled on the grass nearby, the belt around his narrow waist, his fingers caressing its fur, his human throat chanting the meaningless words, he found that standing naked was a cold business, and that it was easy to void his bladder as the books had said he must.

Then it was all over.

He had done everything just as he should.

At first nothing happened, and the cold white moon looked down at him, and fear rode up and down his spine that he would be seen by one of the two-leggeds who always wore blue clothes, and he would be taken and put back into that other zoo that was not a zoo even though it had bars on the windows.

But then an aching began in his erect back, and he fell to all fours, and the agony began, and the pain blinded him to everything, to all the strange functional changes that were going on, and it was a long, long time before he dared open his eyes.

Even before he opened them, he could sense that it had happened, for crisp and clear through the night he could smell as he knew he should be able to smell. The odors came and they told him old stories.

Getting up on all fours, paying no attention to the clothes that now smelled foully of the two-leggeds, he began to run. His strong claws scrabbled at the cement and he hurried to the grass and it was wonderful and exciting to feel the good feel of the growing things under his pads. Throwing his long head back he closed his eyes and from deep deep inside he sang a song to the wolves' god, the moon.

His baying excited the animals in the cages so near him, and they began to roar, and scream, and those sounds were good too.

Running through the night, aimlessly, but running, feeling the ground beneath his paws was good . . . so good . . .

And then through the sounds, through all the baying and roaring and screaming from the animals, he heard his she's voice, and he forgot about freedom and the night wind and the cool white moon, and he ran back to the cage where she was.

The zoo attendants were just as baffled when they found the wolf curled up outside the cage near the feeding trough as they had been when they had found the man in the wolf's cage.

The two-legged who was his keeper recognized him and he was allowed to go back into his cage and then the ecstasy, the spring-and-fall-time ecstasy of being with his she . . .

Slowly, as he became used to his wolfhood again, he forgot about the life outside the cage, and soon it was all a matter that only arose in troubled dreams. And even then his she was there to nuzzle him and wake him if the nightmares got too bad.

Only once after the first few days did any waking memory of his two-legged life return, and that was when a two-legged she passed by his cage pushing a small four-wheeler in front of her.

Her scent was familiar.

So too was the scent of the two-legged cub.

Darting to the front of his cage, he sniffed long and hard.

And for just a moment the woman who was pushing the perambulator that contained her bastard looked deep into his yellow eyes and she knew, as he did, who and what he was.

And the very, very last thought he had about the matter was one of infinite pity for his poor cub, who some white moonlit night was going to drop down on all fours and become furred . . . and go prowling through the dark—in search of what, he would never know. . . .

R. CHETWYND HAYES
Looking for Something to Suck

Whoever, what-so-ever it had been was an open question, but now it was a Shadow.
The night was full of shadows, so no one said: "What's that?" as a pencil thin line of deeper darkness darted along a gutter, or undulated round the corner of a shop or house. Only a very keen pair of eyes could have detected that quivering line as it streaked away on its unending journey.

The Shadow had a glimmer of intelligence, a flickering awareness of its surroundings, but it did not require intelligence to know that light was the implacable enemy. Light was pain, too much light meant extinction. So it moved only by night, resting by day in some cellar, sewer, or any underground place where light could not penetrate. It resented these forced periods of inactivity, for overriding even the instinct for self-preservation was the urge to keep searching. To frequent the haunts of flesh and blood beings; to sip, to taste—to find the one in a million vessel that could give it tangible life.

The Shadow slid under a neat privet hedge, then moved cautiously into a long narrow flower garden, that bordered a crazy paving path. Extra care must be taken, for this particular night was not ideal; the frosty air was clear, the tiny Sky Lights glittered like a million far off street lamps, and the big Night Sky Light, only a little less feared than the awful Day Sky Light, was scarcely hidden by a tall house.

A front door opened and a slab of light crashed down upon garden path and flower bed, causing the Shadow to quickly contract. Two flesh and blood beings came out into the frosty night; they stamped their feet, and the Shadow felt their thought waves of discomfort. It sent out a cotton thin tentacle when a nylon clad ankle came within tasting distance, and sipped. A female, her life force three-quarters spent, the vibrations disappointing, lacking power, and suggesting a creature given up to bodily comforts and placid thoughts. The thin tentacle crept upwards, flowed across a fur coated back and found that a hand, belonging to the other creature, was resting lightly on the far shoulder. A male this time, a little more life force, the vibrations stronger, but unable to provide nourishment.

The Shadow withdrew its tentacle, skirted the light slab, and took refuge under the porch step, contracting its length into an oval ball of blackness. Then it began to quiver with anticipation. The vibrations were strong, the life force only just reaching maturity; but there was something more, a vital, unknown something that made the Shadow forget its caution and streak upwards. A blast of light hurled it back again; it elongated, darted up both sides of the porch door, but to no avail. The cold harsh light protected the two figures standing in the doorway with a dazzling oblong shield, and the dim Sky Lights made it shrink back to the friendly darkness under the porch step.

Then just as despair and hunger, for the Shadow had not fed for many days, was causing its consciousness to dim down, a small foot was placed over the doorstep. It was little enough. The mere tip of a shoe, a scrap of leather, but above that was a set of five blood and flesh toes, and above them, a slim leg. The Shadow flowed up to the shoe, moved slowly over the toecap; it was safe so far, the light was on either side, but not here. It almost reached the round kneecap, before the leg was snatched away. Jerked away so quickly that for a fraction of a second the Shadow was left exposed to the full fury of the over-head hall light. Only the fact that half of its length was still protected by the doorstep, saved it from extinction. The three remaining beings were agitated. They sent out alarmed and angry thought waves, then the older ones went away, their vibrations dimmed, then ceased to be. The door slammed, but the light remained on.

Down below the doorstep the Shadow was content. The one in a million vessel had been found, and eventually the light would go out, night was the time when lights slept. Then there was a long thin crack under the door, and inside all would be dark; and inside all that darkness would be the vessel. And in that vessel was—goodness.

"Oh, for Pete's sake shut up," Jerry Wilton, his face flushed with anger, slammed the dining-room door shut, then flung himself down into a large easy-chair. "Why the hell don't you grow up?"

Jane leant over him, her face pale, her large blue eyes unnaturally bright. "Jerry, will you listen to me for a moment?"

"You listen to me for a change." He pushed her away so that she staggered back against the table. "You are aware who you have just offended by your childish behaviour, don't you? That was my managing director and his wife, and the only reason they condescended to eat in our miserable hovel, was because he wanted to sum you up. He wanted to be certain you were the right kind of wife for a prospective board member."

"Jerry, let me explain."

"And what do you do? When he put out his hand you suddenly put on an expression of extreme disgust, pull up your leg as if you were going to kick him, then turn and run. What the hell, he wasn't going to rape you, only shake hands."

"Jerry, there was something out there."

"Don't talk such bloody rot."

"It's not rot. If I'd stood on that porch a second longer I'd have passed out."

Jerry got up and walked to the fireplace where he stood glowering at her.

"If you felt unwell why didn't you excuse yourself like a civilised being?"

"Because there wasn't time." Her voice rose to a shout "Can't you get it through that thick skull, I couldn't help myself? You've no idea what it's like."

"What?"

The word was spat out like a bad taste, and Jane knew at that moment he hated her. She sank into the chair he had just vacated, and spoke in a quieter tone.

"Jerry, you've got to accept the fact that I'm different."

"And how."

"No, don't interrupt. Please. Some people have a gift for music, others have an aptitude for acting. I have a gift, a curse, call it what you like, for psychic phenomena."

"What, table rapping?" Jerry smiled grimly. "Pity you didn't put on a show for old Smithers this evening. It couldn't have been worse than the one he was given on the doorstep."

"I'm serious," Jane pushed back her blonde hair with a long-fingered hand. "I once made a—thing materialise."

"Don't talk such utter bilge."

"It's not bilge, but cold fact."

"For instance."

Their eyes met, then she lowered her gaze and the fear inspired anger came thundering back.

"For instance," she thumped one clenched fist down upon the chair arm, "the house next door to the one where I lived as a child was haunted. Haunted, do you hear? Not the wind moaning down chimneys, not a loose floor board, but bloody well haunted. A woman could be heard crying. An unmistakable, heart choking sobbing. Everybody had a go at her. The local vicar turned up with a prayer book, the Psychic Research Society, the local church, the lot. And she still kept on crying."

"Can't say I blame her," Jerry remarked dryly.

"Then I had to put my nose in. I was about sixteen at the time, and I thought the whole thing was a big giggle. It was easy to get into the house, mostly all the windows were broken, and I could hear her sobbing all right. My God I could. I ought to have taken to my heels, like I did to-night, but I hadn't that much sense."

Jerry frowned and said nothing.

"The sound came from an upper room. It was said some woman hung herself up there years ago. When I got into the room it was empty. Just dusty floor boards, flaking wallpaper, and a window with most of the panes missing. I was scared all right. Make no mistake about it, I was all but dead with fear ... But at sixteen you're frightened of being afraid, at least I was. She stopped crying, and I couldn't see a thing, but I knew she was still there. Sort of listening. No, that's not right. Feeling is more like it. Then I began to get cold; colder than I've ever been before or since in my entire life. And it started to go out of me."

"What?" demanded Jerry.

She looked up at him like a bewildered child, and he felt his heart soften; shared a little of that remembered terror.

"I wish I knew. But something vital, something that was essentially mine. A white mist was drifting away from me; coming out of my nose, my mouth, my ears, even from the pores of my skin. It made itself into a shape, the mist I mean, if it was mist. Then there was no mist, only a little woman with her face all screwed up, and a rope tied tight about her neck. I remember particularly that her tongue was sticking out."

"I say," Jerry had, at least for the moment, forgotten their row, "you're not kidding me, are you?"

"No, I'm not kidding. But what really terrified me was the sudden knowledge that the ghost, whatever it was, was made out of me. An essential part of my body had been used to shape that—thing. It was like seeing someone walking around with an arm you know has been made from your missing leg."

"What happened?"

"I passed out. When I came to I was home in bed. Someone must have seen me go into the house, for Dad knew where to look. Funny thing is, that woman was never heard crying again."

"Look." He sat down on the arm of the chair. "I'm not saying your story isn't true, although it sounds like autosuggestion to me, but that happened in a reputed haunted house. This place can't be haunted, it hasn't been built long enough. Nobody died here, and before the estate was built, it was all open fields. So why that nonsense on the porch?"

"I can't explain it," she shook her head, "perhaps there are forms of disembodied life that have never died. The only thing I am certain about is, something was drawing the power out of me on that doorstep. There was the same icy feeling, my skin crawled ... No, Jerry, it wasn't imagination."

He got up and looked down at her with genuine concern, then he smiled.

"I'm sorry, but it's all beyond me. I think you ought to go to bed, you look all in."

"Yes," she rose slowly, her face white and drawn, "I think you're right. I'll just stack the things on the draining board."

He followed her into the kitchen and grimaced when he saw the stack of unwashed dishes, then pretended to stagger when she piled six empty milk bottles into his arms.

"Doorstep?" he enquired.

She could not entirely suppress a slight shudder, and he pretended not to notice; fighting down an irritability that she should still be harbouring a memory he was trying to blot out. He opened the dining-room door, frowned when he noticed the hall light was still burning, then walked to, and opened the front door. A blast of cold air made him recoil as he stepped down on to the garden path and, bending over, laid out his milk bottles in a neat line before the porch step, his shadow, foreshortened and grotesque, lay across the path, like, he could not smother the thought, a crouching beast waiting to pounce.

The Shadow sipped. Male, the life force strong, but the vibrations were not in tune; this was not the Vessel. The being moved, and the soft glow cast by the Night Sky Light made the Shadow contract into its former position under the porch step. A small being flashed by; flesh and blood, harsh life force, low vibrations; hunger, a desire for warmth. It sensed the Shadow's presence. Fear. Then the door shut: the light went out.

The Shadow slid over the narrow porch step, under the front door, and into the darkened hall beyond.

Jerry closed the dining-room door and called to Jane whom he could hear moving about in the kitchen.

"The cat's come in."

Her voice came to him over the rattle of crockery.

"Yes, I know, he's in here. Something seems to have frightened him, his fur's standing on end."

"Probably frozen. It's damn cold out there."

"I'll give him something to eat, that should make him happy."

He heard the cat's demanding cry that ceased when a saucer rattled on the tiled floor, then Jane came into the room.

"Think I'll go up now. Coming?"

He sank into his arm-chair, and took up a leather bound book; the faint feeling of irritability made him determined she should go out into that darkened hall alone, so as to convince herself (and him) there was nothing to fear.

"Let me finish this chapter, and I'll be with you."

"Right," Jane only hesitated for a moment, then walked to the door; she looked back over one shoulder, her hand on the doorknob.

"I'm awfully sorry about this evening. Do you think old Smithers was really upset?"

Jerry shrugged, not looking up from his book. "He wasn't exactly jumping for joy when he left, but he'll probably get over it. After all, the rest of the evening went off all right."

She was out in the hall, fumbling for the switch.

"Jerry, you turned the light . . ." She screamed, one terrified cry, and Jerry leapt to his feet, flung his book to one side, and ran across the room. Her hand still

R. CHETWYND-HAYES

clutched the light switch; the hall was bright. But there was a shadow under the hat stand, and Jane stood white faced and trembling against the wall.

"Darling, what's wrong?"

"Something . . ." She looked fearfully round. "Something . . . just before I turned on the light . . . gripped my ankle."

"Not again!" He looked about him helplessly. "We've no rats, at least . . ."

"Rats don't clutch." There was a suggestion of hysteria in her voice. "Rats bite, claw, and mostly run. But they don't clutch. They . . ." She turned her head and looked up at him, her blue eyes expressionless, like one who has already surrendered to the inevitable. ". . . They don't . . . suck."

"Suck!" He shook her gently, not entirely aware of what he was doing, and began to lead her towards the stairs. "Let's get you to bed, you'll laugh about this to-morrow morning."

"Will I, Jerry?"

"Of course you will." He turned on the stair light, and the shadows rushed away. "You know what your trouble is, don't you?"

"No, tell me."

"No self control. The 'orrible thing that clutched your ankle was Timmy. When cats reach an interesting state they are apt to clutch things. I don't know about sucking, but they certainly bite. Timmy probably got you confused with his mother and the Persian next door."

"You certainly explain things away very cleverly, Jerry," she said in a tired voice. "Timmy must be a very lively cat by now."

"How come?" He laughed as they entered the bedroom.

"He must have at least a quarter of my energy in him."

"Now, that's quite enough of that."

Ten minutes later she looked up at him, her pale, young face framed by the blue nylon pillow, and he knew she wanted to hold him back; stop him going down to that lighted hall.

"Jerry, do me a favour."

"Of course. What is it?"

"Don't turn the lights out until you come to bed."

"All right," he nodded.

"Nowhere. Here, or on the landing, or in the hall."

He smiled indulgently. "If you say so."

He kept his promise, but once in the living-room, he turned off the ceiling light, contenting himself with the reading lamp that cast a yellow circle round his arm-chair. Just before he took up his book he glanced down at Timmy: the cat was stretched out on the hearthrug, soaking up the heat, a veritable picture of contentment as it blinked up at its owner with sleepy eyes.

"You don't appear to have much energy," Jerry remarked aloud.

The cat blinked again, and Jerry watched with detached interest, as a bright pink tongue moistened a paw; the face and head were thoroughly scrubbed, particular attention being paid to the ears, then the back and flanks were well licked, the fur on the breast bitten and preened. Timmy was just attacking the area between his hind legs when he froze, became a motionless black effigy of a cat, then slowly, very slowly, raised his head. The yellow eyes glittered in the lamp light like two pieces of polished amber; the sleek head stopped its slow movement, and Jerry saw it was watching something hidden from him by the deep shadow surrounding the bureau.

"What's the matter with you?" he demanded.

The cat flowed into gentle motion; when he drew near to the shadows his progress became slower; now his head was moving from side to side, a deep growl emerged from between his parted jaws, then, with a leap he was deep into the shadows. Jerry heard a scuffle, and Timmy was out again, his fur on end, his tail lashing like a tormented snake; then he took refuge under a chair, where he sat spitting and snarling his rage and fear.

Jerry did not know why he tip-toed across the room, his arm reaching out for the light switch; he was aware of the tricks eyes can play when they are suddenly turned from the concentrated glare of a single lamp, but that did not fully explain the mass of seething deeper shadow that was creeping up the far wall. It seemed to be twisting itself into a coil, and there was even a suggestion of a head at one end; then Jerry's hand found the switch and the room was flooded with light.

"Nothing," he muttered, "a bloody batty cat, a shadow, and I'm getting to be worse than Jane."

He tried to coax Timmy out from under the chair, but the cat refused to move; when he lifted the chair the animal gave a cry of protest and streaked under the sideboard.

"Damn you," he swore, "stay where you are then."

But when he opened the hall door and turned out the living-room lights, there was another snarl, and Timmy tore out and made for the front door, where he sat mewing while staring up at the handle.

"Are you sure?" Jerry asked, "it's damn cold out there."

The cat clawed at the panels, and did not wait for the door to be fully opened before he was out, racing down the garden path, and disappearing through a hole in the hedge.

Thoughtfully Jerry mounted the stairs, turning out lights as he went.

Jane was not asleep, but lay on her back, eyes wide open, staring blankly at the ceiling.

"You've turned out all the lights?"

"Of course."

"Then it's dark downstairs?"

He took his trousers off, folded them neatly, then draped them over a chair back.

"It's always dark when the lights go out."

He put on his pyjamas, came over her side of the bed, and looked down at that pale, childlike face.

"Come off it, Jane, you're not ten years of age any more. So it's dark outside. That's what life is all about; turning on lights, switching them off again. So long as nobody turns off the sun, we've nothing to worry about. Go to sleep."

He went round to his side of the bed, clambered in, kissed her unresponsive lips with the rather casual affection, proper to a husband married five years, then asked:

"Sleepy to-night?"

She did not answer, only turned her head away, and he sighed.

"So am I. Nighty, night," and reached up for the pear-shaped switch which hung down over the headboard.

"No!" she whimpered, "please don't."

"Oh, for heaven's sake."

All the bottled up fear that had lurked deep down, fear which his reason told him had no foundation in fact, turned sour and came out as anger.

"Look, Jane, if you think I'm going to lie here all night with the bloody light on, you're in for a disappointment. I can put up with so much, but there's a limit. What are you afraid of? Things that go bump in the night? A nasty bogey lurking in the wardrobe?"

She turned her head slowly, and the wide open eyes studied him dispassionately.

"I suppose there's nothing I could say that would make the slightest difference?"

"You bet your sweet life there isn't."

With the defiance of a frightened child, smothering his own spark of fear with a red blanket of anger, he pressed the pear switch and flooded the room with darkness. Jane gave one little gasp, then was still. He felt for her hand, and was shocked at its coldness.

"Silly little goose," he whispered, "you've never been like this before. It isn't as if you were alone. I'm here, aren't I?"

Her tiny, little girl voice came to him.

"It's as though you were a million miles away."

"That would put me out in deep space," he forced a chuckle, "and it would be cold out there. Almost," he drew nearer to her, "as cold as you are. Damnation, girl, your feet are like slabs of ice."

"Are they, Jerry?"

"Yes, they bloody well are. I'll turn the electric blanket on."

He turned away from her and fumbled for the switch that dangled a little below the mattress; in a few minutes a warm glow began to seep up through the under sheet, and sleep closed down over his consciousness, blotting out the darkened room, so that for a while he was lost in a deep, black space . . .

He did not at first know why he woke suddenly; became all at once wide awake, every sense alert; the short hairs on the back of his neck standing erect, a condition up to that moment he would not have thought possible. He lay perfectly still and listened; his ears strained to detect the faintest sound. Far away, possibly on the main road, a motor car sent a faint hum through the cold night, and for a moment he clung to this transient line of contact with a homeward bound stranger. Then the sound died away, and a dreadful silence descended upon the darkness; became part of it, pressed down on him, and it seemed as if the electric blanket, conditioned by its thermostatic control to maintain an even temperature, wanted to keep all the warmth to itself. He was cold, very cold, as if he were sharing the bed with a block of ice, then, just as he was about to stir and put on the light, the sound began, or rather, restarted, for he knew now, this was the reason for his sudden awakening.

The fear and cold held him in an icy grip, and he could only lie still and listen; try to find a rational explanation; fit the sound into a mundane frame; associate it with water pipes, a creaking window, the wind moaning down a chimney, or possibly, and now Jerry relaxed slightly, Jane snoring. That must be it. The sound grew louder. He defined it gradually, taking each part in turn and trying to make a pattern of the whole. First there was a drawing in; a slightly hoarse, breath-gasping guggle, then a harsh, obscene, blowing out. This was followed by an entirely unexplainable slithering, like dough being rubbed on a pastry board; then the process was repeated, only now, somewhat faster. The pattern was complete, Jerry placed the combination of sounds into their right category. It was a sucking noise, as though a baby with an abnormal appetite, and an outsized pair of lips, was taking overdue nourishment from a feeding bottle. Once the bed trembled slightly, and Jerry reached out for Jane's hand.

"Wake up, darling," he spoke only just above a whisper, "you're snoring like hell."

He found her hand, just where he had released it before turning on the electric blanket; it was cold, very bony, and felt as if it were loosely wrapped in silk. As he fumbled for the pear switch something crashed to the floor on the far side of the room, followed almost at once by a thud on the carpet by Jane's side of the bed. He found the switch, pressed, and the darkness exploded; was shattered into a thousand splinters by a blast of light; the wreckage lay all round the room, a rectangle of shadow under the dressing table, a broken slab of blackness on one side of the wardrobe, a long smear along the picture rail; all else was light. Jerry tried to understand what his eyes told him, fought to repel the bitter bile that rose to his throat, and stared blankly at the thing that was coiled round the dressing table, curved gracefully down to the floor; a long, white length that rippled gently; and at places rubbed its white roundness against the wainscoting, then curled into a loop, its extremity hidden from sight by the bed. It was all of thirty feet long, and perhaps a foot in circumference; a long snake, or more likely, a worm; covered with a beautiful white, delicate skin, such as might grace a woman's shoulder. In places there was a faint pink flush; a sign of health on a woman's cheek, or perhaps an emblem of modesty, dawning love, or anger; on the white worm those coyish pink hues were the final epitome of obscenity. Jerry sought blindly for Jane's shoulder, alive to a childish need for someone to share this nightmare, but his hand only found the pillow, still crumpled and hollow where her head had rested. But Jane was gone; was down on the floor—with that thing.

He cried out, calling her name, and the worm shrieked in response. A head came up over the edge of the bed; a round, caricature of Jane's face, smooth, veined like a gooseberry, with thick negroid lips that were parted, displaying a line of pink toothless gums. It shrieked again, then fell back on to the carpet, the entire white length quivered as though in great agony, the tail uncoiled itself from the dressing table and threshed wildly against the wall. The head came up again and attempted to smash the overhead electric bulb, but missed and fell across the bed. Jerry screamed as the wide open blue eyes gaped at him, then flinging back the bedclothes tore across the room stumbling over a white coil that felt soft and warm, like a woman's arm. He clambered to his feet, found the wall switch, and the ceiling lamp sent its shadow-killing rays round the room, making the worm writhe and contract in its futile efforts to escape. Jane was lying on the bedside rug, her face was turned away, the bright blonde hair was disarrayed, and she looked like a broken doll, discarded by a destructive child. Jerry crawled over those threshing coils, forgetful for the moment of the white skinned horror—remembering that he had laughed at her fears, had ignored the warning sent out by his own brain—and prayed that the worst had not happened.

"Darling," he called softly, "can you hear me?"

The crumpled figure did not stir, so he gripped the blue satin sleeve of her pyjama jacket, and pulled gently. She rocked slightly as though half asleep, annoyed at being disturbed, then he pulled harder, and the pyjama jacket seemed to collapse, took on a network of creases and ridges. A feeling of complete despair and horror made him forget the dying monster whose hissing screams were growing fainter; he rose up on to his knees, and gave one last violent jerk. Jane flopped over, and he looked down on to what had been her face. It was a skull covered with loose skin; he ripped the pyjama jacket open—and found that was all that remained of a once beautiful young body; a pile of bones in a skin bag; a deflated balloon; a hideous bundle. The soft flesh, the satin skin, the wide open blue eyes; Jane's very essence, lay stretched out across the room, thumping its white roundness on the carpet, trying to smash its head against the electric bulbs. He took the skeleton into his arms, smoothed back the tousled blonde hair, and muttered words of comfort.

"The lights are on, baby. I'll never turn the lights off again. Don't be afraid . . ."

The white worm reared up, making one last effort to reach the ceiling lamp, then came crashing down; the round, veined head lay a few inches from Jerry and he stared at it without emotion. Presently the thought came unbidden, tumbling into his mind, and forced itself out as words.

"It sucked—it sucked all the goodness out of her."

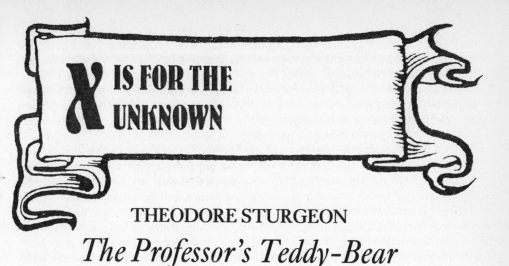

X IS FOR THE UNKNOWN

THEODORE STURGEON
The Professor's Teddy-Bear

"Sleep," said the monster. It spoke with its ear, with little lips writhing deep with the folds of flesh, because its mouth was full of blood.

"I don't want to sleep now. I'm having a dream," said Jeremy. "When I sleep, all my dreams go away. Or they're just pretend dreams. I'm having a real dream now."

"What are you dreaming now?" asked the monster.

"I am dreaming that I'm grown up—"

"Seven feet tall and very fat," said the monster.

"You're silly," said Jeremy. "I will be five feet, six and three-eighth inches tall. I will be bald on top and will wear eye-glasses like little thick ashtrays. I will give lectures to young things about human destiny and the metempsychosis of Plato."

"What's a metempsychosis?" asked the monster hungrily.

Jeremy was four and could afford to be patient. "A metempsychosis is a thing that happens when a person moves from one house to another."

"Like when your daddy moved here from Monroe Street?"

"Sort of. But not that kind of house, with shingles and sewers and things. *This* kind of a house," he said, and smote his little chest.

"Oh," said the monster. It moved up and crouched on Jeremy's throat, looking more like a teddy-bear than ever. "Now?" it begged. It was not very heavy.

"Not now," said Jeremy petulantly. "It'll make me sleep. I want to watch my dream some more. There's a girl who's not listening to my lecture. She's thinking about her hair."

"What about her hair?" asked the monster.

"It's brown," said Jeremy. "It's shiny, too. She wishes it were golden."

"Why?"

"Somebody named Bert likes golden hair."

"Go ahead and make it golden then."

"I can't! What would the other young ones say?"

"Does that matter?"

"Maybe not. Could I make her hair golden?"

"Who is she?" countered the monster.

"She is a girl who will be born here in about twenty years," said Jeremy.

The monster snuggled closer to his neck.

"If she is to be born here, then of course you can change her hair. Hurry and do it and go to sleep."

Jeremy laughed delightedly.

"What happened?" asked the monster.

"I changed it," said Jeremy. "The girl behind her squeaked like a mouse with its leg caught. Then she jumped up. It's a big lecture room, you know, built up and away from the speaker-place. It has steep aisles. Her foot slipped on the hard step."

He burst into joyous laughter.

"Now what?"

"She broke her neck. She's dead."

The monster sniggered. "That's a very funny dream. Now change the other girl's hair back again. Nobody else saw it, except you?"

"Nobody else saw," said Jeremy. "There! It's changed back again. She never even knew she had golden hair for a little while."

"That's fine. Does that end the dream?"

"I s'pose it does," said Jeremy regretfully. "It ends the lecture anyhow. The young people are all crowding around the girl with the broken neck. The young men all have sweat under their noses. The girls are all trying to put their fists into their mouths. You can go ahead."

The monster made a happy sound and pressed its mouth hard against Jeremy's neck. Jeremy closed his eyes.

The door opened. "Jeremy, darling," said Mummy. She had a tired, soft face and smiling eyes. "I heard you laugh."

Jeremy opened his eyes slowly. His lashes were so long that when they swung up, there seemed to be a tiny wind, as if they were dark weather fans. He smiled, and three of his teeth peeped out and smiled too. "I told Fuzzy a story, Mummy," he said sleepily, "and he liked it."

"You darling," she murmured. She came to him and tucked the covers around his chin. He put up his hand and kept the monster tight against his neck.

"Is Fuzzy sleeping?" asked Mummy, her voice crooning with whimsy.

"No," said Jeremy. "He's hungering himself."

"How does he do that?"

"When I eat, the—the hungry goes away. Fuzzy's different."

She looked at him, loving him so much that she did not—could not think. "You're a strange child," she whispered, "and you have the pinkest cheeks in the whole wide world."

"Sure I have," he said.

"What a funny little laugh!" she said, paling.

"That wasn't me. That was Fuzzy. He thinks you're funny."

Mummy stood over the crib, looking down at him. It seemed to be the frown that looked at him, while the eyes looked past. Finally she wet her lips and patted his head. "Good night, baby."

"Good night, Mummy." He closed his eyes. Mummy tip-toed out. The monster kept right on doing it.

It was nap-time the next day, and for the hundredth time Mummy had kissed him and said, "You're so *good* about your nap, Jeremy!" Well, he was. He always went straight up to bed at nap-time, as he did at bedtime. Mummy didn't know why, of course. Perhaps Jeremy did not know. Fuzzy knew.

Jeremy opened the toy-chest and took Fuzzy out. "You're hungry, I bet," he said.

"Yes. Let's hurry."

Jeremy climbed into the crib and hugged the teddy-bear close. "I keep thinking about that girl," he said.

"What girl?"

"The one whose hair I changed."

"Maybe because it's the first time you've changed a person."

"It is not! What about the man who fell into the subway hole?"

"You moved the hat. The one that blew off. You moved it under his feet so that he stepped on the brim with one foot and caught his toe in the crown, and tumbled in."

"Well, what about the little girl I threw in front of the truck?"

"You didn't touch her," said the monster equably. "She was on roller skates. You broke something in one wheel so it couldn't turn. So she fell right in front of the truck."

Jeremy thought carefully. "Why didn't I ever touch a person before?"

"I don't know," said Fuzzy. "It has something to do with being born in this house, I think."

"I guess maybe," said Jeremy doubtfully.

"I'm hungry," said the monster, settling itself on Jeremy's stomach as he turned on his back.

"Oh, all right," Jeremy said. "The next lecture?"

"Yes," said Fuzzy eagerly. "Dream bright, now. The big things that you say, lecturing. Those are what I want. Never mind the people there. Never mind you, lecturing. The things you say."

The strange blood flowed as Jeremy relaxed. He looked up to the ceiling, found the hairline crack that he always stared at while he dreamed real, and began to talk.

"There I am. There's the—the room, yes, and the—yes, it's all there, again. There's the girl. The one who has the brown, shiny hair. The seat behind her is empty. This must be after that other girl broke her neck."

"Never mind that," said the monster impatiently. "What do you say?"

"I—" Jeremy was quiet. Finally Fuzzy nudged him. "Oh. It's all about yesterday's unfortunate occurrence, but, like the show of legend, our studies must go on."

"Go on with it then," panted the monster.

"All right, all right," said Jeremy impatiently. "Here it is. We come now to the Gymnosophists, whose ascetic school has had no recorded equal in its extremism.

Those strange gentry regarded clothing and even food as detrimental to purity of thought. The Greeks also called them *Hylobioi*, a term our more erudite students will notice as analogous to the Sanskrit *Vana-Prasthas*. It is evident that they were a profound influence on Diogenes Laërtius, the Elisian founder of pure scepticism. . . ."

And so he droned on and on. Fuzzy crouched on his body, its soft ears making small masticating motions; and sometimes, when stimulated by some particularly choice nugget of esoterica, the ears drooled.

At the end of nearly an hour, Jeremy's soft voice trailed off, and he was quiet. Fuzzy shifted in irritation. "What is it?"

"That girl," said Jeremy. "I keep looking back to that girl while I'm talking."

"Well, stop doing it. I'm not finished."

"There isn't any more, Fuzzy. I keep looking and looking back to that girl until I can't lecture any more. Now I'm saying all that about the pages in the book and the assignment. The lecture is over."

Fuzzy's mouth was almost full of blood. From its ears, it sighed. "That wasn't any too much. But if that's all, then it's all. You can sleep now if you want to."

"I want to watch for a while."

The monster puffed out its cheeks. The pressure inside was not great. "Go on, then." It scrabbled off Jeremy's body and curled up in a sulky huddle.

The strange blood moved steadily through Jeremy's brain. With his eyes wide and fixed, he watched himself as he would be, a slight, balding professor of philosophy.

He sat in the hall, watching the students tumbling up the steep aisles, wondering at the strange compulsion he had to look at that girl, Miss—Miss—what was it?

Oh. "Miss Patchell!"

He started, astonished at himself. He had certainly not meant to call out her name. He clasped his hands tightly regaining the dry stiffness which was his closest approach to dignity.

The girl came slowly down the aisle steps, her wide-set eyes wondering. There were books tucked under her arm, and her hair shone. "Yes, Professor?"

"I—" He stopped and cleared his throat. "I know it's the last class today, and you are no doubt meeting someone. I shan't keep you very long . . . and if I do," he added, and was again astonished at himself, "you can see Bert tomorrow."

"Bert? Oh!" She coloured prettily. "I didn't know you knew about—how *could* you know?"

He shrugged. "Miss Patchell," he said. "You'll forgive an old—ah—middle-aged man's rambling, I hope. There is something about you that—that——"

"Yes?" Caution and an iota of fright were in her eyes. She glanced up and back at the now empty hall.

Abruptly he pounded the table. "I will *not* let this go on for another instant without finding out about it. Miss Patchell, you are becoming afraid of me, and you are wrong."

"I th-think I'd better . . ." she said timidly, and began backing off.

"*Sit down!*" he thundered. It was the very first time in his entire life that he had thundered at anyone, and her shock was not one whit greater than his. She shrank back and into a front-row seat, looking a good deal smaller than she actually was, except about the eyes, which were much larger.

The professor shook his head in vexation. He rose, stepped down off the dais, and crossed to her, sitting in the next seat.

"Now be quiet and listen to me." The shadow of a smile twitched his lips and he said, "I really don't know what I am going to say. Listen, and be patient. It couldn't be more important."

He sat a while, thinking, chasing vague pictures around in his mind. He heard, or was conscious of, the rapid but slowing beat of her frightened heart.

"Miss Patchell," he said, turning to her, his voice gentle, "I have not at any time looked into your records. Until—ah—yesterday, you were simply another face in the class, another source of quiz papers to be graded. I have not consulted the registrar's files for information about you. And, to my almost certain knowledge, this is the first time I have spoken with you."

"That's right, sir," she said quietly.

"Very good, then." He wet his lips. "You are twenty-three years old. The house in which you were born was a two-storey affair, quite old, with a leaded bay window at the turn of the stairs. The small bedroom, or nursery, was directly over the kitchen. You could hear the clatter of dishes below you when the house was quiet. The address was 191 Bucyrus Road."

"How—oh yes! How did you know?"

He shook his head, and then put it between his hands. "I don't know. I don't know. I lived in that house, too, as a child. I don't know how I knew that you did. There are things in here—" He rapped his head, shook it again. "I thought perhaps you could help."

She looked at him. He was a small man, brilliant, tired, getting old swiftly. She put a hand on his arm. "I wish I could," she said warmly. "I do wish I could."

"Thank you, child."

"Maybe if you told me more—"

"Perhaps. Some of it is—ugly. All of it is cloudy, long ago, barely remembered. And yet—"

"Please go on."

"I remember," he half whispered, "things that happened long ago that way, and recent things I remember—twice. One memory is sharp and clear, and one is old and misty. And I remember, in the same misty way, what is happening now and—and what *will* happen!"

"I don't understand."

"That girl. That Miss Symes. She—died here yesterday."

"She was sitting right behind me," said Miss Patchell.

"I know it! I knew what was going to happen to her. I knew it mistily, like an old memory. That's what I mean. I don't know what I could have done to stop it. I don't think I could have done anything. And yet, down deep I have the feeling that it's my fault—that she slipped and fell because of something I did."

"Oh, no!"

He touched her arm in mute gratitude for the sympathy in her tone, and grimaced miserably. "It's happened before," he said. "Time and time and time again. As a boy, as a youth, I was plagued with accidents. I led a quiet life. I was not very strong and books were always more my line than baseball. And yet I witnessed a dozen or more violent, useless deaths—automobile accidents, drownings, falls, and one or two"—his voice shook—"which I won't mention. And there were countless minor ones—broken bones, maimings, stabbings . . . and every time, in some way, it was my fault, like the one yesterday . . . and I—I—"

"Don't," she whispered. "Please don't. You were nowhere near Elaine Symes when she fell."

"I was nowhere near any of them! That never mattered. It never took away the burden of guilt. Miss Patchell—"

"Catherine."

"Catherine. Thank you so much! There are people called by insurance actuaries 'accident prone'. Most of these are involved in accidents through their own negligence, or through some psychological quirk which causes them to defy the world, or to demand attention, by getting hurt. But some are simply present at accidents, without being involved at all—catalysts of death, if you'll pardon a flamboyant phrase. I am, apparently, one of these."

"Then—how could you feel guilty?"

"It was—" He broke off suddenly, and looked at her. She had a gentle face, and her eyes were filled with compassion. He shrugged. "I've said so much," he said. "More would sound no more fantastic, and do me no more damage."

"There'll be no damage from anything you tell me," she said, with a sparkle of decisiveness.

He smiled his thanks this time, sobered, and said, "These horrors—the maimings, the deaths—they were *funny*, once, long ago. I must have been a child, a baby. Something taught me, then, that the agony and death of others was to be promoted and enjoyed. I remember, I—almost remember when that stopped. There was a—a toy, a—a—"

Jeremy blinked. He had been staring at the fine crack in the ceiling for so long that his eyes hurt.

"What are you doing?" asked the monster.

"Dreaming real," said Jeremy. "I am grown up and sitting in the big empty lecture place, talking to the girl with the brown hair that shines. Her name's Catherine."

"What are you talking about?"

"Oh, all the funny dreams. Only—"

"Well?"

"They're not so funny."

The monster scurried over to him and pounced on his chest. "Time to sleep now. And I want to—"

"No," said Jeremy. He put his hands over his throat. "I have enough now. Wait until I see some more of this real-dream."

"What do you want to see?"

"Oh, I don't know. There's something . . ."

"Let's have some fun," said the monster. "This is the girl you can change, isn't it?"

"Yes."

"Go ahead. Give her an elephant's trunk. Make her grow a beard. Stop her nostrils up. Go on. You can do anything." Jeremy grinned briefly, and then said, "I don't want to."

"Oh, go on. Just see how funny . . ."

"A toy," said the professor. "But more than a toy. It could talk, I think. If I could only remember more clearly!"

"Don't try so hard. Maybe it will come," she said. She took his hand impulsively. "Go ahead."

"It was—something—" the professor said haltingly, "—something soft and not too large. I don't recall . . ."

"Was it smooth?"

"No. Hairy—fuzzy. *Fuzzy!* I'm beginning to get it. Wait, now. . . . A thing like a teddy-bear. It talked! It—why, of course! It was alive."

"A pet then. Not a toy."

"Oh, no," said the professor, and shuddered. "It was a toy, all right. My mother thought it was, anyway. It made me—dream real."

"You mean, like Peter Ibbetson?"

"No, no. Not like that." He leaned back, rolled his eyes up. "I used to see myself as I would be later, when I was grown. And before. Oh. Oh—I think it was then— Yes! It must have been then that I began to see all those terrible accidents. It was! It was!"

"Steady," said Catherine. "Tell me quietly."

He relaxed. "Fuzzy. The demon—the monster. I know what it did, the devil. Somehow it made me see myself as I grew. It made me repeat what I had learned. It—it ate knowledge! It did; it ate knowledge. It had some strange affinity for me, for something about me. It could absorb knowledge that I gave out. And it—it changed the knowledge into blood, the way a plant changes sunlight and water into cellulose!"

"I don't understand," she said again.

"You don't? How could you? How can I? I know that that's what it did, though. It made me—why, I was spouting my lectures here to the beast when I was four years old! The words of them, the sense of them, came from me *now* to me *then*. And I gave it to the monster, and it ate the knowledge and spiced it with the things it made me do in my real-dreams. It made me trip a man up on a hat, of all absurd things, and fall into a subway excavation. And when I was in my teens, I was right by the excavation to see it happen. And that's the way with all of them! All the horrible accidents I have witnessed, I have half-remembered before they happened. There's no stopping any of them. What am I going to do?"

There were tears in her eyes. "What about me?" she whispered—more, probably, to get his mind away from his despair than for any other reason.

"You. There's something about you, if only I could remember. Something about what happened to that—that toy, that beast. You were in the same environment as I, as that devil. Somehow, you are vulnerable to it and—Catherine, Catherine, I think that something was done to you that—"

He broke off. His eyes widened in horror. The girl sat beside him, helping him, pitying him, and her expression did not change. But—everything else about her did.

Her face shrank, shrivelled. Her eyes lengthened. Her ears grew long, grew until they were like donkey's ears, like rabbit's ears, like horrible, long hairy spider's legs. Her teeth lengthened into tusks. Her arms shrivelled into jointed straws, and her body thickened.

It smelled like rotten meat.

There were filthy claws scattering out of her polished open-toed shoes. There were bright sores. There were—other things. And all the while she—*it*—held his hand and looked at him with pity and friendliness.

The professor—

Jeremy sat up and flung the monster away. "It isn't funny!" he screamed. "It isn't funny, it isn't, it isn't, it *isn't*!"

The monster sat up and looked at him with its soft, bland, teddy-bear expression. "Be quiet," it said. "Let's make her all squashy now, like soft-soap. And hornets in her stomach. And we can put her—"

Jeremy clapped his hands over his ears and screwed his eyes shut. The monster talked on. Jeremy burst into tears, leapt from the crib and, hurling the monster to the floor, kicked it. It grunted. "That's funny!" screamed the child. "Ha ha!" he cried, as he planted both feet in its yielding stomach. He picked up the twitching mass and hurled it across the room. It struck the nursery clock. Clock and monster struck the floor together in a flurry of glass, metal, and blood. Jeremy stamped it all into a jagged, pulpy mass, blood from his feet mixing with blood from the monster, the same strange blood which the monster had pumped into his neck. . . .

Mummy all but fainted when she ran in and saw him. She screamed, but he laughed, screaming. The doctor gave him sedatives until he slept, and cured his feet. He was never very strong after that. They saved him, to live his life and to see his real-dreams; funny dreams, and to die finally in a lecture room, with his eyes distended in horror while horror froze his heart, and a terrified young woman ran crying, crying for help.

Y IS FOR YETI

WILLIAM SAMBROT

Creature of the Snows

Ed McKale straightened up under his load of cameras and equipment, squinting against the blasting wind, peering, staring, sweeping the jagged, unending expanse of snow and wind-scoured rock. Looking, searching, as he'd been doing now for two months, cameras at the ready.

Nothing. Nothing but the towering Himalayas, thrusting miles high on all sides, stretching in awesome grandeur from horizon to horizon, each pinnacle tipped with immense banners of snow plumes, streaming out in the wind, vivid against the darkly blue sky. The vista was one of surpassing beauty. Viewing it, Ed automatically thought of light settings, focal length, color filters—then just as automatically rejected the thought. He was here on top of the world to photograph something infinitely more newsworthy, if only he could find it.

The expedition paused, strung out along a ridge of blue snow, with shadows falling away to the right and left into terrifying abysses, and Ed sucked for air. Twenty thousand feet is really quite high, although many of the peaks beyond rose nearly ten thousand feet above him.

Up ahead, the Sherpa porters (each a marvelous shot—gap-toothed, ebullient grins, seamed faces, leathery brown) bowed under stupendous loads for this altitude, leaning on their coolie crutches, waiting for Dr. Schenk to make up his mind. Schenk, the expedition leader, was arguing with the guides again, his breath spurting little puffs of vapor, waving his arms, pointing down.

Obviously Schenk was calling it quits. He was within his rights, Ed knew; two months was all Schenk had contracted for. Two months of probing snow and ice; scrambling over crevasses, up rotten rock cliffs, wind-ravaged, bleak, stretching endlessly toward Tibet and the never-never lands beyond. Two months of searching for footprints where none should be. Searching for odors, for droppings, anything to disclose the presence of creatures other than themselves. Without success.

Two months of nothing. Big, fat nothing.

The expedition was a bust. The goofiest assignment of this or any other century, as Ed felt it would be from the moment he'd sat across the desk from the big boss in the picture magazine's New York office two months ago, looking at a blurred

337

photograph, while the boss filled him in on the weird details.

The photograph, his boss had told him gravely, had been taken in the Himalayan mountains, at an altitude of twenty-one thousand feet, by a man who had been soaring overhead in a motorless glider.

"A glider," Ed had said noncommittally, staring at the fuzzy, enlarged snapshot of a great expanse of snow and rocky ledges, full of harsh light and shadows, a sort of roughly bowl-shaped plateau apparently, and in the middle of it, a group of indistinct figures, tiny, lost against the immensity of great ice pinnacles. Ed looked closer. Were the figures people? If so, what had happened to their clothes?

"A glider," his boss reiterated firmly. The glider pilot, the boss said, was maneuvering in an updraft, attempting to do the impossible—soar over Mount Everest in a home-made glider. The wide-winged glider had been unable to achieve the flight over Everest, but flitting silently about seeking updrafts, it cleared a jagged pinnacle and there, less than a thousand feet below, the pilot saw movement where none should have been. And dropping lower, startled, he'd seen, the boss said dryly, "Creatures—creatures that looked exactly like a group of naked men and women and kids playing in the snow—at an altitude of twenty-thousand five hundred feet." He'd had the presence of mind to take a few hasty snapshots before the group disappeared. Only one of the pictures had developed.

Looking at the snapshot with professional scorn, Ed had said, "These things are indistinct. I think he's selling you a bill of goods."

"No," the boss said, "we checked on the guy. He really did make the glider flight. We've had experts go over that blow-up. The picture's genuine. Those are naked, biped, erect-walking creatures." He flipped the picture irritably. "I can't publish this thing. I want closeups, action shots, the sort of thing our subscribers have come to expect of us."

He'd lighted a cigar slowly. "Bring me back some pictures I can publish, Ed, and you can write your own ticket."

"You're asking me to climb Mount Everest," Ed said carefully, keeping the sarcasm out of his voice, "to search for this plateau here," he tapped the shoddy photograph, "and take pix of—what are they—biped, erect-walking creatures, you say?"

The boss cleared his throat. "Not Mount Everest, Ed. It's Gauri Sankar, one of the peaks near Mount Everest. Roughly, it's only about twenty-three thousand feet or so high."

"That's pretty rough," Ed said.

The boss looked pained. "Actually it's not Gauri Sankar either. Just one of the lesser peaks of the Gauri Sankar massif. Well under twenty-three thousand. Certainly nothing to bother a hot-shot ex-paratrooper like you, Ed."

Ed winced, and the boss continued: "This guy—this glider pilot—wasn't able to pinpoint the spot, but he did come up with a pretty fair map of the terrain, for a pretty fair price. We've checked it out with the American Alpine Club; it conforms well with their own charts of the general area. Several expeditions have been in the vicinity but not at this exact spot, they tell me. It's not a piece of cake by any means, but it's far from being another Annapurna or K2 for accessibility."

He sucked at his cigar thoughtfully. "The Alpine Club says we've got only about two months of good weather before the inevitable monsoons hit that area, so time, as they say, is of the essence, Ed. But two months for this kind of thing ought to be plenty. Everything will be first class—we're even including these new gas guns that shoot hypodermic needles or something similar. We'll fly the essentials in to Katmandu and airdrop everything possible along the route up to your base,"—he squinted at a map—"Namche Bazar, a Sherpa village which is twelve thousand feet high."

He smiled amiably at Ed. "That's a couple of weeks march up from the nearest railhead and ought to get you acclimatized nicely. Plenty of experienced porters at Namche, all Sherpas. We've lined up a couple of expert mountain climbers with Himalayan backgrounds. And expedition leader will be Dr. Schenk, top man in his field."

"What is his field?" Ed asked gloomily.

"Zoology. Whatever these things are in this picture, they're animal, which is his field. Everyone will be sworn to secrecy. You'll be the only one permitted to use a camera, Ed. This could be the biggest thing you'll ever cover, if these things are what I think they are."

"What do you think they are?"

"An unknown species of man—or sub-man," his boss said, and prudently Ed remained silent. Two months would tell the tale.

But two months didn't tell.

Oh, there were plenty of wild rumors by the Nepalese all along the upper route. Hushed stories of the two-legged creature that walked like a man. A monster the Sherpas called Yeti. Legends. Strange encounters; drums sounding from snow-swept heights; wild snatches of song drifting down from peaks that were inaccessible to ordinary men. And one concrete fact: a ban, laid on by the Buddhist monks, against the taking of any life in the high Himalayas. What life? Ed wondered.

Stories, legends—but nothing else.

Two months of it. Starting from the tropical flatlands, up through the lush, exotic rain forest, where sun struggled through immense trees festooned with orchids. Two months, moving up into the arid foothills, where foliage abruptly ceased, and the rocks and wind took over. Up and ever up to where the first heavy snow pack lay. And higher still, following the trail laid out by the glider pilot. (And what impelled a man, Ed wondered, to soar over Mount Everest in a homemade glider?)

Two months during which Ed had come to dislike Dr. Schenk intensely. Tall, saturnine, smelling strongly of formaldehyde, Schenk classified everything into terms of vertebrate, invertebrate.

So now, standing on this wind-scoured ridge with the shadows falling into the abysses on either side, Ed peered through ice-encrusted goggles, watching Schenk arguing with the guides. He motioned to the ledge above, and obediently the Sherpas moved toward it. Obviously that would be the final camping spot. The two months were over by several days; Schenk was within his rights to call it quits. It was only Ed's assurances that the plateau they were seeking lay just ahead that had kept Schenk from bowing out exactly on the appointed time—that and the burning desire to secure his niche in zoology forever with a new specimen: biped, erect-walking—what?

But the plateau just ahead and the one after that and all the rest beyond had proved just as empty as those behind.

A bust. Whatever the unknown creatures were the glider pilot had photographed, they would remain just that—unknown.

And yet as Ed slogged slowly up toward where the porters were setting up the bright blue and yellow nylon tents, he was nagged by a feeling that the odd-shaped pinnacle ahead looked awfully much like the one in the blurred photograph. With his unfailing memory for pictures, Ed remembered the tall, jagged cone that had cast a black shadow across a snowy plateau, pointing directly toward the little group that was in the center of the picture.

But Schenk wasn't having any more plateaus. He shook his head vehemently, white-daubed lips a grim line on his sun-blistered face. "Last camp, Ed," he said firmly. "We agreed this would be the final plateau. I'm already a week behind schedule. If the monsoons hit us, we could be in serious trouble below. We have to get started back. I know exactly how you feel, but I'm afraid this is it."

Later that night, while the wind moved ceaselessly, sucking at the tent, they burrowed in sleeping bags, talking.

"There must be some basis of fact in those stories," Ed said to Dr. Schenk. "I've given them a lot of thought. Has it occurred to you that every one of the sightings, the few face-to-face meetings of the natives and these, these unknowns, has generally been just around dawn and usually when the native was alone?"

Schenk smiled dubiously. "Whatever this creature may be—and I'm concerned that it's either a species of large bear or one of the great anthropoids—it certainly must keep off the well-traveled routes. There are very few passes through these peaks, of course, and it would be quite simple for them to avoid these locales."

"But we're not on any known trail," Ed said thoughtfully. "I believe our methods have been all wrong, stringing out a bunch of men, looking for trails in the snow. All we've done is announce our presence to anything with ears for miles around. That glider pilot made no sound; he came on them without warning."

Ed looked intently at Schenk. "I'd like to try that peak up ahead and the plateau beyond." When Schenk uttered a protesting cry, Ed said, "Wait—this time I'll go alone with just one Sherpa guide. We could leave several hours before daybreak. No equipment, other than oxygen, food for one meal—and my cameras, of course. Maintain a strict silence. We could be back before noon. Will you wait long enough for this one last try?" Schenk hesitated. "Only a few hours more," Ed urged.

Schenk stared at him; then he nodded slowly. "Agreed. But aren't you forgetting the most important item of all?" When Ed looked blank, Schenk smiled. "The gas gun. If you should run across one, we'll need more proof than just your word for it."

There was very little wind, no moon, but cold, the cold approaching that of outer space, as Ed and one Sherpa porter started away from the sleeping camp, up the shattered floor of an ice river that swept down from the jagged peak ahead.

They moved up, hearing only the squeak of equipment, the peculiar gritty sound of crampons biting into packed snow, an occasional hollow crash of falling ice blocks. To the east a faint line of gray was already visible; daylight was hours away, but at this tremendous height sunrise came early. They moved slowly, breathing through woolen masks, the thin air cutting cruelly into their lungs, moving up, up.

They stopped once for hot chocolate from a thermos, and Ed slapped the Sherpa's shoulder, grinning, pointing ahead to where the jagged peak glowed pink and gold in the first slanting rays of the sun. The Sherpa looked at the peak and quickly shifted his glance to the sky. He gave a long, careful look at the gathering clouds in the east, then muttered something, shaking his head, pointing back, back down to where the camp was hidden in the inky shadows of enormous boulders.

When Ed resumed the climb, the Sherpa removed the long nylon line which had joined them. The route was comparatively level, on a huge sweeping expanse of snow-covered glacier that flowed about at the base of the peak. The Sherpa, no longer in the lead, began dropping behind as Ed pressed eagerly forward.

The sun was up, and with it the wind began keening again, bitterly sharp, bringing with it a scent of coming snow. In the east, beyond the jagged peak just ahead, the immense escarpment of the Himalayas was lost in approaching cloud. Ed hurried as best he could; it would snow, and soon. He'd have to make better time.

But above the sky was blue, infinitely blue, and behind, the sun was well up, although the camp was still lost in night below. The peak thrust up ahead, near, with what appeared to be a natural pass skirting its flank. Ed made for it. As he circled an upthrust ridge of reddish rotten rock, he glanced ahead. The plateau spread out before him, gently sloping, a natural amphitheater full of deep smooth snow, with peaks surrounding it and the central peak thrusting a long, black shadow directly across the center. He paused, glancing back. The Sherpa had stopped well below him, his face a dark blur, looking up, gesticulating frantically, pointing to the clouds. Ed motioned, then moved around, leaning against the rock, peering ahead.

That great shadow against the snow was certainly similar to the one in the photo, only, of course, the shadow pointed west now, when later it would point northwest as the sun swung to the south. And when it did, most certainly it was the precise— He sucked in a sharp, lung-piercing breath.

He stared, squinting against the rising wind that seemed to blow from earth's outermost reaches. Three figures stirred slightly and suddenly leaped into focus, almost perfectly camouflaged against the snow and wind-blasted rock. Three figures not more than a hundred feet below him. Two small, one larger.

He leaned forward, his heart thudding terribly at this twenty-thousand-foot height. A tremor of excitement shook him. My god, it was true. They existed. He was looking at what was undeniably a female and two smaller—what? Apes?

They were covered with downy hair, nearly white, resembling nothing so much as tight-fitting leotards. The female was exactly like any woman on earth except for the hair. No larger than most women, with arms slightly longer, more muscular. Thighs heavier, legs out of proportion to the trunk, shorter. Breasts full and firm. Not apes.

Hardly breathing, Ed squinted, staring, motionless. Not apes. Not standing so erectly. Not with those broad, high brows. Not with the undeniable intelligence of the two young capering about their mother. Not—and seeing this, Ed trembled against the freeezing rock—not with the sudden affectionate sweep of the female as she lifted the smaller and pressed it to her breast, smoothing back hair from its face with a motion common to every human mother on earth. A wonderfully tender gesture.

What were they? Less than human? Perhaps. He couldn't be certain, but he thought he heard a faint gurgle of laughter from the female, fondling the small one, and the sound stirred him strangely. Dr. Schenk had assured him that no animal was capable of genuine laughter; only man.

But they laughed, those three, and hearing it, watching the mother tickling the youngest one, watching its delighted squirming, Ed knew that in that marvelous little grouping below, perfectly lighted, perfectly staged, he was privileged to observe one of earth's most guarded secrets.

He should get started shooting his pictures; afterward, he should stun the group into unconsciousness with the gas gun and then send the sherpa back down for Dr. Schenk and the others. Clouds were massing, immensities of blue black. Already the first few flakes of snow, huge, wet, drifted against his face.

But for a long moment more he remained motionless, oddly unwilling to do anything to destroy the harmony, the aching purity of the scene below, so vividly etched in brilliant light and shadow. The female, child slung casually on one hip, stood erect, hand shading her eyes, and Ed grinned. Artless, but perfectly posed. She was looking carefully about and above, scanning the great outcroppings of rock, obviously searching for something. Then she paused.

She was staring directly at him.

Ed froze, even though he knew he was perfectly concealed by the deep shadows of the high cliff behind him. She was still looking directly at him, and then, slowly, her hand came up.

She waved.

He shivered uncontrollably in the biting wind, trying to remain motionless. The two young ones suddenly began to jump up and down and show every evidence of joy. And suddenly Ed knew.

He turned slowly, very slowly, and with the sensation of a freezing knife plunging deeply into his chest he saw the male less than five yards away.

It was huge, by far twice the size of the female below. (And crazily Ed thought of Schenk's little lecture, given what seemed like eons ago, six weeks before, in the incredible tropical grove far below where rhododendrons grew in wild profusion and enormous butterflies flitted above: "In primitive man," Schenk had said, "as in the great apes today, the male was far larger than the female.")

The gas gun was hopelessly out of reach, securely strapped to his shoulder pack. Ed stared, knowing there was absolutely nothing he could do to protect himself before this creature, fully eight feet tall, with arms as big as Ed's own thighs and eyes (My god—*blue* eyes!) boring into his. There was a light of savage intelligence there—and something else.

The creature (man?) made no move against him, and Ed stared at it, breathing rapidly, shallowly and with difficulty, noting with his photographer's eyes the immense chest span, the easy rise and fall of his breathing, the large square, white teeth, the somber cast of his face. There was long sandy fur on the shoulders, chest and back, shortening to off-white over the rest of the magnificent torso. Ears rather small and close to the head. Short, thick neck, rising up from the broad shoulders to the back of the head in a straight line. Toes long and definitely prehensile.

They looked silently at one another across the abyss of time and mystery. Man and—what? How long, Ed wondered, had it stood there observing him? Why hadn't it attacked? Had it been waiting for Ed to make a single threatening gesture such as pointing a gun or camera? Seeing the calm awareness in those long, slanting blue eyes, Ed sped a silent prayer of thanks upwards; most certainly if he had made a move for camera or gun, that move would have been his last.

They looked at one another through a curtain of falling snow, and suddenly there was a perfect, instantaneous understanding between them. Ed made an awkward, half-frozen little bow, moving backward. The great creature stood motionless, merely watching, and then Ed did a strange thing: he held out his hands, palm out, gave a wry grin and ducked quickly around the outcropping of rock and began a plunging, sliding return, down the way he'd come. In spite of the harsh, snow-laden wind, bitterly cold, he was perspiring.

Ed glanced back once. Nothing. Only the thickening veil of swift glowing snow blanking out the pinnacle, erasing every trace, every proof that anyone, anything, had stood there moments before. Only the snow, only the rocks, only the unending, wind-filled silence of the top of the world.

Nothing else.

The Sherpa was struggling up to him from below, terribly anxious to get started back; the storm was rising. Without a word they hooked up and began the groping, stumbling descent back to the last camp. They found the camp already broken, Sherpas already moving out. Schenk paused only long enough to give Ed a questioning look.

What could Ed say? Schenk was a scientist, demanding material proof. If not a corpse, at the very least a photograph. The only photographs Ed had were etched in his mind, not on film. And even if he could persuade Schenk to wait, when the storm cleared, the giant, forewarned, would be gone. Some farther peak, some remoter plateau would echo to his young ones' laughter.

Feeling not a bit bad about it, Ed gave Schenk a barely perceptible negative nod. Instantly Schenk shrugged, turned and went plunging down into the thickening snow, back into the world of littler men. Ed trailed behind.

On the arduous trek back through that first great storm, through the snowline, through the rain forest, hot and humid, Ed thought of the giant, back up there where the air was thin and pure.

Who, what were he and his race? Castaways on this planet, forever marooned, yearning for a distant, never-to-be-reached home?

Or did they date in unbroken descent from the Pleistocene, man's first beginning, when all the races of not-quite-man were giants, unable or unwilling to take the fork in the road that led to smaller, cleverer man; forced to retreat higher and higher, to more and more remote areas, until finally there was only one corner of earth left to them—the high Himalayas?

Or were he and his kind earth's last reserves; not-yet-men, waiting for the opening of still another chapter in earth's unending mystery story?

Whatever the giant was, his secret was safe with him, Ed thought. For who would believe it even if he chose to tell?

Z IS FOR ZOMBIE

W. J. STAMPER

Lips of the Dead

"Down with Théodor! Death to Black Oscar!"

It was the raucous, horrifying yell of the inevitable Haitian mob as it assembled in the historic Champs de Mars outside the palace in Port au Prince, the scene of hundreds of such meetings that had never meant less than murders and gutters flowing red with human blood. The rapacious rule of President Théodor and his favourite general Black Oscar, was tottering to its fall. That day Théodor had violated a sacred session of the Senate and dissolved it at the point of the bayonet because it had, for the second time, refused to support him in a dastardly measure to filch more money from the already pauper citizenry.

As night came on, aged senators lay cringing in the filthy prison, in the courtyard of the palace, and double sentinels paced the flagstones outside.

In the domed council chamber of the palace sat Papillon, the favourite senator of the common people, bound hand and foot, subjected to the jeers and insults of the two beasts. Théodor, lean and emaciated, his yellow, pock-marked face pinched with terror, fingered nervously some loose papers that lay on the table. Oscar, a giant in stature, with a waxed moustache curling up crescent-shaped till the two points almost met above his gaping, black nostrils, pounded his huge fist on the table and fixed his sinister gaze on Papillon.

"Do you think we sleep, idiot?" he stormed. "It is your tongue that has sown the seeds of unrest among the populace and stirred them to rebellion against our authority. What have you to say to this—and this?" He thrust two papers into the face of Papillon, and his black face twitched with rage.

"I should think it would be unnecessary for *le général* to rob the mails for the same information he might easily obtain by listening to any group of citizens conversing on our street corners. It is the sentiment of all true Haitians. You have robbed the coffers of the treasury; you have murdered our best citizens; and now you seek the aid of the Senate in carrying out your cursed schemes," sarcastically answered Papillon.

Stung by the truth of this remark, Oscar lifted his great fist and crashed it against the thin lips of the helpless prisoner. Blood streamed from the cracked lips, ran down the chin and stained the white bosom of the senator's shirt. Papillon, still

344

holding high his proud head, mumbled through his bleeding lips:

" 'Tis no better nor redder than that you spilled at Mole St. Nicholas when you shot down Vilbrun, or when you butchered the patriot, Céléstin, at Jacmel. It is the blood of Haiti."

As Papillon finished speaking, in through the window shone the baleful red glare of the torches of the mob, and through the casement came frenzied yells: "Down with Théodor! Death to Oscar!"

Théodor shivered as he sensed the woeful power behind this thing that he hated and feared, and his lips trembled as he turned to Oscar.

"Has not *le général* some plan? Something must be done," he whined.

"If they become unruly we can toss—we can toss them a head," answered the black brute as he curled his wax moustache and shot a wicked glance at the bleeding Papillon.

"I have ever been the first to draw my sword for Haiti—I have lived for her and her misguided people—and, *mon général*, I shall gladly offer my life and blood for her," came from the puffed lips of the prisoner.

"Cur! Worshipper of Voodoo!" shrieked Théodor as he confronted Papillon. "You shall speak to the vermin from yonder window—order them to return to their homes, or I swear by the great Capoix, your head shall roll at their feet."

"Excellency, I am at your service. Such has been the course of liberty for a thousand years—blood, torture, death. Long live the common people! Long live liberty!"

Without another word Théodor seized him by the collar, lifted him from the chair, snatched the gleaming sword from the scabbard and plunged it through the body of the patriot. With a gurgling groan Papillon sank to the floor, while a crimson stream, gushing from a jagged wound in the breast, poured over the carpet of the room. Then with one horrible stroke Théodor severed the head from the trunk. The gory thing, rolling a few feet, stood upright on the bloody, slippery stub, then slid across the room to the wall. There it sat in the pale light of the lamp, and the hair, still unruffled, was smoothly parted in the middle. Then occurred the most singularly awe-inspiring thing that ever greeted the eyes and ears of mortal man. What do men yet know of the mysteries of Voodoo—its powers—the miracles it may perform?

Two great tears oozed from the eyes and dropped to the floor. The dead lips moved and a voice issued from the crimson mouth.

"To-morrow, Théodor, to-morrow!"

Slowly the quivering lids closed over the glazing eyeballs, then opened, and eyes fixed in the icy stare of death.

Théodor laughed a hoarse, bestial laugh, wiped the thickening gore from his blade on the leg of his trousers and said: "To-morrow, Théodor, to-morrow! A pretty speech indeed, General."

Picking up the ghastly head by the long black hair and holding it as far away as possible, Théodor walked to the window and deliberately hurled it out into the very face of the mob, yelling through the casement as he watched it catapult across the street: "Haitians, this is but the beginning! Depart at once, lest all the others meet the fate of Papillon."

Screams of rage rent the night. Crash on crash of musketry in the street below.

The mob had rushed the gate and the troops had opened fire.

It was the terrified voice of Théodor. "We must flee, General! To the French legation for our lives!"

"My soldiers will defend the palace to the last man, Excellency. If we must go down, let us go down in the blaze of blood. To the prison!"

The helpless senators cringed beneath the covers as the sentinel passed. His clanking bayonet scabbard sent a hollow sound through the corridors, while his footfalls sounded like some weird echo in an empty tomb.

A key grated in the lock. Théodor and Oscar entered, and the murderous work began. Silently they went from man to man. There was a sickening slushing sound as the sharp points of their blades found the vitals of those dark masses beneath the ragged covers of the rickety bunks. Now and then a stifled groan, a rattle in the throat, which was suddenly choked by a rush of blood. This ghastly work lasted but a few minutes, and a crime was consummated that will forever brand Haiti as an outlaw among nations. With his own hands, Oscar put out the one dim light, and following in the wake of the butcher, left the room to darkness and the dead.

Their vile work finished, Théodor and Oscar fled through the night and sought shelter at the French legation.

Daylight revealed their absence from the palace. News of the massacre spread like wildfire to every nook and corner of the city. The troops defending the palace fled when they discovered their chiefs had deserted them. Papillon had been followed in death by all the other senators, and their souls cried aloud for vengeance.

Groups of cursing men and weeping women rushed from house to house, from hiding place to hiding place. Swift horsemen galloped over the roads leading to Gonaives and Saint Marc in search of the fugitives.

The sun was low in the heavens, when at length came word that Théodor and Oscar had been found in hiding at the French legation. The bugles sounded the assembly, and the bloodthirsty mob, armed with axes, spades and whatever other weapons could be procured, moved upon the legation. The streets were choked with a seething, writhing mass of humanity, undulating like some huge serpent as it approaches its prey.

The warning voice of the grey-haired consul, as he stood on the portico of the legation house, pleading with the bloodthirsty mob to remember the sacredness of an embassy, was drowned with rasping yells.

"Give us Théodor! Give us Black Oscar!"

There was a sudden irresistible surge of that black mass. The gate and fence went down with a crash. On, on, up to the very doors it went. There was a splintering of wood, a rattling of broken glass, screams and shrieks. Oscar was dragged out first, and his body riddled with bullets. As his black carcass lay in the gutter, oozing red from a thousand punctures, and the thick tongue lolled out from between the yellow teeth, cheer after cheer went up from the multitude.

The exit of Théodor was more orderly. With downcast eyes his lean figure shambled out of the building between three huge blacks, one of whom carried three stout ropes. The mob gave back to permit ample passage, and strangely enough the street looking westward was without a single soul. There was at last a

peculiar system, even in its innate madness, in which this mob carried out its vengeance.

The prisoner arrived at the edge of the street amid deafening shouts: "Murderer, where is our Papillon?"

A buggy arrived pulled by a strong Haitian mule.

Now, as if by mutual consent, the three blacks took charge of the situation. They proceeded to secure the end of one rope about the neck of Théodor, the other end to the axle of the buggy. The other two ropes were fastened above the ankles, leaving one end of each free. The ropes about the ankles were, however, much longer than the one about the neck. As certain ones of the mob grasped the intention of the three blacks they gave loud and prolonged cheers of approval.

At last all was ready. The buggy was in motion toward the west. Théodor striving to keep on his feet, had his legs jerked from under him by the two men manning the loose ends of the ropes about the ankles. He was bruised beyond description. His neck was scarred and bleeding from the noose, his tongue swollen and covered with dust. Bloody froth oozed from his nose and mouth as he was jolted from one side of the street to the other.

Suddenly he ceased to struggle and strive to keep his feet. There was apparent a certain limpness of the body that gave evidence of unconsciousness. Two trails of red showed in the street behind where the body was being dragged. Sharp stones wearing through the clothing had bit into the bare flesh.

Onward this weird procession went, followed by the crowding, yelling, approving mob, onward toward the west. At length the buggy stopped beneath the shadow of the Sacred Arch. The mob, like hungry vultures encircling a piece of carrion, surged around in a great circle with eyes staring and necks craning lest one single detail of this noisome scene be missed.

There fell upon this vengeful multitude a solemn silence, as from somewhere came the measured beat of the tom-tom—a terrible sound, such a sound as is heard in the fastness of the northern mountains when the priests lead the death-march. One of the blacks was untying the ropes from the gory victim; another was removing the grime and dirt from the distorted face with a damp gunny sack.

What could this mean? Could it be that the hearts of those two men were relenting? Low growls and sharp hisses escaped from the mob. A bottle of spirits, the powerful heathen rum, was held beneath the distended nostrils. A few drops were poured into the gaping, bruised mouth. A convulsive shudder passed through the body. The chest heaved, rose and fell. Consciousness was returning.

The circle had narrowed and the mob was on the point of pouncing upon the reviving victim, when one of the blacks, rising from where he knelt over the prostrate figure, extended his ham-like hand high above his head and shouted with such a stentorian voice that it could be heard by the most distant one of the crowd:

"Are you fools, Haitians? Would you have this beast who has gutted himself upon our reddest blood die before your vengeance has been appeased? Let us torture him; let him writhe in agony; is that not good, countrymen?"

"Yes, yes!" came the answer from every mouth of that vast and blood-craved throng.

A ladder was placed against the face of the Sacred Arch. The last rays of the setting sun shed a purplish light over the city; the drums beat the measured march of the dead. Théodor opened his bleary eyes and shuddered.

Two long ropes were tied under the armpits. Two heavy stones, attached to the other ends, were hurled over the top of the arch. Slowly, but without much difficulty, two men hoisted upward the spare, bedraggled figure of Théodor; upward, till it dangled against the solid wall of the archway. Loud cheers rent the gathering dusk of approaching night: *"Vive le Président! Vive Théodor!"*

Now one of the blacks was mounting the ladder. He carried under his arm a small chest, such as carpenters use.

The mob, expectant, gloating, their hawk-like eyes on the cruel scene, stood breathless—waiting.

At last the top was reached. The black secured the peculiar chest to the topmost rung. The mob surged up about the foot of the ladder. A thousand eager, curious faces were upturned, as he seized the right arm of Théodor, extended it to full length along the wall and, without looking, scrambled among the contents of the chest. He drew out a small hand-axe and a long spike. With one powerful blow he drove the pointed nail through the bony hand, deep into the adobe of the wall.

Beads of black blood trickled down and spattered in the dust below. Mortal agony twisted and distorted the pock-marked face of Théodor, and sharp rasping cries issued from the swollen mouth. Another blow, in strange unison with the beat of the tom-tom, pinioned the other arm. The legs dangled; the body writhed in the throes of approaching death. The skinny legs were drawn apart. Again, and yet again, rose and fell the fatal axe. There was a gritting sound, such as is made by the surgeon's saw, when the cruel spikes pierced the bones of the feet.

"Vive Théodor! Vive Théodor!" shrieked the demoniacal mob.

Mortal man could not long survive such inhuman torture. Slowly the head sank down upon the scrawny chest; the eyes bulged from their sockets. The cooling blood had ceased to flow and now merely oozed from around the nails.

Grasping the dishevelled hair with his left hand, the black straightened up the bowed head, the axe ascended once more and there was a sickening thud as it fell upon the distended leaders of the bare throat.

The mob slunk back as the gory head dropped to the street, rolled a few feet, stood upright on the bloody stub of the neck. As the glazing eyeballs fixed in the cold stare of death, there issued from the purple lips a scarcely audible murmur:

"To-day, Papillon, to-day!"

Had Black Oscar been yet among the living, he alone, of all that multitude, would have noted how strangely these words from dead lips appeared an answer to the words from other dead lips, once sadly murmured at dead of night, in the domed council chamber of the palace.

SOURCES AND ACKNOWLEDGEMENTS

"Vault of the Beast" by A. E. van Vogt from *Monsters* (Simon & Schuster, 1965). Reprinted by kind permission of the author.

"We Never Mention Aunt Nora" by Frederik Pohl from *The Abominable Earthman*. Copyright ©, reprinted by permission of the author and Carnell Literary Agency.

"Last Rites" by Charles Beaumont (first published in *If Science Fiction*, 1955). Reprinted by permission of Don Congdon Associates Inc. Copyright © 1955; Renewed 1983 by Christopher Beaumont.

"And Lo! The Bird" by Nelson Bond from *Far Boundaries* (Consul, 1965).

"The Black Retriever" by Charles Finney. Copyright © 1958 by Mercury Press, Inc. Reprinted from *The Magazine of Fantasy & Science Fiction*.

"The Bird Woman" by Henry Spicer from *Strange Things Among Us* (1863)

"The Hoard of the Gibbelins" by Lord Dunsany from *The Book of Wonder*, 1920. Reprinted by kind permission of Curtis Brown Ltd on behalf of John Child Villiers and Valentine Lamb as literary executors of Lord Dunsany. Copyright © Estate of Lord Dunsany.

"Answer" by Fredric Brown was originally published in *Angels and Specships* (E. P. Dutton). Copyright © 1954 Fredric Brown. Reprinted by kind permission of Roberta Pryor Inc. on behalf of the author.

"The Painted Skin" by P'u Sung Ling from *Strange Stories From a Chinese Studio* (1895).

"The Monster and the Maiden" by Roger Zelazny from *The Doors of His Face, the Lamps of His Mouth* (Avon, 1971). Copyright © Roger Zelazny Reprinted by permission of the author and Carnell Literary Agency.

"The Devil is Not Mocked" by Manly Wade Wellman. Copyright © 1943 by Street and Smith Publications, Inc. for *Unknown Words*, June 1943. Copyright renewed © 1967 by the Condé Nast Publications Inc. Reprinted by permission of Frances Wellman.

"Puppet Show" by Fredric Brown first published in *Playboy*, November 1962. Copyright © 1962 Fredric Brown. Reprinted by permission of Roberta Pryor Inc.

"At Last, The True Story of Frankenstein" by Harry Harrison from *The Freak Show*. Reprinted by kind permission of A. P. Watt and Nat Sobel Associates Inc. on behalf of the author.

"Disturb Not My Slumbering Fair" by Chelsea Quinn Yarbro from *Cautionary Tales* (Doubleday, 1978). Reprinted by permission of the author and Ellen Levine Literary Agency Inc.

"Island of Fear" by William Sambrot from *Island of Fear* (Dell Publishing company Ltd, 1963).

"Doctor Zombie and His Furry Little Friends" by Robert Sheckley from *Can You Feel Anything When I do This?* (Doubleday, 1971). Reprinted by permission of the author.

"The Man Who Liked Dickens" by Evelyn Waugh. Reprinted by kind permission of A. D. Peters & Company Ltd.

"Monsters of the Pit" by Paul S. Powers from *Not At Night* (Selwyn & Blount, 1925).

"Expendable" by Philip K. Dick. Reprinted by permission of the author's agents, Scott Meredith Literary Agency, Inc., 845 Third Ave, New York, N.Y. 10022.

"Born of Man and Woman" by Richard Matheson from *Third from the Sun* (Max Reinhardt, 1956). Reprinted by kind permission of Laurence Pollinger Ltd on behalf of the author.

"The Thing On Outer Shoal" by P. Schuyler Miller from *Not At Night* (Selwyn & Blount, 1925).

"After King Kong Fell" by Philip José Farmer. Reprinted by permission of the author and the author's agents, Scott Meredith Literary Agency, Inc.

"The Doors of his Face, The Lamps of his Mouth" by Roger Zelazny (Avon, 1971). Copyright © Roger Zelazny. Reprinted by kind permission of the author and Carnell Literary Agency.

"Leprechaun" and "Creature of the Snows" by William Sambrot from *Island of Fear*.

"Men of Iron" by Guy Endore from *A Decade of Fantasy & Science Fiction* (Gollancz, 1962).

"The Lop-Eared Cat that Devoured Philadelphia" by Louis Phillips from *The Year's Best SF No. 9* (Futura, 1976).

"Flight Useless, Inexorable the Pursuit" by Thomas M. Disch from *Fun With Your New Head* (Doubleday). Reproduced by kind permission of the author.

"Ghost V" by Robert Sheckley from *The People Trap* (Pan Books, 1972). Reprinted by kind permission of the author.

"Slime" by Joseph Payne Brenna. Reprinted by permission of the author and the author's agents, Scott Meredith Literary Agency, Inc.

"They Bite" by Anthony Boucher from *The Compleat Werewolf*. Reprinted by kind permission of Curtis Brown, N.Y. Copyright © 1943 by Anthony Boucher; copyright © renewed 1971.

"The Foghorn" by Ray Bradbury Reprinted by kind permission of Don Congdon Associates Inc.

"The Plant Thing" by R. G. Macready from *Not At Night* (Selwyn & Blount, 1925).

"The Fools' Pope" by Victor Hugo from *Notre Dame de Paris*. Translated by I. G. Burnham.

"Roman Remains" by Algernon Blackwood from *Weird Tales* (1934). Reprinted by kind permission of A. P. Watt Ltd on behalf of Sheila Reeves.

"The Distortion Out of Space" by Francis Flagg from *More Not At Night* Selwyn Blount, 1927).

"Mr. Waterman" by Peter Redgrove from *Selected Poems*. Reproduced by permission of Routledge & Kegan Paul Plc.

"The End of a Show" by Barry Pain from *Stories In the Dark* (1901).

"Mujina" by Lafcadio Hearn from *Kwaidan* (1904).

"She Only Goes Out at Night" by William Tenn from *The Square Root of Man* (Ballantine, 1968).

"Mother of Serpents" and "Sweets to the Sweet" by Robert Bloch. Reproduced by kind permission of the author.

"Wolves Don't Cry" by Bruce Elliot. Copyright © 1954 by Mercury Press Inc. Reprinted from *The Magazine of Fantasy and Science Fiction*.

"Looking for Something to Suck" by R. Chetwynd Hayes. Reproduced by kind permission of the author.

"The Professor's Teddy-Bear by Theodore Sturgeon from *E. Pluribus Unicorn* (Abelard Press). Reprinted by permission of Laurence Pollinger Ltd on behalf of the author.

"Lips of the Dead' by W. J. Stamper from *More Not At Night* (Selwyn & Blount, 1927).

Whilst every effort has been made to trace authors and copyright-holders, in some cases this has proved impossible. The publishers would be glad to hear from any such parties so that omissions can be rectified in future editions of the book.